THE DOGMOTHERS - BOOK EIGHT

roxanne st. claire

Faux Paws
THE DOGMOTHERS BOOK EIGHT

Copyright © 2021 South Street Publishing

This novel is a work of fiction. Any references to historical events, real people, or real locales are used fictitiously. Other names, characters, places, and incidents are the product of the author's imagination, and any resemblance to actual events or locales or persons, living or dead, is coincidental.

All rights to reproduction of this work are reserved. No part of this publication may be reproduced, stored in or introduced into a retrieval system, or transmitted, in any form, or by any means (electronic, mechanical, photocopying, recording, or otherwise) without prior written permission from the copyright owner. Thank you for respecting the copyright. For permission or information on foreign, audio, or other rights, contact the author, roxanne@roxannestclaire.com.

978-1-952196-16-4 EBOOK
978-1-952196-17-1 PRINT

COVER DESIGN: The Killion Group, Inc.
INTERIOR FORMATTING: Author E.M.S.

Critical Reviews of Roxanne St. Claire Novels

"Non-stop action, sweet and sexy romance, lively characters, and a celebration of family and forgiveness."

— *Publishers Weekly*

"Plenty of heat, humor, and heart!"

— *USA Today* (Happy Ever After blog)

"Beautifully written, deeply emotional, often humorous, and always heartwarming!"

— *The Romance Dish*

"Roxanne St. Claire is the kind of author that will leave you breathless with tears, laughter, and longing as she brings two people together, whether it is their first true love or a second love to last for all time."

— *Romance Witch Reviews*

"Roxanne St. Claire writes an utterly swoon-worthy romance with a tender, sentimental HEA worth every emotional struggle her readers will endure. Grab your tissues and get ready for some ugly crying. These books rip my heart apart and then piece it back together with the hope, joy and indomitable loving force that is the Kilcannon clan."

— *Harlequin Junkies*

"As always, Ms. St. Claire's writing is perfection…I am unable to put the book down until that final pawprint the end. Oh the feels!"

— *Between My BookEndz*

Before

The Dogmothers...

there was

Sit…Stay…Beg (Book 1)

New Leash on Life (Book 2)

Leader of the Pack (Book 3)

Santa Paws is Coming to Town (Book 4 – a Holiday novella)

Bad to the Bone (Book 5)

Ruff Around the Edges (Book 6)

Double Dog Dare (Book 7)

Bark! The Herald Angels Sing – (Book 8 – a Holiday novella)

Old Dog New Tricks (Book 9)

The Dogmothers Series

Hot Under the Collar (Book 1)

Three Dog Night (Book 2)

Dachshund Through the Snow (Book 3 – a Holiday novella)

Chasing Tail (Book 4)

Hush, Puppy (Book 5)

Man's Best Friend (Book 6)

Feliz Naughty Dog – (Book 7 – a Holiday novella)

Faux Paws – (Book 8)

And more to come!

For a complete guide to all of the characters in both The Dogfather and Dogmothers series, see the back of this book. Or visit www.roxannestclaire.com for a printable reference, book lists, buy links, and reading order of all my books. Be sure to sign up for my newsletter on my website to find out when the next book is released! And join the private Dogfather Facebook group for inside info on all the books and characters, sneak peeks, and a place to share the love of tails and tales!

www.facebook.com/groups/roxannestclairereaders/

Chapter One

"Ayla Hollis, are you ready for your entire life to change?"

She was ready for that dagger-sharp bobby pin to not stab her head. "Loosen my veil, Trina," Ayla whispered to her sister. "I already have a headache."

"Sorry, hon. That thing isn't moving out of your bee's nest for love or money." Trina added a playful elbow jab. "Both of which we are gathered here to celebrate."

Ayla couldn't argue with that hard truth.

"All right, let's get you married." Trina guided them both out of the dressing room toward the back of the church where the other five bridesmaids were lined up and ready for the long walk down the aisle of All Saints Episcopal Cathedral. The women all looked straight ahead, game faces on, ready for the walk they'd rehearsed the night before.

All but Jilly. She kept fidgeting and glancing around, and really? Did she pull her phone out of her pocket? Now?

The first few notes of the prelude song rose from behind the closed sanctuary doors, building anticipation among three hundred of Charlotte, North Carolina's most prominent residents.

But no Nana Jo.

Ayla turned to her sister. "You have the ring?"

"I have the ring." She patted the fold of her dress. "Wasn't it smart to have pockets?"

"Jilly thinks so. You're sure you have it?"

Trina rolled her eyes. "Come on, Ayla. You've got costume jewelry worth more than that ring."

"Not to me." Of course, Trina would scoff at the simple diamond that their grandmother wore until the day she died. Trina didn't understand that the ring represented true and lasting love. Neither did EJ, who'd insisted on giving Ayla an engagement ring the size of the Rock of Gibraltar. But he'd agreed that for their wedding, he'd marry her with Nana Jo's ring. It was only symbolic to him, but it meant everything to her.

"Okay, I got it." Trina pulled out the ring as proof, then stuffed it back in her pocket. "Let's roll, the natives are getting restless."

Tamping down the nerves ricocheting through her, Ayla tried to imagine the crowd out there ready to stand and watch her make *the walk.* At least Miz Marie was there. That seventysomething widowed dog rescuer, whom Ayla had befriended at the Westside Shelter when they volunteered together, was the closest thing Ayla had to a grandmother. And Marie Boswell might also be the only person in the church who genuinely cared about Ayla. The only one not impressed or terrified by her father's money.

Oh, and EJ. Her soon-to-be husband. He cared… right? *Right?*

The stab in her heart was almost as sharp as the one in her head.

"Come on, Ayla. Mother's already taken her seat. Don't make her endure too much time one row away from Dad's latest arm candy." Trina looked skyward with disgust. "I still can't believe that little skank wore off-white to a wedding. I mean, who *does* that? Can we just discuss the subtext there?"

Ayla closed her eyes, not wanting to think about her divorced parents' endless drama right now, or what Dad's girl du jour wore today.

As if on cue, a door on the opposite side of the bride's dressing room opened, and her father walked out, his tuxedo stretched across a broad chest. He smiled, revealing perfect white teeth and the timeless features of a chiseled fifty-eight-year-old business mogul, the epitome of success, a man who'd started and sold Paxton Hollis Pharmaceuticals for a rumored hundred million.

Phillip Hollis wore a look of smug satisfaction on his face. No surprise there. After years of dropping hints—also known as manipulation through withdrawal of affection or finances—his little princess was about to marry Eugene John Paxton the Third.

The marriage fulfilled a dream of their fathers, partners on numerous investments, who saw this union as another great Hollis-Paxton merger that would yield endless dividends. And it overjoyed their mothers, who gave birth to EJ and Ayla in the same hospital twenty-nine years ago and claimed this next generation were "fated mates."

EJ had loved that idea for the many years he'd pursued Ayla when they were growing up, but she hadn't been interested in the world-beater who would follow in his father's footsteps. Then, after Nana Jo died, EJ did a full-court press, and her heart softened.

Was she madly in love with the man? Define *madly*. She knew the marriage made everyone happy, and that was always motivation enough for Ayla.

Suddenly, the long, white-tipped nails of her friend Jillian Sutton-Malley dug into Ayla's arm.

"Get back in line, Jilly," Trina insisted in her bossiest voice, and she had many.

But Jilly shook her head. "I have to talk to Ayla."

"Now?" Trina choked.

"I have to!" Jilly whispered breathlessly, dragging Ayla a few steps away from the rest of the wedding party.

"Something important on Instagram?" Ayla joked. "Don't think I didn't see you on your phone."

But Jilly didn't smile. She dug her nails deeper into Ayla's arm as blood drained from her face. "I have to tell you. I'll die if I don't."

For a moment, Ayla saw the entire exchange in slow motion, and her pulse thumped like she was underwater.

"I slept with him," Jilly hissed.

"What?" Ayla breathed the word as confusion set in.

"With EJ. We had sex. A lot. Recently. Like, last night after the rehearsal dinner."

Ayla stared at her friend, a million thoughts at war in her head. Questions and demands and denials and a sudden urge to claw her eyes out. Right after she strangled EJ.

One thought rose to the surface, clear and loud.

I knew it.

Because her fiancé was cut from the same cloth as her father and the whole lot of entitled, spoiled, self-serving people she'd grown up around.

They cheated like they breathed, because getting what you want when you want it was a way of life to this subset of society. Along with judging those who had less while pretending to want to help them, and working to impress those who had more but really wanting to be them. It was why Nana Jo despised them all. It's why Nana Jo…never liked EJ.

Deep in her soul, Ayla knew Nana Jo would have been opposed to this union. She could still hear her voice…

Ayla Jo, it's fine to please people, but don't compromise on love, sweetheart.

But wasn't that what she was doing right now?

"Did you hear me, Ayla?" Jilly's blue eyes widened with fear and guilt. "I feel so bad. You *have* to know before you marry him."

Ayla already did know. Maybe not about Jilly, but she knew…something was missing with EJ. Trust. Respect. Love. EJ didn't love Ayla—he loved the *idea* of Ayla. He didn't even know her deepest, most essential secret.

But she'd let herself be swept along into the wedding of the year with a month-long European honeymoon and hopes for a happily ever after with a man she liked—or had until five seconds ago—but, really, truly, deep inside, did *not* love. Or trust.

If only she could read *people's* minds the way she could read animals'. If only EJ had been a dog instead of a snake.

"Ayla?" Her father's booming voice echoed in her other ear. "Are you ready?"

His words had dragged out like he, too, was underwater.

But Ayla was the only one drowning. She needed air. She needed freedom. She needed…she needed *a new life.*

She jerked back, whipping her bouquet at Jilly, who

somehow managed to grab it. Of course, she'd been practicing how to catch that thing since Ayla and EJ set a date.

"Ayla?" Her sister and father called out at the same time, but it was all muffled by the sound of Ayla's own screaming. Wait. Was she screaming? Of course not. Ayla Hollis would never scream. Only on the inside.

Her father reached for her. "What's going on? What's the matter?" He sounded a little panicked, like all his carefully laid plans were about to go up in smoke.

Shouldn't they be *her* plans? Wasn't this *her* wedding? Not in his head. This was the joining of two massive bank accounts and family dynasties, no different than an arranged marriage from the dark ages.

"Everything is the matter." The words were little more than a ground-out whisper, but he heard her, she could tell by the way his face took on that stern expression that said he did not like being disobeyed.

And normally, that would have been enough to make her acquiesce and be a good girl and follow the plan and say the right thing and never, ever color outside the family lines or do anything but be a Hollis. The good one, too. The one who never caused one drop of whitewater.

Well, too bad, folks. You're in the splash zone.

"Everything's wrong, Dad," she said, her fingers tunneling into the silk of her wedding gown, unconsciously gathering it up. "EJ screwed Jilly. And you screwed me by making me agree to marry him."

"No one is making you do anything."

"Making me feel like I *should* marry him. Well, sorry. I'm not. I'm not marrying him. I'm—"

"Ayla Josephine Hollis! You will—"

"I will *not.*" She hiked the dress higher. "I'm out. Jilly can have him."

Suddenly, the doors opened, and the soft opening notes of Pachelbel's Canon in D drifted out. That was the cue to walk…or maybe it was the cue to *run.*

"Young lady, you will—"

"No. I won't. For once in my life, Dad, I *will not do exactly as you say.*"

The entire sanctuary of three hundred people gasped in unison.

With that, Ayla gathered up the whole dress and took off, shooting past him and a tearful Jilly and a dumbstruck Trina. She used her hip to slam open the double doors and jogged down the wide stone stairs. There, a white stretch limo waited to take the just-married couple to the Peninsula Club for a lavish six-figure reception that already had its own hashtag.

Fitz, the silver-haired man who'd been driving Ayla for half her life, leaned against the door, reading his phone. He looked up and did a double take as she nearly took flight on the last two steps.

"Miss Ayla?" he asked. "What's wrong?"

"My fiancé's a cheater. My father's an ogre. And I've been pushed around for the last time. Out of here! Now!"

Fitz yanked open the back door as she heard her father's voice, but closed it before she could hear what he was saying. It didn't matter. Nothing mattered.

"The shelter!" she called through the separation panel when the chauffeur climbed in.

Fitz knew which shelter. He'd taken her there before, often with an animal in the back on the way to or from. And, thank God, he didn't question the request. Maybe he knew her that well. Maybe he knew that when Ayla

Hollis's life went to the dogs...*she* went to the dogs. Maybe he was on that short list of people who *really cared* about her.

Who else made that list? Now that Nana Jo was gone? Certainly not EJ. Maybe Trina. Definitely not Mother.

Only when they were on the highway did Ayla give in to the tears, which, once they started, wouldn't stop. Tears of fury. Tears of agony. Tears of...*relief*. And not just because she finally ripped the damn veil and heinous clip out of her hair.

With the world passing in a blur, she marched into the front office, cruised past the shocked faces at the front desk, and headed down the hall to where the new arrivals were always rolled up in balls on hard concrete floors.

She could smell wet fur and sadness, and it felt... right. Familiar. And in her head, she could see even more of that sadness. She shook off the energy coming at her with machine-gun rapid fire, spying a little tricolored Chihuahua mix who looked like he needed company.

Flicking the latch, she crawled right into the pen and folded onto the floor with no regard for the Vera Wang crepe halter-top gown that cost enough to feed every dog in this shelter for a lifetime.

The dog with giant ears was thinking about a polka dot blanket he once loved, so he must be cold. She wrapped him in her arms and cuddled him close to her chest, the perfect little creature to catch her tears.

She had no idea how long they were like that, but when she finally looked up, Miz Marie was standing next to her with a wistful smile on her face.

"I had a feeling you might come here, kitten," she whispered.

Ayla swallowed. “Take me home, Marie.”

“Of course.” She stepped in and reached down, scooping up the dog. “This guy, too, now that you’ve bonded.”

“Can we?”

“Honey, I’ve been volunteering at this shelter for a decade. We’ll fill out the paperwork later. And if you don’t mind a bit of a drive tonight, I’m going to take you somewhere special.”

“Take me anywhere.”

So Marie Boswell did what she was famous for among the community of dog lovers all over North Carolina… she rescued the damaged creatures who hit rock bottom and needed a new life.

Chapter Two

Theo Santorini had to face the fact that his charmed existence wasn't so charming anymore. Long considered the "lucky one" in his Greek family, he was one broken-down truck away from becoming one of the country music songs that seemed to be wailing from the speakers in every rest stop he visited from Southern California to North Carolina.

Lost my woman, lost my job, my dog hates me, and my truck won't start.

Okay, he didn't have a dog, and he was currently zipping through the middle of Arkansas in his beloved Honda Civic SI, not a truck. But the job and woman? He hadn't listened to country music since he was growing up in the Blue Ridge Mountains, but the imaginary song was dead-on.

And if he was being honest, he never believed that garbage about "being born under a lucky star" that his siblings had hung on him because he happened to be their grandmother's favorite. That didn't make him lucky—it made him smart enough to know how to handle the old battle-ax.

He was an engineer, for God's sake. He didn't believe in luck.

Things just *looked* like they came easy to him, Theo thought as he passed a blue interstate sign and checked his gas gauge. It was a hair away from a quarter, which was close enough to empty for a man who rarely let his tank go low.

Nothing had been easy about becoming a Navy nuke. It wasn't luck that got him one of the highest scores of any Navy officer who'd taken the test to get into the Nuclear Field Program. They might have sent him directly to Nuclear Power School after that, but he worked his butt off to get all the promotions to become lieutenant commander in charge of the technicians running the power on the aircraft carriers stationed at Naval Base San Diego.

He hit the turn signal and cruised from the fast lane to the exit, unable to resist making a neat mental list of things that had gone wrong in the past month.

The big fat engineering job with a nuclear firm in London that he'd accepted when he left the Navy six weeks ago had fallen through due to an unexpected budget cut. That left him stunningly unemployed, and uncertain of where he'd go or what he'd do next.

His hope that he could stay in the world's most perfect two-bedroom bungalow four blocks from the Pacific Ocean had fallen through, too, since he'd given notice when he thought he was moving to London. And that left him temporarily homeless with no clue where on this planet his next job might be.

As the cherry on top of the crap sundae, the woman he'd thought he loved and had planned to propose to the night they were supposed to have arrived in London had also fallen…in love with her next-door neighbor. That left him more broken and betrayed than he cared to admit.

At least he had his family. The dynamic of the Santorini clan might have shifted quite a bit in the last few years, but the heart of his ever-growing family never changed. They'd proven that the minute they heard about the job, the house, and the neighbor.

His widowed mother, who had remarried and lived with her new husband at his extensive canine rescue and training property, had insisted he stay with them at Waterford Farm. His siblings, most of whom had followed Mom from their home in Chestnut Creek to neighboring Bitter Bark, opened up their homes immediately. Even John, who was about to be a newlywed when he married Summer in three weeks.

The Kilcannon kids, his stepsiblings, and their cousins the Mahoneys had also stepped up and offered places for him to stay while he figured out his next move.

Last but never least, Yiayia, his Greek grandmother who literally believed that the sun was placed in the sky to shine on Théodoros Santorini, had begged him to move into the third floor of the rambling old Victorian in Bitter Bark she shared with her cohort in crime, Gramma Finnie Kilcannon.

True to form, the now huge family had rallied to his aid when his life collapsed. And tomorrow, when he arrived in Bitter Bark, they'd all gather at Waterford Farm, toast his homecoming with pitchers of Bloody Marys and shots of Jameson's—the Irish influence. And then they'd eat and possibly dance—the Greek influence. And if his brother Alex made lamb and spanakopita? And if Yiayia came in with a mountain of kourabiedes—which he knew she would—then Theo could feel like his existence was charmed again.

The thought of his grandmother's butter cookies made

Theo's stomach growl, a perpetual state for him. But the emptiness reminded him it would be a few hours before he stopped for dinner and a place to spend the night. So, after filling the gas tank, he parked in front of the mini-mart and headed in, eyeing the rolling hot dog grill and smelling pizza.

He ordered two dogs and two pepperoni slices and a soda, threw a big bag of chips and a couple of packs of beef jerky on the counter, and paid.

Then he walked into the head to wash his hands.

A minute later, he was shaking off wet hands and glowering at the empty towel dispenser when the door whipped open so hard it smacked the wall behind it, and a wild-eyed woman burst in.

"Wrong roo—"

"Help me!" she cried breathlessly, and he noticed she was dragging a black dog by a chain around his neck. "Please! Take this dog! Don't let anyone know it's here!"

What the hell?

She shoved the dog into the bathroom, and Theo could see the animal was filthy, skinny, and shaking so hard the poor thing could hardly stand on front paws that hadn't been cleaned or clipped in a lifetime.

"A stray?" he asked.

The middle-aged woman looked up at him with genuine fear in her eyes, creases deepening on her face as she frowned.

"It'd be better off if it was," she said. "Dog's been chained to a picnic table for months! I walk my own dog by that place three times a day, and I can see through the trees. No matter what time or what the weather is, this poor animal is out there. Does it get food? I don't know. Maybe. But if so, it means a fight with all kinds of critters and strays. Just look at this wretched thing! I simply couldn't take it one more day!"

"Good for you." He crouched down to get a better look at the animal. The once-white markings on its snout were smoky gray with dirt, and its ribs were visible through short but matted black fur. A mutt, for sure, with floppy ears and pure misery in dark eyes that looked up at him with the same plea for help the lady was making.

"That bastard caught sight of me when I took him, so I gotta leave him here and run. If he sees my truck parked out there…" She shuddered like she didn't even want to think what could happen. "But whatever you do, please don't give back this dog. He's gonna kill the poor thing!"

"Not on my watch," he muttered. "We'll find a shelter."

"*You* will," she fired back. "If that guy finds me, I'm dead. I'm not lying when I say I swear to God he's running a meth lab in that place." She pushed the animal closer to him, her gaze dropping over him with a quick assessment. "You're a big guy. You can take that human vermin who deserves to die."

But he sure as hell didn't want to be the one to kill him.

"Buck won't mess with you unless he's got a rifle."

Great. His M9 was in the car.

"But if that bastard gets his hands on this dog? He'll beat the living crap out of this animal and chain it up again. A picnic table! What the hell is wrong with people?" She spun around, flung open the door, and disappeared.

He stared at the door as it closed behind her, his jaw loose, then back at the sorry creature who cowered in fear.

"Oh man." He held the dog's desperate gaze and spent a few minutes trying to provide some comfort and figure out his next move. "I'm not gonna hurt you, doggo. But, damn, you look hungrier than I am. You like hot dogs? I'll get you some, and then we'll—"

"Don't lie to me, you son of a bitch! I saw her peel outta here, and my dog weren't in that truck!"

At the sound of the man's voice on the other side of the door, the dog dropped to the ground in a ball of quivering, filthy fur, letting out the softest, most heart-breaking whine.

"Where's Muttsy? Where is she?"

The dog covered her head with two filthy paws, a little trail of pee coming out from behind.

Theo swore under his breath and tried to think.

"I'm gonna find her! Where are you, you mangy mutt?" The words practically bounced off the bathroom door, which unfortunately didn't have a lock. If Theo went out there, and the guy had a gun, someone—like a bystander or the cashier or the dog—could get hurt.

"You were supposed to bite people, not let them take you, stupid dog!" he hollered, his voice getting closer to the bathroom.

Theo squeezed his eyes and spun through every possible scenario that a military engineer could imagine to mitigate the situation.

"*Muttsy!* I'm gonna find you, and you ain't gonna like it!"

Screw mitigation. He had to save this dog. He considered a stall, but wasn't about to hide from…human vermin. Looking around, Theo spotted a storage closet door and twisted the doorknob, which opened. It was small, but the dog would fit.

He tried to usher her into it, but she was too terrified to move, so he bent down and scooped the dog into his arms, getting a whiff of…he didn't even want to know. He put the dog on the floor and got right in her face.

"Muttsy." What a despicable name to give a dog.

She whimpered and quivered, looking down.

"Hey." He stroked her head over and over. "Can you be real quiet, girl?" He gently rubbed her filthy snout, easing her nose up so she had to look into his eyes. "You stay real quiet, and there's a hot dog in your future." He kept petting her, keeping his voice low and steady. "Don't make a sound. There's pizza for you, too."

He put a finger to his lips while he stood. "With a side of jerky. Stay so quiet, baby."

Very slowly, he closed the door without making a sound, turning as the other door was flung open by a nasty-looking guy with a pockmarked face and a flannel shirt hanging on scrawny arms. This must be the human vermin.

He might have been Theo's age of thirty-four, but he looked like he'd lived twice that long and drunk his way through most of it. Definitely fit the meth-lab-operator profile.

The man froze at the sight of Theo in front of the closet, his scruff-covered jaw opening as he looked up. Way up. At six-one and change, Theo had this chump by five inches and forty pounds of martial-arts-honed muscle.

"You got a problem, sir?" Theo asked.

He swallowed and narrowed red-rimmed eyes. "Lookin' for my dog."

Stay quiet, girl. Stay quiet. I do not want to have to break this guy, which I could, in one move.

Theo widened his stance, crossed his arms, and blocked the closet door. "So…" He jutted his chin to two empty stalls. "Look."

The man's nostrils flared with a breath as he turned and lifted his hand, grasping something round and small.

"Here ya go, Muttsy!" His voice was fake-nice. "I got you an orange, girl. It's your favorite."

He glanced in one stall, slid a look at Theo, then pushed open the door of the other one. In those few seconds, not a sound came from the closet, not so much as a whimper. But how long would that last? And what would Theo have to do to this miserable excuse for a person to protect her?

The guy glanced at Theo again, as if sizing up his chances of moving him away from the closet. Slim to none, he realized. Then his gaze slid to the floor. Theo followed it down to his shoes, seeing a stream of yellow dog pee trickling out from under the door.

Okay. He might have to replace the dog with the guy in that closet, but it could be done. And they both knew it.

"I got an *orange*, Muttsy," he called again, leaning to the side and looking at the door. But the dog stayed quiet and still. Guess she wanted to live more than she wanted that orange.

After a few seconds, the guy dropped a wimpy f-bomb and pitched the fruit to the ground, yanked the door, and walked out.

Theo waited five, ten, then thirty seconds before he turned and opened the storage closet.

The dog had backed into the far corner of the closet, under a shelf, and behind a bucket and mop, hunched over in fear. After a few seconds, she peered up at Theo with terror and hope and confusion in her eyes.

"It's okay," Theo whispered, crouching down in the doorway. "You have seen the last of him…"

She whimpered, pressing into the back wall.

"Come on, girl." He reached his hand toward her, but she didn't move. Her eyes did, though, sliding to the floor.

He looked down and spotted the orange.

"Not to go full engineer on you, doggo," he said as he snagged the little round fruit, "but this isn't technically an orange. It's a clementine."

By the look on her face? It was the Holy Grail.

"You want this? Must be your weakness if old Human Vermin thought it could lure you." Shouldering his way closer, he tore the rind, hoping the scent would overpower the smell of bleach.

"Here you go. A clementine. Sweeter than an orange and easy to peel."

After a minute, she inched past the bucket, eyes on the prize, and let out a soft whimper. When she got close enough, she gave the fruit a lick. But he didn't give it to her, instead using it to lure her all the way out of the closet.

Then he let her devour the fruit in three satisfying bites once he could get his hand on her collar.

Finished, she looked up, some rind hanging from her lips.

"Better?" he asked.

She answered by licking his cheek, making him chuckle.

"Good girl. Good…" No. He *couldn't* call her Muttsy. She deserved so much better than that. A pretty name for a pretty girl. "Good girl, Clementine."

She licked him again.

"All right. That's your name." Theo slid his fingers into the thick chain around her neck and straightened, guiding her toward the door. "I promised pizza and hot dogs and beef jerky, and I'm a man of my word. And just when you think life couldn't get any better, you'll be at Waterford Farm, where they'll know exactly what to do with you. You know what? We'll drive straight through to Bitter Bark and be there at dawn."

He leaned over and pressed his nose to the smelly beast, not caring that he'd have to air his car out for days after this. It would be worth it to save this sweet dog.

"My luck may have run out, Clementine, but yours just changed for the better."

Chapter Three

The first thing Ayla Hollis saw when she opened her eyes the morning after the worst day of her life was her discarded wedding gown—currently being used as a bed for a black cat named Ziggy Stardust.

"How's that dress feel, Zig?" she whispered, her morning voice raspy. "Like a four-thousand-dollar mistake?"

Ziggy purred and sighed and…pictured his favorite windowsill. His eyes closed, and he imagined the view out that window and the squirrel that liked to sit in an oak tree and stare right back.

Ayla could see the entire scene, exactly as this cat did, in her mind's eye.

Of course, no one would believe her if she told them that, so she didn't. She kept her secret, because being able to read an animal's mind was almost as embarrassing as being a…runaway bride.

She moaned at the memory, plucked at the chenille bedspread, and stared at the chipped maple dresser against one wall of the tiny bedroom. Instead of waking up in the honeymoon suite at the Ritz-Carlton, she was at Miz Marie's Last Chance Ranch somewhere in the foothills of the Blue Ridge Mountains, alone and free.

"Knock, knock! I bring coffee and a raspberry croissant from Linda May's bakery in town."

Not completely alone, thank God.

The bedroom door inched open, and Ayla spied the familiar gray spiky hair and black-framed glasses worn by the most unlikely—and genuine—friend that Ayla had.

"Oh my goodness, Ziggy!" Marie exclaimed. "Get off that expensive dress right this minute, or you will be sorry."

Ziggy looked up at Marie and purred, turned, and pawed at one of the covered buttons before closing his eyes, unable to even conjure up an image of Marie making good on that threat.

"Don't worry about it, Marie. I'm never wearing it again. Raspberry croissant, you say?"

Ayla couldn't remember the last time she ate a croissant.

"Yes, and prepare to have a little party in your mouth." She set a golden-brown croissant with some red jelly oozing from the sides on the night table, next to a small dish that held the exquisite diamond necklace Ayla's father had given her at the rehearsal dinner.

Was that before or after Jilly and EJ decided to hook up, she wondered.

Marie also set down a cup of creamy coffee. "And I put sugar in this because coffee without sugar is not worth drinking. Go ahead. Just eat in bed. Some dog will be by to get the crumbs."

Ayla snorted, thinking about her mother and her bone-deep phobia about being in the same room as actual sugar. Or eating in bed. And forget dogs. Her mother hated them. And they, Ayla happened to know, were not huge fans of her mother.

Ayla pushed up and took the napkin—which, God love the woman, was really a paper towel—and spread it on the bedspread. Glancing down, she read the upside-down words *Waterford Farm* on the oversized T-shirt Miz Marie had helped her into last night, sometime after the second bottle of wine. Under the shirt, Ayla wore nothing but expensive undies meant for her wedding night with Scumbag Paxton.

"How did you sleep?" Marie asked.

"Surprisingly well."

"It's the mountain air out here in Bitter Bark," she said, walking to the wide-open sash window that looked out over spring grass and oak trees bursting with the new life of late April. The Blue Ridge Mountains rose up from the horizon, glorious and green.

"The merlot helped, too." Ayla inhaled the coffee aroma before taking a sip. She drank deeply, then set it aside to start on the croissant, which smelled like butter and…rebellion.

And tasted like the trip to France she was supposed to be taking this afternoon.

"I really don't know how to thank you," Ayla said as she swallowed the first bite and tried not to moan. There were only so many rules a Hollis could break in one morning. "You rescued me."

"Rescuing," the older woman said with a smile that crinkled the thin skin around her eyes, "is what I do."

"Animals and strays." Ayla gave a sad sigh. "I guess I qualify?"

"You did when you were rolled up on that shelter floor crying your eyes out." She came to the bed and perched on the edge. "That whole church was all aflutter with chatter and gossip, and I, the one person who did not belong at a society wedding, was the one who knew exactly where you'd go with your broken heart."

"Thank you." She put her hand over Marie's weathered knuckles, feeling a rush of affection for the woman. If anyone would understand the secret Ayla kept, it would be this woman.

Was it time to share with Miz Marie? They'd been friends for a year, and all Marie ever said was she'd never met anyone who understood animals like Ayla.

If Marie only knew the truth.

"I'm happy to finally see your new place in the daylight," Ayla said, gazing at the vista out the window.

For almost the hour-and-a-half drive here from Charlotte last night, Marie had chattered on about her new ten-acre ranch, probably to keep Ayla from changing her mind and begging to go back. She'd told Ayla the whole story about how she'd purchased the house and land for a veritable song from her good friend Daniel Kilcannon. He owned Waterford Farm, an adjacent property that he and his family had turned into a canine training center where Marie frequently took dogs she'd rescued.

Of course, Ayla knew that Marie's lifelong goal was to "retire" from shelter-hopping around the state, and that she loved the picturesque Blue Ridge Mountains of western North Carolina. Marie always said she longed to open up a "a dream home" exclusively for senior dogs and special-case animals, the "unadoptables," as they got labeled in the shelters. She would take the less-than-perfect animals that simply had nowhere else to go for love and care.

With her recent purchase of the Last Chance Ranch, her name for this property, her dream had come true, even though it had taken her away from Charlotte.

"However," Ayla said, smiling at the other woman, "I'd planned to visit this new home of yours on my own, fully dressed and bearing a housewarming gift."

"Pffft." Marie flicked her hand. "You're here, and that's gift enough." She studied Ayla with the same loving eyes she would a sick puppy, trying to decide if she needed to take it to a vet. "Have you heard from anyone?"

"I don't have a phone, Marie. I don't have a purse, a penny, an article of clothing, or a stitch of makeup except what I didn't cry off while I sat with that dog." She frowned and wiped some buttery flakes from her lips. "What did you name that little guy?"

"I called him River, as in 'cry me a,' and he's currently sleeping in the kitchen."

She laughed at the typical Miz Marie handle. The animals she rescued and found homes for were always named after a song running in her head, or the last thing she ate, or a character she'd seen in a show on her TV, which, based on the names, must be permanently tuned to the 1960s.

"Only you would save a runaway bride *and* the dog she used as a four-legged handkerchief." Ayla gave a wistful smile. "I've never met anyone like you in my life, you know. You're wonderful, Miz Marie Boswell."

Marie put a weathered hand on Ayla's arm. "I'm here for you, kitten."

She swallowed a lump that formed at the gentle tone and the nickname Marie had given her the day they met. It reminded her of how her grandmother called her "Ayla Jo" when no one else on earth did.

Ayla reached up to scratch her head, making a face as her fingers dug into her teased hair. "How am I going to undo this?"

"Your hair or your life?"

"Both," Ayla said with a wry smile. "I can't imagine how upset my family is, or what EJ thinks."

"Who cares?"

Seriously. She let out a low groan. "I honestly don't want to even think about going back there and picking up that…life."

"Then don't. You were about to go to Europe for a month. Stay in Bitter Bark instead."

Now that was as tempting as the second croissant she was considering. "How could I do that?"

"Easily," Marie replied with a shrug. "Call your mother or your sister or your former best friend who can't keep her legs together and say, 'I'm fine, and I'm not coming back for a while. I'm taking a few weeks to myself. Return my gifts, and I'll see you later.' Would it be that hard?"

For a long moment, Ayla stared at this lady who'd become like a mother to her this past year. And certainly a better one than the distant woman she called Mother. Literally. Not Mom or Mama or Mommy, not since Ayla was three. *Mother*.

And whoa, she bet Mother was angry right now. Mortified in front of her entire social circle *and* the white-dress-wearing skank Dad brought as a date. They must all be furious. Usually, it was Trina who refused to be wrestled into submission. Who would have thought that the perennial people-pleasing daughter would be the bride who besmirched the Hollis name?

"Dear God, a *runaway* bride."

"Are you, though? I thought a runaway bride had cold feet, not good reason."

"I don't know the technicalities, but can you imagine

the social media posts?" she asked, shaking her head and suddenly very happy not to have her phone.

"No, because my only use for that particular corner of hell is to get dogs to good homes. In my opinion, you aren't a runaway anything. You are a free and independent woman who deserves to be listened to, loved, and adored, and not cheated on." Marie leaned closer to add, "And it's time you get to be that woman."

"You make it sound so easy."

"It is." Marie stood, moving restlessly around the little bedroom. "I do this with animals all the time. In addition to a home, I give them a job—because every creature finds self-worth through their purpose—and unconditional, trusting, total love."

"A job? I'm not trained to do anything but raise money for causes. And unconditional, trusting love?" She snorted, another thing her mother hated. "I don't believe such a thing exists."

Marie ignored that, studying her. "Nothing? You can't do anything at all? Answer phones or pour coffee or wait tables or…" She gave a soft laugh. "Probably not in your wheelhouse, huh?"

She didn't even have a wheelhouse. "But I do want a job, Marie. I've always wanted a purpose, but the trust fund made a job seem superfluous, so I've volunteered to help animals, like you. And while I'm here, I can feed the chickens and clean litter boxes and I can…" She sat up a little, itching to let it all out. "I can do other things," she said, purposely vague to see if Marie took the bait.

"Well, unless you can fix the goats' fence, clear some trees, rebuild the outdoor kennels, and maybe paint that old storage shed, I don't know what else to give you."

"I can help with the animals." She bit her lip. "Especially the worst cases."

Marie tipped her head, a frown creasing the lines between her eyes, probably at the note in Ayla's voice.

"I know what they need," Ayla added on a whisper. "I know what they want." She swallowed and dove in, dying to get the words out and certain the time was right. "Because I know what they think."

"Excuse me?"

"Marie, please don't judge me harshly, or mock what I'm about to tell you, but the truth is, I can read an animal's mind. It's not a lie or a trick or a game. It's a real thing, like I am able to sense their energy and see the image of whatever they see in their mind. No words, of course, since they don't have language skills, but I'm—"

"A pet psychic!" She slapped a hand on her chest. "Oh my God, you are! Why didn't I ever realize that? I should have, because I've always thought…*yes*. You're a pet psychic."

Ayla cringed. "I'm not a huge fan of that term. The accepted title is animal communicator or animal intuitive."

"Whatever! I've seen them on TV, and I met one once. Sophia." She pressed her hands to her chest. "She was amazing! Literally knew what the animals were—yes, what they were seeing! It was chill-inducing."

What was chill-inducing was this reaction. "You believe me?"

"Of course I believe you! There was a huge article in some national paper not long ago that one of my friends in the rescue world sent me. I think 'pet psychic' is becoming mainstream."

"Really? Because sometimes I'm not even sure myself. It's so…out there. Weird, you know? Like literal paranormal, which I don't believe in at all."

"It's not paranormal," Marie assured her. "It's a gift, like being able to paint or sing or dance on your tiptoes and call it ballet. Have you studied the science of pet psychics?"

"I don't think too many people put 'science' and 'psychic' in the same sentence."

"Well, they should. It's a science. That article said it has to do with waves and vibrations, and oh! You can make money from this, you know. Real money. One lady they interviewed had a three-month waiting list and charged a hundred an hour. Can you communicate with dead pets?"

Ayla shook her head. "Just the ones in front of me. And not a picture, either, or through a computer screen. I have to touch them."

"Well, there are plenty to touch in this town."

"Honestly, Marie, I've spent my life wishing this would go away," she admitted. "As a kid, I thought everyone knew what animals were thinking. As a teenager, I thought I might be crazy. And as an adult? I've learned that I get tremendous comfort from animals, but I keep the fact that they can communicate with me to myself."

"No one knows?"

"My grandmother knew." Ayla added a wistful smile. "She had the same gift."

"Really?"

"I've heard it's hereditary," Ayla said.

"Anyone else?"

"I told my sister, and she threatened to have me committed."

Marie crossed her arms, nodding. "Well, I think you've found your job, kitten. You're a pet psychic." At Ayla's look, she held up her hand. "Fine, fancy pants. You're an animal communicator. And I can't think of a better place to ply your trade than Bitter Bark, North Carolina, the most dog-friendly town on earth."

Could she really do that? The very idea gave Ayla a shiver of excitement. "Maybe I should change my name or—"

"You'll do nothing of the sort," Marie shot back. "No shame, child. Be proud of your skill!"

She was so right about that. Why hide it anymore?

"I'll practice here at the ranch first," she said, closing her eyes as she fantasized about a whole month of doing what she'd always believed she was meant to do. "Didn't you say you have two other dogs?"

"Hoss and Little Joe." She chuckled. "*Bonanza* marathon. There's another stray cat around I call Cheerio, spotted while I was eating cereal, but he hasn't warmed up enough to move in. There are two goats, Waffles and Blueberry—I made blueberry waffles the morning I got them. The chickens, of course. I can't grow this place too fast, not the way I'd like, until I build out the kennels and fix some things. But oh, I've got big dreams for the Last Chance Ranch, kitten. Big dreams. But dreams take time and money."

"I'm happy to help any way I can while I'm here."

"And I love the company," Marie promised. "Actually, I'm on my way to get resident dog number four, if you want to come along."

"Right now?"

"Daniel Kilcannon, the vet who owns Waterford Farm? He called a few minutes ago and told me his stepson picked up a stray on his way here from San Diego. Daniel's given the dog a physical, and she's extremely undernourished, but nothing else is wrong with her."

"You're bringing her here?"

"Yup. Waterford's kennels are bursting at the seams until the big adoption fundraiser next weekend. Plus, this pup had a rough time of it. Why don't you come with me and see Waterford Farm? That place would be a gold mine of business for you. It's all dogs, all the time. And one very large and loving family."

"I'd go, but…" Ayla plucked the T-shirt.

"Well, they'll love that top. As for the bottoms…" She stepped to the dresser and opened the top drawer, tossing a pair of camo pants to her, like Ayla had seen Marie wear a hundred times. "There's a pair of shitkickers in the closet."

"I assume those are shoes?" she guessed, making Marie laugh.

"Yes. Size nine."

"I'm a seven."

"Then wear extra socks—bottom drawer—and get dressed, Ayla. We're headed to Waterford to introduce them to Bitter Bark's newest pet…*animal communicator*." Marie reached down and gave her a hug. "You've got a new job and a new life, kitten. What else do you need?"

She flicked at her hair. "A new 'do."

"There's a bottle of conditioner in the shower. Knock yourself out."

It took half the bottle, but Ayla finally smoothed out her long hair, and then she washed off every drop of makeup except for the lash extensions, which saved her from looking like death warmed over.

Dressed in camos, a baggy T-shirt, and filthy boots that were two sizes too big, she headed out to start her new life and new job.

Wait. Hadn't Marie said there was one other thing that a rescue needed?

Oh yes. Unconditional love.

Two out of three wasn't bad.

Chapter Four

Clementine howled like a hurt wolf, throwing her head back and giving it all she had.

"Oh, please," Theo's stepsister, Darcy Kilcannon Ranier, chided the dog sweetly as she managed to clip one honker of a dog toenail.

Darcy pushed her long blond hair over her shoulder and glanced at Theo from her grooming station at Waterford Farm. "I promise this doesn't hurt her, Theo. She's a little bit of a drama queen."

She was also the neediest female Theo had been around in a long time. And the hungriest. She'd powered through every bite of food he had on the rest of the drive, leaving his car looking and smelling like a dumpster by the time he rolled into Bitter Bark before sunrise.

It had taken about twelve hours and five more rest stops after he left the mini-mart outside of Little Rock, but the minute Clementine finished a meal, she stared at him, wanting more.

More love. More conversation. More food. And more Theo.

When it came time to walk anywhere—anywhere at

all—she curled on the ground and waited for him to pick her up and carry her. Everywhere. His arms hurt from hauling the pup around, and his clothes had reeked until he had finally taken a shower and changed.

While he did, his stepfather had done a thorough exam on the dog in the small vet hospital on the property and pronounced Clementine generally healthy but undernourished, with some sores and infected fleabites. No more oranges, he'd warned, which turned out not to be so great for dogs, making him hate the human vermin even more.

She had a few scrapes and scars that made him think she'd seen plenty of action in her day, not to mention she was neurotic, anxious, and scared of her own shadow.

They'd spent some time giving her flea and tick treatments and the most basic, immediate care. Daniel started her on a special diet and supplements, and when Theo's stepsister arrived that morning, she took over with some much-needed grooming.

When she finished the nails, Darcy turned on a warm stream of water and poured shampoo all over Clem, who whimpered, then finally settled into the sudsy bath given by someone who was clearly an expert at the task.

Even during the luxurious treatment, Clementine never took her dark gaze off Theo.

Next to Darcy, Theo's sister, Cassie, who'd come over the minute she heard he'd arrived early, pointed at Clem's face. "Find someone who looks at you the way this dog looks at you, Theo," Cassie joked.

"But someone who doesn't need to be carried everywhere," he replied. "I'm telling you, she is not going to be happy when we get separated."

"If you're really moving into Waterford Farm, you

can keep her, Theo," Darcy told him. "You're taking Liam and Shane's old room, right? It's dog-friendly. Everything here is."

He considered the offer, but shook his head. "I don't want her to get more attached to me," he said. "This is a short-term deal. The job in London could get reinstated anytime, or something else could come through. I don't expect to be here long."

Cassie stuck her lower lip out. "Why can't you stay, Theo? The whole family is here in Bitter Bark."

"Nick's in Africa," he reminded her, referring to the oldest Santorini, who was working for Doctors Without Borders. "And nuclear engineering jobs are scarce in Bitter Bark."

She came closer and wrapped her arm around his waist. "Well, we've all missed you, big bro. We'll have to make you fall in love with this little dog town the way the rest of us have and keep you here."

"Not falling in love with anyone, anyplace, or anything, Cass," he said grimly. "Not after Heather."

Cassie rolled her eyes. "I can't say I was a huge fan of hers."

"*Now* you tell me?" He eased his sister away and shot her a vile look. "Thanks for the help."

"Where is he? Where is my grandson?" His grandmother's demand came from right outside the grooming building, followed by the loud bark of one of her doxies.

"Right here, Yiayia." He opened the door and was instantly wrapped in a loving hug, while a little dog jumped at his legs.

"Here he is! My Théodoros!" Yiayia pronounced his name with a *t* instead of *th* sound, which was technically on his birth certificate, but no one else called him that. "Finnie, come here. My grandson is home!"

He shot a look at Cassie, who rolled her eyes and laughed. He knew why. Agnes Santorini was never very good at hiding her feelings, and where Theo was concerned? Her feelings were obvious: He was her favorite of the five Santorini kids.

Maybe because the oldest, Nick, had been so close to Dad. Alex and John were twins and had each other. Cassie had been glued to Mom, surprising no one when she moved to Bitter Bark after their mother married Daniel Kilcannon.

As a little boy, Theo had always ended up in Yiayia's care, and for some reason, her razor-sharp personality never bothered him. He laughed at her, and she softened around him. And she cooked him into happy food comas, so it was a win all around.

He reached down to hug the other woman who'd come in with Yiayia. Finola Kilcannon, the tiny Irish woman who'd become his grandmother when her son married his mother. She was the sweet polar opposite of Yiayia, though the two old ladies had become inseparable.

"Oh, good gracious, laddie," Gramma Finnie exclaimed. "I'm always so surprised by how big you are."

"Théodoros means 'God's gift' in Greek," Yiayia told her, gazing up at Theo like he was posed on the pedestal she reserved exclusively for him. "Don't you think he was perfectly named?"

"Perfectly," Cassie said wryly, making him laugh at the long-standing family joke.

"And hello, little Galatea." He bent over to stroke the tan dachshund, who licked his hand.

Clementine whimpered and splashed.

"Somebody's jealous," Darcy said with a laugh and turned on the spray hose.

"Speaking of perfectly named creatures…" Theo looked for Gala's stout little partner, another doxie. "Where's Pyggie?"

"Pygmalion is on strike," Yiayia announced. "We got him out of the car, and he sat on the driveway and won't move. And this must be the stray from the road. Hello, gorgeous."

As his grandmother went closer, Clementine got up on her hind legs and started to growl.

"Hey, Clem," Theo said. "Friendly human approaching now. Usually has cookies. No reason to growl."

He walked over to the dog and put a hand on her head, instinctively knowing he couldn't raise his voice. Instead, he got closer to whisper in a floppy ear. "We're friendly now, girl. We trust strangers. Especially this one."

He put his arm around Yiayia to prove his point. Clem calmed a little and stared at him with almost as much love in her eyes as Yiayia's when she looked at Theo.

"So it appears you've gotten rid of one female and picked up another," Yiayia said.

"And it appears you still say whatever you're thinking," he countered with a knowing smile.

She threw a glance at Finnie. "I try to temper it with a bit of love now, but I can't lie. I never really liked that Heather."

He groaned. "Why was this kept a family secret?"

"Because you liked her."

He had, but obviously…not enough. "So what's wrong with Pyggie?" he asked, wanting the subject off his love life.

"If only I knew. He's mad all the time. Staring at the wall. Not eating."

"Pygmalion not eating?" Cassie's dark eyes flashed. "That's serious."

"Indeed, 'tis serious." Gramma Finnie put an arm around Yiayia, proving that she might be a five-foot-tall octogenarian, but the little lady had done the one thing few people other than Theo had ever attempted—tamed Yiayia. "We're worried about the poor pupper. Something's amiss."

"Maybe he is unhappy that I cut back on his kibble," Yiayia said. "But what about you, Théodoros?"

"Don't ever cut back on my kibble, Yiayia."

She laughed like he was a veritable stand-up comic. "How long are you going to be here, and what can I make you to eat?"

"I'll eat anything you cook," he assured her. "I'm staying for John's wedding in three weeks, but doing a full-court press to get a job since the one in London fell through. Not too long, hopefully."

"Hopefully?" Cassie scoffed. "Like Bitter Bark is *such* a terrible place to live, what with all the fabulous family, gorgeous scenery, great food, and wonderful dogs. It's so *awful* to be forced to stay here."

"You had one foot out of North Carolina not so long ago," he reminded her. "You are the original 'this town is too small for me' girl."

"Well, we changed that, didn't we?" Yiayia crossed her arms with a smug expression. "We got her married."

"That'd do the trick to keep the lad here," Gramma Finnie joked. Although she looked at Yiayia like it was no joke. Uh-oh. These two were the famous family matchmakers. Better put a stop to that nonsense, stat.

"Except you'd be walking over my dead body, because that ain't happenin', ladies. Did we not thoroughly discuss my pathetic love life?"

"Not pathetic once the Dogmothers get involved," Yiayia said. "We have quite the number of success stories under our belt, don't we, Finn?"

"And 'tis time for another," Gramma Finnie agreed. "We've hit nothing but dead ends with Ella, and Nick is on the other side of the world."

"Isn't he coming for John's wedding?" Theo asked.

"Yes, but then he'll be gone again." Yiayia narrowed her eyes at him, examining his face like he was a lamb chop that might or might not be suitable for her moussaka. "But a woman would have to be just right for you, Théodoros. Gorgeous, brilliant, charming, and…" Yiayia slipped her hand through his arm and squeezed his bicep. "The perfect match for my perfect grandson."

Darcy and Cassie shared a look, snorting laughter.

"Don't waste your energy, ladies," he insisted. "I'm temporarily in town and permanently single."

"Oh, is that Pyggie barking?" Yiayia broke away at the sound of the only thing that could steal her attention from Theo. "Better check on him." She and Gramma Finnie headed back outside, with Gala on their heels.

"Word of warning, Theo." Darcy turned off the water and grabbed a fluffy towel. "Don't give them a challenge unless you want to be fending off dates arranged by the two most determined grandmothers in the country."

Cassie nodded in agreement. "Ella's been frustrating them at every turn, and now that Yiayia has a boyfriend—"

"That guy she met at Christmas is official now?" he asked.

"I don't know if they're calling it that," Cassie said. "She tries to play it down, but I think she really likes him."

"She's eighty, for God's sake."

"Eighty-plus, but don't remind her unless you want to be jabbed with her Botox syringe," Cassie cracked. "And so what if she's over eighty? She deserves love since Papu died all those years ago."

"Well, I don't know about this," he said. "Yiayia's kind of special."

Cassie shot a look at Darcy. "As you can see, the Yiayia-Theo Fan Club is really a mutual-admiration society."

Laughing, Darcy reached around to get Clementine out of the sink, but instantly the dog gave a low, threatening growl.

"Clementine!" Theo warned, and the dog stopped, dropped into the sink, and whimpered.

"Now you've done it," Cassie teased.

"Oh man. I forget she's so sensitive." He reached in to pick her up, getting an inhale. "Good smell, Clem. No more trash heap."

"Oatmeal and lilac," Darcy said. "My favorite for the pretty girls."

Theo studied Clementine now that he could see past the dirt and sadness. "She is pretty," he admitted. "And I'm not the right person for her. I'm gruff, and she's tender, and I'm temporary, and this dog needs forever."

"Don't worry, Miz Marie is on the way over," Darcy told him. "She can have her forever life at the Last Chance Ranch."

He'd been grateful to hear that a Kilcannon family friend who took the worst cases lived so close now. It was a perfect solution for Clementine.

"You're gonna be fine, Clem." He whispered the promise into her ear as he lifted her into his arms.

She threw her body against his chest and draped possessive paws over his shoulders. It was as if she understood that the Last Chance Ranch would somehow *not* include her knight in shining armor.

Still carrying the dog, he walked outside into warm spring sun, spying Yiayia and Gramma Finnie talking to a young woman in the long driveway. She was crouched down with Pyggie, looking up and saying something to Yiayia.

From here, all Theo could see was a cascade of dark blond hair spilling over a narrow frame in a baggy shirt and camo pants. Then she pushed her hair back and revealed a striking face with delicate, high cheekbones and a slightly turned-up nose.

"Wow," he muttered. "Not what I pictured when I heard about Miz Marie."

"That's not Miz Marie," Darcy said. "She's in her seventies. I don't know who that is."

Gramma Finnie turned and excitedly waved them over. "Theo! Theo, you have to come and meet this girl. You have to! Get over here right now."

Next to him, Cassie snorted. "That didn't take long."

Just then, Yiayia reached down and scooped Pyggie off the ground, striding toward them, shaking her head.

"Who is that, Yiayia?" Darcy asked.

"A circus act," she muttered, snagging Cassie's arm. "Come with me. And, Theo, don't fall for her tricks."

"What the heck does that mean?" he asked Darcy.

"Beats me."

"Well, at least I'm not being set up."

Darcy's response was a laugh that sounded more like experience than humor. "Don't be so sure."

"This is Ayla Hollis." Gramma Finnie practically cooed the woman's name. "Ayla, this is Lieutenant Commander Theo Santorini, who arrived this very morning after a long career in the Navy. He's a nuclear engineer. And this is my granddaughter Darcy, our head groomer."

They said a quick hello, but dark brown eyes that seemed to contrast with the butterscotch hair flickered over him, interest barely registering despite the impressive and slightly embarrassing recitation of his résumé.

"And who's this?" The young woman reached toward Clem, placing one hand on the dog's back and the other on her head, then closed her eyes. And flinched. With a sigh, she inched back.

"Clementine," he responded. "Fresh from a much-needed bath."

For a moment, she didn't say anything, then looked up at him, sincerity in those bottomless brown eyes. "Could I…could I talk to her for a moment?"

A little perplexed by the request and more than a bit intrigued by the natural beauty making it, he slowly lowered Clem to the driveway.

She folded down to sit in front of the dog, slowly reaching to her.

"She might growl," he warned.

She nodded as if she already knew that. "Poor thing's been through a lot."

"Ayla's a pet psychic." Gramma Finnie sidled up next to him, her voice a thin, excited whisper.

So thin he was sure he hadn't understood her brogue. Because he thought she said—

"But the lass prefers animal communicator," Finnie continued. "She instantly knew what Pyggie was thinking. It was the most remarkable thing."

Theo stared at her, none of this truly registering in his engineer's brain. Did she say *pet psychic*? And here he thought he left the land of nutcases on the other coast.

"And that's why Yiayia marched off?" And why she'd *warned* him. Not that he needed it, but he'd have to tell her how much he appreciated the heads-up.

"It's okay." The woman looked up at him, those haunting dark eyes locked on him. "I understand the reaction. It's…bizarre."

To say the least.

"Well, my grandmother is not easily fooled."

"Fooled? Nonsense, Theo!" Gramma Finnie insisted. "For one thing, you know your grandmother had a near-death experience that took her to the other side. She's very in tune with the supernatural."

"I've heard of people who can communicate with animals," Darcy said. "That's very cool, Ayla."

"Thanks," she replied. "But honestly, there's nothing supernatural about it. I'm kind of sensing the dog's energy. It's…scientific, actually."

Scientific? He had to work to keep from letting out a noisy snort. "I see," he managed, proud for not even adding a goofy smile. But he sure wanted to.

Ayla kept stroking Clementine's head. "I understand you just brought her in. A stray?"

"Not technically," he said. "She's the definition of a rescue from a bad situation."

The woman smiled and plucked at the seriously unattractive camos she wore. "I feel you, girl. Clementine? Is that her name?"

"Yeah." He crouched down to get closer. "I didn't like the one she came with."

"The name confuses her," she whispered.

He stared at the woman who was, he had to admit, a knockout. A whack job, but a great-looking one.

"Is she telling you that?" he asked, trying, and likely failing, to keep the humor out of his voice.

She didn't answer, her eyes closed as she put her forehead close to Clementine's.

"Ayla, I do hope you and Marie will stay for dinner," Gramma Finnie said softly, like she didn't want to interrupt the *communication*. "And not to worry about what you're wearin', lass."

Ayla stuck her leg out straight, showing off a boot that even the Army would reject. "Even these lovely things?"

Gramma Finnie looked up at Theo. "She had to leave kind of suddenly and doesn't have but what's in Marie's closet."

Leave suddenly? Run out of town by people who wanted their money back for her psychic readings?

"Darcy, do you still have any clothes here at Waterford?" Gramma Finnie asked. "I thought we could help out poor Ayla."

"Of course we can," Darcy said enthusiastically. "And if you want to open up an office in town, we can all help you. I own a pet grooming business in Bitter Bark, and my cousin Ella has a dog treat shop attached. We can send each other clients, and you'd be rolling in no time."

Open an office? Was his stepsister serious? Proof that a sucker really was born every minute.

Ayla's delicate features softened as she smiled, making her even prettier. "That is so sweet of you, thank you. I'm a long way from opening up a shop, but I hope to be helping animals—and people—at Marie's ranch."

"Cool. And yes, we can snag some clothes for you today," Darcy said. "There's a lot of women your age and size in the family. What else do you need?"

She laughed, which sounded a little bit like softly ringing bells to him. Bells? *Come on, Theo.* The only bells he should be hearing were *alarm* bells.

"I don't have a thing, so whatever you can spare, and as soon as I buy what I need, I'll return yours."

She traveled without a thing? How much of a hurry had she been in?

"We got you, girl," Darcy assured her. "And yes, you and Marie have to stick around for dinner. The kennel's full, and all the family dogs will be in the pen. Josh will bring our Kookie and Stella for you to communicate with!" She beamed up at Theo. "Fun, huh?"

"Tons."

"Let's go tell everyone," Gramma Finnie said, hooking her arm through Darcy's. "Ayla can finish her reading of Clementine."

"Oh, I'm not doing a reading," she said quickly. "Just getting to know the dog."

As Darcy said goodbye, Ayla shifted her attention to Theo. Still holding Clementine's head in two hands, she pinned her dark chocolate gaze on Theo.

"I can tell you think I'm a fake."

Oh, so she could read people's minds, too.

"No, no. I think you're…" Maybe he better not *think* the truth. "Intriguing," he said, which was definitely not a lie.

A shadow of a smile pulled at her lips, drawing his attention to how full and natural they were, but not slick and glossy like the lips of so many women in the state he'd just left. And she sure hadn't bothered with makeup. But then, she didn't need to.

"I don't blame you," she said. "I struggle with it myself, and I'm the one experiencing it."

"Because you think you might be imagining what you're…hearing?" Except, if she was hearing things, then she would be a certifiable, if gorgeous, lunatic.

"I don't hear anything. I see pictures in my head."

He looked at her, fighting a smile.

"And you think I need to see a professional," she joked. "I get that."

Slowly, he dropped down to the ground next to her, captivated even though he didn't want to be. "What I think isn't important."

"It is to Clementine," she said.

He looked down at the dog, who instantly dropped her chin on his thigh, where that head had spent every waking moment, when she wasn't eating, on the drive from Arkansas.

"Because this dog?" She lifted her brows and smiled. "Is head over heels in love with you."

Something about the way she said it made his whole gut tighten. "How do you know?"

"You're almost all she thinks about."

He laughed softly. "Okay, full disclosure, Ayla." He liked her name, the way it sounded when he said it and how it matched how uniquely attractive she was. "I don't buy into any of this, sorry."

"No need to apologize."

"I know how you do it," he said confidently. "You can say that she's into me because you know I picked the dog up last night on the road, fed her everything that wasn't nailed down, and got her cleaned up and tended to. Of course she likes me."

"Her feelings have gone a little bit past *like*, but..." She finally let go of Clementine. "This isn't easy for me, Theo. I haven't been, uh, practicing for very long. So, if you don't mind, I'd rather not..." She searched for a word, then sighed. "I'd rather not *communicate* with a dog if her owner is doubting what I'm saying."

She started to push up, but he put a hand on her arm, not sure why. Not sure of anything but that he didn't want her to disappear yet.

"Sorry," he said, adding a smile. "Tell me what she's thinking. And me, too, if you can do that trick."

"I can't," she said.

"Because you know I doubt you."

"Because I read body language and can hear the tone of your voice, and I can smell a skeptic a mile away."

His smile grew. "That's the oatmeal and lilac shampoo Darcy used on the dog."

She almost laughed. Almost. And he was a little surprised by how much he wanted to hear that sound again.

"I don't mean to belittle what you're doing," he said. "I know Gramma Finnie and Darcy are enamored, but hey, they're Irish. This big extended family has Greeks, too, and we're a rational people."

"The culture that gave us mythology and the evil eye?" she challenged.

"Point taken," he conceded with a laugh. His hand suddenly ached a little, like it needed to reach out and cup her tantalizing jaw so he could see if her skin felt as smooth as it looked. Instead, he stroked Clementine's head, her chin still glued to his thigh. "So, what's this girl thinking?"

After a moment, she put her hand on Clementine's head, too, and her thumb brushed his, the contact warm. "All I can do is pick up the images in her brain."

She closed her eyes, and her lips parted slightly, and Theo…was glad she couldn't see the images in *his* head.

To erase the thought of kissing her, he dropped his gaze down to the body he couldn't quite get a read on in the Waterford Farm T-shirt, but that didn't stop his imagination from—

"She's thinking about somewhere dark. Like a closet." She frowned a little. "And she's looking at…an orange?"

He jerked back. What the *hell*?

But then he remembered she'd talked to his grandmother, who no doubt had heard the story of how he got Clementine and how she got her name. His mother had obviously talked to Yiayia on the phone before she rushed over here to see him, so this woman was just… playing her parlor game.

"Yeah, that makes sense," he said without challenging her tactic. "Anything else?"

She started to talk, then closed her mouth and shook her head. "Nope." She opened her eyes, and their gazes locked. "That's all I got," she said quickly, pushing up.

Because that's all she knew about Clementine, so she couldn't act like she was psychic-ing anymore.

"Are you sure?" he asked.

She bit back a laugh. "You don't believe me, remember?"

Not for a second. But he had to be careful because she had *some* kind of power. Nothing psychic, though. More of the feminine kind of power…the really dangerous kind.

Chapter Five

"Do you smell that, my friend?" Finnie sniffed noisily.

Agnes picked up her iced tea and sniffed. "You didn't spike me with Jameson's, did you? It's early, even for you, Finn."

Finnie smiled, unbuttoning the top button of her lavender cardigan. "'Tis the smell of love in the air." She practically sang the words, settling into the rocking chair next to Yiayia, where they always enjoyed the panoramic view from Waterford's wraparound porch.

But Agnes wasn't looking at the mountains right now. She was staring at her phone, re-reading Aldo's text that said, *I miss you today*.

Oh dear. This wasn't supposed to happen. He wasn't supposed to miss her. You don't *miss* companions, right? And that's all they were.

Except…last night, Aldo said the D word. At their age, that should mean…dementia. Not *dating*.

She slipped the phone into her sweater pocket and followed Finnie's gaze to where Theo stood talking to the crazy girl who'd shown up with Marie.

"What did you say, Finnie?" she asked, bringing herself back to earth.

"That girl and Theo. Look at them!"

"Oh, I tried to warn him that she's one of those fake psychics like you see on TV."

"She's not fake! She knew immediately what Pyggie's favorite napping spot looks like."

Agnes shot a brow up. "As if a woman who looks like you wouldn't have a flowered sofa."

"But 'tis Pyggie's favorite place to sleep in the sunshine. And she knew that without being told. You don't believe her?"

"Please, *please* tell me you're not that naïve, Finola Kilcannon."

Finnie's mouth dropped with disappointment. "But how would she know that?"

"By doing what those fake people do. They ask the right questions and make intelligent deductions that appear to be mind-reading. She's no different than those people on TV who claim to talk to dead relatives. But she's pretty, I'll give you that."

"Pretty enough for Theo?"

Agnes sat up, suddenly realizing what her friend was suggesting. "For Theo?"

"I know, she'd have to be Miss America for Theo."

Agnes curled her lip, looking at the girl, trying to find a flaw other than claiming to read animals' minds. "Well, she's dressed for a day of dumpster diving. And would it kill her to throw on a little blush and lipstick?"

"Agnes," Finnie said softly, adding the look that always accompanied that gentle reminder.

Fine. But this was *Theo* they were talking about. "Not sure she's quite what I have in mind for my grandson."

"Oh, I don't know," Finnie countered. "I think the lass has an air of elegant sweetness about her."

"There's nothing elegant about those ghastly boots."

"Anyone who can connect with animals probably has a good heart," Finnie continued, undaunted. "And the clothes are borrowed. What other problems do you find?"

Of course Finnie would see only the good and positive in everyone and everything.

"He's too smart for a charlatan psychic mind reader, Finnie," Agnes insisted. "He needs someone of equal intelligence, an impressive career, and maybe wider hips for childbearing."

"Perhaps we should search available royalty for His Highness Prince Theodore."

"Théodoros," she corrected. "And perhaps we should. Or at least get our matchmaking efforts back to Ella. That girl is not getting any younger, you know."

"Don't you want him to stay here in Bitter Bark?"

"Oh, yes. A girl can dream, right?" Agnes sighed with joy at the thought of her darling Theo only minutes away. "But he must find someone extraordinary. Not some common…fortune teller."

"Ye make no sense to me, lass," Finnie mused. "Why not give her a chance?"

"I think she's a fake. A fraud. A schemer. A con. What about that doesn't make sense?"

"Agnes, you've had a near-death experience! You literally walked through the gates of heaven—with a dog, if I recall your story correctly—and returned a changed woman."

"Not *that* changed. I'm still working on being nice." A challenge dear Finnie had taken to heart as one of her primary reasons for living.

And maybe Finnie's constant reminders were working. Aldo thought Agnes was nice. He said so all the time. Had anyone ever called her nice? She couldn't remember anyone, not even her dearly departed Nic, describing her as nice.

It was…nice.

"Then how could you think this woman's gift is that far-fetched?" Finnie demanded. "You've actually been to the other side."

Finnie had a point, but Agnes wasn't completely ready to concede. After all, this was her *Theo*. "I thought we'd save Theo for our last match."

"We might have a lot more matches, dear Agnes."

Looking ahead, she could feel Finnie's unwavering blue-eyed stare on her cheek. Finally, Agnes turned and met that gaze.

"Nick, Theo, and Ella," Agnes said. "Unless you think we should spread our wings and give your daughter, Colleen, a try? Otherwise, between us and Daniel? We've married off the family. The Dogmothers can retire like normal women our age."

"We've matched this family," Finnie said. "But there could be another one. A big…*Italian* family. Aldo has grandchildren, and they could be…yours."

Agnes jerked back with a gasp. "I'm not going to marry him, Finola Kilcannon!"

Finnie looked a little too smug, and she angled her white-haired head and wiggled her brows. "Never say never, Agnes Santorini."

"We're friends. Nothing more."

"Kissing friends."

"Fine, we kissed good night at the door last night. We weren't making out like teenagers. We pecked." Maybe a little more than a peck, but Finnie didn't need to know that because…an Italian family? "That's simply not in the cards."

"It might be." Finnie added a slightly yellowed saucy grin. "We could ask the fortune teller."

When Agnes laughed, Finnie reached her knotted, spotted hand over to touch Agnes's arm. "Give the lass a chance today. Maybe you'll come around. Maybe you'll realize that Marie brought us the answer to our prayers."

"I did?" Marie Boswell's gravelly voice came through the open sliding door that led into the house, and then the woman stepped out, her deep blue eyes pinned on Agnes. "So you like the idea of a talented pet psychic, huh? Is it Pyggie or Gala who needs what my sweet Ayla is offering?"

"'Tisn't a four-legged creature we're thinking of," Finnie said, waving Marie over to where they sat, then flipping her hand to point to Theo, still glued to the ground, talking to the young woman in question.

"Ahhh." Marie eyed the couple as Theo stood. "He is quite a specimen, I'll give you that."

Agnes shot her a look. "That's my grandson you're ogling."

"And your favorite," Marie fired back. "Cassie told me. You really shouldn't have favorites in a family this big." She took one more look. "I certainly can see the appeal. Big. Handsome. Strong."

"Brilliant. Kind. And has a true appreciation for food." Agnes smiled, knowing that last one was an understatement. Maybe that's why she loved Theo so much—he adored her cooking.

"The lass would have to be blind and broken not to notice," Finnie added.

"She's not blind," Marie said, dropping onto the sofa across from them, looking from one to the other. "But broken? Yes, she's had a heartache," she added. "A very bad one. I don't know if she's ready for the kind of shenanigans the Dogmothers are famous for."

Finnie and Agnes shared a look. "Shenanigans?" they asked in unison.

"Like the wedding we're all going to in a few weeks," Marie reminded them.

"John and Summer?" Agnes asked, then smiled. "That was an easy one. Did we shenani…gate?"

Finnie laughed. "You practically lassoed Summer the minute she showed up at Santorini's Deli, and then you started singing *Yianni's* praises like the church choir."

"Worked, didn't it?"

"And Declan?" Marie asked.

This time, Finnie snorted. "Agnes hid their twenty-year-old promise in the piano keys."

"I did," she admitted with a smile. "But you left your bag at the winery to get Alex to go back and see Grace."

For a moment, they looked at each other, familiar, loving smiles pulling. "We're good, Finn."

"'Tis true," Finnie agreed. "We should be known as the Shenanigators instead of the Dogmothers."

Laughing, they all turned to the couple who were still talking as Theo picked up the dog, who looked like she was on strike again, refusing to walk.

"Ayla has been through a very difficult time," Marie told them. "I'll let her share what she wants to, but I can tell you she's been badly hurt."

"So has Theo," Agnes said. "Just had his heart stomped on by a shrew named Heather."

"Ayla's been betrayed as well," Marie said. "Brutally

and publicly. She's dear and genuine and one of the most selfless creatures I've ever met, but she's tender. So, I would ask that you do this very carefully."

"Oh, Marie!" Finnie exclaimed. "We would never push unless the lass is interested and her heart is available. Can you help us by talking to her?"

"Of course."

Finnie leaned forward. "And invite the lad to work at your ranch every day for a few weeks." At Marie's look, she added, "Well, we have to get the ball rolling."

"Working at the ranch." Agnes was unable to keep the admiration out of her voice. "That's some excellent shenanigation, Finola Kilcannon."

Finnie grinned. "So you're in, Agnes? This is our next Dogmothers match?"

She sighed, thinking about it before committing. "If she's for real. This whole psychic thing makes me nervous. It's a little too bizarre for me. Do you really believe her, Marie?"

"I've been volunteering with her at a shelter in Charlotte for a year," Marie said. "And I've seen her help many animals because she knows what's wrong when no one else does."

"And you believed her from the beginning?" Agnes pushed.

"She's only just told me of her skill, so it's not like she's been hauling it out to impress people. But I've always known something was special about her. The fact is, she has a rare and extraordinary talent, and I think if she were allowed to use it instead of being mocked…" She lifted a shoulder. "Then she would be a huge asset to this town, to Waterford Farm, and to my ranch. And maybe to Theo Santorini."

The three of them exchanged looks, silent.

"I won't encourage anything without your support, Agnes," Finnie said. "We are a matchmaking *team*."

As always, Finnie's bone-deep goodness touched her.

"And I won't ask to be on your team permanently," Marie said. "But I'm certainly in a position to be your eyes and ears at the ranch." She lifted a brow. "And I have been needing some help from a strong man around the place. Daniel's been trying to get your grandsons over, but everyone is so busy. Theo would be a perfect solution."

Both of them turned to Agnes to get her final decision.

But before she could give it, Theo and Ayla reached the steps up to the porch.

"There you are, Marie." Ayla came up to join them, going right to where Pyggie was sleeping. "How's this dear boy doing?" She sat and reached down to touch his little head.

"You tell me," Agnes said, trying so hard to keep the challenge out of her voice. "What is he dreaming about?"

"Let me see…" She closed her eyes and kept her hand on Pyggie's head. "Enobklim."

"Enobklim?" Agnes shook her head. "That means nothing to me."

"It's Milk-Bone spelled backwards," Theo said without having to give the word even a minute's thought. Because he was a genius, Agnes mused.

Ayla's dark eyes flashed. "You're right and I can see the box he's thinking about. My Nana Jo told me once that some animals, in very rare cases, see things backwards, like the negative of a photograph."

Of course, a quick explanation, Agnes thought. Plus, one look at Pyggie's belly, and a child could tell he liked treats. And Milk-Bones were the most common treat in the world. So, once again, a lucky guess with a cute twist to give her credibility.

"Your grandmother?" Finnie asked. "Did she have the gift, as well, lass?"

"She did," Ayla said, reaching down to pick up Pyggie, which was no mean feat for someone as skinny as that girl. But she got Pyggie on the sofa next to her and gazed into his eyes for a long, long time.

Finally, she looked up at Agnes and asked, "Who's the man in the pale blue shirt with red and white roses?"

Next to her, Finnie grabbed her arm and squeezed. "I told you! She's real."

Whoa. Maybe she was. That wasn't a lucky guess. That was…impressive.

"What about him?" Agnes asked, picturing Aldo in the soft blue button-down he'd worn last night and the beautiful flowers he'd brought from his garden.

"He's the reason Pyggie's not eating lately."

Agnes felt her jaw unhinge.

"I think he's worried this man is going to take you away."

"Really." Well, that made two of them. "Oh my." She shifted in her seat, not sure what to say. "You're…quite talented, my dear."

"Oh, I knew you'd come around, Agnes," Finnie exclaimed, her Irish blue eyes dancing with the fun of… shenanigans.

Well, they'd find out, wouldn't they? Ayla Hollis was either gifted…or, more likely, a brilliant performance artist. Would Theo fall for that?

She glanced at her grandson, who was staring at Ayla with a mix of fascination and terror in his eyes. Oh dear. It looked like he'd already fallen.

Chapter Six

"Miss Ayla?" The little girl with waist-long ringlets and an arrestingly beautiful face sidled up next to Ayla after dinner as a big group of the family headed to the lawn to play touch football. The child of maybe five hadn't yet said more than hello to Ayla, but she'd been hovering nearby all afternoon. "My name is D-D-Destiny," she said softly.

"I remember," Ayla said, leaning over to get a little closer and running through all the many people she'd met and the tidbits she'd picked up in a dozen conversations with this huge, extended, and extremely warm family. "I understand you're going to be the flower girl in the big wedding everyone is talking about."

She grinned, her hazel eyes dancing. "My mommy is marrying John soon. Wi-wi-will you be there?"

The occasional stutter was endearing and so was the honesty of the question. "At their wedding? Oh, I doubt that."

"Gramma Finnie said you would be," she said. "With Uncle Th-Th-Theo."

She blinked. "Um…no. I don't think so."

"But they do." Darcy joined them with a sassy smile. "The Dogmothers, that is. They're on a mission."

Frowning, she tried to follow, but then Destiny's mother stepped into the circle, with Cassie next to her.

"That's what we call the grannies," Summer said, pushing back sunshine-blond hair and smiling down at her daughter. "And I don't think you're supposed to come right out and tell her, Des."

Ayla looked from one to the other, settling on Darcy, who she now knew was the youngest of Daniel Kilcannon's six kids and married to Josh, a local contractor. They'd bonded earlier when Darcy took her upstairs in the big farmhouse and gave Ayla a whole new outfit that actually fit, including sneakers, along with another pair of jeans and tops and some other necessities.

She hadn't asked Ayla why she'd rushed out of town without clothes—no one had, actually—which was a testament to their class and respect for Miz Marie.

"You're not supposed to tell me what?" Ayla asked Darcy.

"What the Dogmothers do," Darcy replied, sliding a sly look to Cassie, who cracked up.

"The Dogmothers." Ayla shook her head, officially lost. "Okay, from what I can tell, every woman here is a dogmother. Even you, Destiny." She pointed to the young Lab mix next to her.

"Mavvie!" The little girl threw her arms around the dog's neck and kissed him. "I'm not his mother. I'm his best friend!" The stutter seemed to disappear when Mavvie was close, Ayla noticed.

"The Dogmothers are Gramma Finnie and Yiayia," Darcy explained. "They picked up where my dad, who we call the Dogfather, left off."

"Left off from…what?" At their very sly smiles, she added, "Or don't I want to know?"

They laughed, and Darcy got a little closer. "Let's all walk down and watch the game, and we'll tell you."

"Don't let them know you're telling her," Cassie warned, thumbing toward the porch behind them where the two grannies rocked and talked. "They don't like their work to be public until they know they hit a home run. Then they'll be all over town blabbing that they scored again."

Ayla looked down at Destiny. "Why do I think she's not really talking about baseball?" she asked with a teasing smile.

The little girl giggled, but just then, John Santorini, the tall, bearded man who was about to become Destiny's stepfather, walked toward the porch.

"Where's our water girl?" he asked, reaching out for Destiny with both arms.

"Here I come!" She literally threw herself off the steps into his arms, her corkscrew hair flying. "Come on, Mavvie!"

"Come on, Mommy." John looked over the girl's shoulder at Summer. "You're going to play a game of touch football, aren't you?"

"I'm going to sit this one out," she said, tipping her head toward Ayla, "and keep our guest company. I think the conversation is about to get interesting."

Behind his glasses, his dark eyes flickered with some humor, then he spun Destiny in a circle, making her giggle. "Then I got the water girl!"

As they took off, Summer gazed after them, her smile locked in place.

"You wanted to know what the Dogmothers do?" Darcy said, giving an elbow jab to Ayla. "Just look at the joy on that soon-to-be-married woman's face, and you'll know."

Summer did look joyous, but that did nothing to clear the confusion.

"It used to be my dad," Darcy said, slipping her arm through Ayla's to walk them all toward the sideline of the game. "And he was good. Got all six of us hitched and happy, as he likes to say. But then he found his own match in Katie Santorini."

Ayla glanced over her shoulder to the older couple walking the property with two dogs, one a gorgeous but slow senior setter, the other a golden who never left his side. Daniel Kilcannon was a handsome man in his early sixties, a patriarch clearly adored by this clan. Next to him was one of the first people she'd met today, Theo's mother, Katie, who looked at Daniel a lot like Summer had looked at John.

"That's when the Greeks invaded," Cassie added, "and the Dogmothers took over the family business."

"I thought the family business was dog training," Ayla said, gesturing toward the expansive outbuildings, training pens, and dormitories around her.

"That's one of the businesses," Summer said on a laugh. "The other is…"

"*Looove*." All three of them said it together, dragging out the word and punctuating it with hoots of laughter.

Ayla had a feeling that's where they were going, but—

"Are you not playing, Darcy?" A young woman about Ayla's age bounced over on her sneakers, grabbing Darcy's arm. Ella had come late to dinner, and Ayla had briefly met her, but she remembered that a couple of the men here called her Smella, which didn't seem to bother her a bit.

"With Theo home? It's going to get rough out there today."

"Then I'm out, too. I don't play this game without you, Darce," Ella said, sliding her fingers through short, dark hair that accentuated her big brown eyes and striking cheekbones.

"Let's hang and not get all sweaty trying to beat these guys at their game," Darcy said.

"We were going to tell Ayla what the Dogmothers do." Cassie lifted a brow. "You don't want to miss that, do you?"

"Miss it?" Ella's eyes flashed at Ayla. "I could kiss you! Thank you so much for showing up and finally taking the heat off me. I guess it's Theo I should thank, but since they've zeroed in on you…" She made a big sweep of relief over her forehead. "Whew. I can fend off those relentless matchmakers for a while."

"*Matchmakers?*" Ayla choked softly. "Theo? Is that what this is all about?"

"What is what all about?" The question came from another woman who'd joined the group, this one with the stunning contrast of silver-blue eyes and long black hair, a hand comfortably resting on a pregnant belly.

"Oh, Evie!" Cassie said, pulling her into their circle. "You are a perfect example of how they work."

"How *do* they work?" Ayla asked, not sure she wanted to hear this, but knowing she had to. What had she walked into here at Waterford Farm?

They all answered at once, so all she caught were snippets about how good the Dogmothers were and how they'd all been matched—except Ella—and how they'd pounced on their next match the minute they'd seen Theo and Ayla talking in the driveway.

"Their next match?" She laughed and looked from one to the other. "You can*not* be serious," she finally said.

Summer looked at Cassie, who looked at Darcy, who looked at Evie, who looked at Ella, who shrugged.

"I'm the last female standing," Ella said. "So if you want my advice? You either run for the hills, pretend you're already taken, or get ready to stare into the eyes of two very determined old ladies and say no. Which is nearly impossible. I'm worn to a nub from telling them I'm not interested in settling down."

They reached a grouping of blankets that had been laid out for anyone who wanted to watch the game. Right now, that included only Clementine, who was being supervised by a little boy and a German shepherd. Clementine stared intently at the field, and Ayla didn't even need to look to identify the object of her attention.

"So, how do they do it?" she asked as they all sat down together.

Summer held up her left hand, showing off a glistening engagement ring. "Yiayia practically tied me to a chair the day Destiny and I walked into Santorini's Deli for the first time. Next thing I knew, I was moving in with the guy who owns the restaurant. Just as a tenant at first, but then…" She turned to Cassie.

"I saw them coming for me," Cassie said. "I fended them off with a fake relationship with Braden Mahoney—"

"One of my brothers," Ella added.

"But it turned real, real fast." Cassie held up her gold-banded left hand. "We're happily married."

Ayla turned to Evie, her gaze dropping to her fairly sizable baby bump. "Looks like you're happy, too."

"With twins," she announced. "And the man I've loved since I was a kid."

"Oh." Ayla let out a relieved sigh. "So you didn't require their services."

"They certainly helped." Evie gave a wistful smile. "Declan and I had been separated for years, and then… the Dogmothers showed up at my door, and Yiayia planted a twenty-year-old memory in the piano."

"And that got you together?" Ayla asked.

"It helped things along," Evie said.

"And then they obviously played sweet music together," Ella teased.

Ayla shook her head, laughing, but maybe a little overwhelmed. "So, are you saying…" She looked toward the field where five of the men were in a huddle, her eye immediately drawn to the tall, handsome former Navy officer she'd met when she first got here.

They'd talked a few times more that day, but with so many people to meet—and so many who wanted to talk to him—she hadn't had a chance to do much more than look at him. And she'd be lying if she said she hadn't done that every time she had the chance.

But…matchmaking?

Suddenly, she was aware that all of the women were watching her watch him.

"So?" Darcy leaned in. "What do you think?"

"You're about as subtle as they are." Ella poked her. "Let the poor woman at least gather her wits and figure out her strategy. Remember—run, fake, or fold. Those are your options."

Ayla laughed and looked away as Theo grabbed the football and backed up, calling plays, his powerful arm raised to send the ball into the air.

"I think," she said, "that I am recently out of a very serious relationship—"

"So's he," Cassie said. "For which we are all grateful."

"No, I mean *just* out." Like, she was in a wedding gown less than twenty-four hours ago. "It's way too soon for me."

"I think he and Heather broke up a week ago," Darcy said.

"And he is pretty easy on the eyes," Evie added.

"Not to mention brilliant," Cassie chimed in. "The highest IQ of all the Santorinis, and that's saying a lot."

Ayla laughed a little self-consciously. "Y'all are kidding, right?"

They exchanged looks, silent for a moment, but Ayla got the feeling there was some kind of secret communication between the close-knit group of women. Then they broke into easy laughter.

"Totally!" Cassie said, waving her hand.

"We tease!" Ella added.

"He won't even be in town that long," Darcy assured her.

Evie smiled and rubbed her belly, a sparkle in her eyes. "You can't force love, Ayla," she said. "Although the Dogmothers mean well."

"Aunt Cassie?" the little boy called from the next blanket. "Can someone watch Clementine while I run inside?"

"I will!" Ayla jumped at the distraction and the chance to end this conversation. They thought her psychic talent was crazy? The whole lot of them was practically marrying her off to a complete stranger.

She pushed up and moved to the next blanket, taking over holding Clementine's collar as the little boy had been doing. The dog hadn't run off, but she also hadn't actually been more than two feet from Theo all day, so that must be why he'd instructed someone to hold her.

Ayla had heard they'd tried to kennel Clementine

while they ate, but she cried until Theo picked her up, and then she sat under his chair for the whole meal.

"I got her, Christian," Ayla assured him, happy she remembered his name. "And who's this?" she asked, putting her other hand on his German shepherd.

"That's Jag. He's mine."

She smiled, instantly sensing the dog's love for the boy.

"I can tell," she said sincerely, settling between the two dogs.

"We didn't mean to scare you." Cassie crawled over and snuggled next to Jag, her dark gaze on Ayla. "Consider it more of a warning so you both know what hit you."

Both? "Does Theo know?"

"I'm not sure. I haven't had a chance to talk to him today."

A football came tumbling toward them, bumping Clementine, who jumped up and barked. And barked. And pulled so hard that she escaped Ayla's grip, tearing toward the grass, straight to Theo, jumping into his arms with so much force it nearly knocked him down.

Both teams and the small group around the lawn hooted and howled, but Ayla put her hand on her chest and mouthed, "I'm sorry," to Theo.

He shook his head and said something to one of his brothers, then jogged over to the blanket, bringing Clementine with him.

"I tried to hold her," she said, pushing up.

"It's fine." He smiled down at her, a few beads of sweat on his forehead, a smudge of dirt on his cheekbone. He smelled like sunshine and grass and…a sexy guy playing football.

Suddenly, she was aware of so many eyes on their exchange that her cheeks warmed.

Of course. They were all probably placing mental bets on the *family business of matchmaking.*

"I think this girl needs exercise," he said. "Want to take a walk with us?"

Oh, and wouldn't the Dogmothers love that?

"I can take her," she said quickly. "You're in the middle of a game."

"The Bloodhounds are up by twenty-one, thanks to the new star quarterback who blew into town today." He looked down at his sister. "Cass, can you stand in for me while I show Ayla and Clem around Waterford Farm?"

Cassie started to get up, then stopped, catching Ayla's slight look of panic. "Braden's a better quarterback that I am," she said. "I'll walk with you, Theo. We haven't talked all day."

"Oh, but I'd like to show Ayla around. She hasn't gotten the big tour yet." He eyed her for a second. "Unless you'd rather not, Ayla?" he added, probably sensing her reluctance.

"I'd rather…" *Not be matched.* So she better put a stop to it right now. "Actually, a walk would be nice." She pushed up. "I've been wanting to talk to you."

"Really?" His eyes flickered with interest, sliding down to her mouth for a second, then back to her eyes. "That makes two of us."

A whole bunch of female hormones got up and danced around like they were in on the scheme, too.

Um…*no.*

She better put the brakes on this before she found herself looking at him…the way Clementine did.

Chapter Seven

Clementine didn't even notice all the dogs as they walked toward the large pen in the middle of the property. Ayla was right about one thing: The dog had eyes only for him. But Theo couldn't help wanting to lock gazes with the other girl at his side, the one he'd tried to not notice all day…tried and failed.

"So are all these dogs boarding here?" she asked, pausing to look at the many animals romping with not even a single family member in there with them.

"On Sundays, this pen is full of the family dogs," he told her. "I'm not here that often, but I think that's how it works. Everyone brings their dogs on Sundays." They took a few steps closer to the metal fencing.

"They're all so happy," she said, putting her hands on the rail and narrowing her eyes. "Gosh, look at the Husky. What a gorgeous creature."

"Judah. He belongs to Evie and Declan."

"And those three Labs. They look like Destiny's Mavvie."

"Same…mother, I think? I don't know. I wasn't around when they all joined the family, but those three are Alex and Grace's dogs. They own Overlook Glen Vineyards, and Grace found them as strays."

Her gaze drifted around the pen, making him wonder if the dogs were "talking" to her. But he'd teased her enough about that stuff, and he didn't want to antagonize her any further. On the contrary, he just wanted to get to know her.

"So everyone in the family has a dog?" she asked.

"Not Ella. She fosters, but can't commit."

She laughed. "I got that impression from a few things she said."

"And me," he added, then leaned closer to whisper, "but don't tell Clem. She's gonna have a hard enough time when you take her back to Miz Marie's ranch tonight."

"And so will Clem's main squeeze, based on the rumors of how easily you caved when she cried in the kennel."

He chuckled. "How could anyone not have a soft heart for this dog?"

"Marie and I will take good care of her," she promised him.

"And I'll see her a lot."

She looked up, a hint of surprise in her eyes. "You will?"

"Marie's been looking for some help on the ranch and asked me if I could come by and work on a few things." At the change in her expression, he eased back. "Why am I getting the idea that's a problem?"

"It's…not. What are you going to do there?"

"Fix things that are broken, figure out solutions to her problems, make the whole place run like an aircraft carrier." He gave a slow smile. "That's what I do."

"Okay. That's…good."

But she still didn't sound sold on the idea.

"I promise not to tease you anymore," he said. "About, you know…" He tapped his temple, then notched his head toward the pen. "Madame Woo-Woo. Or should I call you Woof-Woof?"

She fought a smile. "It's fine. I have to get used to the skepticism if I'm going to talk about it publicly."

"Let's go this way," he said, gesturing to a wide path that cut through a clearing. "It's really pretty down by the pond."

They turned from the fence and started walking past the kennels, moving slowly as Clementine stopped to sniff and get her bearings. A loud cheer came from the game he'd left, and he turned.

"Hope the Terrible Terriers didn't steal my lead," he mused.

She looked, too, her gaze moving over the property and the huge yellow farmhouse that he was going to call home temporarily.

"So, I'm trying to get the history and families straight," she said. "You didn't grow up here, right? These two families merged recently when your mother married Daniel?"

"Yep, about a year and a half ago."

"Wow. You'd think this gang was raised together, everyone's so close."

"The Kilcannons and Mahoneys were, and they're like one huge Irish blockade. The Santorinis are from a nearby town, but when my mother got married and moved here, Cassie wanted to, as well, and my brothers opened up a location of the family deli here." He frowned at her, hoping that wasn't too much info. "Are you from around here?"

"Charlotte," she said.

"Ah. You going back tonight?"

"I'm not going back for a while. Maybe a month."

A month? It shouldn't have, but that news definitely pleased him. "Well, my crew all lives here now. Except my oldest brother, Nick. The truth is, I still feel a little like an outsider, since I've lived in San Diego all this time while everyone got all, you know, intertwined."

"Intertwined?" There was a slight note of sarcasm in her voice. "Is that what they call it?"

He didn't quite understand the question. "Well, in addition to my mom and Daniel, who is the father or uncle to everyone, my sister married Daniel's nephew, Braden." He gave a laugh. "Yeah, I'd call that intertwined."

She gave him another indecipherable look, then they walked quietly for a while, both watching Clem trot along a few feet ahead.

"Interesting, too," she said pointedly, "how some of that intertwining happened, don't you think?"

Yeah, he was lost. "You know, Ayla, I'm an engineer. I think…linear. And right now, you're not talking linear. In fact, it seems like you're going in circles. What are you asking me?"

She slowed her step on the hill. "About the Dogmothers and their intentions."

"The…isn't that what they call the grannies? Yiayia and Finnie?"

"That's what I've been told."

He frowned, trying to figure where she was going with this, and then he remembered his conversation with Darcy and Cassie, and it all started to make a little sense. Just then, they reached the bottom of the slope and the trees cleared, and Clementine let out a sharp bark.

She turned, whimpered, and ran toward Theo. At his feet, she curled into a ball and started whining.

"What's the matter, girl?" He dropped down to comfort her. "You were doing so well." She put her paw over her face, trying to hide.

Next to him, Ayla got right down on the ground with the dog, putting her hands on her.

"What do you think?" Theo asked.

"It's not about what I think," she said, closing her eyes. "It's about what she thinks. And it's a…a picnic table."

"What?" he croaked the word.

"I think that's what it is. She's seeing it from underneath, looking up, and there's rain. Lots and lots of rain."

The memory of the bathroom lady's desperate tale echoed in his head.

Dog's been chained to a picnic table for months! I walk my own dog by that place three times a day, and I can see through the trees. No matter what time or what the weather is, this poor animal is out there.

"Well, that's a little freaky, because—"

She quieted him with one raised hand. "I see a chain. A thick chain."

"She was wearing one when I got her." How could Ayla know that? "Darcy switched it out for this comfortable collar."

Wait a second. Was he really encouraging this conversation about what *she saw in Clementine's head*?

"No. A long chain. Hooked up to…yes, that's a picnic table." She shuddered a little bit and then bent over, petting Clem. "It's okay, baby. It's okay. No one's going to do that to you ever again."

Someone had to have repeated the story today. Had he mentioned the picnic table? He told Daniel, right? Maybe his mother? All the conversations blurred, and he couldn't remember if he ever used the words *picnic table.* But he knew one thing—this dog was upset.

Reaching down, he wrapped Clem in his arms and lifted her as he stood. "Let's take her down to the pond here. She can run around and forget her past."

"She's not going to forget it easily," Ayla said, pushing up to a stand.

Clementine clung to him for dear life, quivering in his arms the way she had when that woman first left her in the mini-mart bathroom. The way she had at the sound of Human Vermin's voice. The way she had—

He froze as the trees opened to a huge clearing where, in the middle, sat a picnic table that he hadn't known was even there. The family must have added it recently, based on how bright and unfaded the wood was.

"Look at that," Ayla whispered. "That's what she saw."

"In her head? That's what you saw?" Or had Ayla come down here earlier and seen the table then?

"No." She reached over to give Clementine a comforting stroke. "When she got to the clearing, she saw it and had a flashback."

A flashback? But she *was* freaked out, he couldn't deny that. "Poor dog. I feel like she took ten steps backwards after a great day."

"Let's give her a new memory," she said quickly, putting her hand on Theo's shoulder to usher him closer to the table. "You hold her, because you're her source of complete comfort. And we'll sit at that table and love her and love her, and…oh, I wish we had treats."

"They're in my pocket. I never let this dog go ten minutes without food."

Her whole face brightened. "Did you hear that, Clem? Treat. Treats at the table. Come on."

She ran ahead, beckoning him to come faster. So he jogged to the table, the whole time crooning in Clem's ear to calm her down.

"Put her on the table, but don't stop touching her. Keep your hands on her all the time. Touch and stroke and love her."

He did, trying to ignore how provocative the words were. For God's sake, she was talking about the dog.

"Talk to her," she insisted. "Keep talking. It doesn't matter what you say. Fill her head with your voice and give her treats."

He did, saying nonsense, but keeping his voice low and calm while he stroked her back and let her eat the tiny cookies from his hand, then he managed to turn her over and rubbed her quivering belly.

"Let her hear your voice, Theo. Keep soothing her. It's working. It's working."

She certainly was calming down. The shaking stopped, and she welcomed the belly rub like any normal dog. Finally, after a few minutes, she turned over, shook off, and released an enormous sigh, sprawled on the top of the table.

Theo and Ayla sat side by side on one of the benches, both of them letting out their own sighs, like they were sharing simultaneous adrenaline dumps.

After a second, he turned to her. "Who told you she'd been chained to a picnic table?"

Her eyes shuttered closed as if she were a little sick of his doubt. "Clementine told me. It's the truth, whether you want to believe it or not."

He didn't want to, but part of him…did. *Damn it.*

"So now what?" he asked. "Will she be triggered every time she sees a picnic table for the rest of her life?"

"I don't know, but my guess is that this one can help her learn that they're not all bad." She ran her hand over Clem's back. "Let's stay here for a while and let her learn that this is a nice and happy place. Maybe we need to find as many picnic tables as possible and change her whole perception of them."

He held her gaze for a long moment, studying every freckle and the slope of her cheekbones and the depth of her dark brown eyes. There was something about her, something that went deeper than being a pretty woman, which she obviously was. Or a wacky psychic, which she obviously…said she was.

"So," he said, trying to step back and remember what they'd been talking about before Clem freaked out. "What were you going to tell me about the grannies?"

"They're matchmaking us. They're trying to get us together. Like, 'hitched and happy,' I believe was the expression I heard."

"That's…" *Not the worst idea I've ever heard.* "Insane," he finished.

"Right?"

"Like…they think we like each other?" he asked.

"Seriously. You, the engineering skeptic."

"And you, the gorgeous psychic." He made a face. "Whoops. Did I say that?"

She angled her head and looked at him, a tease in her eyes. "Yes, you did."

"I meant *animal communicator*." He winked at her. "Those crazy grannies."

"They are nuts," she agreed. "I'm literally twenty-four hours out of a relationship so serious…"

"I'm six days from one."

She lifted her left hand. "I still have a tan line from the engagement ring."

"And I still have the ring that I was supposed to be giving her in a few weeks."

She winced. "Ouch. What happened?"

"She fell in love with her next-door neighbor. You?"

"He slept with one of my best friends. After the rehearsal dinner."

"*Oof*." He punched his heart with a fake dagger. "Okay, you win."

She gave a humorless laugh. "Didn't feel like winning when I ran out of the church yesterday and Marie poured my sobbing backside into her truck and brought me here."

Holy hell. "A runaway bride?"

She nodded slowly. "Only one notch below a pet psychic."

He couldn't help it, he laughed softly. "Way to pick 'em, Yiayia."

"So…what do we tell the Dogmothers?" she asked.

For a long time, he looked at her, vaguely aware he was dipping his head closer and closer. A couple more inches and…they'd kiss. He knew he should back away, change the subject, or break the eye contact. But he didn't do any of those things.

"I don't know," he said. "You have any ideas?"

"Ella said there are only three choices—run, fake, or fold."

That made him laugh. "Well, I'm not running until I get a job. Then I'm out.

"And I'm not folding twenty-four hours after I left my fiancé at the altar." She let her gaze drop over his face for a quick second. "No, definitely not…folding."

"Then I guess we fake," he said, poking her shoulder with a teasing finger. "Know anything about that?"

She rolled her eyes. "Fake what? We tell them we're still involved with our exes, or lie and say we've both already met someone else?"

"No, that won't work with this family all up in my business." He felt his mouth lift in a slow smile. "Let the old ladies think they struck gold."

Her jaw dropped. "Pretend we like each other?"

"Don't you like me?"

"You're fine, but…" She shook her head. "My life is complicated enough."

"No complications, Ayla." And, God, he liked the idea. Liked it a little more than he should. "You're only here for a month, right? And I might not make it that long. I won't leave before John's wedding, but after that, I could get an offer anytime."

She searched his face like she might actually be considering it. "I think we can tell them no, not interested."

"Clearly, you have never been on the receiving end of a relentless Greek grandmother and her scheming Irish sidekick."

"No, but I had a sweet Southern nana who could take you down with one good 'bless your heart.' I can stand the pressure."

But could he?

"Thanks for looking out for me," she said. "But I'm going to keep my life simple for now."

"S'okay. Your call. But for the record? I'd have totally gone with the fake." And loved every minute of it.

Chapter Eight

Clementine stopped crying around four in the morning. It wasn't until then that Ayla really got any sleep. So when the dog pounced on her at seven thirty, barking, wagging, and begging to go out, all Ayla wanted to do was hide under her pillow and sleep in.

But she could hear more barking outside her open window. And chickens clucking. And a goat…no, that was Marie singing.

"I live on a ranch now," she acknowledged as she pushed herself up and rubbed Clem's pretty face. "So I guess we rise and shine."

Clementine barely gave Ayla time to brush her teeth and pull on a pair of jeans she'd borrowed yesterday before she pawed at the door in desperation. Ayla opened it, and the dog launched out, barking as she ran toward the screen door.

"Okay, okay." As she reached for the handle, she froze and stared at a black Honda coupe out in the drive. Oh, that explained the dog's behavior.

"No wonder you're a wild beast. Your boyfriend is here." She gave a soft laugh and remembered their conversation. "And mine, if I wanted to play his game."

For the four hundredth time since last night, she thought about the offer to pretend to be matched. Right. Like it would be pretend for very long. She'd been two seconds from planting a kiss on his lips.

She pushed the door open, and Clementine bolted, running toward the car and jumping against the side of it.

"Whoa, don't scratch the paint." Ayla walked over to retrieve the dog, glancing in the empty car that she'd also noticed in the driveway of Waterford Farm last night. Only then, it had been a disaster of discarded trash from Theo's road trip with Clem. Sometime between then and now, he'd cleaned out the car, and it looked like he'd just driven it off the lot.

A Navy man would be like that, she mused. She pulled Clementine back as well as she could, but the dog was already in a frenzy looking for Theo.

"Come on, let's go find him." She guided Clementine around the house, but couldn't hold on as the dog broke free and ran past the long coop on the side, ignoring the dozen or so chickens pecking about. She darted along a huge raised garden bed, showing no interest in the vegetables growing there, and blew right by Marie, who was in one of the dog kennels pouring out food.

Marie looked up, surprised by the blur.

"She's on a hunt for her man," Ayla called with a laugh. "The only thing that could make her walk past a bag of dog chow."

Marie stood and straightened the bag, looking at the dog who tore all the way to where the goats were and barked at them, separated by a fairly dilapidated metal fence.

"Theo was there earlier, checking out the fence because he's going to fix it for me."

"How long has he been here? It's not even eight o'clock."

"He came by to borrow my truck," she said. "He told me he was on a mission to get something very important. And while he was here, he looked at the fence."

The dog barked, turned in a circle, then peed, looking left and right in case she'd missed him. Finally, she moseyed back to the other good smell she'd picked up—food.

Marie made her a bowl and set it up separate from the other two dogs who were eating now, too. Hoss, a sweet brown pittie, and Little Joe, a dog of many breeds, with one ear up and one ear down, didn't even look up at Ayla while they enjoyed their breakfast.

"River got tired and went back to bed after we got the eggs." She pointed to the doggy door at the back of the house, then eyed Ayla critically. "You might think about doin' the same, sleepy kitten."

She touched her face and unbrushed hair. "That bad, huh?" She pointed at Clem. "Blame the beast who wept for her beloved until the wee hours. I kept her in bed with me, and trust me, all she thought about was him." And that was Ayla's excuse for not being able to get those oxidized-copper eyes and that sexy smile out of her brain. "But I finally realized she was dying to be under something, so I let her crawl under the bed, and wham, she conked. I think it has to do with that picnic table she was apparently chained to."

"Oh, that picnic table!" Marie grunted. "I can't stop thinking about it, either. I told Theo I wanted to know exactly where it was in Arkansas so I can go back and kill the man with my bare hands. He refused, but only because he knew I wasn't kidding."

Ayla shook her head, almost wishing she didn't see some of the things that Clementine had. To erase the images, she took a minute to really appreciate the beauty of the small ranch, which sat on a remarkable piece of the land.

"It's no Waterford Farm," Marie said, coming up next to her. "But it's home."

"I love it," she said, giving Marie a hug. "Waterford is amazing in its own way, but this is sweet and small and cozy."

"This used to be part of Waterford at one time. Finnie's husband, Seamus, built the original house as the home for their foreman, back when Waterford was an actual working farm in the sixties. Seamus and Finnie eventually sold the land and house, then Daniel and Annie bought it back, and now they've sold it to me." She looked around, uncharacteristic stress pulling at her features.

"It's perfect," Ayla assured her.

"Far from it, which is why I'm a little bit of a nervous wreck this morning."

"You are? What's wrong, Marie?"

"Oh, that's right." She snapped her fingers. "You were off with Theo during this conversation yesterday, and then we took off and got so wrapped up in getting that dog out of there and all her crying, we got distracted."

Ayla shook her head, not quite able to laugh at the memory of Clem clawing at the truck windows and crying. And Theo looking downright gutted, and about to change his mind.

"You'd have thought we were taking her off to the dog dungeons of hell," she said, frowning as she tried to remember what happened before that. "What conversation did I miss?"

"*Rescue Party*. Do you know the show?"

She had to think for a minute. “On the Animal Network? The one where the guy goes all over the country visiting rescue shelters and featuring dogs and the people who take care of them?” Her eyes widened. “Are they coming here?”

“They’re going to Waterford next week,” she said. “Daniel arranged it ages ago. But he got a call from the producers that they have the time and budget to do another shelter in the area and asked him for a recommendation, so of course he said the Last Chance Ranch.”

“That’s amazing!” Ayla exclaimed. “I know that show always goes off the beaten path to find the most colorful and compassionate shelter owners. You’re a perfect candidate.”

“It’s not a guarantee yet,” Marie told her. “The production crew is going to come out here and make a game-time decision about giving us a feature slot. If they do, they’ll stay an extra day and add Last Chance Ranch to their production schedule.”

“But isn’t that show always trying to find the dogs forever homes?” She looked at the three dogs nose-deep in their breakfasts. “Will you adopt these guys out?”

“I guess if they found the right home, or I’ll keep them forever,” she said on a laugh. “The guy on the show doesn’t only visit shelters that adopt, though, but also homes like this one, and starts a GoFundMe for them. That could raise money I need to make this place the haven I want it to be.” She gestured toward the dilapidated fence and weathered kennels. “But we’re a long way from that. And I’m afraid we’re not ready for television.”

It was a little run-down, but Marie had been living there for only a few weeks. “Theo can fix that,” Ayla said quickly. “And I’ll help.”

"Theo told me this morning that all three Mahoney brothers have time in their firefighting schedule this week to help, and Liam, Shane, Garrett, Aidan, and also Trace—the whole Kilcannon crew of men—will come and help."

"Well, there you go," Ayla said. "We'll have this place gorgeous in no time. But, gosh, I don't remember meeting Garrett or Aidan yesterday. Did I miss a few people?"

"They were on a rescue mission. Aidan has a plane, and Garrett supervises all the rescue operations Waterford handles. I think they might have a few new residents for Last Chance when they land this afternoon." She glanced at the kennels. "We're going to eventually want kennels that are warm and comfortable for overnight, too. Right now, these things aren't much more than day shelters from sun or rain. And they look so wretched."

"They're outdoor kennels, they're supposed to look weathered." Ayla slipped her arm through Marie's, wanting her natural positivity to come back. "You're going to amaze the TV guy. Who, if I recall correctly, is quite good-looking."

"Colin Donahue?" Marie looked toward the skies. "If I were forty years younger, I would eat that man with a spoon. And a knife. And two forks."

Ayla snorted a laugh. "Now you sound like Marie."

"But *you're* forty years younger," Marie said, waggling her brows.

"Keep your silverware in the drawer, Marie. Recovering runaway bride, remember?"

"What better way to recover?"

"With Colin the *Rescue Party* Guy?" She squeezed Marie's arm. "You're crazy."

"How about…someone else, hmmm?"

Ayla had to laugh. "Don't tell me you're on the Dogmothers train, Marie Boswell. Theo and I are having none of it."

Marie drew back, mouth open. "First of all, 'Theo and I,' you say? That sounds cozy. And second of all…" Her eyes opened wide with feigned innocence. "What do you mean by the Dogmothers train?"

"The one that apparently leaves the station every time they've decided one of their grandchildren has been single for too long." Ayla laughed at Marie's expression and pointed at her friend. "You're having a hard time looking like you don't already know where this is going."

She bit her lip, trying not to smile. "Am I?"

Ayla rolled her eyes. "It's not happening, so call off the dogs. And their mothers."

"Oh, really?" She sounded genuinely disappointed. "You're not interested?"

"Marie! I just left a fiancé at the altar. I still don't have anything but borrowed clothes and a toothbrush you gave me."

"You should shop today."

"After we get some work done, but please, I can't *think* about a man right now. Even if he's offering to fake a relationship merely to keep them off our backs."

Marie's chin nearly hit her chest. "Why would you do that?"

"Because Ella said once they set their sights on you, the only options are to run, fake, or fold."

"Wait, let me get this straight." Cocking her head to one side, Marie adjusted her horn-rimmed glasses and fought a smile. "He suggested you spend a whole lot of time together to fool them into thinking you like each other so they won't force you to spend a whole lot of time together? Am I getting this right?"

"Stupid, isn't it?"

"I don't know. It's kind of brilliant if you ask me."

Brilliant? Ayla dug for patience. "Please, I'm ten minutes out of an engagement."

"Legit question, Ayla. When was the last time you even thought about EJ Paxton?"

Legit answer: when she ran out of the church. "I'm not thinking about him, to be honest. Except when I imagine him with Jilly, and then my head kind of explodes."

"No second-guessing about that decision?"

"None at all. I talked to Trina late last night, and she said he took off for Europe and left my mother to return the wedding presents." She frowned. "What does that have to do with Theo?"

"You may be ten minutes out of an engagement, but you've been 'alone' a long time. You were never *swoony* over EJ, not since the day I met you."

"Swoony? I don't get swoony. I'm not the swoony type. What does that even mean? That I'm going to hyperventilate and faint at the sight of him? Honestly. I don't *swoon*."

Marie laughed, reaching down to put two hands on Hoss's face, since he'd come up to her for love. "Well, I guess I'll have bad news to report to the grannies, then."

"You were in on this matchmaking?"

She shrugged. "I told them I'd see if you had any interest in the idea. They didn't want to barrel into a match if you were still needing to recover from your ex's betrayal."

"And would they back off if you asked them to?"

"Debatable," Marie answered with a laugh. "I guess we'll find out, won't we?" She genuinely looked sad. "I just thought you two looked wonderful together. You have a lot in common."

"We both got dumped by cheaters," she said. "And we're both only here for a short time. Beyond that? He thinks I'm a fake, and I think he's a…" Her voice trailed off as she tried to find the right word.

"Stud muffin?" Marie supplied.

Ayla bit back a laugh. "That might be, if the calendar said 1987. But, really, how could I like a guy who thinks I'm making up one of the most fundamental aspects of my personality?"

"All the Greeks are skeptics," she said. "We discussed it when you were gone."

"What?" She gave Marie an *are you serious?* look. "You talked about it behind my back?"

"I wanted to know where they stand and if they thought it was a viable business option for you," Marie said. "I honestly only have your best interests at heart, kitten."

"So what did they say?"

"They were divided down family lines. The Greeks are pragmatic and dubious, as Greeks are."

"That's exactly what Theo said."

"But the Irish have a soul for that kind of thing," Marie continued. "Finnie's enchanted, as were many of the Kilcannons. Even Daniel didn't flinch at the idea, mentioning that his late wife was a believer."

"Huh." Ayla considered that and felt a sudden kinship with a woman she'd never met. "Darcy was very open to the idea. And her sister, Molly, the vet."

"Molly is a carbon copy of her mother," Marie said. "They all think you could do well with an office in Bitter Bark."

"Oh, I don't know about that."

At the sound of a truck coming down the long drive, they both turned to see Marie's old Ford rolling in.

Instantly, Clementine barked and jumped up as if she sensed in her bones that Theo had returned. Ayla managed to snag her collar before she could run off, but they all kept their eyes on the big black truck pulling in through the metal gates Marie had left open.

"He's not alone," Ayla said, seeing another man in the passenger seat.

"That's John. And the back of the truck looks full," Marie noted, putting her hand over her eyes to see in the bright morning light. "I thought he was getting wire and posts."

"That's not wire and posts," Ayla said, squinting into the sun. "That's…oh my God. He brought a picnic table." She put her hand over her chest as it hit her how unbelievably kind that was. "He wants to help Clem make more memories to overcome her fear. How sweet is that?"

When Marie didn't answer, Ayla turned to her, catching a smirk on the other woman's face.

"What?" Ayla asked.

"This, my darling…" Marie reached over and lifted Ayla's hand off her chest. "Is known as *swooning*."

Marie let out a big guffaw and headed out to meet Theo.

Chapter Nine

Clementine wouldn't go near the picnic table, which meant she wouldn't go near Theo, who was carrying it with John. Theo was no pet psychic, but he could tell the poor thing was torn between wanting to pounce on him and staying as far away as possible from something that set off alarm bells in her sweet little head.

"This one's for you, Clemmie," he called as they passed, each holding an end of the table. He shot a grin at a surprised-looking Ayla. "Nothing but happy memories on this puppy."

"You bought a picnic table?" Ayla couldn't wipe the smile off her face, which gave Theo a kick of satisfaction for the idea he'd had in the middle of the night.

"Didn't buy a thing," he said as he and John carted the table toward the middle of the huge yard. "This is all my brother."

"Theo texted and said he was going out to Home Depot to get one and wanted me to come along," John explained. "But Summer and I bought a new table and chairs for our yard, because we eat out there all the time with Destiny and Maverick whenever the weather's great.

So this one is free. Comes with great memories and is ready for more."

"And new memories are what you need, Clem," Theo called to the dog.

"Oh, put it right by this tree," Marie said excitedly. "It's a wonderful place to have lunch and be with the dogs."

As soon as Theo took a few steps away from the table, Clementine bolted toward him, jumping into his arms and licking his face. Laughing, he rolled onto the grass.

"I'll get that fence wire in the truck while she has her way with you," John joked as he headed back to the truck.

Ayla came closer, laughing at the frantic dog. "Now she can relax."

"Did she have a rough night?" he asked, easing the dog down as he looked up at Ayla. "Did you?"

"I better scare up some makeup before one more person tells me how bad I look."

"Bad is not the word I'd use," he said, squinting up at the sunshine. Oh hell no. Not bad at all. Tousled, like maybe she hadn't brushed her hair. Naturally beautiful and sun-kissed. But definitely not bad. "You like the table?" he asked.

She knelt down next to him. "Incredibly thoughtful, Théodoros."

He smiled at her. "I'm glad you think so." He didn't know why her opinion mattered so much, but it did. "When did she stop crying?"

"At four in the morning," she told him. "She likes to sleep under the bed, I discovered. I put some blankets there, and she finally crashed."

He winced at the idea of either of these beautiful girls

losing sleep because of him. "I can take her to Waterford, Ayla."

"That would only delay the inevitable when you leave."

"Maybe I can take her with me." He sat all the way up and rubbed the belly Clementine offered. "Not if the job in London comes through, obviously. But I've got feelers out all over the place, so whoever comes in with the juiciest offer will get me." He turned away from her to give Clem a kiss. "Maybe we can be together, after all."

"But just in case, she should probably get used to it here," Ayla said. "And that table is going to go a long way toward helping her. Thank you."

He held her gaze for a minute, feeling the same tug of affection he felt for Clem. Like they belonged together. But that was crazy talk brought on by those grand-mothers, who'd cornered him last night and started a full-court press.

"It was worse than I imagined," he mused.

She inched back, eyes wide. "What?"

"The Dogmothers."

"Oh dear. What happened?"

"A list of reasons we're perfect for each other. A chorus of suggestions ranging from dinner in town to you accompanying me to John and Summer's wedding."

"No!"

He hoped that meant *no* to the chorus of suggestions, not the wedding. He kind of liked that idea.

"Oh, I'm just getting started. They suggested the two of us dog-sit Gala and Pyggie, that we sign up to chair one of the booths at Paws for a Cause, and Yiayia said she'd be willing to teach you how to make Greek cookies. Which should surely seal the deal."

Her mouth opened to a perfectly adorable little O.

"I think they're in panic mode since we both could leave town at any time."

She started to laugh, shaking her head. "What did you tell them?"

"I promised my grandmother I would give it the old college try." He grinned. "And in the Greek culture, if you break a promise to your yiayia, she won't speak to you for forty days and nights."

"Is that true?"

"No, but it could be." He pushed up and looked toward the truck. "I gotta help John. Don't be mad at me for trying. I like you."

Her eyes flickered at his honesty. "That's…nice."

"Talk some sense into her, Clem," he said as he stood. But Clem didn't talk anybody into anything, following Theo like he was made of bacon.

When John came back, they made another attempt to get Clementine to the table by having Theo sit there. That failed because the dog simply wouldn't get within ten feet of the table.

"Well, what do you know? Fear trumps love," Theo said, jumping up to help John with the roll of metal fencing. "Hey, bro, you don't have to do anything else. I know you have to get to the restaurant."

"I have an hour," John said. "The restaurant is running without me, but I promised Summer we'd do some wedding stuff at the winery. You know, when we decided to have the event at Overlook Glen, I didn't think I'd have to do a thing since my brother and his fiancée own the place."

"Planning a wedding is never ending," Ayla said, walking toward them with Clem, who kept a wide berth around the table. "And it only gets more stressful as the day gets closer."

John looked surprised. “Spoken like a person who’s been through it.”

“Um…all the way up to the part where you walk down the aisle,” she admitted with an embarrassed smile. “That’s as far as I got.”

“Really.” John tried to hide his surprise. “That couldn’t have been easy.”

“She had a good reason,” Theo said quickly, hoisting the fencing roll over his shoulder. “A really good reason.”

John nodded, but he didn’t say anything as he and Theo—and Clem—walked toward the goats, well out of earshot of Ayla.

“She left a guy at the altar?” John asked softly as they started unrolling the long spool of metal that would replace what weather and goats had destroyed. “Whoa. Heartless.”

“He slept with her best friend,” Theo said. “On the heartless scale, that’s higher.”

“If it’s true,” John said.

“Why would she lie?”

His brother notched a brow, but didn’t elaborate. Instead, he eyed Theo from behind glasses he’d worn as long as Theo could remember. “You like her, don’t you?”

He didn’t answer right away, but glanced over his shoulder to see her wiping down the picnic table, talking to Marie. “I’m attracted, I’m not going to lie. But that might just be Yiayia pressure.”

“All they do is dangle the bait,” he said. “Taking it is up to you.”

He smiled. “So let them think I took it,” he said. “That way, they’ll stop.”

“They won’t stop until you’re down on one knee.”

Theo almost choked. “All I want is to hang out with her while we’re both in town.” He searched his older brother’s face. “Bad idea?”

“I don’t know, little brother. A woman that freshly out of an engagement might not be a safe bet.”

“I’m not placing bets, John. I’m enjoying her company while I put my life back together after it imploded.” He ground out the words, a little frustration growing.

“All I’m saying is you should be careful,” John said. “You’re a week out of being cheated on, too. Both of you are vulnerable.”

“I appreciate the concern, man. I will take it on advisement.”

“What the hell does that mean?” John asked.

“It means don’t gripe when I bring her to your wedding, ’cause I plan to. That’ll shut the grannies up. Come on, let’s put up a fence before you go off and do wedding stuff with the woman *you* were set up with. You know, the one with a kid and a job in Florida and a million reasons why it was all wrong at first?”

John smiled, effectively silenced.

Five hours later, long after John had taken off, the fence was done. It might have been more physical labor than he was used to after ten years below deck on an aircraft carrier, but the project had required some measuring, math, and muscle, so Theo’d had a blast.

Now he was having another one. Having just finished two massive BLTs and a bowl of fruit at the picnic table, he didn’t want to move. He sure as hell didn’t want to go home and check for emails from headhunters and return phone calls on the job hunt. He had to, but he didn’t want to.

“Do you need Marie’s truck this afternoon?” Ayla asked as she offered him more iced tea. “I want to run into town and do a little shopping. I can't wear Darcy's and Cassie's hand-me-downs forever."

"I can drive you," Theo said. "I have to hit the hardware store for more supplies for when I work on the kennels tomorrow, and I can drop you off and pick you up after you get what you need."

"I can't thank you enough for all you're doing." Marie reached her hand across the table to pat his arm. "Look how content Blueberry and Waffles are behind their new fence."

"Happy to help you out, Miz Marie. After all, you adopted my Clementine." He glanced at the dog, who lay on the grass several feet away. She'd moved a little closer a couple of times, but only because Theo had tossed her some scraps. As soon as she got one, she'd hustle away with the prize in her mouth.

They'd all agreed that she needed to accept the picnic table at her own speed, and he shouldn't upset her by carrying her to it.

"*Your* Clementine." Marie raised her brows. "If you think of her that way, then I haven't adopted her. I'm only keeping her until you decide she's coming home with you forever."

He shook his head. "I adore her and feel responsible for her, but wherever I go, I'm going to travel a lot. I don't want the responsibility of a dog, especially one this needy. She'll do better here."

"She's very happy now," Ayla said, turning to look at Clem. "Just seeing you sitting here, even at this dreaded picnic table, is doing wonders for her psyche."

He studied Ayla over the rim of his glass, remembering his brother's warnings. She sure didn't seem like a fraud or…whatever accusations John had thrown around.

She was as genuine as any woman he'd ever met, easy to talk to, quick-witted, and kind.

And he didn't want to be warned off her, damn it.

An hour later when they rolled into Bitter Bark with Clementine in the back seat of his Honda, after more easy, comfortable conversation, those feelings hadn't changed a bit.

"Oh, is that Darcy's grooming shop? Friends With Dogs? And Ella's Bone Appetit next door?" Ayla peered at the charming red-brick building off Bushrod Square in the center of Bitter Bark. "I'd love to stop in there. And there's a boutique where I can get some clothes. Can you drop me off here? I'll take Clem."

"And cause a scene when our little toddler has a public meltdown?" he joked. "Bitter Bark's a hundred percent dog-friendly. I'll take her with me to the hardware store and for a walk in the square. You take your time and text me when you're free."

"I don't have a phone," she admitted with a sad smile. "And I'm spending Miz Marie's cash, which I will repay when my new bank card arrives in the mail in a few days. So I won't be long, I promise."

"A woman shopping? Not long?"

She smiled. "I'll meet you in the square in an hour." She looked over his shoulder at the park area behind him. "Be careful out there."

"In the hotbed of danger that is Bushrod Square?"

"I see picnic tables." She turned to the dog snout that was inches from hers. "Be a good girl, Clementine. No crying."

She tapped the dog's nose, blew Theo a kiss, and climbed out of the car, leaving both of them panting a little.

Chapter Ten

When Ayla stepped into Bone Appetit, she was greeted by a huge smile from Ella at the register, talking to a customer. "Hey, Ayla! Make yourself at home."

How could she do anything but? The adorably cluttered little shop smelled like cookies and coffee, thanks to the table in the front that offered free treats for the four-legged visitors and fresh coffee for those with two.

Almost immediately, Ella's mother, Colleen, who'd been at Waterford the day before, greeted her with a hug.

"Nice to see you again, Ayla. Did you come in for some treats to take back to the Last Chance Ranch?" she asked.

"I'll definitely take some back," Ayla assured her, looking around. In addition to a wall of organic treats and a section of toys, clothes, and accessories, there was everything for the dog lover, from paw-covered dish towels to clocks with breed-specific faces. "This place is so cute."

"All credit to my daughter," Colleen said, drawing

her into the store, past a customer with a gorgeous goldendoodle in tow. "And it helps that Darcy opened up her grooming shop right here."

They stepped toward an arched doorway that led into what looked like a beauty salon for dogs, with several getting bathed, trimmed, and loved by Darcy and two other groomers.

"Hey, Ayla!" Darcy called, up to her elbows in soap suds with a snow-white Westie in the sink. She notched her head, making her long blond ponytail swing. "Come on over and meet Angus."

"Oh, I have another customer," Colleen said. "Hang with Darcy, and I'll get you a little package to take back to Marie's."

Thanking Colleen, Ayla walked through the salon, slowing down to appreciate the pups, big and small, in various stages of beautification.

"How's Clem doing?" Darcy asked as she turned on the water to rinse the pup in the sink.

"She's okay. Theo showed up with a picnic table from John's house, and she had mixed emotions about that."

Darcy nodded, since by now all of them had heard about Clementine's reaction to the table. "Loves Theo, hates the table?"

"Exactly," Ayla said on a laugh, a little buzz in her head that she attributed to all the doggie thoughts and feelings in the place. "You'll be happy to know I'm in town to do a little shopping so I can return your clothes." She plucked at the T-shirt she wore. "Thank you again."

"No rush. Where are you going?"

"I saw a little boutique a few doors away I thought I might try."

"La Parisienne?" She gave a dubious look. "Expensive,

but sometimes Yvette has good sales. Great lingerie, if you're in the market for that."

Not anymore. "I'm looking for jeans and tops, maybe a cotton T-shirt dress."

"I know where to take you. We can try—oh!" She looked out the window and laughed at a woman standing outside, her face practically smashed up against the glass. "Look, Angus!" she said to the dog. "Your mommy's here."

Darcy waved the woman in and turned to Ayla. "Fair warning. Linda May owns the bakery, and she doles out town gossip like it's pats of butter, so anything you say can and will be on the lips of half the town tomorrow."

"Thanks for the heads-up," Ayla said.

The woman rushed in, brushing back some of her silver-blond hair, her gaze locked on the dog.

"How's my Angus doing?" she crooned as she reached for the soaking-wet dog, who looked a little like a drowned rat at the moment.

"He's okay," Darcy said. "Definitely not his normal self."

"I know." Her shoulders slumped. "Something is wrong with him."

"Linda May, let me introduce you to Ayla Hollis. She's staying out at Miz Marie's Last Chance Ranch."

The other woman extended her hand, her eyes crinkling with warmth from what looked like a lot of smiles in fifty or so years. "Hello, Ayla. Linda May Dunlap," she said.

"Ah, the croissant queen," Ayla joked. "I had two yesterday. Raspberry. Insane."

"Oh, thank you," the woman said. "Those are my signature pastries. If you're new in town, you get a free one if you stop by."

"Don't tempt me." Ayla tipped her head toward the dog in the sink. "Angus is a doll."

"Isn't he?" She added a noisy sigh. "But something's not right. I have an appointment with your sister tomorrow, Darcy," she said, and Ayla knew she was referring to Molly Bancroft, whom she'd met yesterday. "He's not eating well, and he quivers and pants now and again, which I know is a sign of pain. And…I don't know. I sense in my gut he's out of sorts."

"You should never ignore that," Ayla said.

"Hey, Ayla, why don't you…" Darcy lifted her brows and cocked her head in Angus's direction. "You know. See what he's thinking."

"Excuse me?" Linda May asked.

For a moment, Darcy was quiet, giving Ayla a questioning look, obviously asking for permission to share. Ayla took a breath. It had been one thing with Miz Marie at her side and a farm full of friendly family members. But a stranger? Who also happened to be the town gossip? What Darcy was really asking was, did she want the news about her gift…out?

After all those years of hiding? Yes, she did.

And anyway, Angus was buzzing with the need to communicate. She had felt it the minute she'd come to this sink.

She gave a quick nod to Darcy.

"Ayla is a professional animal communicator."

Ayla felt a rush of gratitude not only for the title, but the genuine respect Darcy had cloaked it in.

Linda May's blue eyes popped. "Excuse me? Did you say—"

"That's right," Darcy insisted. "Ayla has a gift that allows her to know what dogs are thinking and feeling.

She was at Waterford yesterday, and we were all blown away. She could tell instantly that my little Stella was moping because Kookie came late with Josh."

Ayla recognized the look Linda May was giving her. Plenty of doubt, a little humor, and a dollop of *Do you take me for an idiot?* God, she was sick of this. She hadn't asked for this particular skill, but what if she could help Angus?

Turning from the woman to the dog, Ayla stepped closer and put her hands right on his wet head.

"You want a towel?" Darcy asked.

Silent, Ayla shook her head and blocked out the other dogs, the running water, the hum of a dryer in the back of the shop, and all the conversation. For a moment, all she could feel were the waves of energy coming from the little terrier.

He was seeing red. Pulsing, aching. Right in his… mouth. She slid her hand around his little snout to the left side, and instantly the pulse grew more intense. The dog looked into her eyes and sent out waves and waves of pain. And he was seeing a bowl of food, focused on something white.

"He has a toothache," she said.

"What?" Linda May asked.

"But it's not a normal toothache," she said. "It might be an abscess."

"Is that why he's not eating?" Linda May asked in a shocked whisper.

"He's eating the chicken you give him," Ayla said. "But he's frustrated because you mix it with hard kibble, and that hurts to chew." She stroked his face. "It's here on the left. And it's bad."

"I can't…I don't…are you serious?" Linda May choked out the words.

Ayla turned and looked at her. "It's really bad," she said. "I don't think you should wait until tomorrow to have this taken care of."

Her expression was pure doubt. "You didn't even look in his mouth."

"I don't have to," Ayla replied with a quiet confidence. "He told me what's wrong."

"Did you hear that?" she said to Darcy and the groomer at the next station who'd stepped closer. They both nodded. "That's crazy!"

Darcy grabbed a fluffy white towel and started drying off poor Angus, careful to avoid his sore mouth.

"Molly's working today, Linda May," she said. "Why don't you take him over to her office now? I'll text her and let her know what's going on so she'll see him right away on an emergency basis."

Linda May nodded as if she were speechless. Then she slid a look to Ayla. "I don't know what to think about this."

Ayla smiled. "That's okay. I hope Angus feels better soon."

She scooped the dog out of Darcy's arms, towel and all. "You poor baby," she crooned, cuddling the dog. "Is it okay if I take him right now?"

"Go, off with you." Darcy flicked her hand. "Take the towel so he doesn't get chilled. We can settle up another time. Bye, Angus! Hope you feel better!"

Linda May rushed out, tucking Angus tightly to her chest.

"Nice work, Ayla," Darcy crooned.

"Did you really just do that?" the groomer from the next station asked. "Like, you read that dog's mind?"

"I felt his energy," she corrected. "And that dog needs to have a tooth pulled, like, yesterday."

Darcy dug out her phone from an apron pocket as another groomer joined them, and they all started talking about it.

"Okay, I texted Molly. And I don't have any more appointments today. So, I have an idea." She snapped off her grooming jacket and ushered Ayla through the salon and into Bone Appetit. "Aunt Colleen, can you cover for Ella?"

"Of course. Where are you off to?"

"Shopping! Get your bag, Smella Mahoney!" she called to her cousin. "We have to show Ayla where to get some clothes. I have a feeling she's about to have a lot of attention on her."

She couldn't disagree. In fact, Ayla could already hear the low-grade buzz of conversation about what she'd done going through the two stores.

Before she knew it, the three of them were headed down the street, with Darcy replaying the whole event for Ella, who didn't even question the believability factor.

Already, Ayla adored these two.

That feeling only intensified during a fun shopping expedition. Ayla wasn't used to shopping on a budget, so with only Miz Marie's cash in her borrowed purse, she was grateful Darcy and Ella knew where to get the best deals.

But she also wasn't used to this genuine kind of friendship, especially from two women she barely knew, who asked questions, shared tidbits about their lives and families, and were clearly the best of friends who communicated without words. But not once did they make Ayla feel like an outsider.

Every once in a while, Ayla thought about Jilly and realized what really bad choices she'd made in friends *and* men.

An hour later, they left one store with a few pairs of jeans and khakis, some tops, desperately needed underwear, and a bra, heading to the square to get to another boutique on the other side. As they did, Ayla looked around the tree-filled park, noticing a lot of picnic tables, a playground, walking trails, and a huge bronze statue in the center.

"That's Thaddeus Ambrose Bushrod, our founder," Darcy told her. "You look like you want to go pay your respects."

Ayla laughed. "I'm wondering how I'll find Theo after he finishes at the hardware store. One of you might have to text him for me."

"A man at the hardware store?" Darcy scoffed. "When Josh goes, I need to send a search party. We have time to hit one more shop. You need something a little nicer than jeans to meet with clients."

"You really think I'm going to have them?"

"Of course!" she said. "Unless you doubt your own abilities."

"I doubt…how people react to them," she admitted. "I don't come from a very accepting family. Just the idea that I connected with animals was not exactly celebrated. My mother would…" She shook her head. "Implode."

The women exchanged sympathetic looks.

"Well, she's not here," Ella said.

"And we are," Darcy added. "Look around at all the dog lovers in this town. You'll have a line around the corner."

"You think?" Ayla had never believed there was a

burning need for her skill. Sure, a few skilled communicators had made it big on YouTube and even some TV shows, but she'd never really considered her gift as a…business endeavor. "Most people think it's pretty… woo-woo." She fluttered her fingers with the expression.

"Most people are narrow-minded," Darcy said.

"And you gotta own it, girl." Ella elbowed her. "So we need a way to—"

"Darcy! Ella!"

They all turned at the woman's voice, seeing Linda May darting across the square. "And, oh my God, Ayla!" Her blond hair fluttered as she rushed to catch up with them.

"You were right!" she exclaimed. "Molly's doing the extraction now." She put her hand on her chest. "I went back to the shop to find you and…" She panted, catching her breath. "You were absolutely right. And there was no way to see the abscess since it was way in the back, under her molar. Molly said it could have been a while before we figured out what was wrong, and Angus would have lived in such pain."

"I'm so glad Molly found it," Ayla said.

"No, *you* found it!" She threw her arms around Ayla in an impulsive hug. "Thank you so much. You're incredible!"

Ayla laughed and waved off the compliment. "I'm just happy I could help Angus."

"I don't know how to thank you."

"That free raspberry croissant for newcomers will do the trick," she teased.

"Free raspberry croissants for life!" Linda May said. "I'm so grateful. Are you taking new clients? Because when I start telling people—"

"Told ya!" Darcy sang the words, making Ayla laugh.

"I'm out at Miz Marie's ranch for a while," she reminded Linda May. "That's the best way to reach me."

"Okay, then, but, well. Do you have office hours?" Linda May asked.

She laughed again, looking at Ella and Darcy for an assist.

"You could work from our office in the back of my shop," Ella said.

Ayla shook her head, which was reeling. "I don't think that's necessary, but thanks for your support, Linda May. I'll pop into the bakery for a croissant. Be sure to let me know how Angus is doing, okay?"

"I will." She beamed and hugged Ayla again. "God bless you, sweetheart."

With that, she took off, leaving them standing there, Ayla still a little bewildered. This was all happening fast.

"Color me overwhelmed," Ayla admitted. "I've been thinking about this my whole life, always wanting to find a way to practice, but I never thought it was possible. And now…office hours? I can't imagine hanging a shingle and…" She laughed. "I wouldn't know where to start."

"I know where to start," Ella said, her big brown eyes bright with an idea. "I know the perfect place to start." She looked at Darcy. "Paws for a Cause."

Darcy gasped. "Ella! That's brilliant!"

"The fundraiser?" Ayla asked. "Theo mentioned it."

"The kickoff is this weekend, and fortunately for you, Cassie's event-planning business runs the whole thing now. She'll get you into the Waterford tent, which is front and center and huge. Garrett's doing a big adoption thing, and Shane's running some dog training seminars."

"You can do a booth," Ella said. "Any money you

raise would go to dog-related charities. It's a perfect environment for you to get comfortable."

"Will you do it?" Darcy asked.

It would be the most public exposure of Ayla's gift ever. She thought about it for a moment, looking around the small, sweet, pet-friendly town, then at the two bright-eyed, eager cousins.

Well, she wanted a new life. Why not start now?

Chapter Eleven

"Wait…what? You're going to sit at the fundraiser and read animals' minds?" Theo glanced at Ayla in the passenger seat as he drove back to Marie's ranch, his smile wavering at the gut-punch look on her face. "I mean…it's like a fun thing for kids, right?"

All humor faded from her expression as her gaze shifted down to her lap. "I'm doing it for the dogs, not for the kids," she said, the note of disappointment—and maybe hurt—in her voice enough to make him want to kick himself.

"Sorry," he muttered. "I don't mean to—"

"Yes, you do." She gave a mirthless laugh. "I'm sure I'll get plenty of that kind of teasing. But I'm not going to let that stop me from using my gift with animals. I've hidden it for too long."

Gift? He tamped down the reaction. He didn't want to be a jerk about this, especially when he felt such a spark with this woman. But he also didn't want to be a chump.

"Surely your family and friends know."

She shifted in the seat, turning toward Clem, who stuck her face between the two seats, panting lightly in

Theo's ear. On a sigh, Ayla stroked the dog's head, thinking. "The first person I ever told was my grandmother Nana Jo, who reacted with pure, unadulterated joy."

"Because she had the same gift," he said, remembering what she'd said at Waterford.

"She spent her life hiding it because of what people would say, but she hoped I wouldn't. But when I told my sister and my parents, they..." She gave a wry laugh. "This news was not well received in the Hollis family, where things are supposed to be done a certain way."

"Even though your grandmother had the same ability?"

"Well, they were kind of ashamed of her."

He whipped his head to face her. "Of your grandmother?" Now that was a family dynamic he didn't understand. No matter how annoying Yiayia could be—and she sure tested his mother on a daily basis when Dad was still alive—respect was given to the grandparents, no questions asked.

"Nana Jo was my father's mother, and they didn't have much money. My dad is a self-made man, but my mother came from a fairly prominent family. She's one of those Daughters of the American Revolution types who traced their lineage back ten generations and never missed a cotillion. Even before my dad amassed a fortune, my mother only cared about one thing—what other people think of us. But not Nana Jo. She was a country lady who liked to 'put up tomatoes and make blueberry buckle.'" She let her slight North Carolina accent thicken with the air quotes, making him smile.

"You were close to her?" he guessed.

"Very. She's been gone two years, and I still miss her terribly. She always told me 'be true to yourself,' and it's taken me a while and a really dumb detour, but I'm going to."

"Dumb detour to Bitter Bark?" he asked, hoping he was wrong.

"Dumb detour almost down the aisle to a guy Nana Jo would never have wanted me to marry. But when she died, I was a little lost, and he'd been waiting in the wings forever, saw an opportunity, and swooped in." She shrugged and tried to sound nonchalant, but he knew how much a breakup could hurt, no matter what the details. "And as far as my ability with animals? I never told him."

"Really?" He threw her another look, even more surprised by this revelation. "I'd think you'd tell your fiancé everything." But then, Heather had totally failed to mention she'd been spending every minute they weren't together with the new guy who moved in next door.

"Nope. He'd have laughed in my face." She sounded so sad at that, it hurt his heart. And made him *not* want to be that guy.

He reached his hand over the console to touch her arm and underscore that point. "Will you tell me about it if I promise no scoffing?"

"Will you believe me?" she countered.

"I don't lie," he said softly, using his arm to ease Clem back so he could read Ayla's expressions better and not take his eyes off the road for too long. "So, if I act like I believe that you are really reading an animal's mind, it would be a lie. But that doesn't mean I'm not interested in how it works for you. Is that fair, or will you not like me anymore?"

"Who said I like you?" she teased, the smile coming back and reaching her gorgeous dark eyes. Thank *God.*

"The Dogmothers," he replied.

"Wildly optimistic, those two." She turned a little in her seat, relaxed again. "But you're the reason I haven't told people. I mean, your reaction."

He nodded, truly sorry he'd disparaged the whole idea, but that didn't automatically make him accept telepathy with animals. Not a nuclear engineer who minored in physics.

"So, when did it start?" he asked. "How did you, uh, know you could do this?"

She thought about it for a long moment before answering. "Well, growing up, we never had pets, so I never spent any appreciable amount of time with animals. But when I was twelve, I took riding lessons, and right away I sensed my connection with the horses was a little more, well, profound than other people's."

"How did that connection manifest itself?"

"I felt their energy," she said. "I could see the images that they saw in their heads. I knew when they were tired or hungry or thirsty or hurt. I knew when they wanted to go down a different path because they'd been on one that morning and there was mud that would slow us down."

"But couldn't that be chalked up to you being very smart and intuitive? Maybe being able to feel the way the horse led you and not…what he was thinking?" There had to be a logical explanation.

"No," she said simply. "Once I saw a fallen tree, clear as day, and my instructor took me that way, despite what the horse was telling me. Sure enough, there was the tree on the path, exactly the way I saw it—and I do mean down to the broken branches and how they were placed. The horse told me it was there."

He considered that, silent while he tried—really

tried—to figure out how that could scientifically work. He couldn't.

"At first, I really didn't think it was something unusual," she continued. "I thought everyone who loved animals could do this. When I turned fourteen, I started volunteering at a local animal shelter, and that's when I realized that I could communicate with almost every animal, and no one else could." She looked out the window in thought, maybe remembering. "I told Trina, my older sister, who thought I was nuts. After a little while, I told my mother."

"Who also thought you were nuts?" he guessed.

"Who was being cheated on by my father for the second or third or whatever time by then, so she could not possibly have cared less."

"Oh." He gave her a sympathetic look. "Sucks."

"It did. They finally divorced right after I went to college, which was years after they *should* have split up. That's when I did try to tell my mother about my gift and talked about becoming a vet tech, which I really wanted to do…" She rolled her eyes. "I might as well have said I wanted to join the circus. I was told in no uncertain terms that I would not ever tell anyone ever that I had this 'weird problem,' and I would especially never tell EJ Paxton."

"Did you date him all that time? Were you guys, like, high school sweethearts?"

"Not even close," she said. "But our parents had us paired at birth and I wish I were kidding when I say that."

"And I thought not being able to make a decent tsoureki disappointed my dad."

That made her laugh softly, as if she appreciated the joke during her heavy tale. "Honestly, I didn't like EJ at all growing up and only saw him at country club functions and business events my dad held. My father and his father were—are, I guess—very close associates. They started and sold a company together, so EJ was always around. But about two years ago, he seemed to change. He absolutely bulldozed me with attention and promises and…what he thought was love. I guess I got a little flattened by it."

"You? I can't imagine you getting flattened by anyone or anything."

"I like to make people happy," she admitted, sighing as if that were her worst character flaw. "I like to cause the least amount of whitewater and conflict. And to his credit, EJ had grown up, developed a decent sense of humor, and really had his act together. I was mourning my Nana Jo, and he was in the right place at the right time."

"So you weren't madly in love with the guy you were going to marry?"

She flinched a little at the question. "I'm ashamed to say I wasn't, and obviously neither was he, or he wouldn't have slept with my friend the night before our wedding." She let out a light laugh, trying to sound nonchalant. "Anyway, I'm glad I got out."

So was he. But he doubted she felt flippant about her fiancé's infidelity. He certainly didn't, not if he had to truly and openly admit it. Ayla had pain, he didn't want to contribute to it by scoffing at something so important to her.

"So," he said, trying to show support. "What's Clem thinking right now?"

He expected her to snap back a joke or a reason she couldn't *perform on demand*, but instead she turned in her seat to see the dog. "She's thinking about you."

"She's looking at me."

"No, she's thinking about you…" She was very quiet, her eyes closed. "Were you running your fingers along a row of keys that are hanging in…a store?"

He sucked in a soft breath. He'd just stood at the cash register at Bitter Bark Hardware, absently grazing the rack of unmade keys while he waited in line. How the hell…

"Okay, but plenty of small-town hardware stores in America have racks of unmade keys by the register, and you know exactly where I was while you shopped. Very smart, very lucky, very specific."

"But is it accurate?"

He couldn't argue with that. It didn't convince him, but he'd made his point, glancing at the white gates of Waterford Farm as they passed and realizing how close they were to Marie's ranch. He didn't want the afternoon with her to end, and he sure didn't want it to end on a note that sounded like he was testing her.

"So tell me more about your family," he said.

"My family is…" She eyed the gates for a moment with a look that reminded him of Clem the first time she saw pizza. "The complete opposite of yours. Not fun and fabulous, not close and competitive, and not…interested in each other."

She sounded so broken, he actually felt it in his own chest. "That's a shame."

"Well, we're also ridiculously rich, which takes some of the sting out of it. And my sister can make me laugh when she doesn't drive me crazy, so there's that." She added a sigh. "But your family—all of it—is amazing. I thought about everyone all evening last night. The brothers and cousins and dogs and grandmas and stepsiblings and some of the cutest little kids I've ever seen."

"There's a lot of those around," he agreed. "But like I told you, I'm really only close to the Santorini branch of the family. This whole Kilcannon and Mahoney stuff started while I was living in San Diego."

"How can you bear to leave?"

"Because I'm a nuclear engineer and want to make money," he replied.

"Money isn't everything."

"Easy to say when you're…what was the phrase? Ridiculously rich."

She eyed him for a moment. "Is money that important to you?"

"Money is freedom," he said without hesitation. "And a validation of talent and hard work. I was on military pay for well over a decade, doing a very difficult job that commands a huge salary in the civilian world. What London offered was three times, or more, what I made even at lieutenant commander grade."

"But you have such an incredible family here."

He could hear the longing in her voice. "I guess the grass is always greener," he said. "You have money and want the big gang. I have the gang and want the cash."

"You can have the cash," she said quickly. "I'll take those wonderful, meddlesome, adorable grandmothers. I miss mine so much."

"Yeah, they're good. And I'm Yiayia's far-and-away favorite grandkid, so that's nice."

She laughed. "I held that position with Nana Jo, too."

"Well, you're welcome to get your grannie fix with mine."

"Thanks. I guess I'll see them all this weekend when I'm in the Waterford tent embarrassing the hell out of you."

He slowed the car to a stop in front of Marie's drive, turning to her. "Why would you embarrass me?"

"Doing my magic tricks, as you call the single thing that makes me the most unique human I could possibly be."

Oh man. He closed his eyes as the comment sliced. "For the what? Fourth time? Fifth? I'm sorry."

"It's okay. You're trying." She angled her head toward the house. "You coming in to do more work today? Or do you want to drop Clem and me off here?"

"I don't want to drop either one of you off," he confessed softly, turning to her. "I feel like Clem is part of my body, and you are…" A riddle wrapped in an enigma cloaked in confusion and so pretty it hurt to look right into her eyes.

"I can't wait to hear the end of that sentence." She poked his shoulder. "A fraud, fake, charlatan, fortune teller, looney bird, woo-woo witch, and—"

"Gorgeous."

"Oh." She smiled. "That's even nicer than one of those five apologies. Compliment accepted."

"Good, because it's true. But I still…"

"Don't believe," she finished for him.

He sighed. "I could lie, but then you wouldn't believe the compliments *or* the apologies. Does it matter?"

"Matter for what? You can still come over to fix the ranch. You're welcome to give your love to Clementine, and I don't dislike your company."

"Don't dislike? You hear that killer compliment, Clem?" he joked to the dog, but held Ayla's dark gaze, enjoying the hell out of the banter and flirting.

"Well, I'd like you better if you believed me."

"Is that all it would take?" He gave her a slow smile.

"Then convince me, Ayla."

"What do I get if I do?" she asked. "Other than bone-deep satisfaction."

He inched a little closer as if the answer had to be obvious. "Look, we're just playing here, right? And we have a lot in common, you and me."

"We do?"

"Yeah, both a little bruised from an ex."

"Okay, I'll give you that. But nothing else."

"Not true," he argued. "Both the favorite grandkid. And both…" He dug for more. "Leaving town soon. Right?"

"Maybe. So what are we 'playing,' as you put it?"

"A game," he said without hesitation. "And games are fun."

"A game?" She lifted one brow. "Like a game of make-believe? I told you I don't want to do that."

"But—"

She put a finger on his lips, quieting him. "Here's a game of make-believe we can play. Can I *make* you *believe*?"

No. Not in a million years. "I guess it depends on the prize," he said, feeling his whole body slipping a centimeter closer.

"I'll play for bragging rights."

"And I'll play for one, long, unforgettable, completely breathless…" His mouth was inches from hers.

"Kiss," she finished.

"Night," he said at precisely the same second.

And they both laughed.

"We'll have to work up to that." She cupped her hand on his cheek, her eyes dancing with humor. "But be careful if you play a game of make-believe, Theo. I might make you believe."

Never gonna happen. "When do we start?"

"Saturday," she said without any hesitation.

"Dinner?"

"If you like, but first you have to sit next to the pet psychic at the fundraising fair all day Saturday, and you cannot make a single comment that's anything but praise and support."

Well, at least he'd have a chance to be close to her all day. "Okay. Sounds fun. What are we playing for?"

"Points. For every person who says I'm right about their dog, I get a point. And for everyone who says I totally missed the mark, I lose one. If I have less than ten, I'll buy you dinner. How's that?"

Good, but not great. "Do I get points?"

She thought for a moment. "I'll give you a point for every time you support, acknowledge, and otherwise do not mock my talent. Loser buys dinner."

"Okay, but…" Not quite enough. "How about a kiss for every point? Then we both win."

"Oh." Her eyes flashed in response. "Then I guess we'll both be very…motivated."

He sure was.

Chapter Twelve

The sun bathed Bushrod Square in a spring light that seemed to make the sky bluer, the grass greener, and Clem's coat an even shinier black. The entire square was already humming with activity for the Paws for a Cause kickoff. On the way over, Marie had told Ayla how the fundraiser had grown in the past few years, from a few booths and daily activities over the month to a much bigger event that drew tourists, dog lovers, and animal-centric organizations from all over the country.

For the kick-off, tents and booths of various sizes had been set up to sell products, offer services, adopt animals, and raise money for a range of causes. Bitter Bark Fire Department trucks lined the whole east side of the town square, ready for kids to crawl all over them. A stage had been erected for a lively dog show that would take place later that afternoon, crowning lucky puppers for Best Wagger and Loudest Howler. Already, even an hour before Paws for a Cause officially opened, the grassy, expansive town square was filled with excited furbabies and their owners.

Clem was handling the distractions and dogs like a pro, trotting between Marie and Ayla with a newfound confidence that made Ayla's heart soar at the amazing progress they'd made this past week.

She still wouldn't go near the picnic table on her own. And she ate twice as much and three times as fast as any of the other dogs, always keeping one eye on them, like Hoss or Little Joe might steal her food. Yes, she whined sometimes for no reason, still slept under Ayla's bed all night, and growled at strangers.

But Ayla happened to know that Clem wasn't quite as obsessed with Theo as she had been at first, thinking more now about her new world than only the man who saved her.

If only that were true for Ayla.

For three of the past four days, he'd shown up in the morning and worked on the ranch until late in the afternoon. And how could Ayla not help him? Or have lunch with him? Or take walks with him and Clem around the property? Or go into town and buy tools and supplies to rebuild the kennels?

So, they'd spent hours together, talking and laughing, making jokes about the game they'd be playing today, and getting to know each other in the most organic and natural way.

And then, when Theo wasn't around, Ayla found herself thinking of him then, too, or talking to Miz Marie about him. They'd managed to keep things very platonic, but that was because they both knew they had a dinner date Saturday night.

And a day-long session of animal communication that started in…ten minutes.

Ayla let out a little groan as she and Marie walked past the founder's statue and around a massive tree with a plaque proclaiming it as the town's namesake tree.

"Are you nervous?" Marie asked, glancing with concern at Ayla.

"Yeah," she admitted. "I'm a little tense."

"Are you worried you'll make mistakes or not get any readings on the animals?"

Ayla thought about it, shaking her head. "No, I trust my skills. They rarely let me down. It's the audience that freaks me out."

"One audience member in particular, I imagine," Marie teased.

"Yes, he would definitely be making me nervous. I hope having him watch me all day wasn't a bad idea."

"Not at all," Marie assured her. "You'll have fun with your flirting and joking around, constantly finding lame excuses to casually touch like you two do."

They did, didn't they? Ayla felt a smile pull. "Lame?"

"To an outsider. I'm sure it seems perfectly natural when you two kid around."

"Excuse me, but have you seen those kennels?" She held up her nails, two of which were chipped, the expensive week-old wedding manicure all but gone. "That was work, not flirting."

Although holding tools and carrying wood and watching Theo sweat in the sun while he rebuilt the kennels had been pretty darn enjoyable.

"Harmless and fun," Marie said. "I think this little friendship's done some nice things for both of you."

This little friendship. That sounded innocent enough. Far more innocent than some of the thoughts that had been keeping Ayla awake at night.

"We're having dinner tonight," Ayla told her. "I guess I should have told you that you're babysitting Clem."

Marie laughed. "Yes, you should have, but fortunately

for you, I'm available. Can I tell Finnie and Agnes? They'll be over the moon."

"If Theo hasn't already. But no reason to go over the moon," she added. "It's only a game."

"Oh, is that what the kids are calling it now?" Marie bumped her with a playful elbow. "Maybe *that's* why you're tense," she suggested. "Because you have a date tonight."

Ayla slowed her step, tugging on Clem's leash. "I'm tense because I've never been 'out' in the public before," she confessed. "The few times I've practiced my skills have been in the privacy of the shelter, usually with you. Once at Darcy's grooming shop, and last Sunday at Waterford. I want to be sure I can handle the doubters."

"So you invited one to sit with you all day?"

"That may be *why* I invited him," she mused. "I think if he sees my work, he'll know I'm for real. But even if he doesn't, he's not going to sit there all day and crack jokes about what a fake I am." Her eyes widened. "Is he?"

"What would you do if he did?"

"Well, I wouldn't go out to dinner with him."

"Then he won't," Marie said. "The boy's smitten over my kitten. Come on." She nudged Ayla forward. "There's the Waterford tent, and it's already packed."

"Packed with dogs," Ayla noted, holding tight to Clem's leash as she scanned the long white overhang with the new family Waterford Farm logo visible everywhere.

"This is a huge day for Waterford," Marie told her. "Not only do they raise a lot of money for the ever-growing rescue side of the business, they can probably find homes for a dozen or more dogs today. Look, there's Garrett wearing his hat. That's always a good sign."

"I haven't met Garrett yet," she said, noticing the tall, good-looking man in a beat-up cowboy hat with a toddler on his hip. "What's the significance of the hat?" she asked.

"It's his 'doggone hat,'" Marie said on a laugh. "That's what his mother, Annie, used to call it when he was a teenager. You can see how old the hat is. He only wears it when, well, a dog is gone. When one gets adopted. He must have started early today. Come on, let's go find out who's going to a forever home."

As they got closer, Clem let out a low growl, pulling at her leash.

"It's okay, Clementine," Ayla assured her. "Everyone's friendly here."

But the growl grew deeper, punctuated by barks, and with each step, she grew more agitated.

Some of the family came over to greet them, but Ayla could give only cursory hellos as she worked to calm down Clem.

"What's going on here?" Daniel Kilcannon knelt down next to Clem and put a gentle hand on her head. She ducked out of his touch, yanked on the leash, growling and barking at…Garrett.

As the man came closer, Clem started jumping and trying to break from Ayla's grip. Garrett stayed back a few feet, holding the little child on his hip protectively.

"Clementine," she said, a little harsher than they normally were with the dog, but she was spiraling fast, barking, growling, and staring directly at Garrett. Ayla closed her eyes and held Clem to figure out what was bothering her.

Waves of energy wafted from her, but the images in Clem's head were changing so fast, Ayla couldn't grab one to analyze it. There was darkness. Rain. A man she couldn't make out. That picnic table. A flash of light. Another flash. And that man…

Clem lunged toward Garrett, teeth bared, her barking the most aggressive Ayla had ever heard from this dog. Daniel managed to snag the dog, who was one hundred percent focused on Garrett, and she wanted to attack.

The hat!

It suddenly showed up in Ayla's head as clear as if someone had handed her a picture.

"Take off your hat," she called over the barking. "Please, lose the hat for a moment."

"Sure." He slipped the hat off and tossed it to someone a few feet away.

Almost immediately, the barking stopped, though Clem continued to growl.

Then a strawberry-blond-haird woman whom Ayla remembered meeting at Waterford took the child from Garrett's arms, calmly removing him with the ease that showed she was his mother.

Ayla's heart shifted that anyone could be afraid of Clementine, but that had absolutely been an attack mode…and it stopped the minute the hat disappeared.

Suddenly, a strong hand landed on Ayla's shoulder, and she looked to her side to see Theo inches from her, concern etched on his handsome features.

"Are you okay?" he asked.

"I'm fine, but Clem…"

"Doesn't like my doggone hat," Garrett said, slowly and carefully coming closer. "It's okay, girl," he said in a low and comforting voice. "I'm friend, not foe."

Clementine stared at him, her dark gaze unwavering, but the lethal look had softened.

Ayla could tell Garrett was far too experienced with dogs to move fast. He kept his distance and slowly crouched down, carefully getting a treat from his pocket that he slid on the ground toward Clementine.

She didn't budge, still staring in warning.

Theo came around Clem's other side, replacing Daniel, who stood to watch the scene unfold, along with many other members of the family.

"It's okay, Clemmie," Theo whispered in her ear. "This is my stepbrother. Not the best-lookin' guy in the squad, but you don't need to eat him."

Garrett laughed softly, moving an inch closer. "Hey, Clementine," he said, once again holding out his hand.

Clementine stared.

"He's okay," Theo assured Clem, reaching a fist toward Garrett's hand. "See? I like him." They bumped fists, and Clem finally blinked. "He's good."

Garrett came a little closer, and the fight went out of Clem as her body relaxed. She turned to Theo and started giving his face a tongue bath, her tail wagging like crazy.

The whole group let out a relieved laugh.

"Good call on the hat," Theo said to Ayla as he eased Clementine's snout from his face. "That's what was bothering her."

"Does that count as a point?" she asked, smiling at him.

"Yes, so you're off to an auspicious start, Captain Clairvoyance."

She laughed, then reached over to give Clem a hug.

"I guess we have to make sure you're on the lookout for men with hats," Garrett said, settling in front of the dog to give her some love.

"Then we're in trouble on this sunny day." Theo looked around. "I count five just in this crowd."

"Those are ball caps," Ayla said. "This dog only reacts to something more like a cowboy hat."

Garrett gave her a surprised look. "You must be the pet psychic the family's been buzzing about."

Before she could answer, Theo put his hand over hers. "Actually, it's animal communicator, Garrett," he said in perfect sincerity.

"Thanks," she whispered. "I should give you a point for such incredible respect and nonmocking."

"I'll take all the points you're giving out, Ayla."

She felt her heart flip a little just thinking about it.

A few minutes later, they were whisked off to a table by an efficient and delightful teenage girl Ayla met the previous weekend. Prudence, or Pru, as everyone called her, was Molly and Trace's daughter. But today? She had an impressive air of authority for someone who couldn't be much older than sixteen. She carried a clipboard, wore a headset under a thick mane of dark hair, and seemed born for leadership.

"I went ahead and made you a sign," she told Ayla as they walked to a row of tables and booths at the front of the tent. "I hope you like it."

"As long as it doesn't say 'Ayla the Magnificent,' I'm fine," she assured the girl.

"Darcy told me to keep it super professional, so..." She gestured toward a long white table with a simple cardboard sign that said "Ayla Hollis, Animal Communicator." The table held a stack of bright green flyers.

"That's nice, Pru, thank you."

"I'm your contact for anything you need, but I'll stick around and get things going." Her hazel eyes sparkled. "I gotta say I'm dying to see you at work."

"Stay as long as you like," Ayla said. "I think Theo's got his hands full with Clem."

He was crouched down, trying to get Clem to slide under the table, but the dog was having none of it.

"She hates tables," Ayla said.

"Did she tell you that?" Pru asked, a little excited.

Ayla laughed softly. "No, I've been living with her for almost a week. She'd rather starve, sweat, or stand in the rain than get under a table."

"I wonder why," Pru said. "Can you ask her?"

Theo looked up. "The lady who dumped her in a mini-mart told me she was chained to a picnic table, so that's probably why she hates tables."

Pru looked horrified. "Oh my gosh, the poor, sweet doggy."

"I'll keep an eye on her while you get started, Ayla," Theo said. "She isn't going to sit quietly and people-watch."

Pru helped Ayla get situated, showing her the flyers and explaining how they were handling payments, but the minute anyone approached the table, Clem got upset.

Her energy went a little haywire, and she shot out a warning bark. In fact, when the first person who seemed like an interested customer came by with a sweet but slightly rambunctious boxer, Clem growled and scared them off.

"She is not good for business," Theo acknowledged, standing up with her. "Why don't I take her for a walk around the square and tire her out?"

"I can take her for you, Uncle Theo," Pru offered. "You can stay with Ayla."

"Thanks, Pru, but you're working. And I honestly don't want you to have to deal with her if she sees…a guy in a cowboy hat." He threw a look at Ayla. "Not even sure I can."

"I think it's a great idea to get her used to this environment," Ayla said. "I'm here all day, so it's fine. Enjoy the walk."

They took off, and Pru instantly settled into the seat next to Ayla. "He's nice, huh?" she said.

"Very." She skimmed the flyer, which was beautifully designed and well written. "Did you make this?"

"My boyfriend helped," she said. "He's really good with graphics."

"It's amazing." Ayla smiled at her. "I might have to hire him if I do this professionally."

"Oh, look." She surreptitiously pointed to a young couple with a wheaten terrier reading the flyer at the end of the long table. "They seem interested. Can I pitch them?"

"Sure."

Pru stood and beamed at them. "Would you like to know what your beautiful wheaten is thinking?" she asked. "This lady is an expert at reading an animal's energy."

"Oh?" The woman looked at her husband. "We'd love to know, wouldn't we?"

He rubbed a receding hairline and laughed. "Good luck with that. Spencer is a very, uh, challenging dog to understand."

The couple checked out the prices, and Pru informed them that all the money raised was for Waterford's adoption program. The man was dubious, but his wife persuaded him to spend the money for a good cause, so they brought Spencer around the table to meet Ayla.

"Hello, big boy," she said, admiring the perfect grooming job and his somewhat regal stance.

Instantly, she knew why.

"He's a show dog?" she guessed, making them both nod enthusiastically.

"He hasn't done that many yet, but—"

Ayla held up a hand to stop them. If they told her too much, she knew it would interfere with what she wanted to get from the dog.

"Let me talk to him," she said with a smile.

"Cool, huh?" Pru asked with awe in her voice.

The couple exchanged looks, but leaned in as Ayla put her hands on Spencer's head and rubbed gently, blocking out all the sights and sounds to concentrate exclusively on what was in this animal's head.

"The bar?" she asked, glancing at them. "You're training him on a jumping bar in your…driveway." That's what it looked like to her.

Again, they shared a look, doubt sliding into surprise.

"Yeah," the man said. "We are."

Ayla nodded and shifted her attention back to Spencer, her own confidence slowly building as she closed her eyes and searched for images, seeing only that jumping bar, which was…too high. In Spencer's mind, it was more like a pole vault than a low jump.

"You might want to lower it," she told his owners. "He's not ready to jump as high as you have it."

"But he's done it twice," the man said.

"Hush, Gary," his wife instructed. "I want to h
what she says."

"Because you actually believe this," he mumbled.

Ayla wiped the comment from her brain and added the slightest pressure to Spencer's head, and then she could see a small, brown, stuffed…moose? A reindeer? Something with antlers that had all of Spencer's attention. The toy was sitting on top of a coffee table that had some very chewed-on legs.

"He's chewing on the table," she said softly, "because I think you might be using the wrong reward in the training."

"Really?" The woman shot forward. "We have caught him gnawing on the table after a training session. I think he's frustrated."

"What are you using as the reward to train him?" Ayla asked.

"Treats."

She shook her head. "He wants…" She narrowed her eyes, thinking. "Is it a moose or a reindeer?"

The woman sucked in a noisy breath. "Moosie! His favorite toy! I've sewn it up three times." She turned to her husband. "Did you hear that, Gary? How did she know?"

Gary's frown deepened. "Are you saying train him with a stuffed animal as a reward instead of treats?"

"I think you should try that," she said. "I really think he'd stop chewing on the table. And maybe lower that bar a few inches so he's not quite so scared of it."

"Oh my God, that's amazing!" The woman looked at Pru. "Did you hear that? Amazing."

Pru gave an excited clap. "She's so good, right?"

"Wherever you got Moosie," Ayla said, "go back and get a few more. Can I give him a treat?" she asked, reaching into a container on the table.

"Yes, yes, and thank you!" The couple gushed a little longer, then took off with a promise to send over Gary's mother and her Shih Tzu, who'd started biting when she got tired at night.

"Holy Moses," Pru said, sliding back into the seat. "How did you do that?"

"I honestly don't know," she admitted. "But it was fun."

"I'm glad, because I have a feeling you are going to be very busy today. I can't wait to tell Yiayia," she said. "She's skeptical."

"Ahh. I heard the Greek side is taking my talent with a major grain of salt."

Pru laughed. "I will admit you were the topic of conversation at family dinner Wednesday night."

"I was?" She let her eyes go wide. "Believers versus the nonbelievers?"

"Oh, no. The usual family discussion about the Dogmothers' latest project." Pru inched closer. "I'm an honorary Dogmother, you know."

"Is that why you wanted to take Clem and let Theo stay with me?"

She gave a guilty grin. "Possibly. Oh, look. There's Lucas and Tor." Waving, she leaned in to add, "My boyfriend. We just had our four-month anniversary."

"Dogmothers?" Ayla guessed, following her gaze to a good-looking teenage boy.

"Actually, they had a hand in it."

"Beautiful greyhound," Ayla said, her attention riveted on the tall, graceful dog loping next to the boy. "Tor, did you say?"

"Short for Toreador, which was his racing name. Or Tornado, if you've got something shiny." Clipboard and job momentarily forgotten, Pru darted over to the boy, who gave her a hug and then said something that made her laugh.

Pru practically dragged Lucas and Tor back to the table, the whole time giving him a rapid-fire recap of what had happened with Spencer.

After she introduced Ayla, Pru eased Tor closer. “Quick, before you get any more customers. Can you read Tor?”

A former racer? She wasn’t sure she wanted to. Those dogs could have some dark memories after years of being used for their talents and given next to nothing in return. But Pru looked so enthused, she didn’t want to let her down.

“I sure can.” Ayla stood and leaned over, the tall dog easily able to dip his head across the narrow table. She slipped him a treat to hold his attention for a moment, closing her eyes.

All she could see was…a place that looked very familiar.

“He loves Waterford Farm,” she said.

“It’s like his second home,” Lucas told her.

“And…” The next image came in crisp and clear. A tree so big and bright it had to be in… “A mall at Christmastime?”

Pru literally screamed, making the dog prance a little, and the boyfriend laugh.

“How did she do that?” Pru exclaimed, attracting attention from people nearby. “She couldn’t know about the mall! Oh, Uncle Theo! There you are. Wait until you hear this!”

Ayla caught sight of Theo with Clementine, but then another person came up to the table while Pru, Lucas, and

Tor took off to tell Theo—and everyone within earshot—what had happened.

There was a line for the next two hours, and all the while, Theo stayed nearby, watching, listening, and managing Clem.

Everything went by in a blur—except for the wonderful animals who provided a kaleidoscope of changing images—but if Theo was still keeping points for every time she made a believer out of a dog owner, she knew she was winning.

Chapter Thirteen

"It'd be easier to get a moment backstage with a rock star." Theo smiled down at Ayla as he pulled food from a bag. "So I'm happy to settle for lunch from the family deli on a park bench with no Clementine."

"I'm glad Marie took her home," Ayla said, opening the to-go box of spanakopita he'd gotten at the restaurant that bore his last name. "This was not her happy place."

He made a face, thinking of how many times he'd had to calm Clem down that morning. "I saw two more guys in cowboy hats. Same thing. Total beast mode."

"Obviously, someone who wore one hurt her." She blew out a breath, sounding exhausted. "Fortunately, I didn't have anything like that so far today. It's something I dread. I don't want to make a dog relive his or her pain, and I honestly have a hard time seeing it."

He wasn't sure how to react to that, so he decided to start eating his gyro and stop talking. What could he say? *You're the most intuitive person I've ever met, and I'm more sure than ever that's how you do this.*

No, he should be honest. Whatever she was doing—reading minds or faking it—had him feeling tense. It was so fundamentally far from his view of the world, that the whole thing had tested him more than he really wanted to admit.

Could he really like a woman who did that? Well, yeah, he liked her. But—

"You still don't believe," she said as she stared down at the flaky golden pastry.

"How can you tell?" he asked after swallowing.

"I'm intuitive like that."

He almost choked on the food going down as her word echoed his thoughts. "Jeez. It's like you read my mind."

"I did not and cannot. I told you, I don't do people."

She didn't do animals, either. Because there was no way, *no conceivably possible way*, that she was *reading* all those dogs' *thoughts*.

Ayla Hollis might not call herself a *people* "communicator," but really, what she could do, and do amazingly well, was inform, educate, entertain, and make people feel like she somehow gleaned information from their dog's brain. And no doubt about it, that was a skill and, based on the cash that she'd earned Waterford Farm's adoption programs today? It was a marketable one.

But when he took off the crush goggles he wore around this woman, he was able to see that she was simply masterful at deducing, guessing, reading people, and asking the right questions. She could hear one random fact, make a little supposition, maybe do some mental math. Then she'd read a verbal clue, pick up on exchanged looks, or even get a little insight based on the dog's name and…wham.

How long have you been putting Jinx in your walk-in closet at night? He doesn't like sleeping in there at all.

Now, that one was a beauty. And the couple had been gobsmacked. Oh, and Jinx had had his last night in the walk-in closet, he was pretty sure.

"What are you smiling about?" she asked, studying him after she had a bite of spanakopita.

"Thinking about Jinx and the closet," he told her, leaving out the part about how tense the whole thing made him, and wanting to change the subject. "And I'm smiling about the Santorini gyro." He lifted the sandwich. "I was raised on them. No other Greek restaurant from here to San Diego can match my father's secret tzatziki recipe. I have to give credit to John for refusing to let any old line-cook come into his restaurant and change it."

"What did you think about Jinx and the closet?" she asked.

"I think…you're good, that's all I'm going to say. You have a freakish ability to…to…"

She stared at him, waiting.

"Figure people out," he finished. "And then tell them what they need to hear."

Her shoulders sank with a quick, unhappy breath. "So, I'm right. You do not think I'm legitimate."

A legitimate entertainer? Absolutely. A psychic? Come *on*. "Does what I think matter?"

She lowered her plastic fork and turned, pinning those impossibly dark brown eyes on him.

"A little bit more each day, yeah," she admitted in a near whisper. "I don't want it to matter, but it does. Good to know, I guess. So I don't…fall…smack on my face on the pavement again."

"Let me see if I got that." He took a slow breath and a sip of soda. "You like me, but if I don't 'believe' you, then you don't *want* to like me. You can only like someone who's buying your schtick."

"Buying my *schtick*?" Her voice rose slightly. "Condescend much, Theo?"

Damn it, he had. "Sorry."

"You say that a lot."

He shifted on the bench, frustrated that he could be a gruff engineer and terrible with words around someone so gentle and articulate. "Are we having a fight, Ayla?"

"We're having lunch. Which might be our only meal together today after all. I'm already blind with exhaustion, and I'm still committed to work the rest of this day."

He felt the punch of disappointment. "So, you're canceling dinner tonight?"

"That's probably for the best."

And he was blowing it left and right today. "Okay, let me say this the right way, because I'm definitely not the communicator you are, and I don't want to dig myself any deeper."

She waited, eating quietly while he took his last few bites of the gyro and folded the paper on his lap.

"I think you have an incredible talent and instinct. What I saw you do out there with person after person and dog after dog was…" He shook his head, digging for words, which was never easy for a man who understood numbers so much better. "Effortless. Masterful. And really, really helpful for people. And for dogs."

"Okay. Thanks. But you still don't really…believe."

"In clairvoyance or ESP or the supernatural?" He shook his head. "No. But I believe in your intuition. I see a powerful, well-honed sensitivity to a hundred different details that a less perceptive person would miss." He studied her for a minute, hoping that he'd said that right. "So maybe we're merely using different words for the same thing."

She searched his face for a moment, looking into his eyes, listening, processing, thinking. Surely she'd see what he was saying was true—and a compliment. He meant it as one.

"No," she said simply. "It's way more than that. Sorry, but it is."

He put a hand on her arm, her skin warm from the sunshine and so smooth he wanted to feel more of it. Which took his brain back to dinner. He didn't want to cancel that date. He wanted to go out with her. To kiss her and hold her and listen to her laugh.

"Is it really that important what I think?" he asked. "'Cause I'm willing to overlook a difference of opinion and…semantics."

She turned to him, her eyes tapering as she readied whatever point she was going to lob at him.

"It's not semantics, and yes, it's important. This is my new life, Theo. And like it or not, you're the first man in it after I got crushed by another man who didn't take me seriously. After being raised by a father who didn't take anything I said or did seriously. I grew up in a world surrounded by men who didn't take me seriously."

"I take you very seriously," he said. "I'm not using the right words to describe your…skills."

Her eyes shuttered on the last word, and he mentally kicked himself for another verbal stumble over something this important to her.

"They didn't take me seriously as a *person*," she replied. "Forget my gifts. They didn't see beyond my looks and excellent hostess skills and ability to make sparkling small talk. My…*soul*…was not important to those men."

"Well, your looks are kind of blinding, to be fair. And your ability to work a crowd—whether it's at a society event or a fundraiser in the park—is a testament to all that I just mentioned. So, don't lump me in with men who don't take you seriously."

She studied him for a minute, letting out a sigh.

He inched closer, holding her gaze to make his point. "And I bet your father and your fiancé saw more than simply the obvious in you."

She snorted. "To my father, I was the second daughter who would not be able to take over his business, even though he couldn't admit that level of sexism to anyone. Sorry, but it's true. And my fiancé?" She closed her eyes and dropped her head back. "I think I was the easier of the two Hollis daughters to manage."

"And by manage, you mean cheat on."

"Bingo. Trina would have run, too, absolutely. But she would have castrated him first. That's the difference between the Hollis sisters."

He made a face. "I hate that there are still men like that out in the world," he said. "Men who don't take women seriously."

She gave him a blistering look, silent.

"Ayla, you can't believe that I think like that. These men obviously treated you with zero respect."

Lifting one brow, she whispered, "My 'schtick'?"

He deserved that. "Jeez. I'm sorry." Then he gave a dry laugh. "And you're right. I say that a lot."

He was quiet for a moment and so was she, nibbling at the last of her spanakopita, staring ahead. Even in her profile, he could see the hurt in her expression and despised himself for putting it there.

"I don't mean to make excuses, and this isn't another apology, but you know, I'm an engineer. I don't think in terms of…" *Feelings and words.*

Suddenly, Heather's voice came back to him from the night they broke up.

You can't talk about your feelings, Theo. And he does.

Ayla looked at him, a question in her eyes. "Woo-woo things?" she supplied with a tiny bit of sarcasm when he didn't finish his thought.

There was nothing woo-woo about feelings. They were just…uncomfortable. "I'm a scientist, Ayla," he said. "I live by mathematical formulas and empirical evidence. It's hard for me to understand what you do. But I honestly didn't intend to disrespect you or not take you seriously."

After a moment, she lifted the last of the flaky crust.

"Thanks, I appreciate that. And thank you for lunch, Theo. Don't take this the wrong way, but maybe you shouldn't hang around my table any longer. In fact, I'd be more comfortable if you didn't."

"Is there a *right* way to take that?" He felt all the air whoosh out of him.

"I think I can do the job better without being so aware of you."

"Got it. And…tonight?"

She looked long and hard at him, obviously thinking and considering and please, God, giving him a chance. He liked her. He really—

"I think I'll be too tired to go out tonight, if you don't mind."

He minded *a lot.*

She folded her paper and closed the lid on the to-go box. "You don't have to apologize anymore, Theo." She stood and let out a sigh. "You really have helped me more than you know."

"How?"

"Because now I know I won't fall into old habits in my new life. It would be very easy to agree with you or even hide, when I'm around you, what happens to me with animals. It would be very easy to get swept up in our attraction and connection, letting this go to the next natural step. Easy to avoid conflict and be a people-pleaser and let a strong man lead the way for me."

"So how does that help you?"

"You reminded me how much I don't want to do any of that. So, thank you." She put a hand on his arm. "Really, I mean that sincerely. Thank you."

With one more smile, she stood and headed back to the Waterford Farm tent, leaving him sitting alone, frustrated, and remembering exactly why he avoided talking about feelings.

After a long, pointless walk around town, Theo found himself in front of the familiar blue awnings of Santorini's Deli. John's version of their father's—and grandfather's—Greek restaurant was brighter, lighter, and more modern than the one Theo had grown up in.

But there was still a powerful air of familiarity and family. Something that reached down to his bones and made him want to eat olives off his big brother's plate and steal ouzo when Yiayia wasn't looking and hang out in the kitchen to watch his father work magic on the grill.

He closed his eyes at the thought of Nico Santorini, punching down a threat of grief. It was the smell of the place that made him miss Dad. And maybe the need to work out a problem he was having with a girl.

He pushed open the door to Santorini's, relieved that the lunch crowd that had been here earlier had died down, freeing up a dozen or so of the tables in the large dining room. A young woman he didn't know greeted him with a smile at the hostess stand, but before he could introduce himself, he heard his name called.

Instinctively, he knew to look to the far back booth, the place where the family gathered in the off-hours. Sure enough, Cassie was waving to him.

This dining room was set up a little differently than the original Santorini's in Chestnut Creek, but of course there'd be a table or booth where whoever was managing the restaurant might be tabulating the day's receipts.

In the past, Yiayia would be there, sipping coffee and complaining that whoever made her cookies had not used rose water, so she'd have to go back and make them herself for tomorrow's customers. Alex would be testing a new recipe. John might be doing inventory for Dad.

Bitter Bark was a great place, and Waterford Farm was an amazing piece of picturesque property where these three branches of a family tree could gather and grow into one. But Santorini's Deli, even this version in Bitter Bark, was like walking into *home*.

And right now, he needed that.

"You guys give up on the dogs?" he asked as he reached the oversized booth where Cassie, Yiayia, John, and Alex all sat together.

"My makeup was melting in that heat," Yiayia said, tapping her cheek that had very few lines considering her age of eighty…something. She never said. "Finnie had to work the church table selling raffle tickets, and Cassie needed a break from standing all day."

"Yeah, I'm wiped," Cassie agreed. "Theo, you want some tea? I can get—"

"Relax," he said, grabbing a chair from the next table to place at the head of the booth, and nodded to Alex. "How'd the wine-tasting booth do?"

"Great. Grace wanted to walk around with Chloe and Andi, and I needed to see how things were running in the kitchen here since I left."

"Smoothly." John didn't even look up from the tablet he was tapping, no doubt the twenty-first-century version of "doing receipts," as Dad called the job. "Ask Theo. He walked out of here with spanakopita and a gyro a while ago."

"You ate both?" Alex snorted. "Good to know the Navy didn't diminish your record-breaking appetite."

Theo grinned, long used to the ribbing his family gave him for his voracious need to eat frequently and in large quantities.

"I didn't eat both," he said. "But I could have. Tell Bash the tzatziki was Santorini perfection. Dad would be proud."

John nodded his thanks, attention still riveted on the numbers.

"So you ate the gyro," Yiayia said, inching closer. "Then who ate the spanakopita? I know that Clementine went back to Miz Marie's, so…" Her voice rose in a playful question.

"As if you don't know, Agnes Santorini."

She looked a little smug. "Really?"

"Then what are you doing here?" Cassie asked.

"Or have you had enough of the psychic-sidekick gig?"

"I've had enough of the whole day," he admitted on a slightly defeated grunt. "And this psychic stuff? Jeez, if I don't buy into the whole thing, I'm some kind of doubting, heartless ogre. If I do, I'm…"

"An idiot?" Alex suggested.

"Gullible?" John mused.

"Naïve," Cassie added.

But Yiayia stared at him. "Maybe it means you like her, and you don't want to admit that."

He tried for an eye roll, but probably didn't nail it because…the truth hurt.

"Am I right?" Yiayia asked, leaning across the table.

"Chill," Cassie said, putting her hand on Yiayia's arm. "What do you think of her, Theo?" his sister asked, keeping the question open so he at least had an out if he wanted to take one.

"I think she's…" *Way too embedded under my skin for someone I've known a week.* "Very impressive."

"I hear a 'but,'" Alex said.

"Definitely," his twin brother agreed.

"But you're leaving soon, and she's just visiting?" Cassie suggested. "Is that the but?"

He looked from his sister to his grandmother, weighing how much to share. He needed some help and advice, but Yiayia had an agenda where Ayla was concerned, and Cassie looked like she'd collapse if she had to solve one more problem today.

"I know what the 'but' is," John said. "He likes her, but the whole pet psychic business rubs him the wrong way, and he would like to…" He glanced at Alex.

"Rub her the right way," he finished, a smile pulling at his face.

Cassie cracked up, and even Yiayia's shoulders shook with a soft laugh.

"It's worse than that," Theo said softly, surprising himself as the admission came out. But obviously, he needed to talk to this trusted group of close family.

In fact, he couldn't remember the last time they were together and didn't have significant others or a whole lot of Kilcannons or Mahoneys around. The moment was too rare, too special not to take advantage of it.

His sister scooted closer, humor gone from her expression as she studied him. "What do you mean, Theo?"

"I do like her," he said, relieved to finally acknowledge that to these people who mattered so much to him.

"I know what the problem is," Yiayia said. "She's a fraud, and you're a…well, you're perfect."

Even John had to look up from his work to share an *is she serious?* look with his siblings, making Theo laugh.

"Isn't that the problem?" Yiayia continued, oblivious to the fact that she could not hide her favoritism. "I knew it from the very beginning and told Finnie this was a mismatch, which, as the three people sitting at this table can tell you, we don't do."

He gave her a wry smile. "I don't think we're a mismatch at all. At least, I didn't…" Until that conversation over lunch.

"But I knew that she was a little too wacky for you, Théodoros," Yiayia continued. "Pretty, yes. Very sweet and witty, and we love Marie, so you can see why we zeroed right in on her. But…" She blew out a breath, shaking her head. "You're a *nuclear engineer*!"

She said it with about the same emphasis as if she'd proclaimed him the King of the World, which only made

Alex and Cassie crack up and moan, the way they had when he'd brought home the straight-A report card every semester while they were high-fiving their B's. John got A's, too, but somehow Theo's were better.

"It's not going to work out," he said after they had their moment.

"Why do you say that?" Cassie asked.

"Because I'm a science guy and she's a…" He grunted at the impossibility of words. "I'm sorry, but reading a dog's mind is…"

"Weird?" Alex suggested.

"Ridiculous," John added.

"Cuckoo for Cocoa Puffs?" Yiayia joked.

"Important to her," he finished, ignoring their comments. "It's not a character trait I need to overlook or understand. It's the essence of who she is and if I can't embrace her…her truth? Then I don't get to embrace her."

"And you want to embrace her," Cassie whispered. "Am I right?"

So right.

"Hate to break it to you, bro, but"—Alex gave a tight smile—"you might have to bend a little. That's how people build relationships."

"I suck at relationships," he said. "Just ask Heather."

"We really didn't like Heather," Cassie muttered.

"Well, I did," he shot back. "And I did such a pathetic job of talking about it that she literally fell in love with the guy next door, who was *not* a nuclear engineer, but apparently he could yammer about feelings all night long."

For a moment, all four of them stared at him, a little taken aback by his honesty.

It was Yiayia who broke the silence, leaning forward. "So you think Heather chose the neighbor over you because you don't like to talk about your feelings?"

"That's what she said. And, honestly, I'd rather break atoms than discuss…things. I don't like to talk about…" He shrugged and looked around, suddenly desperate for a distraction.

"Theo." Cassie gave him a serious look. "You have to talk. And some of that talk has to be about feelings. How else are you going to really know someone?"

He looked at Alex, but already knew he wasn't going to get an assist from his famously passionate chef brother. "Talking it out is the…second-best part."

While they laughed at that, John put the tablet down and adjusted his glasses.

"I know how you feel, Theo," he said.

"Yeah?" Theo studied his brother, pretty sure he'd get the support he needed from this man, if not the others. He and John were, in some left-brained ways, more alike than John and Alex, despite the fact that they were twins.

"But sometimes, if something is worth having, you have to go out of your comfort zone. And personal communication about esoteric things, especially something you don't like or understand, is not in your comfort zone."

No, it was not.

"But my guess is that it is very much *in* the comfort zone of someone who is so in tune with a creature's energy that she literally feels it."

"Literally?" Theo challenged, frustration mounting because he knew his brother was right.

"That's the point," John said. "It is literal to her. Summer said Ayla made a lady cry when she did a reading on her German shepherd, who was thinking about another family pet they'd lost."

"I was there," he said. "The little girl had a kitten bag and was wearing a kitten T-shirt. That's the kind of thing that Ayla would see and deduce that they also had a cat. And when she mentioned it, the little girl probably reacted, and Ayla picked up on that."

"Fine," John said. "So that's how she does it. Who cares? That's not the root of this problem, is it?"

Once again, they were all quiet, looking at him.

"No," he finally said. "I'm the root of the problem."

Yiayia reached over and put her hand on Theo's, and he knew exactly what she was going to say. *You're not the problem. You can't be the problem! You're perfect!*

"Anything worth having is worth fixing," she said.

He drew back, surprised.

She grinned. "Blame Finnie. She's always pouring those Irish sayings into my head. But"—she angled her head and tried to lift a Botoxed brow—"there's some truth to it, isn't there? And if anyone can fix anything, it's my Théodoros."

Cassie, John, and Alex looked at each other and, in perfect unison, all stage-whispered, "Because he's perfect!"

His siblings laughed, but Yiayia's dark gaze was intense and wise, and there was no smile on her face. "Because if you're smart enough to figure out the problem, Mr. Engineer, then you're smart enough to fix it. That is, if you want to."

He nodded slowly, certain. "I want to. We were supposed to have dinner tonight, but she cancelled." After his thoughtless 'schtick' comment? How could he blame her? "I don't know when I'll see her again."

"I do." Yiayia pulled out her phone and tapped the

screen, her long fingernail clacking as she texted someone.

When she finished, she turned the phone so he could read the text she'd sent, and he couldn't help smiling as he put her plan together.

"And that, my friends," she said smugly to the others as she tucked the phone back in her grannie bag, "is how the Dogmothers always make their match."

"What did you do?" Cassie asked.

"Nothing but clear the path. How your brother wants to proceed down it is entirely up to him."

He already knew and couldn't wait.

Chapter Fourteen

"Are you sure you don't want me to stay here?" Marie leaned against the doorjamb of Ayla's room, her expression a little sad. "I don't like to leave you alone, especially when you were planning to go out tonight."

"Well, those plans changed, and you got a great offer from Agnes and Finnie, Marie." Lying on the bed, Ayla kicked off her sneakers and fell back on the pillow, unable to resist stretching out after the long day at Paws for a Cause. "Dinner at their house in town will be a hoot."

"I know. I was so surprised when Agnes invited me, right after you told me I didn't have to babysit Clem. But we could bring her, if you want to come along."

Dinner with three delightful old ladies…or a hot bath and wine after a very emotional day. Honestly, tonight, it was no contest.

"I'm done in, Marie," she said, reaching over and down the side of the bed where Clem was. From under the bed, she licked Ayla's fingers, so happy to have the next-best-thing-to-Theo back in her sight. "So's Clem."

"You were a huge hit." Marie came in and rested on

the edge of the bed. "They raised a record-breaking amount at the Waterford tent today, and a large part of that was due to your work. Of course, Daniel already pledged quite a bit to the Last Chance Ranch, which is amazing."

"I'm so glad, but it wasn't just me. They had the wine tasting. And the Greek food. And the free training classes by those Kilcannon men. And I heard the raffle to win a flight in Aidan's plane went for well over a grand." She smiled. "The animal communicator was only one of many great ways that family raised money today."

Marie put her hand on Ayla's sock, wiggling her toes. "Why'd you cancel with Theo tonight, kitten?" she asked.

"Because I'm tired…of men who don't think I'm legit." She lifted her brows. "How's that for honesty?"

"It's real and raw," she said. "But are you sure? He seems to be quite enamored of you."

Not enamored enough to give credence to one of the most important aspects of her entire being. The conversation over lunch still stung, and she was glad she'd made the decision to break the date.

"Well, he could be faking that, like he thinks I'm faking…me." She flicked her fingers at Marie. "Now, get on with you, lady. Go have a fun dinner."

"But I'm leaving you without a phone or a car. I don't like that."

"When is my sister going to mail my phone?" she asked, exasperated. "But don't worry. You're leaving me with four dogs, a cat, a bottle of merlot, and an industrial-sized bottle of bubble bath. I'm already in heaven."

"You want me to leave my phone? You could call

Yiayia or Gramma Finnie if you need me." She smiled. "Or Theo."

Rolling her eyes, Ayla shooed Marie off the bed. "I don't want you driving at night without a phone. I'm good."

Marie finally gave up, blew a kiss, and left for her evening with friends and, one by one, Hoss, Little Joe, River, and Ziggy came into the room.

"No one's ever alone at the Last Chance Ranch, are we?" Ayla mused as she went to the kitchen to pour wine into a big plastic cup and then borrowed a fluffy bathrobe from Marie's room. A few minutes later, she was buried in bubbles, which she enjoyed with quite the menagerie of a four-legged audience.

Closing her eyes, she blissfully shut out all their thoughts, which was easy enough to do when she was this tired, and let her mind wander back to…Theo.

Replaying the moments of the day, she tried not to think about how he'd looked at her when another satisfied customer left her table. That wasn't doubt in his eyes, not always. He did seem a little…enamored.

And if they hadn't had that conversation over lunch, she'd be dressing for a dinner date right now—on a woefully thin wardrobe. But what she wore wouldn't have mattered, because maybe they'd have talked and laughed and…

She groaned. All those points for kisses.

Had she sacrificed a wonderful night…on principle? Yes, maybe she had. And that's what New Ayla did. No more doing what was expected of her without getting what she wanted in return: respect.

As she leaned back to rinse her hair under the tub faucet, one of the dogs barked. Then another. Clementine jumped up, got a little wild-eyed, then barked, running out of the room.

Someone rang the doorbell, which made Clem even crazier.

He wouldn't…would he?

Trying to ignore the unwanted bolt of hope that went zinging through her, she wrapped her soaking-wet hair in a towel and slid into the borrowed robe, heading out front to answer the door. She squinted to peek through the sheer curtains at the driveway, and that bolt ricocheted all the way through her when she saw a familiar Honda Civic.

Well, yes, he would.

Clementine was practically clawing at the door for her to open it. And, dang it, Ayla totally got that reaction to this man.

"Easy, girl. Easy." She flipped the lock, but left the chain on, opening the door a few inches.

He stood on the porch holding a large paper bag, a bouquet of flowers, a bottle of wine, and…a stuffed animal.

"Hello," she said, feeling her lips lifting in a smile. "Can I help you?"

"Apparently, I am not done apologizing."

"Is that so?" Her gaze dropped over all he carried in his arms. "With props this time?"

"I bring dinner, drinks, dessert, flowers, a toy for Clementine, treats for the rest of the crew, and some kneepads so I can truly grovel while I offer my apology."

And her heart turned over a few times, like she'd barrelled down a roller coaster with her hands in the air.

"No groveling necessary, but I'll take the rest." She opened the door, but got her hand on Clementine's collar to hold her back from an embarrassing display of…of exactly the elation Ayla was feeling.

She really had wanted to go out with him tonight, but she couldn't compromise her newfound integrity. Had he finally figured that out?

He came in and managed to get most of his stuff unloaded on an entry table, then crouched down to accept Clementine's exuberant show of affection. When his face was good and lapped, he looked up at her.

"Don't expect that from me," she said with a tease in her voice.

"I don't expect anything," he said, his emphasis on the last word not lost on her. "Can I stay for dinner? I'll make it for you."

"Of course."

"But first…" He stood, not really smiling, but his gaze did drop over her, and then he reached for the towel around her head. She felt it very slowly loosen and fall into his hand, her wet hair sliding toward the robe.

Every single cell in her body heated, dissolved, and tried not to whimper.

"I can't beg for forgiveness to a towel." He slid his fingers into her wet hair, the move sending shivers down her spine. Palming her scalp, he gently eased her head back so she was looking up at him.

"Ayla," he whispered, "there's something you need to know about me."

That his very touch made her bare toes curl against the floor? "What?"

"When something doesn't make perfect logical sense, it's like a physical pain to me. I want pieces to fit together. I want code to function. I want all alpha particles to have two protons and two neutrons. I want the change in reactivity to be caused by a change in temperature."

"You lost me."

"And I *don't* want that," he admitted, adding a little bit of pressure to ease her closer. "I don't want to miss out on spending time with a really amazing woman because of my need for things to make logical sense. Because some things, I know, don't make sense."

"Like what goes on in my brain?"

"Like how attracted I am to you. What goes on in your brain—whether I can explain it in scientific terms or not—*is* very appealing to me. I don't understand that, obviously, but the appeal is very real. And I don't understand what you do, but…"

"It's real to me," she supplied, because he really was trying so hard, and she ached to help him out.

He nodded. "I know it is, and I swear I respect that."

She felt a sigh escape her lips, ready, as always, to accept this apology. "Is that what you want me to know about you?"

"No, although it's good to have in your back pocket when dealing with me."

She gave him a confused look. "Then, what?"

"You know how you want a new life and want to be…different? That's why you came here after what happened with your ex?"

"Yes?"

"Well, I want that, too." He swallowed, clearly wrestling with the whole conversation and how much he wanted it to come out right.

"In what way?" she asked.

"I don't want all that logical crap to be my excuse anymore. I don't want it to cost me one more relationship.

I don't want it to be the reason I can't get all the thirty-seven-and-a-half kisses you racked up today."

She smiled. "And a half?"

"That one couple with the little brown dog? Gizmo? The guy didn't believe you, but his wife did. So, half a point." He searched her face, his gaze lingering over her lips for a moment, as if he was going to collect on those points right that minute. "And for every time I took you seriously, you were going to give me a point, remember?"

"So…goose egg for Navy Guy."

He shook his head. "I took you seriously over lunch," he replied. "I heard you loud and clear, Ayla Hollis. And that's why I'm here. So the score is thirty-seven-and-a-half to one."

She looked at him, falling into the coppery green of his eyes, drawn to the expression of hope and warmth in them.

"You know what I want, Theo?"

"I hope it's pasta and red wine with my grandmother's cookies that I snagged from Waterford Farm for you. That way, we can have a really long, really deep, really memorable…" He drew back and left her a little breathless as she waited for what he'd say next. "Conversation," he whispered.

"Oh." The word slipped out, a mix of awe and surprise. "You want to talk?"

"Not, you know, desperately," he admitted on a laugh. "But I think that's what…we need. And it's what you want, right?"

"Yes," she said. "But I also want…" She took a deep breath, holding his gaze. "To collect on your one lonely point. Now." She lifted up on her toes, bringing her mouth to his. As her eyes closed, she felt his lips on hers, as warm and soft as she knew they'd be, and his arms wrapped around her to pull her into him.

Clementine barked, and so did one of the other dogs, but Ayla melted into Theo's strong, solid body and enjoyed the sensation of every nerve in her body coming alive while they kissed.

It might have been a few seconds, it might have been a few minutes, but the connection was sweet and tender and meaningful and…*real*.

They sighed into each other's mouth and finally separated.

"Now that," she whispered, "was a good apology."

"Yeah? Wait until you taste my cooking. You'll never want me to leave."

She already didn't want him to leave, but she decided to save that, and the next kiss, for later.

One of the most common things Ayla saw when she closed her eyes and took in the energy and images that resided in a dog's head was the sight of a person cooking. Dogs, she'd learned early on, loved nothing more than resting on a kitchen floor, watching their beloved prepare a meal, inhaling the aroma of good things to come, waiting for a sample that would "accidentally" fall to the floor.

Right now, settled at Miz Marie's tiny kitchen table, sipping wine, smelling the fresh flowers on the table and sizzling butter in a pan, she locked her gaze on the fine and fit form of a very strong and handsome man doing the cooking and…yeah. She totally felt like a dog in every good way.

She smiled and glanced down at Clem, who was at her feet, staring at Theo with unabashed adoration. River, the little Chihuahua mix Marie had saved from the rescue, was next to Clem. The two of them were forming a lovely little bond. Hoss and Little Joe were snoozing on the living room sofa, and Ziggy was probably on Marie's bed.

"I'm guessing cooking comes naturally to a man raised by a restaurant-owning family," she mused, mellowed by the wine and still humming from that kiss.

"We all spent our entire childhood in the kitchen of Santorini's," he said, handling the pan like a pro. "I wasn't interested in the business, like John, or the fine points of the cuisine, like Alex, but as you may have noticed, I love to eat. Therefore, I love to cook." He glanced at her from the stove. "And not only Greek food, though I will juice up this pasta with a little dill and sage, but only because my dad was amazing with aromatics, and he taught me."

She studied him, still smiling, probably wearing the same expression as Clem. "Aromatics. That sounds exotic."

He turned from the stove and came over to the table to drink from the other wineglass. "So…you didn't learn to cook at home?" he asked.

"Only if I wandered into the kitchen and talked to the house chef," she said with a self-deprecating laugh. "So, I can do the basics, but nothing with *aromatics*."

"Poor little rich girl," he teased, tapping her glass with his. "Come on, honey. I'll teach you all about the aromatics." With his free hand, he reached for hers, easing her to her feet and bringing her to the stove.

She stood close to him, enjoying the sheer size and

warmth of his body as he added chopped herbs and vegetables to the sizzling pan. While it all sautéed, he studied her for a moment, a question in his expression, but none on his lips.

"Yes?" she prodded. "You can ask me anything."

"Anything?" He laughed softly. "I was wondering about your family. You so rarely mention them, except your Nana Jo."

She smiled, liking that he remembered her grandmother's name. "I don't have many others, just my parents, a few aunts and uncles and cousins."

"Tell me more about your dad?"

Did she have to? "My dad is the Hollis in Paxton Hollis Pharmaceuticals."

"I never put that name together with…" He blew out a whistle. "Yeah. No wonder you had a house chef."

She sighed and leaned against the counter, taking a sip of wine. "My father is everything you would imagine a self-made tycoon would be. Controlling, demanding, expectations through the roof."

He grunted in sympathy. "And your mother?"

"Worse," she said on a laugh. "'Mother isn't pleased' might be what gets carved in her gravestone. So, the divorce we all suffered through wasn't entirely my dad's fault, though he did cheat on her. I honestly don't remember a day in my life where they didn't argue. Believe me, I'd have given up the chef and all the trimmings of wealth to have a family like yours," she said.

He nodded. "Sometimes they're pretty damn great, I can't lie."

"I can tell from everything you say, your parents loved each other. And honestly, the reason I don't talk about my parents is because I don't want to. I'd rather talk about yours than mine, unless it's too hard to talk about your father. I imagine you miss him."

He gave a tight smile. "Every day. He was an awesome guy. But he was sick a long time, and we came to terms with his death long before it actually happened. His illness took a toll on my mother and our family. I wasn't there, either, so that made it hard. But…" He shook his head as if he couldn't or wouldn't discuss it. "But my parents did have a great marriage. I told you they were high school sweethearts."

"Detoured only once when your mom dated Daniel Kilcannon." She smiled, thinking of the story he'd shared with her earlier that week. "And props to you and your whole family for accepting a stepfather as gracefully as you have. Although, who wouldn't like Dr. Kilcannon?"

"Most of us have accepted him. He's awesome, and my mother is incredibly happy with him. Nick, my oldest brother, who you know is Daniel's biological son, hasn't quite embraced the concept. He got past his issues with the guy, but I think their marriage has kept him in Africa longer than he planned to stay."

"Shame," she said. "It would be nice if you could all be together."

"It'll be good to see him when he comes in a couple of weeks for John's wedding," he said.

"Any word about the job in London?" she asked.

"The headhunter said they are discussing putting the position back into the budget, and if they do, it's mine. But I have a few other irons in the fire, although none of the fires pays quite that much." He laughed and caught himself. "I know, I know. It's just money."

"Said the girl with the chef," she added with a self-deprecating laugh. "I do understand getting paid for your talents."

He stirred the aromatics, seeming to concentrate on them, then glanced at her. "What about you? Are you thinking about your next move and how to get paid for *your* talents?"

"No irons in any fires," she said. "I'm literally taking life one day at a time. I like it here at the Last Chance Ranch. It feels more like home than my ritzy condo that doesn't allow pets."

He studied her for a minute, quiet again.

"Another question?" she prodded.

"Did you love this…this EJ guy you almost married?"

"EJ Paxton," she said. "As in…Paxton Hollis."

"Ahhh." He nodded. "Sounds like it was all pretty cozy."

"Way too cozy," she agreed. "And I thought I loved him, but it turns out I only kind of liked him. I mean, hooking up with one of my bridesmaids after the rehearsal dinner aside, he's a generally good guy. And he was… there when I needed him, when my Nana Jo died, and I was scared there'd never be another person to truly love me again."

He nodded, swallowing again, making her wonder if this conversation was uncomfortable for him. She hoped not, because she was enjoying it enormously, and didn't want to back off right when they started hitting the important topics like family and exes.

"Did you love this…this Heather girl?" she asked.

"I thought I did, but it turns out I only kind of liked her." He grinned and winked at her.

She laughed at the echo of her own words, but the humor evaporated from his face as he put pasta in boiling water.

"Other than hooking up with her next-door neighbor, she's a good woman."

She could hear the hurt in his voice, enough that she put a hand on his arm and gave it a light squeeze. "From things you've said, it sounded like it was more than a hookup." He'd told her that she was moving in with the guy, so it wasn't casual like between Jilly and EJ.

"Does it matter?"

"It wasn't rehearsal-dinner sex," she said. "You said she has a legit relationship with the guy. They…fell in love." She cringed. "I'm not helping you, am I?"

He laughed. "Are you trying to?"

"I'm trying to talk, which was part of the promise you made at the door. But I don't want to ruin dinner with this particular subject."

He blew out a breath, working the pasta in the bowl. "You want to get the salad from the fridge? This'll be ready in a minute."

"Sure." She got it and set the table, trying to think of a way to draw him out again, but not drag him back into the completely uncomfortable topic of his cheating ex. She opened her mouth to ask him another question about work when he turned from the stove to look at her, hurt in his green-gold eyes.

"It was my fault," he said in a rough whisper.

Oh, that was genuine pain in his expression, and it did something to her heart. "It doesn't sound like it was your fault."

"I didn't give her what she wanted. I wasn't there in the ways she wanted. I was too…" He gnawed on his lower lip, quiet for a few very uncomfortable heartbeats. "Risk-averse," he finally said. "What she wanted, what…

what women want…" He finally gave in to a smile. "All that isn't easy for me. It doesn't feel natural."

She nodded slowly, understanding deep in her bones not only what he was saying, but how difficult it was. And somehow also knowing that's why he was here tonight.

"I think," she said, "that when you find the right person, it will feel natural."

"I hope you're right." After a moment, he turned to the stove and finished the pasta in the butter aromatic sauce, tossing it with confidence and making them both plates garnished with a few sprigs of herbs.

"That looks amazing," she said as he brought the plates to the table.

He set them down and leaned over, planting the lightest kiss on her hair. "You did help by letting me in the door tonight."

"If I hadn't," she said as they sat down, and Clementine instantly put her chin on Theo's shoe, "Clem would never have forgiven me."

"Clemmie." He dropped her a noodle and another for River. "Now there is one female who gets me."

"And here"—she lifted her glass—"is to hoping you find another."

They looked into each other's eyes for a long time, a very long and lovely few seconds that made Ayla's heart do a little double time. After sipping the wine, they ate and talked and shared stories about their families, making Ayla certain his childhood was far more enviable than hers.

After they cleaned up, all four dogs congregated at the kitchen door, making their needs known by looking up with anxious eyes.

"Let's hit the head, kids," Theo said, opening the door to the fenced-in backyard. "Oh, it's nice tonight. Come on out, Ayla."

She grabbed one of Marie's hoodies from a hook and joined him, inhaling the pine-scented smell of a woodsy Carolina spring night. The air wasn't quite summertime hot yet, although she suspected it was always cooler out here near the mountains.

The dogs spread out into the shadows to find their places on the grass—all but Clem, who stayed within a foot of Theo. The only light was from the kitchen window, leaving the picnic table in almost complete darkness.

"Should we?" he suggested, nodding to it. "Maybe Clem will go near it at night."

"Probably not, but we can try."

True to form, Clem stopped about ten or fifteen feet from the table, lowering herself down to stare at Theo while he walked over to it. He sat on top and reached his hand out to Ayla.

"Sit with me. See if she gets jealous and comes over here."

Laughing softly, she climbed on the bench seat, then let him draw her closer. "Good trick, Navy Guy."

Smiling, he scooted her onto the table next to him, putting his arm around her. "Not Navy anymore."

"Sad about that?"

"I had a great run. I was ready to move on. Of course, I thought I had a job and a new life and…"

And Heather. She turned to him, snuggling a little closer because it felt good. "You do have a new life," she said. "You just don't know what it looks like yet."

He looked at her for another few heartbeats, their faces close, holding off on the inevitable kiss because the anticipation was almost as much fun. "You're starting a new life, too," he said.

"Another of the many things we have in common," she said, tapping his chest. "Maybe those Dogmothers were on to something."

"Maybe they were." He still didn't move, but he looked into her eyes, taking a slow breath. "What does your new life look like, Ayla?"

Like…this. She closed her eyes and tamped down the thought. "Well, it looks like I might be an animal communicator, which you think is ridiculous."

"First of all, I do not think that. Second, what I think shouldn't matter," he said softly.

"It shouldn't," she agreed, opening her eyes to look at him. "But for some reason, it does."

"Why do you think it does?

She held his gaze and smiled. "Because I like you. And that means what you think matters."

"Yeah? Wow, we came a long way between lunch and dinner today." He moved a centimeter closer. "And I'm pretty sure we have thirty-seven more kisses on the book."

"At least." She felt her eyes close with the anticipation.

He placed his finger on her chin, then slowly dragged it down her throat to send six billion chills exploding all over her body. "Starting right…now."

His lips brushed hers, light as air at first, then he applied the gentlest pressure to deepen the warm, sweet kiss. He broke the contact long enough to look at her, silent as they both let the newness of the kiss settle over them. The rightness and niceness of it.

"It was inevitable," he murmured. "I knew it the minute I saw you."

"The camo pants and shitkickers?" she asked on a laugh, leaning in for another kiss.

"That's what did it." His words were lost as they kissed. He slid his hand up to thread her hair through his fingers and controlled the angle of her head, finding a place where they fit perfectly.

She grasped his shoulders, loving the breadth and power of them, arching her back to offer him her throat to kiss. But he lifted his head, frowning at the sound of a siren in the distance. It was far enough away to imagine it was on the highway that led to town, but it was coming this direction.

Clem barked once, standing up at the sound, suddenly on full alert.

"Oh, Clem doesn't like sirens," Theo mused.

But Ayla closed her eyes as images flashed in her head. Red lights swirling, brighter and brighter. "I've… seen this before with her," she whispered.

Next to her, Theo stiffened, but she didn't have time to analyze the reaction.

The siren got louder, and Clem went progressively more nuts, barking, growling, and suddenly, she launched at the picnic table.

"Whoa!" Theo reacted without a second's hesitation, lifting Ayla off the table and swinging her away before Clem came at them. Ayla let out a soft shriek, stumbling a bit, as much from the impact of what Clem was thinking than the shock that she'd tried to attack them.

"Easy, Clem, easy." Theo came closer, two hands out protectively, but Clem growled at him, positioning herself between Theo and the table with a look like… wow, she would definitely attack if he got closer.

He backed away on instinct, and Clem stood in front

of the picnic table, teeth bared as the siren got louder, probably at the intersection to turn off to the ranch.

The other dogs barked a few times in response, then lost interest when there was no reason to be barking. But Clem had a reason.

"What the hell is wrong with her?" Theo muttered.

Ayla closed her eyes and kind of knew what was wrong. Clementine was seeing one thing—a man in a hat, wearing something big and white on his arms. The image got crystal clear as the siren reached a crescendo, then started to soften as it passed. Clem growled and barked and held her ground until it was gone and quiet, the only sound her soft panting from the exertion.

"Clementine?" Theo took a step closer.

The dog turned and very, very slowly crawled under the picnic table, lying down flat and staring out.

"Can we get near her?" Ayla asked, sensing she was coming out of attack mode, but not completely.

"I don't know, but I've seen some of the Kilcannon trainers do this." He dropped onto the ground, getting right down to her level, then he scooted toward her, whispering her name the whole time.

"Do you want me to get a treat?" she asked.

"Yes, please."

She darted inside and grabbed a cookie, giving each of the other dogs one when they followed her. Back outside, Theo was closer to Clem, but still flat on the ground, making his way toward her.

"Toss it to me," he said. "About a foot away."

She did, and it landed about eighteen inches from him, but Clementine made no move for it. Theo grabbed the cookie, offered it, and she came right out to eat it from his hand. While she did, he sat up and held out his arms.

After she swallowed, she dropped into his lap and whimpered. Her mind, as far as Ayla could tell, was cool blue and blank.

"She's happy," Ayla whispered, coming closer.

"That was strange, huh?"

She folded onto the ground next to him, petting her. "She's trained to attack when there's a siren," she said.

"Meth lab."

"Excuse me?" She looked up at him, not sure he'd said what she thought he had.

"The lady who left him at the mini-mart said she could have sworn his owner was running a meth lab."

Suddenly, a whole lot of images she'd seen made sense. "He was," she said softly.

Theo glanced at her, a frown pulling. "How do you…" He closed his eyes. "Yeah, the siren. That would be the clue. Definitely."

Not the siren, but she didn't feel like begging him to believe. They'd taken so many nice steps forward, she had no desire to send them back to that.

Chapter Fifteen

The incident with Clem at the Last Chance Ranch really bothered Theo. He'd shared it with Daniel, who immediately suggested that Theo bring Clementine to Waterford a few days later when they were between training sessions. It would be a good time to give her the run of the pen and let the experts check out the dog's issues.

He'd invited Ayla to come with him, but she had her first client coming that day.

As Theo turned into the Waterford Farm entrance, he thought about how quiet and introspective she'd been after Clem's outburst that night. He sensed that it had something to do with what she was feeling. Or, more specifically, what Clementine was feeling. Or thinking.

With a grunt, he shoved the thought into a compartment he'd rather not open and rolled down the long driveway at Waterford. The canine rescue and training center, which was normally noisy and busy this time of day, was surprisingly quiet. A class of trainees had recently left, and another wasn't due in for a few days.

He was starting to catch the rhythm of life at Waterford now that he'd been here for ten days or so. It was easy to see why the family of Kilcannons who'd been raised on this property had arranged their lives to work here as adults. The place was beyond bucolic, especially painted in the vibrant blues and greens of late spring, and the vibe was laid-back and happy.

It couldn't be more opposite than life working on an aircraft carrier, and he was surprisingly okay with that.

As he parked in the spot that had become his in the driveway, he noticed a whole pack of Kilcannons was gathered outside a nearly empty training pen. In fact, all six of the Kilcannon kids were out there, plus Trace, Molly's husband. Obviously, they weren't *kids*, but he could imagine what life had been like at Waterford when those six were being raised here. Loud, fun, happy—much like the Santorinis' home, only without the kourabiedes and with more dogs.

Yep, if anyone in the world could fix Clementine, it was the crew he was looking at.

As he climbed out of his car, the kitchen door opened, and his mother came out.

"They've gathered the entire family for you, Clementine," she said as he let the dog out of the car. "It's a special occasion."

He could see his mother was slightly tentative as she came closer, and he hated that anyone would feel that way around this sweet dog. She loved dogs and was rarely apart from Daniel's setter, Rusty, or Goldie, the retriever they'd adopted together. But she knew what happened the other night, and she'd been in the tent when Clem went after Garrett.

He walked closer, knowing Clem would follow. "You don't have to worry, Mom," he added. "She hasn't had one moment of anything but peace for a few days."

Daniel came out then, a cup of coffee in his hand and a smile on his face.

"There she is," he said, coming right up to Clem without any hesitation. Of course, he was known as the Dogfather for a reason.

Holding the cup steady, he crouched down to get face-to-face with the dog, stroking her head with the gentle, capable hand of a man who'd been a vet for most of his sixty-three years.

"She's looking so good, Theo," he said. "Putting on weight. Bright eyes." He lifted her lips and took a good look at her gums. "Good color, but we definitely have to schedule a teeth cleaning with Molly. Not giving her any more oranges?"

"Not one," he promised. "But I'm concerned about what happened the other night. I don't know what all can set her off, but I want to untrain her. Is it possible?"

"Hey, this is Waterford Farm," Daniel said, his blue gaze warm and as grounded as the man himself. "Anything's possible. Come on, let's take her to the troops."

The three of them walked across the drive to the empty training pen.

"There's the lady of the hour," Shane said, meeting them halfway to greet Clem and slip her a treat with the sleight of hand of a trained magician.

Clem's tail wagged, but she turned quickly to make sure Theo was right there.

As they ushered her into the training pen, Liam, Shane, and Trace stepped in, too, taking a few minutes to establish a rapport with the dog.

Liam, the tall, quiet de facto leader of this sibling group, came close to her and showed his dominance by the way he stood. Shane played with her some more, and

Trace exhibited a very gentle touch, while his wife, Molly, leaned against the outside of the pen, watching.

Next to her, Darcy, Aidan, and Beck chatted.

In the pen, Garrett approached Clem, too. No hat, so the dog seemed perfectly fine. Every few seconds, she looked for Theo, but with the treats and attention and play, she was well distracted.

"It's a terrible feeling to be on edge with your dog, isn't it?" Molly asked Theo, putting a hand on his arm.

"I'm not going to lie, her behavior kind of scared me. I can't have an attack dog living with Miz Marie and Ayla."

"Well, what did Ayla say?" Darcy, on his other side, asked. "She must have known exactly what Clem was thinking."

"She didn't say much except the obvious. The siren set him off."

"But could she read Clementine's thoughts?" she asked.

He felt his eyes shutter closed. "She was as stunned by the whole thing as I was."

"She probably knew and didn't want to say."

"Why would she do that?" he asked.

"Because you'll be a drip and tell her she's making it up." She tempered that with a sweet smile.

"A…drip? She—"

Clem barked, pulling his attention, but it was because Shane was rolling on the grass with her.

"It sure would help to know what breed mix she is," Shane said, sitting up and nuzzling Clem fearlessly.

"Would it matter?" Theo asked.

"It helps to know a dog's temperament," Daniel, now in the pen, explained.

"She's obviously got a good dose of Staffy in her," Shane said, rubbing her snout playfully. "Plenty of pittie to make her pretty. And Lab, no doubt."

"Lab?" Liam looked at his brother like he was crazy. "Look at the color. That's a border collie, with a boxer in the family tree."

"That's no border collie." Aidan choked at the suggestion. "There might be boxer, but I'm looking at a bull terrier who met a Dane he couldn't resist."

Daniel shook his head, studying the dog. "Frankly, I think she's part English foxhound, and Shane's right about the pit," Daniel said.

"And Lab." Molly added her two cents, pointing at the dog. "More than a little."

Theo looked at his mother, who was fighting a laugh.

"It's a family pastime," she joked. "Disagree on the breed, and then, you know, they'll bet on it and get a DNA test done. Winner gets the first Bloody Mary on Sunday."

"Or"—Darcy said, leaning into him—"you could ask Ayla so Clem could *tell* her what her parents looked like."

He rolled his eyes. "You married into a nuthouse, Mom."

His mother put an arm around Darcy and grinned the way she would while hugging Cassie, her own daughter. "And I love every nut in the house."

"Okay, so she's some mix of forty different breeds," he said. "But she's still an attack dog when you don't want her to be."

Liam shook his head vehemently. "Nope, you're wrong about that. An attack dog would have needed a command from her owner."

"Maybe she was trained to attack at the sound of sirens," he suggested.

Liam looked doubtful, and if anyone would know, it was this former Marine who trained law enforcement K-9s for much of his life. "It's possible, but my guess is she isn't an attack dog at all, but a guard dog."

"Is there a difference?" Theo asked.

"Big difference," Trace said, pushing up the sleeves of a T-shirt to reveal his tattoo-covered arms. "A guard dog is trained to protect and won't likely bite anyone, but will scare the crap out of them."

"Well, she did that."

"Then she did what she was trained to do," Shane said, getting right in Clementine's face and rubbing her head. "And I wouldn't worry too much, Theo. She's a happier dog already than when you brought her here ten days ago. On this trajectory, she's going to heal and recover and forget her dark days."

"The thing is, she doesn't really have the nature of a guard dog," Liam said. "So she might not be a very good one. Maybe that's why her owner was so rough on her."

"I was thinking the same thing," Garrett agreed. "She probably wasn't formally trained."

"She was definitely not formally trained," Theo confirmed, the unwanted image of that disgusting man's pockmarked face and ratlike features popping into his head. "The dog's been chained to a damn picnic table."

Looking skyward, Liam grunted. "People *suck*."

"But we can definitely do some work with her," Shane, a natural dog whisperer who could train a stuffed animal to heel, assured him. "Let's start with seeing how she reacts to Garrett's hat. You okay with that, Theo?"

He hated the idea of upsetting her, but they needed to

know what set her off so they could change her reactions. "Sure."

"Lemme go get it," Garrett said.

"And the bite suit," Liam called to him as he headed into the kennel.

"What's the plan?" Theo asked.

"Heavy reward training to counteract whatever she's been trained to do," Liam told him. "If the hat makes her aggressive, we'll reward her every time she's not aggressive. It'll take the better part of a few days, but we can turn her around."

"And what about the next time she hears a siren?"

"We're going to try and recondition her overall responses, so that should probably help. We can take her down to the fire station and have one of the Mahoneys test her, too. Once we get her reconditioned, we can give you some tools to help her overcome the fear of picnic tables, too."

Nodding, he leaned against the mesh railing, his heart hurting a bit when Garrett came out with a full-body bite suit he knew they wore when training law enforcement K-9s.

"Don't worry," his mother said, getting closer to Theo as if she instinctively sensed one of her kids was stressed. "This is what they do with German shepherds all the time."

"German shepherds are specially trained to be vicious on command. This is Clem." He tipped his head and looked at her. "She's just a scared little…Lab-pittie-boxer-collie-Dane-bulldog-terrier…thing."

"Don't forget foxhound," Daniel said, laughing.

Theo's smile was tight as he watched Liam step into the full-body jumpsuit, the arms and legs puffy with protective padding. For Clem? Really?

His mother curled her hand around his arm, her gaze on Theo, not the pen. "She'll be fine, honey. My biggest question is how can you let her go when you've clearly fallen hard for her?"

He looked down at her, frowning, lost in concentration on the dog for a moment. "Who?"

She inched back, a look of amusement in her soft, brown eyes. "Um…your dog? Would I mean anyone else?"

He let out a grunt instead of swearing in front of his mother. Stupid response. "Don't get crazy, Katie Santorini… Kilcannon." He gave in to a laugh. "You're as bad as Yiayia."

"Who isn't bad at all anymore," she said, turning to the pen. "But I was merely asking how you'll be able to give Clem up. I can tell you're attached to her."

"Because I'm leaving eventually and have no idea where I'm going or if I could take Clem with me. Plus, she's in very good hands at the Last Chance Ranch."

"You ready?" Liam interrupted their conversation as he called to Garrett. "Bring on the doggone hat, brother."

Garrett came through the pen carrying the hat behind him, but Clementine was too busy sniffing the suit Liam wore to notice.

Garrett tossed the hat, and Liam caught it with one hand, put it on and inched back, giving Clem a moment. When she looked up, she immediately took a step back, growling.

"You don't like this hat, do you, Clem?" Liam asked.

She barked once, then again, looking around the pen, then back at Liam, who got down a little bit and produced a treat from an exterior pocket in the suit. He tossed it to Clem, who ignored it, her focus on the hat. She growled and barked, but definitely did not attack.

Once again, Liam offered a treat, and this time, he kept it in his hand. "Cookie, Clem?"

She wouldn't take it, baring her teeth, but nothing worse. After a minute, Liam took off the hat, tossed it back to Garrett, who hid it outside the pen, and instantly Clem settled. She ate the treat on the ground and came closer to Liam, sniffing for the other one, which he gave her, along with a lot of praise.

"Guard dog," Liam said, standing up and unzipping the suit. "So you don't have to worry she's going to attack anyone. Can you give me a few hours with her this afternoon?"

"Maybe tomorrow, too," Shane said. "That dog is imminently trainable. She loves food almost as much as you do, Theo."

"Of course," Theo said, a wash of relief and gratitude rolling over him. "And she's safe with Ayla and Marie? Even if they hear another siren?"

"Absolutely," Liam assured him. "If she were going to attack, she would have."

He smiled at the dog. "Good girl, Clemmie."

As they all praised her and went off to get a few more dogs to join them in the pen, Daniel put a hand on Theo's shoulder.

"Do you have a minute?" he asked Theo. "I want to run something by you."

"Sure." He glanced at Clem because he never left unless Ayla or Marie was with her, but she was distracted, running with Aidan's big boxer, Ruff. "What's up?"

"I want to ask you for a favor, and please feel free to say no."

He laughed. "Auspicious beginning. I doubt I'll say no, but what do you need, Daniel?"

"Come on, let's talk in my office."

A few minutes and two cups of fresh coffee later, Theo stood in front of a wall of Irish setters in Daniel's office, some of the photos dating back to when Gramma Finnie was a young mother living in the original version of this house.

He knew there'd always been a setter living here, from that early one who'd accompanied Finnie and Seamus from Ireland, to the very old one who snoozed on the floor in front of Daniel's desk.

"Hey, Rusty." He gave the dog's head a rub, but barely got a flick of the tail in response.

"My Rusty's getting old, I'm afraid," Daniel said as gestured for Theo to take a seat, giving the dog a sad smile. "His sight's going, his hearing's bad, and I carry him up the stairs every night now." Theo could hear the heartbreak in the man's voice as he took a seat behind his desk.

"He's a beautiful dog," he said, giving Rusty an extra bit of love on his graying head.

"He's been at my side for darn near sixteen years, through some of the best, and some of the worst, times in my life. Truly, a faithful companion." He gave a tight smile. "But Goldie's brought some life back into his step. Kind of like your mother has to me," he added, lightening the topic.

"Mom's happy, Daniel," Theo said, and meant it. "I can really see the difference in her since I've been away all this time. It's good to hear her laugh."

Daniel nodded in agreement and took a sip of coffee while Theo did the same.

"So, what's up?" he asked.

"I think you know that I was recently appointed to the

board of trustees at Vestal Valley College here in Bitter Bark," Daniel said.

"Mom mentioned it. Congratulations on that. Is it time-consuming?"

"Molly's taken over my vet practice, and my sons are running the day-to-day operations of Waterford, so I have the time to indulge my nonwork passions. As an alum, Vestal Valley is dear to my heart."

Theo nodded and drank his coffee. "I know you're a big committee guy," he said on a laugh. "Your kids joke a lot about how there's no Bitter Bark program you won't chair or join."

He shook his head with a guilty smile. "But this is definitely the biggest commitment I've taken on that's not vet- or family-related. As a matter of fact, I was on a conference call for two hours this morning, and something came up that I thought I'd talk to you about, but…"

"Feel free to say no," he echoed Daniel's earlier words.

"Absolutely. Look, I know you're a graduate of Duke, educated in quite an impressive manner by the Navy, and a superstar nuclear engineer."

He winced. "You sound like Yiayia reciting my résumé to a potential spouse," he joked. "I only took a natural path, and considering my currently unemployed status? You can drop superstar anything from that list."

Daniel shrugged. "You've got impressive credentials, son, so you might look askew at what I'm going to ask, but I will anyway."

Theo leaned forward, intrigued. "Talk to me. I'm open."

"One of the school's strategic visions is to improve our engineering department, which is up-and-coming, but not anywhere near the quality that it could be. Attracting top-notch professors is difficult out here in Bitter Bark, so, like many colleges and universities, we rely on academic conferences and seminars that are worked into the school year. They bring in guest speakers and lecturers for intense sessions that translate into credits for students."

He nodded, knowing exactly what Daniel was talking about. "We had them at Duke and in the Navy." He lifted his brow. "You want me to speak?"

"Oh, I'd love that, but the sessions are in the fall, and you may be long gone by then. What we need is someone with access to people we could schedule for next year. And I know you probably have that access." He lifted his brows. "Would you make a few phone calls?"

"Sure," he said without hesitation. "My expertise is nuclear, obviously, but I have a few friends who'd be perfect presenters. Some in general physics, some nuclear. I'd be happy to give them a call and gauge their interest. I'd need to know what specialities the department wants."

"Absolutely," Daniel agreed. "You'd get that information from the dean of the Engineering Department. Would you be willing to meet with him? An hour of your time, tops."

He laughed. "Daniel, with the exception of helping Marie fix up the ranch, I don't have that much else on my plate at the moment."

"Thank you, and…about that." His face fell a little. "I hope Marie's expectations are realistic for that TV show coming to film this week."

"Why? Do you think the chances of them doing a feature on the ranch are slim?"

"I'm afraid it's a long shot," Daniel said. "And if they turn her down, I know it's going to be a huge disappointment."

Theo nodded. "She's counting on it."

"I wish I could give her our slot, but they really want to feature Waterford and the irony is that we don't need the publicity as much as she does," Daniel told him. "We make our money through the training programs, and that helps fund the rescue operations. But Marie has big dreams for the Last Chance Ranch. She wants real kennels, some full-time staff, including a vet tech. That all takes an incredible amount of ongoing fundraising. A half-hour program that reaches millions of people and touches their hearts with what she's trying to do? That's like a goldmine for her."

"I didn't realize it was that big a deal."

"Oh, it is," Daniel told him. "That's why I pushed the producer, who, I'm afraid, agreed to be nice since he's looking for a bigger locale, more like Waterford. But that host? Colin Donahue? I'm hoping once he sees the place and meets Marie, something will click for him. Because of that, I have to tell you how much I really appreciate how you've helped her fix the ranch up on this short schedule."

"No problem. I've had some help from the family, as you know. And I've loved going over there and helping out. Plus, I get to see Clementine."

"And Ayla," Daniel added with a tease in his eyes.

"And…Ayla," he agreed, reaching for his empty cup as he stood. "Is this entire family made of matchmakers?"

"I'm retired from that, too," Daniel said with a chuckle as he stood.

"Doesn't sound like it."

"Well, your mother—the whole family, of course—wants to see you happy and settled, and your connection with this young woman is pretty evident. Or are we matchmakers who are imagining things?"

Maybe a little of both. "Well, we've got a surprising amount in common, and I…like her," he admitted. "But…"

"But you're leaving soon," Daniel finished for him when Theo's voice faded.

"That's not…the only issue," Theo said, leaning forward, hungry for this man's input, which he knew would be thoughtful and, considering his vet credentials, surely would support Theo's thinking about pet psychics. "I'm struggling with the whole 'communicates with animals' thing. As a scientist, it…challenges me."

Daniel smiled. "I bet it does."

"Well, you're a vet. What do you think? It's a little far-fetched, don't you agree?"

He considered the question for a moment, his blue gaze on Theo. "I know exactly how you feel," he said. "I struggled with the same thing when my late wife, Annie, took me to see a woman with similar abilities down near Asheville."

"*You* went to a pet psychic?"

"Annie was a believer, and even thought she could have a little of the second sight herself. She didn't," he added quickly. "There's a difference between being an empathetic and understanding dog person, like my late wife and my kids, especially Shane, and what Ayla does."

What Ayla does. He let the words sink in, riveted.

"Annie had this one unforgettable and troubled Lab as a foster," he explained. "This guy simply wouldn't respond to any training. Annie had quite a few connections in the dog world, and heard about this pet psychic who had success with some really tough cases. I was skeptical, but I certainly couldn't figure out what was wrong with that dog, so I went with her." He tipped his head. "Truthfully? I went partly out of curiosity, and partly to make my point that the whole idea was, well, not in keeping with anything I'd learned in vet school."

Exactly. "What happened?"

"My mind was blown," Daniel said.

"Don't tell me," Theo said. "She asked a few seemingly innocent questions and did a little bit of research before you arrived. Then she made it sound like she knew what the dog was thinking, and you bought it."

Daniel looked at him for a long time, the hint of a smile pulling. "Actually, she instantly recognized a pain in the dog's ear. He'd lost his hearing in one ear and was on his way to total deafness, but he exhibited no signs of pain. We'd have never known he needed surgery on that ear. Because of her, I did the surgery and saved his hearing." He gave in to that smile. "I learned a lesson that day."

Theo wasn't sure he wanted to learn that lesson, but had a feeling he was about to. "Add a hearing test to your standard physical?"

Daniel laughed. "Well, that, too. But sometimes you need to have faith in something you can't see, quantify, or understand, son, no matter how out-there it might seem."

He nodded, reaching down to give old Rusty one more good scratch, adding Daniel's anecdote to the evidence that kept piling up. Was it possible…she really could get in an animal's head?

He wasn't sure, but she'd sure gotten into his.

Chapter Sixteen

On Friday morning, before the *Rescue Party* people were scheduled to arrive, Marie was a hot mess of nerves. Clem picked up on her stress, along with River. The dogs followed her around the kitchen, watching her carefully. And so did Ayla.

"I've never seen you like this," Ayla said, holding the coffeepot over the empty cup Marie held out like a desperate person. "Maybe you don't need another cup."

"Pour. I need coffee. And more cereal. And another croissant."

Ayla laughed and tipped the pot to fill her mug, not surprised when Marie turned right to the sugar bowl to sweeten the brew.

"Contrary to popular belief around here, sugar does not cure what ails you, Miz Marie."

"It helps." Marie added a second teaspoon and took her mug to the kitchen table, looking out the back window. "It's beautiful, isn't it?"

"The ranch?" Ayla joined her. "Looks like a different place since I got here."

"Thanks to you."

"Oh, please." She lifted the pink bakery box lid and

eyed a croissant. "Okay, maybe sugar does cure what ails you. Let's split one."

"Split schmit." Marie snagged one of the pastries and took a healthy bite. "Stress eating is a part of life."

Ayla chose a croissant for pure pleasure, not stress. "But no credit to me on the ranch. Theo's been working tirelessly. The kennels look so good, I could sleep out there. And all those flowers he planted?"

"You helped."

"He did the hard labor. I just enjoyed the scenery."

"Like when he took his shirt off," Marie said, grinning around her next bite.

"Yeah. Good scenery." Ayla gave a little shiver. "*Great* scenery."

"Have you two kissed yet?"

Suddenly, Clem jumped up and barked at the sound of a car in the driveway. "You can ask him." Ayla winked and stood up, brushing some croissant flakes off her hands.

"Theo's coming today? Are you sure that's not the *Rescue Party* people? Daniel said they showed up a half hour early yesterday."

Ayla peeked through the doorway toward the living room window. "Nope. Honda Civic SI."

"And listen to that little trill in your voice," Marie mused. "Someone has a crush on the man who plants shirtless."

Ayla didn't bother to deny that. "Making me a woman with functioning hormones, working eyes, and a beating heart."

"Amen, sister," Marie said on a laugh. "Although my hormones went on strike a while ago. Sooo…" She added a wiggly brow to the singsong word. "What's stopping you from…you know, the next step?"

"The chance of tripping over that step, falling flat on my face, and crying." She smiled. "Again."

"He would never hurt you like that," Marie said without any doubt or a moment's hesitation, her voice barely audible over Clem's insane barking at the door. "One thing I've learned in all this time—he's a good man."

"He's a great man," Ayla agreed. "But he can't, won't, and never will believe in me or understand me. That's a deal breaker for me, even if the deal is just a good old-fashioned make-out session." Which she'd love to have with him.

"So you *have* kissed him?"

Several times.

"Hey, Clemmie!" Theo's deep voice boomed through the house. "Ladies, are you ready for the big day?" he called.

A moment later, he came into the kitchen, Clementine in his arms and draped happily over his broad shoulder, a look of insane satisfaction on her face.

I feel ya, sister.

"We are ready," Ayla told him, gesturing toward the bakery box. "Help yourself, and we have more for the *Rescue Party* crew."

"We are not above bribery," Marie joked.

"Great. I had breakfast an hour ago, and I'm starved."

"You're breathing, so you're starved," Ayla joked, imagining him joining a noisy Santorini kitchen table and getting teased as he powered down his third pastry.

A longing she hadn't expected tugged at her heart. Oh, to have had a childhood like that.

He put Clem down and pulled out a kitchen chair, turning it and straddling the backrest in a move so deeply masculine, it nearly took Ayla's breath away.

"Relax, Miz Marie. They're going to love you. And remember, when you need a human-interest story, drag Clem into it. You have my permission to describe the entire situation as I've told you."

"Maybe you should go on camera," she said.

"Nope. This is about you and the Last Chance Ranch." He looked up and thanked Ayla for the coffee she brought him with a warm smile, his green-gold eyes locked on her. "Clem sleep last night?" he asked, which was always one of his first questions.

"Yep, like a baby." Ayla, on the other hand…

"Oh my God, they're almost here!" Marie grabbed her phone, reading a text. "The producer texted me that they are about two minutes away. They're early!" She popped up and stabbed her fingers into her short gray hair. "We're ready. Aren't we ready? I think we're ready."

Once again, Clem picked up her tension and started barking, and that got River to chime in.

Ayla was next to Marie in a flash. "Calm down. You are ready. I promise. This is your baby. You can talk about the Last Chance Ranch and bring a person to tears. Remember how we practiced last night?"

She nodded, wiping her palms on her khaki pants. "Okay, you're right. I'll be fine. Tell my story, and Clem's, maybe. Walk them around, let them meet Waffles and Blueberry, tell them the plans. If we have money." She closed her eyes. "God, we need this for the money."

Just then, they heard a vehicle in the driveway, and the dogs headed to the front door, followed by the people.

A huge white van with the *Rescue Party* logo on the side drove up. Almost immediately, Clem jumped up and started barking and did her low growl.

"Oh no. White vans trigger her, too?" Theo dropped to the ground to put his hands on Clem's face to calm her. "Clementine, stop," he said, slipping her a treat from his pocket in conjunction with the tone of authority that Ayla knew he'd learned during training sessions at Waterford.

"I'm going to greet the crew," Marie murmured. "Please don't let Clem eat them before they say yes to doing a show."

"Clem's not going to eat anything but the treats I plan to shove at her," Theo said, blocking her view of the van out the window and producing another from his pocket. "Clementine. Look at me."

She did and took the treat, but it wasn't truly calming her. She pranced a little, then whipped around and growled at the van again, the same threatening sound Ayla remembered from the night of the siren.

"I'm going to take her out back," he said. "When they go back there, I'll work with her at the van. I know what to do." He looked up at Ayla. "We have to get her calm if we're going to tell a success story."

She nodded in agreement. "Keep her in the kennel where she can't see the van. When we go in the back, you can come back out here and do… What are you going to do?"

"Treat and train so that she comes to love the sight of a white van, the way she now loves the sight of a cowboy hat. She's slowly learning to come around on picnic tables, too."

"Great. If there are no fire trucks racing down the highway, we should be golden."

He stood, scooping Clementine into his arms and over his shoulder. "I'll calm Clem. You get out there and calm Marie."

For a moment, they looked at each other, feeling the

pull and thrill that always seemed to be there when they were this close. It was magnetic and magical and…oh, why didn't he believe her?

She tamped down the thought and headed out the door to offer Marie much-needed moral support.

"Oh, hello." The tall, dark-haired man talking to Marie stepped aside to smile at Ayla. Then she recognized him as the host of *Rescue Party*. "I'm Colin Donahue."

Whoa, he was even better looking in person, with deep blue eyes and nearly black hair, a classic square jaw, and a smile that the camera loved. Ayla could see why this man had built his fun concept show into a little cult phenomenon.

"Ayla Hollis," she said, shaking the hand he'd offered. "I work here." She and Marie had agreed it would look good to have "staff" on-site, as if the ranch were healthy and growing.

Three more people were in the back of the van, which looked like a mini TV studio. She met Kyle, the producer, and Jimmy, a camera operator. An assistant named RaeAnn also greeted her, then peppered Marie with questions about the ranch and its history. After a moment, Theo came out of the house—with no Clementine, so he must have gotten her eating in the kennels.

While he was introduced, River pranced around Colin's feet, begging for attention, which the man lavished on the little dog, picking him up and wrapping strong arms around him. "And what's your story, little guy?"

"He's River," Marie told him. "Most of my rescues are named after songs, TV shows, or the last thing I ate."

Colin's eyes lit up as if this little piece of information was worthy. "So River came from…"

"'Cry Me a River,'" Marie told him. "Because I found

him being used as…" Her voice trailed off as if she suddenly realized where this story was going. "Never mind," she said.

"No *never mind*," Colin said. "This sounds like the kind of story I like. Why is he named River?"

Marie looked at Ayla, a question in her eyes. Yes, the way they got River would make a good human-interest story. Lots of color and personal information. Would it help? Was it worth it? To help Marie?

"I was crying," Ayla finally said.

"I'm sorry to hear that." Colin stepped a centimeter closer, the power of his direct stare cutting right through her. "Do I have to beat someone up for hurting you?"

She could have sworn she felt Theo's whole body stiffen at the question.

"You do not," she said. "I punished him thoroughly by leaving him at the altar."

Colin's jaw dropped, and then he let out a hearty laugh. "Good for you. Okay, show us around, team."

With the ice broken a bit, Marie led the way with the producer, assistant, and Colin all asking her questions as they walked into the house.

"Are you going to bring Clem out here?" Ayla asked Theo.

"Yeah. Unless I have to stay and growl at Tall, Dark, And Flirtatious over there."

She bit back a laugh. "You're jealous?"

He didn't answer, but gave her a sexy smile. "Hey, whatever it takes to get them to decide to film the show, right?"

"This is for Miz Marie," she agreed.

He narrowed his eyes. "You never told me you cried a river in that shelter."

"You never threatened to beat up someone who hurt me."

"The day is young," he teased, then headed back to get Clementine, leaving her with that little thrill he always managed to sprinkle over her.

Colin spent a lot of time with Hoss and Little Joe, asking Marie questions, while the producer and the assistant wandered the property, hanging out near the goats, who were endlessly entertaining. Jimmy stayed in the van, editing yesterday's work at Waterford, according to Colin.

With each passing minute, Marie seemed calmer and more confident, telling her life's story that, sadly, included the loss of her son in the military, and some colorful tales about her travels around the state's shelters.

Theo came back with Clem, who now seemed like she wouldn't growl at a bear, but he didn't push it by trying to get near the picnic table.

"Here's an animal with a colorful story," Marie said as Theo brought her closer. "This man saved this dog, who had been chained to a picnic table, if you can believe that."

Colin made a face as if the image physically hurt him. "Good on you, sir," he said, almost looking Theo in the eye, as they were close in height and stature.

"I only did what anyone would do," he said, the modesty making Ayla smile from where she watched.

"Do you want to hear all about that?" Marie asked. "It's quite a story."

Colin angled his head, acknowledging that. "I'm sure it is. All your stories are good. I think we should definitely shoot a segment here this afternoon, and you can fill me in then. It'll be more spontaneous."

"Wonderful!" Marie clapped her hands and beamed at him. "I would love—"

"Hold up!" Kyle called, marching across the grass toward them. "Major change in plans."

They all turned to him, and Ayla could swear she heard Marie's heart drop to the ground.

"RaeAnn's on with the network right now, and we have work to do."

"What kind of work?" Colin asked.

Kyle reached them, shaking his head. "I don't know how we're going to do this, but *Live With My Pet, Peeve* can't air this afternoon, and corporate is in a total snit."

"How is that our problem?" Colin asked, then looked at the others. "You probably know the show. The host has a dog, Peeve, and they do dog-on-the-street interviews all over New York City."

"I've seen it," Marie said. "I love how they end every interview by asking the person what their pet peeve is."

"It's our number one moneymaker," Kyle said, sounding a little less than thrilled about that. "*Peeve* sponsors expect a live show every week, and it rakes in the ratings. When we put something else on, the numbers plummet, the ad revenue drops, and expensive shows that travel around the country"—he gave Colin a dark and meaningful look—"get cut from the schedule."

Colin swore softly. "What's the plan?"

"I have a plan!" RaeAnn came jogging over, waving her phone. "They said we can shoot live here, and they'll air our show in *Peeve*'s slot today."

"Here?" Marie gasped.

"Well, no," she said. "In town, so we can do dog-on-the-street interviews. If we hurry, we can set up the van near the town square. Lots of dogs there."

"We can do that," Kyle said, checking his phone. "We have four hours to get there, set up, and go live. Come on, crew."

"Oh." The word, laden with sadness, slipped through Marie's lips.

"I'm sorry," Colin said, reaching out a comforting hand to Marie. "We'd do something here, but the gold in *Peeve* is that it's spontaneous, live, and riveting. Last Chance Ranch is great, but not right for this slot."

"Could we shoot tomorrow?" Marie asked.

"We'll be gone," Kyle said. "Really sorry. But we have to have something amazing, or those sponsors—"

"We have something amazing." Theo stepped into the small group, bringing the conversation to a halt.

Clem? Ayla looked up at Theo, expecting him to pitch the story hard. If he told it, then maybe—

"This woman right here"—he put a hand on Ayla's shoulder—"is what is known as an animal communicator."

Ayla nearly choked.

"A pet psychic," he added when their three guests stared at him. "And I doubt you're going to find anything or anyone more riveting in Bushrod Square."

Colin blinked at her. "Is that true?"

So many emotions washed over Ayla, she almost couldn't answer. Theo was pitching her? And was he smiling down at her like…like he *believed*?

"Of course it's true," Theo said when she didn't answer. "She did readings on about thirty dogs at a fund-raiser in town, and honestly, if you talk to people who were there, Ayla Hollis is what they are going to talk about, I guarantee it. Why don't you interview her here?"

Colin glanced at him and then back at Ayla. "You're a communicator?"

"I am," she finally acknowledged, once her brain accepted the fact that it was Theo who'd suggested this life-saving idea.

Kyle came closer, openly staring and appraising her. "I've been trying to book a psychic for a year, but the few I had initial interviews with were either whack jobs or total fakes."

"I'm not fake," she said.

"I can vouch for that," Marie chimed in. "I've been volunteering at a shelter for over a year with this young woman, and I've never seen anyone who can do what she can do."

"Is it like magic?" RaeAnn asked, mesmerized.

"Nothing like magic," Ayla said, glancing up at Theo. "But I understand skepticism." Did he understand what this meant to her?

Kyle and Colin exchanged looks and shrugs.

"Can you work this nonmagic on some of the dogs here?" RaeAnn asked.

"Of course I can. All of them." She reached down to Clem and rubbed her head. "Clem's been sending me pictures for a while now."

"No, no." Kyle shook his head. "It can't be a dog you know. What's the fun in that? It has to be unfamiliar dogs. Come to town, and we'll film there."

Which would defeat the purpose of giving Marie's ranch its time in the spotlight.

"I can't," Ayla said. "I have to do it here at the Last Chance Ranch. I mean, this is going to be live, right?"

"Yes, it is," Kyle said. "Which means no screw-ups, no retakes, and no editing. We're not as experienced as the *Peeve* crew on the live dog-on-the-street-stuff, which can be fraught with surprises."

"All the more reason you don't want to be in town," Theo said. "This is a controlled environment."

The producer narrowed his eyes at Ayla. "I need to know you're not a fake."

"Then bring me an animal I don't know. Dog, cat, whatever." She lifted her chin. "I'll give you a better show than *Peeve*, but we have to do it right here at the Last Chance Ranch."

"Oooh." Kyle made a face. "I would love to kick *Peeve*'s ass in ratings and tweets."

"Ayla will get tweets," Theo assured them.

"Oh, yes!" Marie added. "Hashtag dogtalk!"

"Hashtag betterthanPeeve," Colin said, eyeing his colleague. "Come on, Kyle. This is our chance to kick that guy's butt. We're here, it'll be easy. We have everything we need in the van, including a satellite upload. We can shoot inside, where we can control lighting and ambient sound. We don't have the type of equipment the *Peeve* people have to do a live show while marching around a small town."

"We need animals," Kyle said.

"Those we can get," Marie told him. "I'll make a few phone calls and have friends from town bring their dogs. Ayla won't know them, I swear. She just got here a couple of weeks ago."

Kyle looked like he was ready to capitulate, but he needed one more nudge. What could Ayla—

"I know how you feel," Theo said, stepping closer and putting a strong hand on Ayla's shoulder. "It's the damn weirdest thing you ever heard, and all you want to do is roll your eyes."

The other man looked at him. "And laugh my ass off."

"You won't laugh when you watch her work," he said. "You can trust me on this."

Without thinking too much about it, Ayla reached up and put her hand over his, smiling at him. She didn't know what to say, but he had to see the gratitude in her eyes.

"All right, let's do this," Kyle finally said. "Let's get to work and do a live show! Holy crap, we're doing this."

As they dispersed, Ayla turned to Marie, who still looked a little gobsmacked.

"I promise I will push the Last Chance Ranch," Ayla told her.

"I know you will. Let me go help them." She reached out and squeezed Theo's hand. "Thank you so much."

Marie shot off after the others, leaving Ayla alone with Theo.

"I can't…" She bit her lip, shaking her head. "You, of all people."

"I hope you're not mad that I offered you up on the altar of Marie's lifelong dreams."

"Mad? Theo, that was brilliant. And…you believe?"

For a long time, he looked at her, studying her face and holding her gaze. "I believe that you believe," he said slowly, and she knew that even those words were difficult for him.

"And I believe," she whispered, "that we just took another step in the right direction."

He smiled and held out his arms to hug her. "Knock 'em dead, Ayla the Magnificent."

Right then, in his arms, feeling his heartbeat, knowing how hard that conversation had to have been for him… she did feel magnificent.

Chapter Seventeen

Considering what was involved in the process, the TV professionals moved at lightning speed. Some of Marie's local friends volunteered to bring their animals and showed up as things got ready. With help from Theo, who worked with Jimmy, a brilliant technician, they'd gotten the camera and sound and computer wired up for a live transmission, while Ayla had been off getting made up by the assistant.

And now they were live on the air.

Clem had barked relentlessly at the new dogs—and the van—but she was quiet now, next to Theo as they looked out on the "set" in the living room from the hallway with Marie.

Marie was on a cloud. They'd ended up taping an opening segment with her walking around the Last Chance Ranch, talking about the place and her plans. They took some video of River, Hoss, and Little Joe, and let Marie introduce the goats. It was only a minute or two tagged onto the beginning of the show, but now the live segment was all Ayla, currently talking to Colin like they were both television professionals.

"Man, she's owning this," Theo whispered to Marie.

"And so pretty," Marie responded.

That was an understatement. Ayla rarely wore makeup, or if she did, it was so natural that he'd never noticed. But whatever she had on now made her eyes look magical and her cheeks sweet and smooth and her mouth all begging for a kiss.

Darcy and Ella had come over with some clothes, and Ayla had chosen a simple black dress that fit her slender body like a glove…a glove he wouldn't mind sliding off. But the biggest shocker of all? She was an absolute natural in front of the camera.

She didn't flinch or stutter or seem remotely uncomfortable as she described a process that would have made almost anyone else feel a little odd. She laughed with Colin and answered his questions with humor and warmth that made watching her a pleasure.

"I always relax first," she told Colin after he asked her to describe the process that went on in her head when she worked with an animal. "My mind has to be clear, so I really wipe out anything that might distract me, and then I am open to feeling the animal's energy."

Oh man. Energy again.

Theo pushed down the skepticism that rose up and forced himself to enjoy the sights and sounds of a woman doing her job, and doing it well.

"How do you start?" Colin asked, looking at her like he was as mesmerized as Theo was. But Theo knocked that little bit of jealousy away, too. Ayla wasn't interested in that guy, but based on the way she looked at Theo this morning? She was definitely interested, and he couldn't let his innate skepticism screw that up.

Plus, if this show raised big bucks for Miz Marie, then how many dogs like Clem would get a last chance? This was bigger than his views on the subject.

"I think the dog's name," Ayla said.

"Like, telepathically?"

"I usually manage to get the dog's attention by thinking his or her name. Then I ask a question, silently, in my head."

"No words?" Colin asked.

She laughed lightly, a musical sound that probably made millions turn up their TV and get closer.

"Sorry to break the news, Colin, but animals don't speak English or any other language. They have an image they associate with a word. You say 'treat,' but they see an image of the treat. Same meaning, different way of mentally processing it."

"Can you talk to dead animals?" he asked, leaning forward as if hanging on every word.

"No," she said simply. "I'm not that kind of communicator. Nor do I look at a picture or communicate with a dog through a computer screen. But when an animal is in front of me, I allow myself to sense the energy waves emitted from their brain. I see what they're seeing. Animals don't always live in the present moment. They can be thinking about experiences, smells, people, moments that stand out in their lives."

Damn it, he had to admit that made a tiny bit of sense. But maybe because the words were coming from someone he liked so much, he wanted to believe her. She was truly convincing.

"Well, let's get our first guest out here and watch you work. RaeAnn? Do you have a four-legged friend and his or her human?"

"We do. Meet Christine and her furbaby, Gandolf."

The name got a laugh as an older woman came in, carrying a beagle. She sat on the sofa and Ayla took her little dog to snuggle and kiss right on the nose. Lucky dog.

"All right, Ayla. Is it true you have never met this dog or his owner?"

Ayla smiled at Christine. "We've never met, but…" She flipped the dog's floppy ears. "Gandolf is precious."

"What's he telling you?" Colin asked, cutting right to the chase.

Ayla closed her eyes, as Theo had seen her do many times that Saturday in the square. She didn't say a word, but almost instantly, Gandolf reacted with a whimper, then his tail swooshed madly.

"He's thinking about a kiddie pool," she said, and Christine gasped. "The one with stars all over it."

"We got that for the warm weather!" Her jaw loosened, and she looked at Colin and then Jimmy behind the camera. "How did she know that?"

Ayla stroked the dog's head. "But that little yellow toy. Is it a banana?"

"The stuffed banana, yes!"

"It keeps getting wet in the pool, and he does not like that."

The tail stopped swishing. Holy crap on a cracker. *Really?*

Next to him, Marie gave him a big old *I told you so* look. On the set, Christine was practically crawling out of her skin.

"That's right! He keeps taking it in the pool when I'm not looking, then he gets so sad when it's soggy."

Colin leaned in with a serious reporter's expression on

his face. "How about his health, Ayla?" he asked. "Can you sense any pain or any issues that Christine should know about?"

She nodded, running her hands over Gandolf's whole body. "He feels really good," she said. "A little upset in the stomach, but that could be nerves. Or...did you switch food? He doesn't love the dry stuff."

Christine put her hands on her cheeks in shock. "I tried to tell my husband that he hates those little brown triangles."

"Who wouldn't?" Ayla joked.

"Well, if your husband's watching," Colin added, "he knows now. No more brown triangles."

As everyone laughed, Ayla graciously gave the dog back to Christine. Colin closed the segment like a pro, breaking for commercial, and then he and Ayla talked and laughed about something with the producer. Marie slipped away to the kitchen to make sure RaeAnn was ready with the next dog.

Just as Kyle called out ten seconds to go live, Clementine stood up next to Theo, her ears perked a little as if she heard something.

Oh God, not a siren.

He reached down, trying to decide whether he should get her out of here in the five seconds before they went live, because once the producer called for quiet, they couldn't really move.

He didn't hear a siren, but he reached into his pocket for a treat anyway. Kyle held up his hand and hollered, "Five seconds!"

His raised voice must have startled Clem, because she bolted from the hall, through the living room, and barked right in Ayla's face.

"Oh boy." Colin laughed, glancing at the camera and the red light that indicated they were definitely live. "Who do we have here?"

Theo took a few steps closer, but Ayla picked the dog up and settled her with a few calming strokes. "This is Clementine, Colin, and I can tell you, this sweet pooch communicates with me all the time."

"Tell us about that," Colin said.

As Theo reached the camera stand, Kyle held his hand out to stop him, letting the host and guest take this unexpected route. Okay. This was live TV.

Theo sucked in a silent breath, praying Clem could handle the spotlight. Literally. Because one was shining right in her face.

"Her story is dramatic and amazing," Ayla said, stroking Clementine's head. "She is the perfect example of why Miz Marie's Last Chance Ranch is a sanctuary for animals who didn't get a fair shake in life."

"Has Clementine told you about her past?" Colin asked.

"In great detail." She turned Clem's face so they were nose-to-nose, which was probably the most precious thing ever broadcast on live TV. "She was chained to a picnic table, left out in the elements, and badly mistreated."

Colin's eyes shuttered as he shook his head in disgust. "I'm so sorry for her."

"But she's happy now," Ayla assured him. "This is her last chance, and she's enjoying every minute at this amazing place."

Of course she'd turn the situation into an unexpected commercial for Miz Marie. Theo glanced at the kitchen and caught sight of the woman grinning from ear to ear, her hands in a prayer position as she gazed at Ayla like she was the most incredible creature God ever made.

Theo knew exactly how she felt.

"Does she remember her past very often?" Colin asked.

Ayla nodded enthusiastically. "That's why she jumped in here, I think. The bright lights took her back to a memory. One, I have to say, I've never seen before."

Colin shot closer. "Tell us. What is she seeing?"

Ayla closed her eyes and put her face very close to Clementine's, her hands lightly grasping the dog's head.

"She's digging," she said. "Or…someone is. She's watching someone dig. Very bright lights are shining on a hole in the ground, and she…she wants to dig, too." Ayla smiled. "She is, after all, a dog."

Colin laughed. "Anything else?"

"Yes. There's a box coming out of the ground."

"A coffin?" Colin asked on a gasp, totally caught up in the moment.

"No…" Ayla cocked her head, frowning. "But I see a word on the box."

"She can read?" Colin choked the question. "Now you might lose me, Ayla."

She didn't let that throw her, eyes still closed. "Maybe this box once stored Christmas decorations," she said.

"Excuse me? How can you tell?"

"Or it's owned by someone named Noel. It says 'Noel' on the box and…something else." She shook her head. "Clementine isn't focused on that, but she doesn't like the lights." Ayla used her hand to shade Clem's eyes. "She doesn't like them now, either."

"I'm sorry, Clementine." Colin leaned closer and petted Clem's head, but his gaze was on Ayla. Making him human, Theo had to admit. "You are amazing, Ayla Hollis!"

"I'm not doing anything except telling you what I see in Clementine's pretty head." She kissed the dog. "And I hope that as time goes by, these darker memories are replaced by happy ones here at the Last Chance Ranch."

"I'm sure they will be," Colin said, glancing at Kyle. "Do we have time for one more? Awesome. Let's take a quick break, and then Ayla's going to tell us what's going on in the head of…" He glanced to the side, where RaeAnn stood with a gorgeous black Lab on a leash. "Sable! Stay tuned, folks! We've got a beauty coming up." He smiled at Ayla. "Another beauty."

Seriously, dude?

But Ayla shifted her attention to Clementine, then looked out into the lights. "Theo?"

"Right here," he said, coming closer to scoop up the dog. "Impressive work," he said. "Noel? Pretty specific, isn't it?"

"That's what Clementine saw." She looked up at him with the slightest challenge and tease in her dark eyes, and all he wanted to do was…kiss her.

"You're doing a phenomenal job," he added, leaning a little closer. "Not that I'm surprised."

She smiled at him, holding his gaze for a long, long moment.

The fact was, maybe she did see this stuff in her head. And maybe Clem did or didn't. They'd never know and honestly, it didn't matter. And that, he decided, was a huge step forward for him, and for them.

As he stepped away from the set, he heard Colin say, "Oh, so he's your boyfriend. I should have guessed."

Theo didn't hear her response, but he couldn't wipe the smug smile off his face. It was still there when the show ended. And when the little production company packed up and left. And when the last of Marie's friends and dogs took off, after getting free "readings" from Ayla to thank them for coming, even though they didn't all get to be on air.

He was still smiling when Ayla came out of her room, back in jeans and a T-shirt, but still looking a little glamorous with the glittery makeup and dark lashes.

"You were amazing!" Marie leaped from her chair and threw her arms around Ayla. "How can I ever thank you?"

"The whole idea was Theo's," she said, looking at him over Marie's shoulder. "How can I thank him?"

He came closer and put his arms around both of them. "Let me take you to dinner tonight."

Marie slipped out of the circle. "You take Ayla. I'll watch Clementine. Nothing could make me happier."

And nothing could make Theo happier, either.

Chapter Eighteen

When the restaurant owner himself brought out the tiramisu, Ayla knew she'd been a hit that afternoon. Her first clue had been the person who'd stopped them while they were crossing the square on their way to Ricardo's, the upscale Italian restaurant in Bitter Bark.

Her second clue was the reaction of their server, who gushed about the show.

But Ricardo and the tiramisu?

"I guess I'm famous," she said to Theo on a laugh after Ricardo heaped praise on her, then left so they could enjoy the dessert on the house. "Who knew that so many people watch a live animal show?"

"Well, it is Bitter Bark, and this place has gone to the dogs," he joked. "But I understand the Kilcannon-Mahoney-Santorini communication effort was in full force before it went live. Word got out to the Mahoneys at the fire station, and they all watched, and Ella and Darcy had their employees tell everyone who came into the stores, and Waterford Farm sent out a newsletter."

"Really?"

"And my stepcousin Connor and his fiancée, Sadie, are

co-mayors, so there was an email blast to all the residents. Oh, and Cassie told her biggest client, Family First Pet Foods, and they tweeted about it to a few million followers because they do so much promo here in Bitter Bark, so…"

With each word, she felt her eyes get bigger. "I'm kind of glad I didn't know all that."

"Why? Everyone wants to help Miz Marie, of course, and you." He leveled his golden-green gaze on her. "The newest sensation of Bitter Bark and now, I guess, the world."

"Please." She flicked off the compliment, certain he was being sarcastic. Or was he? "Are you mocking me?" she asked. "I'm so used to it now, I can't tell anymore."

His smile wavered. "I am not. I'm impressed. I told you that. You were like a seasoned television professional today."

"I had fun." She held a forkful of creamy dessert in front of her lips as she made the confession. "I have to say that doing that show was one of the most enjoyable things I've ever done."

"You sure weren't nervous."

"Not a bit." She took the bite and resisted the urge to moan in a way that would make her mother want to curl up and weep. "Wow."

He ate with the same gusto, not hesitating to moan. "Best tiramisu I ever had."

She laughed. "This is in the food category, isn't it? Then you like it."

"Guilty." He tipped his head in acknowledgment. "But this is perfection."

"The whole dinner has been," she agreed. And not just the luscious pasta and tangy marinara sauce that made Ricardo's famous.

Theo had been…as good as the tiramisu that slid between her lips.

He'd picked her up, looking sharp in dress clothes, and held her hand after they parked and walked through the square. Dinner had flown by as he told her stories about working on an aircraft carrier, and living near the Pacific Ocean, and growing up in a big Greek family.

She'd shared bits of her life, which wasn't nearly as exciting or bursting with family love, but somehow he managed to draw her out and let them really get to know each other.

"Wow, you do love that tiramisu," he said, searching her face as she swallowed. "Your eyes are actually bright."

"I do, but that's not what has me so happy right now."

"Great day in the old psychic biz?" he teased, and she laughed because the bite had gone out of his jokes. They'd made great strides today.

"Yes, it was, but that's still not it." She put her fork down and reached out to place her fingers lightly on his knuckles, loving the feel of even that little bit of him. "I honestly cannot remember the last time I enjoyed a dinner date so much."

"Another thing we have in common, then." He turned his hand and threaded his fingers through hers. "And I didn't even have to fight Colin for your attention."

She laughed. "He was a flirt."

"He didn't flirt with Marie," he joked. "Or Clem."

"Clem! Wasn't she wonderful today? I was so proud of her."

He searched her face, quiet for a moment, and she knew what he was thinking.

"Yes, I saw all that I described in her head," she said

before he had a chance to voice his skepticism. "Clear as day. Except it was night in Clem's mind."

For a long moment, he didn't say anything, and she could feel her heart rate increase. *Please take it seriously, Theo. Please.*

"How big was the box?" he asked.

She almost exhaled with relief. It was all she needed to hear, just that. No snark, no snide comments, just… that.

"Not very. It was actually more like a metal suitcase, but it was definitely in the ground, as far as what I—well, Clem—could see."

He looked down at his plate.

"What?" she prodded, giving his hand a squeeze. "We're making such progress here, Theo. I can't tell you what it means to me to even have this conversation with you. What are you thinking? That I'm faking this? That you don't know why you'd like a woman with this gift? That you want to forget about it and…leave?" She heard the strain in her voice, but she couldn't help it. She was falling for him, and that scared her.

Finally, he looked up. "I don't know what to think about your ability, Ayla, but I can guarantee you I am not asking myself why I like you. I just do." He said it with enough vehemence to give her chills. "And as far as getting up and leaving? Yeah, I do want to do that, but not alone. And sadly, you live with Marie, and I'm staying at Waterford, so what I really want to do for the rest of this night…" He moved closer a centimeter and lowered his voice. "Is probably going to have to wait."

Her chills turned to a pool of heat. "Oh." She sighed, slightly increasing her grip on their joined hands. "Well, that's…" Sexy and thrilling. "Even scarier."

He drew back, blinking at her. "It shouldn't scare you. I would never…hurt you."

"But I don't know that," she whispered, once again getting a look of abject disbelief from him. "Oh, I know you'd never hurt me intentionally, but I'm still bruised from what I've been through, and I assume you are, too."

"I can't remember her name," he said with a totally straight face, making her laugh.

"Heather," she supplied.

"EJ," he shot back. "But I have never and will never cheat on someone."

"I know that," she said. And she did. "You're not cut from the same cloth as EJ." She gave a dry laugh. "You don't even reside on the same planet."

"Thank you." He lifted her hand and pressed a kiss on her knuckles in gratitude. "Then what's scaring you?"

She thought about it for a long time, looking at him as she tried to find her words. "You're kind of…perfect."

"Hardly. Also, ditto."

"I don't know what to do about that," she admitted.

"Sit back and enjoy the ride?"

"Until it ends," she said softly.

His own smile wavered. "One day at a time? I'm running out of clichés here."

"How about…our days are numbered? You're leaving," she said simply. "As soon as you get a job somewhere, likely London."

"It does seem that way more every day," he said. "The headhunter is certain that position is back in play."

She wanted to smile and say how wonderful, but… was it?

"Hey," he said, squeezing her hand. "You're free. You could…" His voice trailed off as if he didn't know how to say what he was thinking. "I know it's soon, but there are options. There's no reason to assume…a tragic ending."

"We shouldn't even be talking about anything ending. We've barely begun."

He held her gaze and stroked the pad of his thumb over her knuckle. "I would like to begin."

Her heart rose and fell and rolled around. "What exactly are we beginning?"

"I don't know, Ayla, but I want to find out." He kissed her hand again. "I really want to find out."

The words left her nearly breathless and humming with anticipation. That feeling only intensified when he paid, and they left the restaurant—with two more patrons congratulating her on the show that afternoon—and walked out into a warm early-summer night. White lights flickered on the trees all through the square, and the small town bustled with locals, students from the college, and tourists. And, of course, dogs.

"I miss Clem," she said as Theo took her hand.

"Clem's fine." He guided her to a secluded spot in the corner of the square, tucked away in the shadows under one of the trees that had no lights. "C'mere."

She followed, her whole body already fluttering.

He eased her onto the bench, then drew her closer. "No picnic tables, sirens, dogs, or other interruptions."

Laughing softly, she closed the tiny bit of space between them. "Don't forget my adoring fans, who could be lurking around the statue of Thaddeus Bushrod, founder of Bitter Bark."

"Your adoring *fan*," he whispered, "is right here, dying to kiss you."

"Please do."

He tunneled his fingers under her hair, angling her head as their lips met and parted to deepen the connection. He tasted sweet like the tiramisu and peppery like the wine. With a barely audible moan, they wrapped their arms around each other, and heat spiraled through her as he intensified the kiss.

She didn't know what they were beginning, either, but if it felt like this, she didn't want it to end.

That was the problem: She didn't want any of this to end, and it would.

As his tongue flicked over her teeth and teased her mouth open, she managed to push that thought out of her head and fall deeper into this moment, loving the pressure and promise of his lips and the warmth and power of his hands.

Theo Santorini would be a lover like no one she'd ever known, and all she wanted to do right then was find out.

When they stopped to slowly catch their breath, they were silent for a moment, taking the time to look into each other's eyes, not needing words.

He kissed her lightly, then let out a long sigh, tightening his arms around her.

"Good thing you can't read people's minds," he murmured into her ear.

"It's probably the same thing I'm thinking," she said. "And it's…oh. Nice."

He drew back to look into her eyes, then kissed her again, letting the heat build for a moment before slowly ending it.

"We can't make out on a park bench," she said softly.

"We can't? We are."

She laughed. "We shouldn't."

"Why not?"

"Théodoros?"

They both blinked at the sound of Yiayia's voice.

"That's why not," they said in perfect unison, reluctantly letting go of each other before turning toward the sound of his grandmother, who was walking side by side with a man.

"Oh my goodness, it *is* you." She came closer, giving a nervous chuckle, as if she'd been the one caught making out in the park.

Ayla and Theo stood to get up and say hello, meeting them halfway, where there was a little more light.

"Hello, Yiayia," Theo said, but his attention was on the man next to her. Ayla recognized his shock of thick white hair and dark eyes immediately, but only because little Pyggie thought about this man a lot.

"Aldo, this is my grandson, Theo!" Her voice rose in excitement. "I didn't think you two would meet until John's wedding next week."

The man's face lit up as he extended his hand to Theo. "Théodoros," he said, giving it the Greek pronunciation that Yiayia liked. "I've heard *so* much about you."

Theo shook the man's hand. "I'm sure you have if you've been hanging out with Yiayia. Good to meet you, Aldo." He put his hand on Ayla's shoulder and drew her even closer. "And this is Ayla Hollis."

Yiayia looked past them to the bench where they'd been sitting. "What are you doing out here?"

"Agnes," Aldo said in a teasing voice. "They were on *our* bench. The most private spot in Bushrod Square."

Yiayia gave him a quick look and another nervous laugh, but Theo wasn't laughing at all. His gaze was locked on Aldo, looking a little more like a suspicious father than a guilty grandson.

"We often bring Pyggie and Gala here," Yiayia said quickly, as if they used the bench for dog-sitting and not exactly what Ayla and Theo had been doing.

"And you're the psychic," Aldo said, shifting his attention to Ayla. "Agnes made sure I watched today, and that was quite the show you put on."

"Finnie and I recorded the whole thing," Yiayia added. "Watched it four times."

"Oh, wow." Ayla laughed. "Not sure I could stand to watch myself on TV that much."

"You were fantastic," Yiayia said. "And I don't give compliments lightly. Isn't that right, Théodoros?"

"Only to me," he responded.

"Well, thank you," Ayla said. "I had a lot of fun."

"You have to tell us how you do that," Aldo added. "Agnes and I were just chatting about how the whole trick works." He glanced at Yiayia, looking for agreement, but she stayed quiet. "I'm the guy who always wants to talk to the magicians and find out the secret. Do you share yours?"

"Well, it's not a trick," she said slowly. "I read the animal's mind."

Aldo laughed. "All right. There's a sucker born every minute."

Next to her, she felt Theo bristle. "Actually, she's telling the truth," he said.

Ayla's heart nearly burst at the words. It was one thing for him to pitch the producer when they all wanted the same thing—publicity for Marie's ranch. But this? Not necessary…and so incredibly appreciated, she was speechless.

But Aldo gave another scoffing laugh. "All right. I understand if you don't want to say, but it was a marvelous act. I'd pay to see you do it in Vegas."

"It's not an act," Theo said, a little tension in his voice. "I've been with her for the better part of two weeks, and I have to tell you, she's not pretending."

Aldo's brows lifted. "Really. Well, as you can tell by the color of my hair, I wasn't born yesterday, so…"

Ayla knew Yiayia liked this man and that she'd been seeing him since Christmas, and he seemed nice enough. She couldn't fault him for skepticism, she expected it. But something inside her wanted to prove Aldo wrong.

"Yes, really," Theo said.

"Well, they say love is blind, so…" Aldo looked at Yiayia. "You're right, Agnes. You might have another match on your hands."

Ayla reached out and touched the man's arm. "Aldo. Do you remember the time you came to Yiayia's house and were alone with Pyggie in the kitchen?"

He stared at her. "Excuse me?"

"You were in a dark green polo shirt."

He blinked in surprise.

"You picked up Pyggie, looked him right in the eyes, and said something. I don't know what, because dogs don't communicate with words."

He looked speechless.

"You tried to give him one of the cookies from the counter, but he wouldn't eat it. He wanted to. It smelled good, but I guess he wanted to let you know he wasn't happy. He knew you were taking Agnes out of the house."

Yiayia choked a little laugh. Theo crossed his arms and looked smug. And Aldo looked like he'd need help closing his dropped jaw.

"That really happened," he managed to say. "I really wanted that dog to like me, but how did you *know*?"

She laughed. "Pyggie told me. It's fine if you don't believe me—"

"I do!" he exclaimed, turning to Yiayia. "Agnes, did you hear that? She…wow. *Wow.*" For the rest of the conversation, his entire demeanor changed from sarcastic and dubious to…amazed.

A few minutes later, they said goodbye, and Theo and Ayla started walking toward his car. She slid both her hands around his arm, holding so tight.

"Thank you," she whispered. "Coming to my defense when you are still riddled with doubts can't be easy."

"Ayla, I'm not going to stand there and let someone disparage you."

"Well, that had to have been difficult."

He smiled down at her. "First of all, 'difficult' is resisting the urge to find another dark bench and finish what we started. Second, the guy was a little smug, and who is he to go make out with my Yiayia? And third…"

She waited, curious to see where he was going.

"I'm buttering you up so you say yes."

"Yes to…" She could only imagine, and yes was probably going to be her answer.

"To going to John's wedding with me next week. Will you? I'd really like you there as my date."

A smile pulled, and she hugged him again. "I would love that. Thank you for asking."

He kissed her again, this one taking longer and getting heated. When they broke apart, he glanced around. "The square isn't going to work," he said. "Let's go back to Miz Marie's and find an empty kennel."

She laughed at that. “There’s always that picnic table in the back.”

He groaned. “How did we find ourselves at this age with no privacy?”

“Who knew we’d need it? I escaped to Bitter Bark to start a new life, not fall for a new man.”

“Fall for?” He smiled. “Are you?”

She searched his face, drinking in every feature she was rapidly starting to adore. “I might be,” she admitted.

He dipped his head so their foreheads touched. “I might be, too.”

Chapter Nineteen

"I'm not kidding, Mr. Santorini."

Theo stared at the older man across the desk, seeing nothing but genuine hope in Dean Simmons's green eyes as he stroked his beard and let the offer hang in the air.

"Academia?" Theo inched back. "I've never considered it."

"You wouldn't have to teach," the dean said. "Just hire the right people and make sure the curriculum keeps up with the latest in nuclear engineering. Department head, with all the perks."

None of which would add up to a third of what he was worth on the open market. He'd be back to Navy pay.

"Well, I'm flattered by the offer," Theo said, pushing up as the meeting came to its natural ending. "In the meantime, I'll be able to get you at least three speakers for your presentations. If you can cover expenses to get them here, then I'm confident the people I have in mind will say yes."

"Thank you." Dean Simmons stood, and they shook hands warmly. "And thank Daniel again for the introduction."

"I will," he promised.

When he found his way to the front of the Engineering Department building, Theo spied Daniel waiting for him under a massive wisteria tree in the quad of the small campus.

"All set?" he asked as Theo joined him.

"It'll be easy," he said, thinking back on the meeting. Daniel had made the introductions, then stepped out while Theo enjoyed a long conversation with the dean, talking about the changes in engineering academics since he'd been in school. "Smart guy, too."

"So you think you can find him some speakers?"

Theo nodded. "I sure can, and if I weren't likely to be living somewhere else, I'd do a few of those symposia myself."

"Maybe you'll still be here."

"Then I'm in trouble," he said on a laugh. "It's almost May. If I'm here in the fall, my career is effectively over."

"I wouldn't worry. Dean Simmons was drooling over the very idea that someone who has had their hands all over a nuclear-powered aircraft carrier was standing in his office."

Theo laughed. "He did offer me a job to head a new Nuclear Engineering Department on the spot."

Daniel slowed his step and looked at him. "Really? I guess that would be a real notch down for someone with your skill set."

"Starting a college department?" He shrugged. "Not a notch down for anyone. I don't see myself in academia, but it's an interesting option. Not the highest-paying one, but..." He glanced around at the picturesque campus, the mountains in the distance, and all the other intangibles this place had to offer, like familiarity, family, and…the woman he'd managed to spend every waking minute with this week.

"Some things are more valuable than money," Daniel said, his words eerily echoing Theo's thoughts.

"And maybe someday I'll pursue those things," Theo told him. "But right now, in my thirties, after all those years in the military? My skill set is valuable, and I can make a lot of money. Don't you think it would be silly not to try?"

Daniel didn't answer for a long moment as they walked. "I never pursued a career for money, though being a vet has given me a comfortable life."

"And I love engineering," Theo added, somehow feeling like he should defend his position.

"So, you're focused on power plants? Research operations? Tech companies? I can imagine the sky's the limit for you, son."

"There's a limit, but I do have options. I don't want to go somewhere…undesirable."

"I know you had your heart set on that job in London."

"I still might get it." Except he hadn't looked at his email in two days. "And who wouldn't want a few years in Europe?" Didn't he? He used to. He and Heather were going to live there and use London as a home base to see the world. Now he was in Bitter Bark and pretty damn content.

"Well, I'm very grateful that you can help the dean out," Daniel said as they reached the parking lot. "Headed back to Miz Marie's ranch?"

"Yep." Theo laughed. "Speaking of things that are more valuable than money. I'm building her a cathouse."

Daniel's eyes sparked with admiration. "A noble task that I fully support. Your mother and I are driving to Charlotte to pick up Nick at the airport this afternoon."

"Oh, that's right. He's coming in today for the wedding this weekend."

"Should be a lively Wednesday night dinner," Daniel said. "I hope you'll be there. Bring Ayla and Marie." He grinned. "And that sweet dog Clementine. How's the training going, by the way?"

"Actually, really great. Liam and Shane gave me some terrific techniques, and we almost have Clem able to get all the way to the picnic table without freaking out. We're working on sirens, too, though that's a little tricky. And Liam's taught her an attack command which I thought would be a good thing for Ayla and Marie to know." Once he was gone. "Although I hope they never have to use it."

"You've done amazing work with that dog," Daniel said.

"Thanks. Your sons did all the work. Have fun getting Nick. I'll see you tonight."

He made a few stops for some things that Miz Marie needed, grabbed lunch for all of them, and headed down the familiar highway to the Last Chance Ranch. As he pulled in, he caught sight of Ayla in the chicken coop, wearing cutoff denim shorts, a not completely clean T-shirt, and Marie's oversized shitkickers, which she always chose when she had to replace the straw or get the eggs.

She turned at the sight of his car, her whole face brightening with a smile. For a minute, he looked at her as he parked, because there weren't very many things he liked looking at quite as much as Ayla Hollis.

Her dark gold hair, her slender and feminine body, her blinding smile, her incredible brain.

Clem barked wildly and shot toward his car, getting right outside the door and trying to paw her way closer to him. Opening the door, he let Clem launch toward him, her dirty paws dragging down the oxford cloth shirt he'd worn to Vestal Valley.

Laughing, he smothered the dog with some love and kisses, and when he looked up, Ayla was right beside the car with some hay caught in her thick hair, a smudge on her face, and that vague odor of the coop about her. And all he wanted to do was smother her with the same love he was giving Clementine.

"Hey, chicken lady."

She laughed, holding up a basket of eggs. "*Bawk.* How'd it go at the college?"

"Good." He glanced down at his now-dirty shirt and khakis. "Good thing I brought work clothes." He eased Clementine down to the ground and stepped out, going right for the hug Ayla offered.

The minute their bodies met, they seemed to simply mold together like they belonged. They'd spent an awful lot of the past few days exactly like this, finding excuses to touch, kiss, and hold each other as much as possible.

They both wanted more, and he actually had a great plan to make that happen. But first, a kiss.

She tasted like North Carolina sunshine and a little bit of… "Raspberry croissant?" he guessed.

"My weakness," she admitted, putting her hands on his chest. "One of them, anyway."

"Mmm." He lowered his head and kissed her again. "Guess what I found out this morning?" he murmured into the kiss. "Groomsmen have the option of getting a room at Overlook Glen for after the wedding, and I…" He inched back to see her reaction, casually trying to get some hay from her hair. "Just happened to snag one."

Her eyes flashed enough for him to know she was perfectly happy with that plan. Finally, a whole night together, alone.

"So pack a bag for the wedding," he told her on another kiss, and this one he trailed down her jaw.

"Guess what?" she whispered. "Marie's gone to pick up a pregnant stray cat in Boone. You know what that means?"

"New residents for the house I just built?"

She laughed. "She'll be gone until after lunch."

He lifted his head to respond to that idea. "You don't want to wait until Saturday."

The look in her eyes told him the answer, and when she arched slightly into him, there was no doubt. "I will if I have to."

"I will, too." His body was defying that logic, but he knew it would be better than a quickie while Marie was gone. "I won't like it, but…" He kissed her again and started rethinking that response as they heard a car coming down the road toward the house.

They had just broken the kiss and stepped apart when a late-model BMW appeared at the end of the driveway. Theo frowned at a car he'd expect to see more often in Southern California than western North Carolina. God willing, the occupants were here to make a hefty donation to the ranch.

Still holding Ayla, he felt her stiffen and gasp.

"What's wrong?" he murmured.

The driver's door opened, and a man stepped out, staring at her. No, he glared at her, silent.

"I can't believe this," she barely whispered the words.

"Who is that?" Although, based on the look, the clothes, the car, the vibe, he knew deep inside exactly who it was. The ex.

She stayed stone-still, staring back, all color draining from her face.

Then the passenger door opened, and a fair-haired woman with a little too much makeup and diamonds for these parts stepped onto the dirt drive.

"Trina?" she whispered, sinking deeper into Theo. "What are they doing here?"

"My guess? They've come to collect you."

"Well, they're going home empty-handed. And she better have my phone and wallet with her, which I know she's been holding hostage to try to get me home."

Theo turned toward the lanky man in a linen shirt and dress pants and did the only thing he could do—put his arm around Ayla and resisted the urge to howl, *Mine!*

Clem howled, though. She barked and added a well-deserved growl of warning. Theo let her go one second longer than he normally would, enjoying the look of trepidation on the other guy's face. Then he tossed Clem a treat and gave her the signal to stay still and calm. The miraculous training worked.

"Ayla!" Her sister shot forward, wobbling on wedged heels that could not be more out of place at the Last Chance Ranch. "Oh my God, look at you! Are you being held prisoner against your will?"

Ayla fought a laugh. "Hi, Trina. You're going to kill yourself running in espadrilles."

Her sister reached out to hug her, but then inched back, looking Ayla up and down. "Work camp, right?"

"Stop it." She turned from her sister to the man

coming toward her, who stabbed his designer-cut brown hair with his hand, narrowing his eyes. He was too slick, too rich, and too arrogant for Theo to take seriously, but he'd take his cues from Ayla.

"I can't believe you ran off, Ay." He let out a put-upon sigh and spared a quick glance at Theo. "We need a little time alone. You can go back to…" He let his gaze drop over Theo, lingering on the paw dirt on his chest. "Work."

"EJ, this is Theo Santorini, a former lieutenant commander and nuclear engineer in the Navy."

"Well, I—"

"He's also my boyfriend."

EJ's jaw dropped. "Your boy—"

"And he's perfectly capable of assisting you in getting back in the car so you can return to whatever rock you crawled out from under, no doubt with Jilly, and never speak to me again." Ayla crossed her arms and stared at the other man.

"Ayla." He shook his head. "It was a total misunderstanding that you've completely blown out of proportion."

"It really was, Ay," her sister said. "You need to hear him out."

"I do not need to hear anything except the sound of your car leaving."

Theo threw her a look, hiding a smile at her strength.

Trina let out a groan. "I told you," she said under her breath to EJ.

"How did you even find me?" Ayla asked her sister.

"Honey, you were on TV doing that…that *thing* with dogs." She inhaled like it pained her to even obliquely refer to it. "We got a bunch of calls from people, because no one had had any idea where you've been since the wedding. So we found the show on demand, and they said the name of this place. Daddy watched." Her eyes widened. "That did *not* go well. And Mother? Let's just say there's been a run on Ativan at the local pharmacy."

"You didn't need to come all the way out here, Trina."

"Yes, I did, so they wouldn't. Seriously, Mother is apoplectic, and Daddy?" She let out a whistle. "Honey, I would check your trust fund accounts ASAP."

Ayla dropped her head back with a grunt. "I don't care. How hard is that for you to understand?"

"Um, very?" Trina said with an awkward laugh.

"Listen to me, Ay." EJ came closer. "Even if we can't work this out, you need to come home. And as far as Jill? You do not understand the situation."

"You banged one of my best friends after our rehearsal dinner," she shot back. "What part of that don't I understand?"

"The circumstances."

With each moment, Theo could feel himself get more and more tense, resisting the urge to ball his fists. This was Ayla's fight, yes, but he was happy to serve as her backup.

"Listen to me, pal," he said through clenched teeth, and his tone made Clem come closer and growl. "Ayla wants you to leave. I want you to leave. And my dog wants you to leave. So, goodbye."

Trina moaned. "Ayla, please think about what you're doing."

"I am. I'm not leaving. I'm here now. I…live here now." She struggled with the last few words, Theo could tell, but she punctuated the statement by lifting her chin and squaring her shoulders.

EJ shook his head like the whole thing baffled him.

"What the hell has gotten into you, Ay?"

Trina cocked her head and pinned Theo with a look. "I think the question is *who* has gotten into her."

Fury shot through him, but Ayla put a hand on his arm as if she sensed how tight he was.

"Trina, tell Mother I'm fine. Tell Daddy I don't care if he's not happy with me. And tell me you have my wallet and phone, since I asked you to mail it to a PO box almost three weeks ago."

Her sister's shoulders slumped. "They're in the car," she said, gesturing for her to follow. "Come with me."

"Get them, please."

"Ayla." She reached out. "Come with me. Please?"

She stood firm for a second, then let out a sigh and followed, leaving Theo standing alone with EJ. Who took a slow, deep breath and, to his credit, met Theo's gaze.

"So, question," EJ said. "Are you two really together, or is that fake, too?"

Too? Theo didn't want to even dignify that with a response, so he stared at the man, silent.

"I mean, she's seriously on the rebound, and I get that, but you do know that whole psychic thing is, well, her way of rebelling, right? Acting out, if you will. She has a tendency to…embellish the truth, if you get my drift."

What he was about to get was Theo's fist in his teeth.

"She's always been in Trina's shadow," he continued as if Theo had asked for this psychoanalysis. "So this gets her the attention she craves. You know, like the whole drama of leaving the church in front of everyone. She lives for that stuff. You know that, don't you?"

Clem growled at him, exactly as Theo wanted to.

"Okay, whatever, tough guy." EJ turned to where the sisters stood by the car, face-to-face and engaged in what looked like a heated exchange. “She’s jealous of her sister, too.”

“I can’t believe you, Trina!” Ayla’s voice, sharp with emotion, bounced back at them, making EJ throw a smug *I told you so* look at Theo.

Trina got in the car and slammed the door, leaving Ayla slack-jawed at whatever their last words had been. After a second, she stepped back from the car, shaking her head.

EJ turned and gave Theo one more look. “She’s doing this for her ego, trying to drum up sympathy from her family, which, granted, is more broken than most. But don’t expect her to stick it out here…” He notched his head toward the ranch. “She wasn’t born with a silver spoon, she was born with a gold one. When the novelty of whatever you two are doing together wears off, she’ll come back to me.”

Theo took one step forward, leaned down an inch to get in the guy’s face, and leveled him with a look. “Get the hell out of here.”

“You think you’re so tough in your dirty shirt.” EJ curled his lip. “Ayla’s gonna regret this. I’ll make sure of it.”

“Take your lame ass threats and go.”

EJ let out a breath and pivoted, walking to the car as Ayla returned to Theo’s side, carrying a purse, with a defeated slump in her shoulders.

EJ peeled out, spitting dirt and gravel and scaring the crap out of Clementine.

“You okay?” he asked, reaching for Ayla. “What was that all about with Trina?”

She looked up at him, her eyes swimming with tears. “She’s punishing me,” she said with a break in her voice.

"She's literally punishing me. She has our grandmother's wedding ring and refuses to give it back. She knows how much it means to me."

"What?"

"She called it ransom. When I come home, I can have it."

"Is it worth that much?"

She shook her head. "It's worth next to nothing, at least to her. To me? It's everything. Nana Jo loved that ring, and my grandfather. She said it represents love that lasts a lifetime. You can't put a price on that kind of sentimental value."

"Then we're going to get it back for you."

She held up a trembling hand. "I don't want to talk about it right now, Theo. I don't want to think about it. It's very hard for me not to want to make people happy, and Trina and my parents are very, very unhappy with me for leaving."

He pulled her into him and wrapped her in a hug. "They have a weird way of showing love."

"It's control, not love," she said on a sigh. "God, I got so cheated in the family department."

"Well, you can borrow mine." He pulled back and looked at her, the echo of her ex's words still in his head. He had to stomp those words out. "Come to Waterford for dinner tonight. Wednesday night's always a big family night, and even better, my brother Nick gets in this afternoon. It'll be great and you'll forget about this."

She searched his face, thinking. "Can I be honest?"

"I don't want you to be anything else."

"I don't think I can take all that family love tonight. Not when I still have the stench of mine all over me. I'll stay home with Marie tonight, if you don't mind."

"I do mind, but I understand." He burrowed his fingers into her hair and brought his mouth to hers, kissing her long and hard to show her that.

Chapter Twenty

Ayla had talked enough about the day's events with Marie. Right now, the only thing she wanted to do was stand in this shower until her skin was red from the hot water and then go to bed. She didn't want to think. Didn't want to cry anymore. Didn't want to…

What was that noise?

She flipped off the faucet and realized it was the very unfamiliar sound of her cell phone ringing. She'd forgotten what that sounded like. She pulled the shower curtain back and squinted at the screen, half expecting the call to be from EJ, but then she remembered she'd blocked his number.

She'd also let Theo put his number into her phone, which would explain why the caller ID said Navy Guy. Smiling, she grabbed a towel to wipe her hands.

"Navy Guy, huh?" She couldn't help laughing a little at that.

"What are you doing?" His voice was low, sexy, and nearly drowned out by the noise in the background.

She glanced down at her soaking-wet, naked body, an unholy thrill dancing through her as she thought about telling him the truth. "Not much. Why?"

"Please borrow Marie's truck and come to Bushrod's."

"Bushrod's?" She made a face. "What is that?"

"Oh, the Bitter Bark Bar is what you'll need for GPS. Not that it's hard to find. It's on Ambrose Avenue across from the square."

She frowned, wiping a droplet of water from her eyes. "What's happening at Bushrod's?"

"An informal family after-dinner party. We always come here after Wednesday night dinners. My brother's in town, and everyone's in such a great mood, and…" She could practically hear him take a steadying breath. "I miss you so much, Ayla."

She closed her eyes as the words rolled over her with the same heat as that shower water. "Well, you had me at 'family after-dinner party,'" she confessed. "The part where you miss me is icing on the cake."

"So you'll come? I know you were feeling kind of blue about your family, and I want to help you. And hold you."

How could she say no to that?

"Yes, but I need to get dressed. I'm…in the shower."

"Oh." She heard the soft grunt. "I could come and get you."

She laughed softly. "I can drive there." She heard an outburst of laughter in the background. "Don't have too much fun without me."

"No promises. The Greeks are rowdy. Plates could break."

Chuckling, she said goodbye and suddenly had more energy than she'd thought possible.

Less than an hour later, she was still charged when she opened the heavy wooden door of the Bitter Bark Bar and was immediately hit with noise and music and the lingering smell of fried food and beer.

Then she saw Theo, threading his way through the tables to meet her at the door, looking sexy and tall and gorgeous. Somehow, his short, military-cut hair looked a tad bit tousled and his soft-blue button-down a tiny bit rumpled, the sleeves rolled up to show a dusting of dark hair on his forearms. And the smile? Like someone had turned the lights on.

"You made it." He kissed her right on the mouth, giving her a light hug in greeting.

"Did I miss the plate throwing?"

"No plates broken yet, but the freaking Irish are drinking us under the table. Come on." He put an arm around her and guided her to a huge group of tables pushed together near a dance floor, giving her a chance to say hello to the many people in his family she already knew.

This was mostly the younger set, she realized, with no sign of Daniel, Katie, or the grannies. And none of the little ones, obviously. But all of the Kilcannons and their significant others were gathered, along with the Mahoney brothers, and Ella perched on a table like she was holding court.

Cassie immediately came over and gave Ayla a hug.

"So happy you're here, Ayla!" The words were as warm as this wonderful woman's smile, and all of the friction from the afternoon encounter with her sister and EJ seemed to melt away. "We're drinking pitchers tonight. Want a beer?"

"Sure." But before she could follow, John and Summer joined them, arm in arm, glowing like two people who'd been sprinkled with fairy dust.

"I have a feeling this is going to be three days of partying," John said as he gave her a hug. "You'd think no one in the Santorini family ever got married before."

"Ahem!" Cassie returned with two glasses, giving one to Ayla. "I was the first to fall. You are the second."

"Well, you're the first Santorini *son*," Summer said, smiling up at John. "So maybe that's why all the excitement. And didn't you and Braden have a surprise wedding, Cassie? That was before my time with this crew."

"We did. And it cut out all this prewedding stuff."

"A surprise wedding?" Ayla drew back. "Why does that sound like a reality TV show?"

Cassie laughed and held her hand out to the good-looking man in a navy Bitter Bark Fire Department T-shirt who came to her side. "Because we're crazy like that, right, Braden?"

He said hello to Ayla, too, and in a matter of seconds, Alex and Grace joined the circle.

"You two should have been the ones getting married next," Cassie said, poking Alex.

"Yeah, you should have done it this weekend," Theo added. "While Nick and I are in town."

"We're too busy putting on weddings at the winery," Alex said, draping his arm over the cool and beautiful winemaker who was never far from his side. "We're actually planning a quiet elopement followed by a big bash. Right, Grace?"

"If you tell them about it, it's not eloping, Alex. But he's right. When you host weddings every weekend, running off to Vegas has a certain appeal."

Theo looked over Ayla's head, a frown pulling. "Where's Nick? I want to introduce him to Ayla."

"I'm right here." A tall, dark-haired man who looked

like he might have eight or ten years on Theo stepped up from behind him. "You must be the enigmatic animal communicator this family is buzzing about. Nick Santorini."

She shook his hand, offering a warm smile. "I was lured here pretty easily, so I don't know how enigmatic I am. All it took was the promise of Greeks throwing plates. I'm Ayla Hollis, Nick. Nice to meet you."

"The plates break at the wedding," Cassie said.

"Not in our winery," Alex cracked. "You can spit at Summer, and she can step on John's feet, and for God's sake, someone write something on the bottom of her shoes. But no plates will break."

Ayla looked from one to the other. "Confused," she admitted. "They're going to spit on you, Summer?"

The other woman laughed. "Not literally, but I understand it's to protect me from evil spirits."

"Yiayia has already had her way with you," Cassie joked. "But do be sure to step on John's foot, so you always have the upper hand."

"Like she doesn't have it now," John said. "Along with Destiny, who is the real boss of the family."

"And you'll dance last," Alex added, "so we can all stick money on you." He glanced at Grace, whose eyes were wide. "And now she *really* wants to elope."

"And miss all that awesome Greek tradition?" Ayla asked. "I think it sounds like fun."

Nick leaned closer to Theo. "If she's not afraid of Greek weddings…" He was as good-looking as his brothers, but different, too. "You might have yourself a winner, brother."

"I've been talking you up to Nick," he admitted to Ayla, leaning down to whisper the explanation.

She smiled over her glass at Theo, wondering if he noticed the chills that his words and soft breath had caused to cascade all over her.

"I understand you're here from Africa," she said to Nick. "Doctors Without Borders?"

"Yep. I'm the one who gets back here even less frequently than Theo. But that could change."

"Really?" She sipped and waited for a little more elaboration, but he only gave a smile and ran his fingers through his dark hair, making her notice a few silver threads at the temples. She seemed to recall Theo saying Nick was nearly ten years older, which would put him around forty-four. And his brown eyes weren't as ebony as Cassie's or the twins', nor did they have the green of Theo's.

But then, he was Daniel's biological son, and knowing that, she could imagine she saw something of a Kilcannon in the angle of his jaw and his nose.

"Are you thinking of leaving the organization?" she asked so he didn't notice how carefully she was examining his looks.

"I'm thinking of a lot of things," he said, smiling to acknowledge that if anyone was being enigmatic right then, it was him. "Theo tells me you have a fascinating job."

"Well, it's not really a job yet, and Theo is…" She looked up at him, a little surprised at how he was smiling at her. "A little skeptical of my skills."

"A lot skeptical," Nick said. "But if there's anything my brother does well, besides nuclear engineering, it's protect people. And I've heard him tell more than one person—myself included—that you are pretty good at what you do."

The compliment warmed her as much as Theo's continued defense of her abilities. She slid her arm around his waist.

"He's sweet like that."

"Sweet?" Nick snorted. "He can take a man down with one well-placed kick."

And thought about doing that earlier today, she thought, sharing a quick, secret look with Theo.

"Are you here alone, Nick, or did you bring someone to the States with you?" Ayla remembered Theo saying Nick had a serious girlfriend.

"I'm solo," he said. "Lucienne didn't want to make the long flight."

"Your girlfriend is French, right? An anesthesiologist?"

He nodded and glanced at Theo. "You can all stop planning the trip to Paris for the next wedding, brother. That isn't in the cards." The disappointment in his voice was evident.

"All the more reason to come to Bitter Bark," Theo said, lifting his glass. "Let Yiayia and Gramma Finnie loose on the female population of North Carolina, and you'll forget Luci soon enough."

Nick's eyes flickered like...he didn't hate that idea. Which surprised Ayla. Why would he want to forget his girlfriend?

But before she could ask any questions to glean more about this man, John asked Summer to dance as the first few notes of a familiar country song started playing.

"That music's not for Greek dancing, I'm guessing," Ayla said to Theo.

"They want to save that for the big night," he said. "John's the dance leader, and I think he wants to hold his bride and not circle around her." He looked toward the floor as Tim McGraw started singing "It's Your Love."

"Do you like country music?" she asked.

"When in North Carolina..." He took her hand and urged her toward the dance floor. "And when I'm with someone I want to hold in my arms, then yes. Big fan."

She happily set her glass down and walked with him, wrapping her arms around his neck as the music filled the bar, and couples filled the dance floor. She leaned into him, picking up musky scents that were getting all too familiar and feeling the carved muscles that she so wanted to know better.

Tucked close, she looked up at him. "So. You missed me, huh?"

"I did. Blame Nick."

"I can't blame anyone, but what did Nick do?"

"Made me realize some things when I talked to him."

She searched his face, thinking. "He's not happy in his relationship."

"What was your first clue?" He shook his head. "The man wants a family, and he's with a woman who flat out says no."

"Oh, then he should break up with her and find someone else."

"I think they're tangled up pretty good," he said, adding a little pressure as if *tangled up pretty good* was exactly what he wanted.

"So, what about that made you miss me?" she asked, trying to imagine the brothers' conversation.

He looked at her for a long time, holding her gaze, hardly moving to the music. "You're going to make me say it, aren't you?"

"I'm curious, that's all. Nick is in a less-than-great relationship and talked to you, and that compelled you to call me and ask me to meet you here. How does that work?"

He grunted a laugh and looked skyward, making her laugh at his reluctance to talk about things like this.

"Okay," she said, adding some pressure to the muscles in his shoulders that she gripped. "Let me ask in language you like. How do you connect A and B to get to C?"

"Do math, and I'm yours forever," he joked.

His forever. Why did that sound so…tempting?

"A is Nick in a bad relationship, and C is inviting me to town for a drink and a dance. What was B?" she asked.

"B." He coasted his hands up and down her waist, splaying his huge hands like he wanted to get as much of her in them as possible. "Is my brother telling me that life goes fast and that I should make sure I have my priorities in line. You, Ayla Hollis, are a priority."

Her chest tightened at the thought. "How did that happen?" she whispered as much to herself as to him.

"I don't know. But what I do know is that I'm reaching my quota on talking about feelings."

She smiled. "And then what happens?"

His gaze grew heated, and he lowered his face to lightly kiss her lips. The contact was electric, with the sound of a love song and the feel of his warm body making her lightheaded.

When he lifted his head, he gave her a look that curled her toes and threatened to buckle her knees. Then he eased his hand up her back, somehow managing to nestle her even deeper into him, so she turned her head and let it relax on his deliciously broad shoulder.

Only then, when she opened her eyes, did she realize they were surrounded by his family.

Braden and Cassie were a few feet away, gazing into

each other's eyes. Alex and Grace laughed and stopped dancing long enough to share a kiss. John and Summer looked lost in palpable bliss. And beyond that, his extended family was scattered around the dance floor.

Darcy had her eyes closed against Josh's shoulder, and Declan held his pregnant wife like she was made of crystal as they smiled at each other. Shane and Chloe were cracking up more than they were dancing, like Liam and Andi. At the edge of the dance floor, Trace had his arm around Molly, and Beck sat on Aidan's lap, her arms draped over his shoulders as they talked.

Connor and Sadie were kissing, and Garrett and Jessie looked like they could be the ones getting married this weekend.

All this *love*. The impact of it nearly knocked Ayla over more than the kiss.

What a family. What an incredibly, unique treasure of a people Theo had in his corner. It made her whole body ache with a different kind of longing, not like the need for food or sex or even another kiss.

This was bone-deep and different. This was a need that reached down into her very soul and grabbed at her. She'd been cheated in the family department, as she'd told him, and he said she could borrow his.

But she couldn't borrow his family…without him. So now, when they parted ways, she would not only lose the most intriguing and attractive man she'd ever met, she'd lose the family of her dreams.

She tightened her hold on him a little, out of fear and frustration and that visceral longing for everything he offered. *Everything*.

She squeezed her eyes shut, and when she opened them, her gaze landed on Nick, standing way back at the tables, his arms crossed, his expression a mirror image of what she imagined hers looked like. Nick looked like a man longing for something, too.

She lifted her head and gazed up at Theo, lost in eyes that were smoky green in the bar light.

As much as the warmth and love that surrounded this man, she wanted *him*. His attention, his intelligence, his body, and…his heart.

For now, she'd better settle for the easy stuff. That was probably all she was destined to get, as this interlude in Bitter Bark would have to end somehow. No family, no great love, no…forever.

Lifting herself a little, she let her lips brush his. He intensified the kiss, adding heat and letting out the softest moan as they connected.

If that's all she got, she'd take it. She wanted him that much.

Chapter Twenty-One

Theo had seen a lot of cute things in his life, a lot of beauty in the world that made him purely happy to be alive. But a five-year-old girl with flowing curls and a poufy pink dress walking side by side down the aisle with a barely one-year-old Labrador to the tune of "You Are My Sunshine"? That pretty much took the winning slot for Most Adorable Sight Ever.

Destiny clung to her little basket of rose petals, fluttering them to the floor as she walked, her dear little face locked in a serious expression. Maverick kept pace with her, the box holding the wedding rings wobbling from a ribbon around his neck.

Theo's vantage point as a groomsman gave him a perfect view of the little girl, who was stealing hearts with the same speed she was dropping the petals. To his right, Nick stood as straight as any military man, fighting a smile as he watched. Next to him, Alex, the *koumbaro*—best man at a Greek wedding—shook his head at what the chef would probably call a saccharine overdose.

Next to him, John's face radiated so much love, Theo almost fell off the raised altar platform.

Had anyone ever loved a stepchild the way John Santorini loved Destiny? Doubtful. Although there were a lot of "steps" in this family, and John certainly had some competition for that special kind of love. But Theo had never seen anyone more up for the task of fatherhood than his older brother.

Theo's gaze moved over to the bridesmaids, sharing a smile with Cassie, who'd become so close to Summer that she was the maid of honor. Next to her was a woman he'd just met—Raven Jackson, who was Destiny's aunt and Summer's late husband's sister. Raven's stunning Halle Berry vibe showed how much of Destiny's remarkable beauty came from her father's side.

In the front row, Summer's parents beamed at their grandchild, and Theo's mom dabbed at tears with one hand while holding Daniel's hand with the other.

Next to them, Yiayia and Gramma Finnie were also holding hands, probably to keep themselves from high-fiving for yet another successful match.

That thought made him shift his attention back a few rows to the woman he'd brought as his date tonight. Ayla sat with Marie, both of them smiling at the sight of Destiny.

It was literally impossible for him to breathe for a second, and not just because the tie around his neck was tight. Ayla was…breathtaking.

She wore a strapless black dress with bands of white along the edges, her impossibly thick hair piled up into some kind of knot with a few wavy caramel-colored strands falling over bare shoulders. Around her neck was a thin choker made of what looked like hundreds of diamonds sparking the candlelight the way her eyes did.

With her full "glamour" makeup, including shiny pink

lips, he found it hard to take his eyes off her. He stared long enough for her to meet his gaze and hold it for three or four body-rocking heartbeats, the corners of her glossy lips lifting in a secret smile.

Then, the cutesy music stopped, and something loud and dramatic started as the doors opened to reveal Summer, who had chosen to walk down the aisle alone. It made sense since she was a young widow who'd done the big wedding once before.

In deference to that, she wore the palest pink dress that skimmed the floor and a short veil that was somehow understated but perfectly traditional.

She looked up, her gaze locked on John, and Theo could have sworn he felt the whole church vibrate with the love that arced over that aisle.

This was the way it should be, he thought, a little surprised by how his eyes stung. Just like this. Kind of *magical*.

He'd never felt that way with Heather. He'd never felt that way…period. Was he even capable of that kind of emotion? It seemed foreign and terrifying and daunting and…

Once more, he caught Ayla's gaze.

Possible.

Didn't that woman prove over and over that magic *was* possible?

Blowing out a breath, he forced himself to stop his wildly out-of-character thoughts and watch the ceremony, which was a wonderful blend of Summer's Protestant upbringing and the color of his family's culture.

At the moment when vows were about to be exchanged, John and Summer walked over to the bridal attendants in a move that had definitely not been practiced at the rehearsal last night. Destiny's face registered shock as they both took her by the hand and walked her up to the altar for the vows.

There, in a faltering voice that brought everyone to tears, John promised in front of God, family, and the world that he would not only love, honor, and cherish Summer Jackson, but he also vowed to love, protect, and adopt Destiny as his daughter…until death parted any of them.

At that moment, Nick slid a look to Theo. "I'm dead," he muttered.

"Seriously," Theo agreed.

By the time they'd exchanged rings, received a blessing, and wore the traditional Greek crowns, everyone in the church was drained from the emotional ceremony.

"I forgot what a *thing* a Greek wedding is," Theo whispered to Nick.

"An amazing thing," Nick said, both of them as solemn as the rest of the occasion.

John and Summer kissed and, with Destiny and Maverick, headed back down the aisle to thunderous applause and a standing ovation.

After that, true to a Greek wedding, nothing else was solemn. Even the trip to Overlook Glen, where the early May weather cooperated with a perfect late afternoon, was raucous with laughter and toasts in the limo.

Ayla traveled with Marie, meeting Theo at the winery. But not until after he'd posed for what felt like a million pictures with family, sharing hors d'oeuvres and champagne on the huge veranda with a 360-degree view of vineyards and mountains.

After all that, he was finally free and more than ready to be done with groomsman activities. He scanned the sea of tables dressed with white linen and hundreds of flickering candles for the woman in the strapless black dress.

He found her at a table with Marie, Yiayia, Gramma Finnie, and the man he'd met in the square the other night, Aldo Fiore. He could hear their laughter as he approached the table.

"There he is now, lass," Gramma Finnie said, putting a gnarled old hand on Ayla's shoulder to turn her toward Theo.

"And trust me, your name is written on the bottom of Summer's shoe," he heard Yiayia say. "I put it there myself."

"I'm sure you did," Ayla said on a laugh, standing up to greet Theo. "I now know the meaning behind every Greek, Irish, and Italian wedding tradition," she told him, gesturing to the three octogenarians who'd been entertaining her. "I hope you have a sugar cube in your pocket."

He produced his, a heart-shaped thing that they'd been given in the dressing room. "I hope you practiced your fake spitting on the bride."

She chatted and laughed a little more with the oldsters, giving him the impression this little group had already formed enough of a bond to have inside jokes. He stayed and talked politely, especially to Aldo, who seemed like a nice enough guy.

But what Theo really wanted to do was whisk Ayla away to go check out the sunset, sip some champagne, and get about as close to her as he could.

Finally, he got his wish when Aldo got up to refill everyone's glasses, so Theo and Ayla joined hands and said goodbye.

"This is the most beautiful winery," she cooed as they walked across the huge patio. This venue had been the site of many weddings since Alex had left Santorini's Deli to be the head chef here and live with Grace, who owned the winery. "And that wedding we saw today? Unbelievable."

"Destiny kind of stole the show," he said, grabbing them two flutes of champagne and thanking the server who'd offered them.

"She deserved to." She lifted her glass to him. "The groomsman on the end was pretty fine, too."

He smiled at her. "He was distracted by the beauty in black and her sparkly diamonds." He grazed the necklace with his fingertips.

"The only piece of my wedding attire I saved," she admitted.

"I can see why." It had to be worth a fortune.

She touched his glass. "What are we drinking to, Theo?"

He thought for a minute about all the things he could say. *To us. To tonight. To tomorrow morning when we wake up in each other's arms.* To crazy possibilities and upside-down lives and those priorities his brother Nick kept talking to him about.

"Uh-oh. That's a lot of…feelings on your face," she teased. "You're scaring me, Navy Guy."

He laughed a little. "There are so many things with you," he admitted.

"What kinds of things?"

Things that scared him and thrilled him and made everything in his life feel like it needed to shift. "To… priorities."

"That sounds serious for such a festive occasion."

Maybe it was. "We're here because my brother has his all straight," he said.

"Well, to hear Yiayia and Finnie, we're here because they snagged Summer right off the street and convinced her to marry *Yianni* right then and there."

He laughed. "That sounds about right." He raised his glass. "Then we'll drink to the Dogmothers."

As they touched glasses, his gaze moved over her shoulder and met the eyes of his grandmother, who stared right back with that same victorious look she'd worn in the church.

Before he sipped, he added a slight lift of the flute in her direction, and she raised her glass right back at him.

By the time dinner, toasts, slow dancing, more toasts, and cake was served, the wedding guests were juiced and ready for the Greek dancing. And once it started, there was no stopping the ever-growing circle of people arm in arm and surrounding John and Summer and Destiny.

There, everyone howled with laughter and hooted their best "Opa!" even if they didn't have a drop of Mediterranean blood in them. Especially if they didn't, based on how well Braden Mahoney could dance the sirtaki.

"He's good at that," Ayla mused, watching him.

"He married a Santorini," Theo replied. "He better be."

Holding Ayla and sharing belly laughs with her as they danced, Theo suddenly noticed Nick was missing.

As one song rolled into another, he gave Ayla a tug. "Break?" he asked.

"Definitely. Water would be great."

They slipped out of the circle, along with some others, and walked to their table. "Have you seen Nick?" he asked.

"Wasn't he dancing?"

He shook his head. "I think he might be struggling with it."

"Struggling? You just said all Santorinis can dance like that."

"Oh, he can do the dances. My dad and grandfather did them every week, but…" He scanned the smattering of people, very few at tables now, as they mingled, drank, and danced. "You know, when he found out that he's Daniel's son, he became…not Greek. Literally. They found out the truth through a DNA test, and he doesn't have a single percentage of Greek in him."

"Oh." Frowning, she took her water from her place setting. "I know that can be true on a scientific level, but look at Summer. She's no more Greek than I am, but she embraced so many of these wonderful traditions."

"But Nick got the rug yanked out from under him. One day he was fifty percent Greek, the next day he was half-Irish instead."

She took a deep drink of water and shook her head. "I'm not picking up any kind of resentment from him at all. Other things, like maybe he is on the verge of breaking up with that French girl, but he gave a beautiful toast as the head of the family. Touching, really. And he treats Daniel with the utmost respect."

"I don't know." He looked around again because it wasn't like his brother to disappear.

She pressed a hand to his chest. "Look at you, getting all emotional and feely." She grinned. "I like it."

He put down his glass and held her warm gaze, putting Nick out of his mind and Ayla back in it. "I like you."

"Mmm." She leaned in, looking up at him. "It's mutual, you know."

Kissing her was so natural now, he never hesitated, and this time was no different, especially standing alone in the shadows like this. Pulling her into him, he pressed his lips to her ear.

"I got a room with a vineyard view," he whispered, feeling her shudder in his arms. "Not that I plan on looking at anything but you."

She drew back, her dark eyes nearly black as she leveled her gaze at him. "How long does this shindig go on, Théodoros?" she asked in a husky voice that made him want to kiss her again.

So he did.

"That's the bad news about Greek weddings," he told her, touching her lower lip with his index finger because it was so damn soft. "We can't leave until after the last dance. And that has to be John and Summer."

"They're not going anywhere for a while," she said on a laugh. "But I can wait."

Heat pulsed through his whole body with the need to kiss her again, but another couple walked by, laughing and talking. "Let's take a walk in the vineyard."

"In these?" She held out a slender ankle, showing him a deadly pair of four-inch heels. "I forgot my shitkickers."

"There's a stone path and I'll hold you tight," he promised. "Let's go down this way…" He eased her over the stone floor to the edge of the huge outdoor deck, leading her to some stairs.

The music faded a little as they walked down toward the vineyards, but maybe that was Theo's blood thumping with the familiar drumbeat of need for Ayla. The lights dimmed, too, as they walked deeper into the dark, following a stone path that led to lush rows of grapes, the earthy, sweet smell almost as intoxicating as the wine they made.

"Are you cold?" he asked. "I could have grabbed my jacket."

"No, I'm fine." She snuggled into him, arm in arm, leaning against him for balance in her treacherous but hot-as-hell shoes. "Where are we going?"

"Somewhere…" He slipped them down another row and around to a small building. "Private."

"Inside?"

"This is the wine-press room," he said. "I'm sure it's locked. But look, what's over there?"

She followed his gaze to a huge tree. "A picnic table."

"Calling our name." He stopped and kissed her, dragging his hands up and down her waist and hips, easing her into him to let their bodies press against each other. As they kissed to the table, he was lost in the heat and touch and ache that pulsed through his blood.

"C'mere," he murmured, lifting her onto the side of the table and getting close to kiss her.

She lifted her legs, and her swooshy dress slid higher so he could get right where he wanted to be. Body to body, mouth to mouth, they moaned in unison as the heat built.

"We gotta make it to the room," she murmured on a laugh, arching her back in a way that made him think they might *not* make it to the room.

He slid his hands over the dress, over her breasts and up to her throat. She lifted her chin so he could nuzzle and kiss the sweet, soft flesh while she wrapped her legs tighter around him.

Her whole body vibrated with each breathless gasp she released, tempting him to explore her parted thighs so he could finally know what she felt like.

Suddenly, they heard laughter, much closer than the wedding, and the slam of a door.

They both froze, still wrapped around each other.

He turned toward the sound of a whispered conversation and another laugh.

There was enough ambient light from the wedding for him to recognize the couple slipping out of the press building. The man he knew, of course, but the woman in the long bridesmaid's dress? Yeah, he recognized her.

Ayla took in a very soft breath of surprise as she recognized the couple, too. They both stayed perfectly still while the other two people, possibly arm in arm, laughed again and disappeared into the vineyard, heading back to the stairs Ayla and Theo had just come down.

"Well," she said. "Now you know where Nick is."

He broke into a slow smile. "Nick and Raven?"

"They're gorgeous together," she said. "And can you imagine the babies?"

"Babies? You sound like Yiayia."

"Whose services weren't needed, unless she sent them down to tour the winemaking facilities. I don't put anything past her."

He laughed, looking back in the direction the other couple had disappeared. Nick and Raven?

"Hey," she said, her hand on his chin to turn him back to her. "Now we know the door is unlocked." She dragged her hand down his chest, looking up at him with unmistakable lust in her eyes. He damn near buckled.

But then he heard the music and a loud shout, and the strains of the song were familiar and welcome. "The Kalamatiano," he said.

"Something tells me that's not an olive."

"The Bride's Dance," he said. "And that means…the end is near. Or…in our case…" Another kiss as he hungrily caressed her body over the dress he couldn't wait to take off. "The beginning of our first night together."

She let out a sigh and reluctantly eased him away to pull down her dress. "That sounds…heavenly."

"It will be. I promise."

Chapter Twenty-Two

Ayla's high heels were off halfway up the stairs to the third floor of Overlook Glen, making it easier to climb to the cozy room with a fireplace and a four-poster bed that Theo had arranged for them to share that night.

After the dizzying dance around and around the bride and groom, not very many women in the place had managed to stay in their shoes. And, no surprise, Ayla's hair had fallen into a tangled mess from all the dancing.

Thank God Theo was an engineer with a plan and had gotten her bag long ago from Marie's truck and left it in the room. Grateful for that, for the privacy, and for the amazing night, Ayla let out a blissful sigh as she headed to the balcony and looked out at the moon rising over the mountains in the distance.

"You sound tired." Theo came up behind her and wrapped his arms around her, dropping a kiss on her bare shoulder.

"Tired from dancing, which are words I never thought I'd utter."

He moaned softly, lifting her hair with one hand to plant more kisses and splaying his fingers greedily over her stomach.

"It's a test of your endurance," he murmured. "Greeks have been doing it since Sparta."

"Did I pass?"

"With…" He nibbled her skin, making her shiver. "Flying…" He dragged the tip of his tongue along the nape of her neck. "Colors." His mouth pressed harder as his hand moved lower and lower down her body.

A little dizzy at his touch, she turned slowly in his arms, reaching up to clasp his head in her hands.

"What other tests can I take?" she asked with a sultry tease in her voice.

His eyes shuttered as his whole body grew tense and hard. "Doesn't matter. You'll get an A for…Ayla." He breathed her name, the sound of it almost reverent on his lips. "How did you do this to me?"

She lifted a brow and let her gaze flicker south. "It wasn't that, um, difficult."

"I don't mean the obvious physical response," he admitted gruffly. "I mean all of this." He kissed her again, turning her whole body to walk her to the bed.

"I am crazy about you." He punctuated that pronouncement with another kiss as he eased her onto the silky comforter. "How did that happen?"

"Clementine," she said on a laugh as they laid down together, but he stayed slightly propped over her. "Blame the dog who thinks about you almost as much as I do. Or should I not be reminding you of the one thing about me you don't like?"

He gave her a look like she was out of her mind. "There's nothing about you I don't like," he said, trailing a finger over her collarbone and sliding it lower toward the rise of her breasts. "Except…this dress."

"You don't like it?"

"I'd like it better on the floor. What's underneath?"

"Not much," she admitted, biting her lip. "Just a little lacy thong I picked up at that French boutique in town. Very little."

His eyes softened the way they did when his grandmother put spanakopita in front of him.

"A thong, huh?" He put a hand on her thigh and let it travel up. "I better get a good look at that to make sure it's…regulation."

She chuckled, but that melted into a sigh as he slowly rolled her over and found the zipper to her dress. Sliding it open at a maddeningly slow pace, he placed kisses down her back every few inches.

When he reached the end, she turned and lifted her hips so he could take it off, baring everything but the black lace thong she'd chosen for tonight. His gaze moved over her like she imagined his hands were about to, hot and hungry and wildly appreciative.

"Not even fair," he murmured as he took the dress all the way off, but he didn't toss it on the floor at all. Instead, he slid off the bed without taking his eyes off her and very carefully placed the dress on the back of a chair, like the neat military man he was.

She propped up on her elbows, loving the way he looked at her, feeling sexy and confident and strong. His gaze zeroed in on her thong.

"Not regulation, Hollis." He knelt on the bed, looming over her as he loosened his tie. "That little thing you call underwear will have to go."

She wanted to smile, but her whole body was quivering

with need. She wanted to reach up and unbutton that tux shirt, but watching him strip was too much fun. She wanted to keep joking about things that kept this light, but suddenly it didn't feel light at all.

It felt real.

He popped the studs like a pro and dragged the shirt over his shoulders, revealing every insane muscle. She'd seen them before at the ranch. She'd touched them under his T-shirts. But somehow, this was different.

He wasn't so gentle with his own shirt, which did end up on the floor, along with his belt and pants and socks, leaving him in black boxer briefs. He straddled her on the bed, his hazel eyes tapered and focused and fiery.

"Nope," he whispered, sliding his hand into the tiny bit of lace that happened to be the first thing Ayla had put on her credit card when she'd gotten it. "Not regulation at all."

He lowered himself slowly, sliding the thong down her legs with more kisses planted along the way. Each time his mouth pressed against her flesh, she shuddered and moaned and melted a little more.

She clung to his shoulders, wrapped her legs around his hips, and closed her eyes to let every other sense take over. She inhaled his scent, a mix of barely-there cologne, the winery wedding, and the musky fragrance of a very turned-on man.

All of it filling her head, making her dizzy.

He explored every inch of her body, touching her with capable hands that were somehow both tender and tough, gentle on her skin, but callused from the work on the ranch. With each delirious moment, her nerves seemed to tighten and dance, and her skin grew hot and tight.

When he kissed her, she took his tongue against hers,

tasting the remnants of almonds from the candy they'd shared after the last dance and the salty flavor of his kisses. She pressed her lips to his neck and chest and abs, wanting to devour every inch of hard, male muscle that made her feel so incredibly alive and fiery.

She listened to his ragged breaths, his sexy words, his breathless repetition of her name as he kissed his way from thigh to throat and let his fingers touch everything in the wake of his mouth.

He sat up and snagged a condom he must have put on the nightstand when he'd dropped off her bag. Yes, looking at Theo might be the headiest sensation of all, drinking in the cuts of his muscles, the purple ink of a Navy tattoo on his shoulder, the dark dusting of hair on his chest.

As he opened the packet and put on the condom, she reached up and touched his chest, not surprised to feel his heart hammering like hers.

"You have it, you know," he whispered, pressing her hand harder over his heart.

His heart? "I do?" The declaration stunned her. "I thought I only had…" Her gaze dropped over his body. "The rest of you."

"You have it all." He dropped down on top of her again, kissing her gently on the lips. "Don't look so shocked. You can read minds."

But he didn't believe that. Because if he did, if he *truly* did? Then she *would* have it all. She'd have his body, soul, heart, and mind. And she wanted that.

"I can't read yours," she said.

"Then I'll tell you what I'm thinking…" He nestled against her, pulling her legs up so they circled him again. "Later."

"Now," she said as he entered her. "Tell me what you're thinking right now."

"I'm not thinking," he said, letting his eyes close as the pleasure of the first contact washed over both of them. "I'm feeling." He closed all the space between them, putting his mouth by her ear to whisper, "That's what's so damn scary."

But nothing seemed scary about the way he moved inside her, or the way he held her and kissed her and found places to touch that made her want to scream. Maybe he was scared, but Ayla was…lost.

She forgot to concentrate on her senses, because everything rolled together in a crescendo of heat and bliss and exquisite pleasure. Everything was intensified, deeper and brighter and sweeter and lighter than anything she could remember.

Digging her fingers into his muscles, she forgot where she was…who she was…and all she could do was ride the rolling sensations until she let go and spun right out of control.

Not Theo. He never lost control. He never seemed to forget where he was or who he was, his concentration intense and forceful, like he could ride right along the edge of pleasure without giving in.

But, finally, he did, and she held him while he fell over that edge and whispered her name over and over and over.

For what felt like an hour, but was probably only a few minutes, they lay breathless and spent, unable and unwilling to move a muscle. He managed to kiss her cheek lightly, then rested his head next to hers.

"You never told me what you were feeling," she whispered.

"I'm not sure," he said, "because I've never felt it before. But I know there's a word for it."

Her heart skipped a beat as she waited. She knew there was a word for it, too. A wild, terrifying, impossible, perfect word that neither one of them could say.

Though maybe he meant…faith. Because they couldn't each love until he truly believed she was who and what she said.

Love would be easy and natural, but believing her? That was the real test.

Ayla woke from a deep, deep sleep with a start. She'd been dreaming about Clementine under a picnic table, crying. The image of that made Ayla whimper in her half-asleep state, and instantly, Theo tightened his grip around her waist and pulled her closer to his chest and hips.

"What's wrong?" The words were little more than a breath in her ear.

"Bad dream."

"Nothing can be bad tonight." He stroked her stomach and glided his hand up to caress her breasts, her whole body rested and ready for him again. "What did you dream about?" he asked.

"Clem."

His hand stilled. "Is that…like, a thing you do? See her dreams?"

She could tell he was trying to sound like he took that very seriously, but he might have been too tired to hide the truth.

"No, I can't see her dreams." Slowly, she turned

over, blinking into the darkness while she waited for the first hint of dawn to come in through the balcony doors. Then she could really see his expression. "But I can see what she's thinking." Did she want to take this up right now? Kind of, yes. "Whether you like that or not."

"I don't dislike it," he said quickly. "I never said I disliked it."

"But you don't believe it."

He let out a little groan like maybe it was too early for a discussion about anything. Too warm under these covers. And they were too naked and too crazy about each other to argue.

But the dream had upset her. And the truth was, she couldn't say all that she wanted or feel all that she wanted or even *do* all that she wanted until…this was settled.

"You have to believe me," she said softly. It really was that simple.

He searched her face, his eyes visible in the darkness now. "Do I?" he asked. "Can't we simply agree to…not completely agree?"

"Then what?" She sat up a little. "You think I'm lying?"

He put a hand on her shoulder and guided her back to the pillow. "I told you. I think you see what you see. And you think, or *believe*, that it's what's going on in the dog's head. But there's no empirical way to know that."

"So without empirical evidence, you don't believe me?"

He studied her for a long time. "Why do I feel like the honest answer is going to cost me the best wake-up sex I ever had?"

"It'll cost me, too." She moaned, knowing she really didn't want to pay that price, but had to. "But to be perfectly honest, it's not sex on the line." She smiled. "I won't punish myself because you're a stubborn engineer with no faith or imagination."

He didn't move except to frown. "Then what is on the line?"

"Everything else," she said softly.

His whole face fell.

"And if you ask what else is there, Theo Santorini, I will…laugh at myself for being a fool." She looked down, a little embarrassed by what she'd admitted. Because for all she knew, sex was the only thing he was thinking about with her. But it wasn't like that for her.

"You're not a fool."

When she didn't answer, he put his hand under her chin and lifted her face so she was forced to look at him.

"But let me make sure I understand what you're saying, Ayla. Anything we have—everything we have—is contingent on my believing you?" She could tell by the way he asked the question that he hated the idea of that. "We couldn't find a way around that?"

"We could," she said, "if we agree that this…this…" She gestured from him to her. "Is temporary. You're leaving when you get a job, and I…I don't know what I'm doing. Here or Charlotte, I haven't decided. This started as a game, got a little fun, and both of us were licking our wounds after being cheated on. If that's what we're doing here, then fine. We can agree to disagree."

"Are you kidding me?"

She was probably kidding herself, so she didn't answer.

"Because I wasn't *licking my wounds* last night," he said.

"Well, you were licking—"

He cut off her attempt at humor by putting his hand

over her lips. "I don't exactly know what this is between us, Ayla, but I don't see it as temporary."

He didn't?

"I don't see it as a way to pass time and have fun while I'm stuck between gigs. I don't see it as a way to get over my last relationship, which I have essentially forgotten existed, for the record. And I sure as hell don't see it as some kind of game."

She searched his face, the very first light of predawn letting her see how serious he was.

"Do you?" he demanded.

"No," she admitted. "If I did, this wouldn't matter. But the fact is, I can't fall for a man who thinks I'm either lying or too dumb to know if I'm right or wrong."

He choked softly. "I know you're not lying, and I know you're not dumb."

"But do you know that I have an ability that is real?"

He stared at her, painfully silent.

"I can't…" *Love someone who doesn't believe me.* "I can't change how I feel," she managed.

"Neither can I."

Then the truth was, he wasn't the man for her. She closed her eyes as she tried to accept that.

He'd never love the *real* her, and she'd never stop wanting him to. All the other stuff—where they lived, what they called this, how they moved forward from here? Nothing mattered if, at the most fundamental level, he didn't *get* her.

And he had to know that.

"Theo." She took a breath as she launched into what had to be said. "I swore that I would never again hide my true self for a man—not for my father, not for a husband, not even for a lover as incredible as you."

"Ayla, listen—"

She shook her head. "No, you listen. I came here at the lowest point of my life. The very lowest. And all I wanted was a new life. I got one. I let my inner voice sing out for the first time, and I ended up on national television and with clients who want my services. I found a way to not only help animals, but become truly independent. And with that new life came the smartest, cutest, sexiest, most intriguing and appealing and amazing man I've ever met."

"Can't we—"

She put her fingers to his lips. "And not only did I find that life and that man, I discovered…a family." Her voice cracked. "A veritable community of love and joy and dancing and laughter and support, filled with people willing to open their arms and give me a blanket of comfort that I have never known and have longed for every day of my life."

With each word, she saw his expression fall a little more. She didn't want to hurt him, but he had to know. He had to.

"But I will give it all up, Theo, to not return to the weak, spineless, people-pleaser I was. I will never again let myself be dismissed, disregarded, and bulldozed by people who think they're stronger and smarter."

He sat up slowly, shaking his head. "I am not that man," he said softly.

"But I'm afraid you are."

He frowned, looking around. "What is that? A phone vibrating?"

"It's coming from my purse," she said. "Ignore it."

He huffed out a sigh, looking like he'd much rather deal with a call than have this conversation. Then his phone rang, noisily, cutting through the silence in the room.

Wordlessly, he rolled over and reached to his pants on the floor, lifting them and fishing his phone from the pocket.

He snagged it and glanced at the screen. "It's Marie."

"Oh." She sat up with a pinch of worry. "That must have been her calling me."

He tapped the phone twice, putting it on speaker. "What's up, Marie? Before you say anything, I'm with—"

"She's gone!"

"What?" They asked the question in unison.

"Clementine! She's gone. I don't know where she went." Her voice rose to a screech. "I brought the dogs out early and went inside to get coffee and take a shower, and…I heard them barking, but I ignored it. Then…" She broke down into a sob. "I came back, and she's gone. Got through the fence in front somehow, I don't know. I don't know! But I cannot find her anywhere!"

"We'll be there as soon as possible, Marie," Theo told her. "Just keep looking. Keep calling for her. She can't have gone far."

Ayla dropped her head as the remnants of the dream punched her again, but she didn't dare say anything. She didn't dream about dogs when something went wrong… or *did* she? She'd never loved a dog quite as much as Clementine, who'd slept under her bed every night since Theo brought her to the ranch.

Theo was up already, pulling jeans out of an overnight bag. "We have to go find her."

"Should we get help?"

"We'll see who's at Waterford. Everyone else is here or nearby. Alex is making some huge wedding brunch for the family. I don't want to ruin that." He stepped into jeans and yanked up the zipper, staring at her. "Don't you want to come with me?" he asked, coming closer. "Please."

She simply couldn't move, paralyzed with…fear.

Something was wrong. Something was very wrong with Clem. How did she know that? If she didn't know, she sure didn't expect Theo to.

She pushed the covers back and dressed, both of them silent all the way back to the Last Chance Ranch.

Chapter Twenty-Three

A few seconds after Theo whipped onto the ranch drive, Daniel's Tahoe came barreling up the road from the direction of Waterford Farm. Theo wasn't surprised to see him, or Mom in the passenger seat, since Daniel had answered his phone on the first ring half an hour ago. And if they were surprised to see Ayla with him, neither one of them showed it.

Instead, they greeted each other solemnly as Miz Marie came tearing out of the front door.

"Any news?" Theo called, but from the ravaged look on her face, he sensed that if there was any news, it wasn't good.

She shook her head and went right to Ayla, hugging her. "I don't know what happened!"

"Were these gates open?" Theo asked, gesturing to the two long barricades that she normally closed if the dogs were out and about.

"Not locked, but closed. And latched."

Daniel walked over and examined the latch, while Theo's mother went to comfort Marie.

"Did you hear anything besides barking?" Daniel asked. "Voices or a car?"

"I was inside," Marie told them. "TV blaring, then in the shower. While I was in the shower, I heard the dogs bark, but I didn't think much of it. They get into tussles with the chickens and stuff. They bark." She pressed her hands to her face. "I've never lost a dog before."

Ayla hugged her again, whispering in Marie's ear, then stepped away, walking toward the side of the house along the chicken coop.

"We need to organize a search of the whole area," Theo said. "Who's at Waterford? Who's nearby?"

"Everyone else is out at the winery or at hotels near there," Daniel told him. "I don't have any staff at Waterford today."

"But if you call your brothers," his mother said, "they'd be here in a heartbeat."

"And everyone in my family," Daniel added.

Theo winced at the thought. "The wedding brunch is in a few hours. I can't do that to John. Who else could we call? Neighbors? Friends? We need to fan out and search."

Daniel had his phone out already.

"It's Sunday morning," Marie said. "People aren't around. If we walked into a few churches, we might get help."

"There's no other break in the fencing, right?" Theo asked, flipping through everything he knew about this property. "I know I fixed some on the other side of the goat pasture."

Marie shook her head. "Nothing I know of, and I just walked all of it. If she got beyond the fence? There's no telling where she could have gone."

His heart dropped at the thought. Clementine didn't know her way around here that well. Could she find her way back? Would someone find her?

"We called Garrett," his mother said. "He's put out one of his notices on social media. He's got an incredible network of contacts."

"I left messages at all the local shelters in case someone finds her and turns her in," Marie added.

"And she's chipped now," Daniel reminded. "Don't forget that."

If anyone found her, they could have her easily identified. It was a small consolation.

"Then we should start looking." Theo turned again, squinting at the surrounding areas. "We can break up into—"

"I don't think that's going to help us find her." Ayla came back, a weird expression on her face he couldn't quite read. But then, he hadn't been reading her so well since they woke up this morning.

"Why not?" he asked.

She glanced at him, seemingly hesitant to answer, then she looked at Marie. "She's not here."

"I know…I…" Marie frowned and inched closer. "What is it, kitten?"

Ayla sighed and turned a little away from Theo. "She's really gone," she said to Marie, her voice almost a hushed whisper. "I don't know how I know this, but she's not anywhere near here."

Daniel came closer, and so did Theo's mother, both of them looking intent and interested. Theo stayed stone-still and looked at her, worried where this could be going.

"Where do you think she is?" Daniel asked.

Ayla hugged herself, rubbing her arms. "I feel like…" She closed her eyes as if she were catching herself. Then, almost imperceptibly, she lifted her chin and threw Theo a challenging look. "I feel…I sense…that she's far away. I think someone's taken her."

"Did you see that?" Daniel asked.

Ayla shook her head. "I'm not getting images or visuals, no. But I feel something I've never experienced before. An emptiness, like she's…distant. Ever since we got Clementine, I've been able to sense her near me."

"Because she's never five feet away from you," Theo said, doing everything he could to temper his reaction. He didn't want to belittle her or…disregard her. He did *not*. But every minute they were standing here talking about feelings, Clem could be lost in the woods or hit by a car or attacked by a predator.

Ayla sighed softly. "It's very hard to explain," she said, "and even harder to believe, I *know*." She slid him a look on that last word. "But I walked the property, and I know, without a doubt, that she's far away. I think she's been taken in a car."

"She'd never willingly go with a stranger," Theo said. "And she's not trained enough to let someone she doesn't know pick her up."

Ayla shrugged, obviously not willing to argue with him.

"Well, then, we should call the cops," he said. "And while we wait for them, we need to fan out and search for her."

Daniel held up a hand, taking a step closer to Ayla. "Do you think there's something that might trigger more information?" he asked her. "Walking the street? Looking at a picture of Clem?"

Good God, Daniel, *seriously*?

"While you guys do that, I'm going to start walking," he said. "I'll head east down the road, in the direction of Waterford."

But Daniel followed him. “I think you should listen to the expert,” Daniel said softly, bringing Theo’s next step to a halt.

“Excuse me?”

“You’ve never heard of a psychic who solves crimes?” he asked. “They find missing children and see things that ordinary people don’t.”

“Because it’s not ordinary,” he shot back.

“It’s extraordinary,” Daniel responded, “and entirely possible. Someone could have driven up here and taken Clem.”

“Clementine wouldn’t go with a stranger,” he said.

“Maybe it wasn’t a stranger.”

But everyone else Clem knew was still asleep. Theo let out a sigh. “So what do you suggest we do?”

“I don’t know, but you can walk all over the woods and foothills if you like,” Daniel said. “I’m going to try and help Ayla to see if she can come up with something that can give us a clue that we can then give to law enforcement, shelters, and a search party.”

Okay, that made sense. A little sense.

Daniel turned and headed back to where the women stood. Theo kept walking, looking down as he tried to figure out how to handle this with Ayla. At the edge of the gate, his eyes caught something orange, but he kept on walking…until it registered.

Was that…

He whipped around and jogged back to what he now realized wasn’t just the color orange…it was an actual orange rind. He bent over and picked it up, taken back to the mini-mart.

This wasn’t the rind of an orange. It was from a clementine.

I got you an orange, girl. It's your favorite.

Chills popped on his skin as he heard the voice of a man he'd hoped he and Clementine would never see again.

Holy hell. Holy, holy *hell.* That human vermin came to get her.

And Ayla...*felt* it.

"I know who has her," he said, his words barely a whisper.

Ayla and the others jogged toward him, all of them staring at the rind he held. "What is that?" she asked.

"It's...empirical evidence."

"Of what?"

"That you're...absolutely right." He held the rind up. "Only one person knows her weakness for this fruit. He must have seen you on TV, and he came for Clementine."

"The guy from the mini-mart in Arkansas?" Her voice rose in shock. "Why?"

"I have no idea. Not for love, based on the way he treated her."

"The meth lab," Ayla whispered, putting her hand on her chest as the blood drained from her face. "He's scared I'm going to see something that he doesn't want me to see, so he came to get Clem."

It made perfect sense.

"Do you know this man's name?" Daniel asked. "Or what he drives?"

Theo shook his head. "But I know where he lives. Well, I know the town." He managed a laugh. "Okay, I know the exit where the mini-mart is. I'll start there."

He turned, but Ayla grabbed his arm. "I'll come with you."

"You should stay here and lead the search, in case we're wrong."

"We're not wrong."

He tipped his head in concession, no shred of doubt in his heart. "Ayla, I'm about to break a whole lot of laws getting there, and maybe a few more when I arrive."

"Theo."

For a long moment, they stared at each other, silent. Theo felt something shift in his heart. Maybe that was his whole heart moving. Coming alive and telling him to start feeling more and thinking less.

"If you come with me…" he said slowly.

He watched her expression harden as she braced for him to dismiss her or disregard her or bulldoze her.

But he was *not* that man.

"You'll be able to sense where Clem is, and somewhere in that remarkable head of yours are images that Clem has shared. You'll recognize places. You can help me find this guy." He took her hand and felt her whole body melt as she closed the space between them and hugged him.

"Finally," she whispered. "You believe."

Yes, he did.

When the fog cleared, it left his brain crystalized, sharp and certain. Like the moment when a mathematical operation to measure a gravitational field using scalar magnitudes of vector quantities suddenly, shockingly made sense.

The symbols of the formula weren't floating around his brain trying to make order out of chaos. They fell into place like a finished puzzle, revealing the truth.

That's what happened when he'd seen that clementine

rind, now sitting in the console cupholder as though it had the power to guide them straight to the missing dog. It didn't have any power, but Ayla did. Good God, she really, truly did.

He couldn't see Ayla's gift in the traditional form of an equation with calculations that, with thought and trial and error, eventually balanced and made sense. There was no coefficient for "brain energy" like there was for, say, nuclear energy.

But what she was able to do with her mind was not only as obvious as the second law of thermodynamics, it was far more impressive than anything he could do with his.

And, wow, they could have astounding kids.

"What's making you smile, Théodoros?" she asked from the passenger seat, where she'd been navigating for hours, checking messages from Bitter Bark, talking to Marie, or staring hard at every single license plate to see if the attached vehicle was from Arkansas.

But he wanted to save that thought for a better time, for a happier scene, not when the two of them were barreling at eighty-five miles an hour from Bitter Bark to a mini-mart off I-40 two states away.

"I can't believe I didn't see it sooner," he said, not for the first time since they'd been in the car.

"It's okay," she said, putting her hand over his on the gearshift. "You see it now, when it matters."

"It mattered before," he said. "To you. To us."

She stroked his knuckles lightly, closing her eyes on a sigh. "I was getting scared."

"Of me never believing you?"

"Of losing you," she admitted. "Because I don't want to, Theo."

He flipped his hand to thread their fingers together. "I

don't want to lose you, either," he admitted. "Or Clem. Are you…getting anything?" For once, the question was completely and totally sincere.

"Nothing in my head, but my heart hurts like hell."

He grunted in agreement. Theo didn't want to think of what the human vermin could or would do to Clementine. So, for the many hours it took to drive to the exit off Interstate 40, Theo refused to let his brain go there.

Instead, he let it go somewhere else that was uncomfortable and a little scary, but so important.

"Tell me more," he said softly. "Other than your Nana Jo, have you ever met anyone else with this talent? What's it like, really?"

As he drove, she shared every little detail of what happened in her mind when she "read" an animal. Mostly, he listened, interrupting her with dozens of questions as it all finally made sense. The veil of doubt dropped as he inhaled her explanation of the inexplicable.

"Would it really have cost me you?" he asked. "If I hadn't gotten to this place, you would have given up on me?"

She was quiet for a little while, then turned to him. "I will never again give up the essence of me for someone else," she said. "But I was hopeful you'd come around."

"Thank you for being so patient," he said, humbled by that. "And you shouldn't accept less," he added. "You deserve total and complete faith." He brought her hand to his lips. "You now officially have my heart, body, *and* mind, Ayla Hollis. I'm yours."

She let out a little whimper of satisfaction, then closed her eyes and slept. While she did, something curled around his heart like grabby fingers, squeezing so hard he almost couldn't breathe.

Maybe he was the lucky guy after all. Maybe his luck hadn't run out, as he'd been so certain of last time he was on this very road, going in the other direction. After all, he'd found Ayla Hollis. If he'd gone to London, that wouldn't have happened. He'd have gone to Bitter Bark for a long weekend and John's wedding, but would he have even met her?

Maybe, but without Clem, would they have had the connection? He didn't know, but they did. And the feeling was truly unlike anything he'd ever felt before. So what was he going to do? Where was he going to go? And how could he—

"Oh." She blinked awake. "Sorry, I crashed."

"No worries. You earned a nap. We're not that far from the mini-mart."

She smiled. "Where you met the girl who changed your life."

"One of them." He took her hand again, wanting so much to share the thoughts he'd had. But it was so hard for him to put those things into words. Couldn't he just kiss her fingers, and she'd figure it out?

He did, and she gave his hand a squeeze. "I changed your life?"

"You changed my…perspective." He glanced at her, hoping those words could be enough, but he could tell by her expression she wanted more. And deserved it. She'd shared so much, and it wasn't easy telling him about the feelings and images and sensations. "And, as my oldest brother liked to point out, my priorities."

"What are your priorities now, other than getting a job and figuring out where you're going to live?"

"You're a priority."

She smiled, but stayed silent, her dark gaze on him.

"You could be *the* priority," he said. "And from there, the other two—job and location—would figure themselves out."

"Wow," she whispered. "That's…big."

"Could be," he agreed. "I mean, assuming you agree."

"Wholeheartedly, but…I'm not so sure I'd want to live in London, if that's what you're saying."

"I don't blame you," he said. "Right now, I don't, either. So maybe luck was on my side the day that job fell through after all."

Suddenly, she sat up and looked at a big building visible in the distance. "How close are we to that exit?"

"Why? Did you get…a feeling?"

"No, but I've seen this place before. Well, Clem has. We're close, aren't we?"

"One exit away," he told her.

Tapping her phone, she studied a satellite image, quiet as she stared at it. "That building is called Remington Arms Company."

He snorted. "Kinda hope Clem's kidnapper doesn't work there." Not that he was going to pay any calls to the guy without the gun that was under his seat. "Do you… feel her?"

She looked up at him, agony in her expression. "I don't know what I feel, Theo. This is all-new territory for me. I'm trying anything." She blinked as her eyes filled. "I want to find her so much, I can't breathe. My chest hurts. My head's humming. I don't know if that means she's nearby, or I'm…terrified."

"I get that. Let's find out what we can."

Ten minutes later, they pulled into the mini-mart parking lot, which was empty. Inside, he took a long look at the cashier. Same guy? He had no idea. Same hot dogs and pizza, though.

"'Scuze me," he said to the young man. "I was in here a couple weeks ago, and some lady brought a dog in that she'd taken from a local guy."

He got a blank, dead look in response. When Ayla came closer, the guy glanced at her, a little interest evident when his gaze fell on the diamond necklace she still wore.

"Any chance you were working that day?" Theo demanded.

The man, maybe twenty-two years old, gave his head a slow shake. "Sorry."

"Well, then maybe you can help us. Do you know of a local guy who kept a dog chained to his picnic table?"

There was the faintest flicker in brown eyes, then they went dead again. "Can't say I have."

Damn it. "How about a woman…" Why hadn't he gotten a single name? "About fifty. Lives nearby. Drives a truck?"

The other man actually laughed. "Just about everyone in this town drives a truck, pal."

He wasn't willing to hit a dead end. "Well, I'm looking for a guy who could be described as…human vermin. And…" He took a breath. "Most likely runs a meth lab."

Again, the cashier glanced at that necklace. "Well, I might have some ideas…" He drew the words out.

"And you want to be paid for those ideas," Theo guessed, reaching for his wallet to drop two twenties on the counter. "Would that be enough?"

He eyed the cash, then seized it with his left hand, stuffing it in his back pocket. "You want Buck Calloway."

The minute he said the name, a memory came back to him. The woman, pushing Clementine at him...*Buck won't mess with you unless he's got a rifle.*

"Yes, I do. Where can I find him?"

"He's got a couple of, uh, places. Most likely, he'd be up on Gentry Road. East of the Carson Bridge."

Next to him, Ayla madly tapped her phone. "Okay, I see those streets. Do you have an address?"

He shook his head. "And, ma'am, if you'd be so kind as to never tell him I said anything. 'Cause I don't want to die."

"I don't want you to die," she said softly. "Come on, Theo."

"We need an address."

She looked up at him. "No, we don't. I'll recognize it."

With that, they left, heading north on a side street called Carson Bridge Road, looking for Gentry. He found it, turned right, and slowed a little, looking for a picnic table and a meth house.

But it was rural out here, and the few houses they saw were set so far back, they'd have to go down individual driveways to see anything or slow to a stop to see through the trees.

"Okay, we're close." Ayla pointed to a group of trees with a mailbox on the side of the road, the number 653 on the box, though the five had slipped to its side. "I've seen that. I've seen that a lot in Clem's head. She *hates* that mailbox. The image is always dark and threatening."

Good God, what had happened to poor Clem in this place?

Theo pulled to the side and stopped the car. "All right, I'm going in."

"Walking?"

"Yes. You're staying here, behind the wheel with the car running. If anyone comes anywhere near you, you haul ass, understand?"

"And leave you here?"

He reached under the seat and pulled out his nine millimeter, the semiautomatic he'd carried since he trained on one. "I'll be fine," he said.

"Whoa." She stared at the gun. "Wasn't expecting that."

"Navy Guy, remember?"

"Nuclear engineer, remember?"

He smiled and tucked the handgun under his T-shirt in the back. "Well, now I'm a nuclear engineer with a Beretta. Come on, climb over. You have to drive away if you see anyone coming toward you. I have my phone, and you have yours." He leaned across the console. "Kiss me and tell me you forgive me for ever doubting."

"I forgive you." She put her hands on his cheeks and pulled him closer, kissing him light and quick. "Come back fast, safe, and with Clem, and I'll be so in love, you might talk me into London."

That was all he needed to hear.

With one more kiss, he climbed out, made sure she was behind the wheel and ready to roll at the sight of anyone. Then he headed down the drive of 653 Gentry to get what he wanted. He wasn't worried. His luck had obviously returned.

Chapter Twenty-Four

Ayla's whole body hummed with so many nerves, she had to take deep breaths to remain calm. A gun?

Of course a former military guy had a gun. And that was good. That was smart. But it was so…out of her comfort zone.

How had she gone from being a runaway bride fleeing a society wedding to a pet psychic sitting outside a meth house in Arkansas while her boyfriend marched in with a gun?

If it hadn't been the scariest thing she'd ever experienced in her life, it would almost be funny. Someday, this would be funny.

When they were living in London together.

A shiver went through her that had nothing to do with nerves.

Was that what she wanted? Maybe, maybe not. She wanted Theo Santorini, that much she was sure of. Especially now when they'd finally conquered the one huge barrier to love. His faith in her was real, no matter how awful the situation was that got them here. He believed her, and that changed everything.

It freed her to love him, and she was a hundred percent sure she could. Maybe she already did. Maybe she—

She heard a dog bark. Sudden, sharp, aggressive. A little far away, but it could be coming from where Theo was. She closed her eyes and listened, almost certain that it wasn't Clem, even at her most aggressive. Just then, her phone buzzed with a call and startled her, but then a flood of relief washed over her when she saw Navy Guy on the screen.

"Are you okay?" she asked as she answered. Instantly, she could hear the echo of the bark, which was obviously much closer to him.

"I'm fine. No one's here. Except Sid Vicious, who is, I hate to say this, chained to a picnic table." He whispered a dark, angry curse.

"So we save Sid?"

"Not this dog. He'd kill anyone who got near him. I now understand the difference that Liam explained between a guard dog and an attack dog. This guy is seriously looking at me like I'm his next meal. If he weren't chained, I'd be dead."

She closed her eyes, sympathetic for the dog and fearful for Theo. "Maybe we beat the guy here," she said. "You did drive really fast, and he only had, what? An hour or so on us? Come back, and we'll wait across the street until he comes home."

"I don't know. I might get law enforcement here. I peeked in some windows, and I couldn't see much, but what I did see was enough to know what's going on in there."

Meth lab. "Then why chain the guard dog to the table?" she asked, picturing the scene. "If the dog's purpose is to protect the guy who's inside, why make it so he can't get to an intruder? It doesn't make sense."

"It doesn't," he agreed. "So he must want the dog to scare people off with barking."

"But you're not scared. You walked right up to the window, and all the chained dog could do was bark."

"The barking would alert someone inside or nearby," he said. "I'm going to take one more pass around and be back."

"I'll be here." She tapped the phone and dropped it on her lap just as she heard the sound of a car coming up the road behind her. She sat up and looked in the rearview mirror. Not a car, a van. An old, beat-up white work van.

Was that Buck Calloway? Of course he'd drive a van. That's the vehicle that had freaked Clem out.

She grabbed the phone to call Theo and warn him as the van slowed to a stop at the driveway, but he didn't pull in. Instead, he kept going, very slowly.

In a few seconds, he was next to her, both vehicles facing the same direction, his speed down to about two miles an hour as he passed.

What if *he* had a gun?

White-hot fear blinded her as she froze, then she picked up her phone, pretending to look at it like she was lost and reading GPS, then she casually glanced at him. All she saw was a cowboy hat, then he hit the accelerator and rumbled away.

Buck Calloway? Maybe, but why hadn't he turned into the driveway? She was glad he didn't so she could call Theo, but suddenly, about fifty yards away, the van stopped dead in the middle of the road.

And the driver's door opened.

What was he doing?

She leaned forward, squinting. Nothing happened for a few seconds, then out jumped a black dog into the middle of the street.

"Clementine!" she screamed the dog's name.

The driver's door closed, and the van took off, leaving Ayla stunned at the sight of the dog they'd driven hundreds of miles to find.

Clem stood still for a second. Just as Ayla put her hand on the handle to throw her door open and call her, Clem started running in the opposite direction.

And Clem could outrun Ayla.

She smashed the accelerator, eating up the road as Clem shot left, darting toward the woods on the side of the road. Ayla barely pulled over, slammed on the brakes, and threw open the door.

"Clem!" She launched across the two lanes after the dog, leaving her car door wide open. "Clementine!"

The dog stopped and turned, her tail whipping as she barked at Ayla, then started running to meet her.

"Oh my God, we found you!" Ayla stumbled and fell onto her, wrapping Clem in a desperate hug. "Are you okay, my sweet girl? Are you good?" On a sigh of pure relief, she dropped her head to Clem's and instantly saw pictures flashing through the dog's head.

A cowboy hat. A picnic table—this time so clear Ayla could practically see the scars in the wood. And a box. That Christmas box again, being pulled out of the ground.

Then it was gone while Clem bathed her face in grateful kisses.

"Come on, girl. You're not going back there. Let's go call Theo and tell him the best news ever." She stood and clasped Clem's collar, looking left and right before crossing the road, but as she did, she heard, then saw, a van barreling toward her. Not just any van. That van.

He'd come back for her. He'd lured her out of the car with Clementine.

Swearing, she tugged on the dog's collar. Into the woods or beat the van and get in the car? The open car door was only twenty feet away and the woods left her vulnerable.

"Let's go!"

But Clem froze, staring at the van as it approached, then trying to back away and get out of Ayla's grip.

"Come on, girl. Come—"

But it was too late. The van screeched to a halt inches from Ayla. She whimpered at the sight of a pockmarked face half hidden by a cowboy hat and the gun aimed directly at her through the open window.

"Get in or die," he said.

She blinked, truly shocked, unable to think.

"Leave the dog," he ordered. "It's you I want. Dead or alive, missy. It's your choice."

She really had no choice. She let go of Clem's collar and opened the door, praying the dog could somehow lead Theo to wherever this monster took her.

Theo jogged back to the road with his phone in hand, ready to call the local sheriff's office when he got in the car with Ayla. As he stepped around the last tree and saw the mailbox, he turned right, expecting to see his Honda where he'd left it, somewhat hidden in the only curve in the road.

But it wasn't there.

Wait. Was that it? All the way down the road?

Swearing, he took off at a full run. What the hell was she doing sitting there with the door hanging open?

"Ayla!" he called as the wind whistled in his ears.

Get out of that car and wave to me.

"Ayla!"

He sprinted the last twenty yards and threw himself at the open door, swinging down to see—

"Clem?"

The dog was curled onto the passenger seat, whimpering.

"Clementine!"

As soon as she dove across the console into his arms, Theo saw Ayla's phone on the seat, making his heart fall down to the ground with a thud. She couldn't have left on her own. She would never do that.

He closed his eyes as horror and disbelief sucker-punched him, trying, but failing, to piece together the puzzle. It didn't matter. She wasn't here, and Clem was, so he needed help.

Smashing 911 on his own phone, he stroked a shaking Clem, wishing like hell he could read her thoughts and find the woman they both loved. She couldn't be far. The sheriff would close off every road and find her. They had to.

While he talked to the dispatcher, he walked around the area, his gun in his right hand, his gaze never stopping as he scanned the road and the woods. Could someone have taken her in there? The thought sickened him.

As he walked, Clem followed, barking and sniffing and then suddenly breaking away and heading down a dirt road.

He followed her then, not willing to lose both of them, but Clem was suddenly moving fast.

"Stay right where you are, sir," the dispatcher said. "We'll have an officer out there shortly."

"More than one," he insisted. "This is a meth house, and my girlfriend has been kidnapped."

But he didn't hear her response, because Clem trotted off with purpose.

"Clementine!" he called. "Come back here."

He took off after her as the dispatcher kept talking on speaker. "Sir, please don't leave your location."

"Okay, but…Clementine!"

She wouldn't stop, tearing down over the dirt, barely pausing to sniff. Did she know something he didn't? Could she see Ayla in her head? Did this psychic thing work both ways? Theo had no idea, but he followed, ignoring the instructions coming from the phone.

Suddenly, the dirt road split into a Y, and Clem went left, then stopped cold, long enough for Theo to catch up. She shoved her nose into the ground and sniffed, her tail flipping madly.

"What is it, girl?"

When she looked up, Theo saw exactly what she was sniffing. A sparkling strand of diamonds dropped into the dirt.

Not diamonds…*breadcrumbs*.

With hope surging, he lifted the necklace he'd last seen around her throat and peered down the road, barely able to see the outline of a rusted trailer at the edge of the thick woods.

He stood and started toward it, glancing back for Clem. She was staring at the trailer, too, but she'd fallen to the ground, her ears down in fear, a little stream of pee trickling onto the dry dirt.

Whoever was in that trailer scared the life out of Clementine…and probably had Ayla right this minute.

Chapter Twenty-five

Human vermin.

Ayla clung to the phrase that Theo used any time they talked about the man who'd mistreated Clementine, the nickname that came to mind every time she could see him in the dog's head. Right now, she could see how clear Clem's mental image of this beast really was. Although, interestingly, Clem saw him in reverse, like a photograph.

Didn't matter. He was even uglier in real life.

"Everything." The man spat the word for the tenth time since he'd brought her behind the trailer.

Not *in* it, which gave her some small measure of relief. Something told her if she went in that thing, she wouldn't come out alive. But at least out here, with the woods in sight and the blue sky above, she had hope that she might get away from him.

But right now, pushed up against the rusty metal, a gun in her face and his vile breath in her nostrils, she couldn't figure out what that escape might look like.

"I told you everything. She saw your hat. She saw a picnic table. And she saw a box of Christmas decorations. That's all she's ever told me."

"Then how the hell did you find me?" He shook the gun a little, making her gasp.

"Because you lost her in a nearby mini-mart, so I came back here." Every time she recounted the story, she was careful to say *I* and not *we*. He couldn't know Theo was out there.

When Theo found her car, he'd call the police. The longer she stayed alive out here, the better chance she had.

"How did you know which store?"

"The man who gave me the dog told me," she said, hating that her voice was reed-thin with fear. "After you took the dog, I asked him, and he remembered the exit."

He curled his lip, revealing yellow teeth. "How'd you know it was me?" he demanded. "Could you see me in that witch's head of yours?"

A drop of spit hit her when he hissed, making her close her eyes and force herself not to gag. "The man told me about the clementine you had," she said, grinding out the words. "The orange," she added when she could see *clementine* meant nothing to him. "I put two and two together."

"Well, ain't you smart?" His beady eyes coasted over her face. And lower. "Pretty, too."

Oh God.

"I don't know what Leon's gonna want to do with you when he gets back, but I hope he's willin' to share."

Bile rose again as her nails dug into the metal behind her.

In the distance, she heard the first faint scream of a siren. Yes! Theo had found the empty car. He'd called the police. There was hope, and she seized it with everything she had.

But Buck's eyes flashed with fear, blood draining from his acne-scarred face. "Hope they didn't get Leon. I knew he shouldn't have left, but he had to get a dog over there and fast."

A dog? Sid Vicious?

He pushed the pistol into her neck. "You better hope them sirens don't get closer, missy. 'Cause we're goin' in that woods if they do. And then you went on TV for the last time talkin' about what Muttsy knows."

"I don't know anything else, I swear."

He snorted in disbelief. "I looked for you at that dog house in North Carolina. I'da just taken care of you there, like Leon wanted. But you weren't nowhere, and I didn't want the old lady."

Marie. He'd been poking around the ranch while Marie was alone. Once more, her stomach turned.

"So I took the dog. At least you couldna get no more out of her." He inched closer. "You sure she didn't tell you nothin' else?"

She shook her head, aware that the sirens were definitely getting louder.

He looked toward the road, then turned, spit, and swore, quiet for a minute while his pathetic little wheels turned in his brain.

The sirens screamed closer. Much closer. Probably not far from where she'd managed to drop her necklace out the window without him seeing. It was all she could think of to leave as a clue when he veered off that road.

Theo might not see it, but would Clem? A stretch, but it was all she had.

But the chances one of them would find it while she was still alive? Slim to—

"Move it!" He grabbed her arm with a menacing grip,

yanking her away from the trailer toward the woods. “They’re too close for comfort.”

She dug in her heels and refused to move, making him whip around and spear her with an evil look.

“Don’t think about it, missy. I ain’t got no problem takin’ care of you, if you get my drift. That’s a big woods, and my guess is you won’t be the first body Leon left.”

Who the hell was Leon? Whoever he was, this guy was a little afraid of him. But she knew damn well that if she went in that woods, Theo and the cops would never find her. Not alive, anyway.

“I’m not going,” she declared. “I’m not moving. And I’ve already asked enough people around here about Buck Calloway that if you kill me, they’ll arrest you so fast you won’t know what hit you.”

He drew back ever so slightly as the truth of that hit. “How’d you know my name?”

She tapered her eyes to slits. “Witch’s brain.”

He literally shuddered, making her hope he might be a little afraid of her. Doubtful, but she had to try.

“So let me go, and I won’t put a spell on you.”

He actually looked like he was considering it, then he shook his head. “Leon would kill me.”

Yep, the boss. “Then let’s wait for him.”

He gave her a sharp look. “You seen Leon? From that dog’s head?”

Had she? Leon. Leon. Had Clem ever pictured a man’s face other than this one? Just that…Christmas box with the name Noel on it.

Or *Leon*, since Clem saw things backward.

“No,” she said, sensing it was the safest way to go. “And I swear I won’t tell anyone anything if you’ll—”

The sirens screamed louder still, and she saw the

moment that panic hit him. His eyes widened, and he shoved his arm under hers, lifting her up with a surprising amount of strength for someone so scrawny.

Without a word, he started running, carrying her with his left arm, the pistol in his right hand jabbed into her ribs. If she kicked or screamed or fought at all, she could be dead. So she bit her lip, closed her eyes, and forced herself to stay silent as he tore into the trees.

This wasn't happening. This couldn't be happening. Was she really never going to see Theo—

"One more step, asshole, and you're eating lead."

Theo!

She turned her head, fighting to see, but before she could, she fell to the ground with a thud. She spun around to see Theo standing with his legs wide, his pistol drawn, and a deadly expression on his face.

Slowly, as if she sensed she was in the middle of a duel, she crawled backward toward Theo, managing not to whimper in relief.

"Drop your gun, Calloway."

He lowered it, but only enough so it was aimed at Ayla. "You shoot me, I shoot her."

Theo stayed dead silent, his jaw clenched, looking as if he was trying to make a decision. Or waiting for… something.

Suddenly, the sirens wailed again, screaming this time like there were many of them. In the instant Calloway looked in that direction, Theo lifted one hand, flicked his fingers, and said, "Bite!"

Clem shot out from the woods, startling the man. The dog lunged toward him with one vicious growl and snapped her teeth over his right arm, sending the gun to the ground and her former owner into a painful rage.

His screams were drowned out by the sirens as half a dozen police cruisers barreled into the area, circling the trailer. Officers started yelling all of them to drop their weapons.

Clem jumped into Ayla's arms as she sat, dumbstruck, on the ground, and both of them looked up at the man who'd saved them, an equal amount of undying appreciation and love in their eyes.

Long after Buck Calloway had been taken off in handcuffs, the deputies wrote reports, took pictures, and systematically dragged everything they could out of the trailer, logging it as evidence. At their request, Theo and Ayla stayed, sitting in the sun with Clem and answering questions about their roles in what happened.

Ayla was hot, tired, and hungry, but so happy to be alive that she clung to Theo with one hand and Clem with the other, knowing that the end of all this had to be near.

Theo and Officer John Mason had talked a lot, bonding over both being former Navy men. After what felt like forever, Officer Mason came over to them, looking like he might let them go.

"We're done here," he said. "We've got a team at the other house, and I don't think we need you there, but we'll need to contact you for any additional statements."

"Did you find what you're looking for?" Theo asked.

"Not exactly," he said. "And I don't expect Leon Garrison will be coming back to this particular hideout anytime soon."

"I take it he's got some kind of authority over this drug operation?" Ayla guessed.

He nodded. "He's the one we want. He can lead us to the rest of the ring, which we suspect is about fifteen people around these parts who're responsible for the distribution of meth, heroine, and cocaine all over this state and beyond. We keep chipping away at them, one at a time, but Leon's elusive. And he knows where the money is."

"The money?" Theo asked.

"We shut down their laundering about six months ago. Since then, they haven't been able to move cash, so our guess is a hundred grand, maybe more, is stashed somewhere. If we had any idea where Leon was, we'd set up a stakeout and get him, and the money, that way."

Suddenly, a set of chills unlike anything Ayla had ever felt jolted her.

"Well, good luck with that," Theo said. "If there's anything we can—"

She put her hand on Theo's arm, gasping softly. "I know."

Both men looked at her.

"I know where the money is." How could she have not figured that out? "I know exactly where the money is."

"What?" Officer Mason looked at her with no small mix of incredulity and hope. "Where is it?"

She inched back, putting her hands on her cheeks as everything fell into place. "The picnic table. The dogs chained to it." She looked at Theo. "They're not there to protect the people in the house. The dog's purpose is to protect…what's buried under the picnic table."

The deputy choked softly. "How the hell do you know that?"

"Because…" She looked down at Clem. "She showed me."

"When? How?"

Theo held up a hand. "Ayla is an animal communicator, Officer. She's a pet psychic, and a damn good one."

The other man blinked. "No kidding? We used a brilliant psychic on a murder case about seven years ago. Solved it." He inched closer. "Where's this picnic table, ma'am?"

"At the other house. I know exactly what the box looks like. It has Leon's name on it." She let her eyes shutter closed as all the quick flashes of images Clem had been sending suddenly made sense. "I've seen them filling it with plastic shopping bags. They unchain the dog and move her to the side, but she sees everything. Then they chain her back up again so no one will go near that table."

"Let's go!" Theo and the officer said in perfect unison.

Twenty minutes later, Ayla, Clem, and Theo stood about fifteen feet away from the picnic table outside Buck Calloway's house. Clem was shaking a little, but Theo picked her up and held her like a baby so she didn't have to see anything that upset her.

But Ayla and Theo could see everything. Including the metal box buried in the soft dirt under the picnic table, the name Leon Garrison etched into the side. An officer pulled out several plastic Dollar Store bags that held, well, a whole lot of dollars.

Almost immediately, the sheriff had hustled Ayla and Theo away, with no explanation why.

As they got to Theo's car, and he put Clem in the back seat, Officer Mason jogged closer, calling Theo's name.

"Sorry for the bum's rush," he said as he reached the car. "You've been unbelievably helpful. We're reburying the box and setting up an operation to catch Leon Garrison when he comes to get it. We're even putting that other dog back to guard it. But we'll get him, thanks to you two."

He extended his hand to Theo, and they shook, and then the officer turned to Ayla. "Ma'am, you are to be commended. I've no doubt the media will want to talk to you once we have Garrison in custody. Would that be all right? Can I give the press your contact information?"

"Absolutely," she said. "I'm so glad we could help."

"I'm sorry you were in such a terrible place with Calloway," the officer said. "You earned that reward money."

"Excuse me?"

He gave a soft laugh. "You didn't know? There's a $25,000 reward for any tip that leads to the arrest of Leon Garrison. We bring him in, it's yours."

Her jaw loosened. "Wow. That's...great. Go get him, Officer."

Once they were in the car, Theo turned to her and leaned in for a kiss she'd been waiting for since he'd left her hours ago.

"Twenty-five thousand smackeroos," he said. "What are you going to do with that?"

She pressed her hands together as joy ricocheted through her. "It's going straight to the Last Chance Ranch so Marie and I can bring in more animals that need a wonderful place to live."

"Aww." He kissed her again. "I don't know what I like more. The fact that you're donating it, or that you're sticking around for a while at the Last Chance Ranch."

She held his gaze for a long time, the emotional events of the day leaving her raw and vulnerable and excruciatingly aware that life was short and precious.

And she was looking at the man she wanted to spend it with.

Chapter Twenty-six

A week later, Theo was still feeling *all* the things, and they intensified with each passing day…and night. And today, at Waterford for Sunday dinner, those feelings were nothing but happiness, surrounded by family and dogs.

Much of that family, and Ayla, was huddled around Miz Marie in the kitchen, discussing several dogs that Garrett and Aidan had saved from a bad situation. Thanks to the work Theo had been doing, with some help from family, the kennels were bigger and could handle more dogs, especially now that they were well into the warm month of May, so Marie happily announced she could accept the oldest and weakest of the rescues.

While they talked, Theo took his Bloody Mary out to the sun-drenched patio, where he found the grannies sipping "iced tea," as Gramma Finnie called her Jameson's. The two ladies were deep in conversation, the doxies asleep at their feet.

"Oh, come sit, lad." Gramma Finnie patted the sofa next to her rocker. "We were talking about you two."

"Me and Clem?" he joked, reaching down to give Clem's head a rub.

Yiayia rolled her eyes. "You know what we were talking about. The next Dogmothers success story." She grinned at him. "I called it from the minute I laid eyes on that girl."

He snorted. "You told me to run, Yiayia. Thought she was full of it."

"I merely wanted you to be careful."

Gramma Finnie rocked closer. "I, on the other hand, smelled romance in the air instantly. This one goes to the Irish grandmother."

"Who's next on your hit list?" he asked as he sat down. "Somehow, Nick managed to leave yesterday unengaged. You two are slipping."

They shared a look. "Oh, he'll be back."

To see Raven? All his brother had said about her was that they'd talked at the wedding because she wanted to arrange an adoption of an African orphan, and Nick could certainly help her through that process. When pressed by Theo if the connection had been more than that, Nick acted totally innocent. But something told Theo they weren't discussing adoptions in the wine press building the night of John's wedding, but he hadn't pushed it.

"There's always Ella," he said, propping his feet up on the hassock.

"We're not quite finished with you," Yiayia replied. "The job isn't complete until that knee"—she leaned forward and tapped his leg—"hits the ground, if you know what I mean."

He knew. "Calm down, you two."

"What?" they asked in unison, looking alarmed.

"Are we mistaken, lad?"

"I saw you sucking her face over by the kennels."

Yiayia launched one of her heavily drawn brows. "Did I not?"

"You did," he acknowledged on a laugh. "We… sucked face. But no one is going down on one knee."

Yet. Theo and Ayla had fallen hard—into each other's arms, into bed every night, and in…love.

At least that's what this felt like to him. He loved everything about her. Did that mean he loved her? He hadn't told her yet, but he would, and soon.

"You've practically moved into that ranch," Yiayia noted.

"Well, I do a lot of work there. Did you see those new kennels I built? Those are actually a feat of engineering that I'm darn proud of."

Staying with Ayla in Marie's house hadn't really been that awkward, although Clem didn't love it when they kicked her out of the bedroom for a few hours. During the days, they worked on the ranch with Marie. The three of them had fallen into a rhythm that felt right.

"Has there been any word on that reward money?" Gramma Finnie asked. "'Twould buy a fine diamond ring."

He belly-laughed at their total lack of subtlety. "First of all, that money belongs to Ayla, because I didn't do anything."

Yiayia gasped. "You rode in like the cavalry and saved the day."

"I saved the girl and the dog, but she was the one who put two and two together and came up with a hundred grand buried under a picnic table."

Finnie clucked. "'Tis remarkable."

Yiayia shook her head. "I'm ashamed that I was so skeptical."

"*You* are?" He looked skyward, still pained that it took him so long to see the light. "But Clem knew." He bent over and gave the dog some love, getting a happy sigh in response. "And when Leon Garrison showed up for his money on Tuesday, every deputy in that county was there to greet him, thanks to Ayla Hollis."

"She's getting so famous!" Yiayia crooned. "How many interviews has she done now?"

"I lost count," he admitted. "Every TV station around Little Rock, and the newspapers, and then the interview she did for the Animal Network in addition to the live show. She's told the story quite a few times."

"And what are you doing while she's talking to her all her fans?" Yiayia asked.

"Being fan number one," he cracked, winking at his grandmother. "Actually, when I'm not rebuilding kennels…" He blew out a breath, not sure how this news would go over. "I've been on the phone with Nova Nuclear."

"Who's that?" Gramma Finnie asked.

"I know who it is," Yiayia said. "The company in London."

He nodded. "The engineering position I was supposed to take last month is back in play. They're waiting for numbers on the final offer."

"What kind of numbers?" Yiayia asked.

"Really, really big ones." The offer had risen in the month that had passed, so he knew they were sincere, and the money was fantastic.

"You can't leave, lad!" Gramma Finnie exclaimed. "Ye've just found yer lassie."

He smiled, knowing by now that her brogue got thick when she got emotional, and he appreciated how invested she was. "No worries, Gramma. I think she's going to go with me."

"She is?" Again, perfect unison. This time enough to make all three dogs at their feet lift their heads with interest.

"Looks that way," he said, remembering the long talk they'd had last night tucked under the covers, when Ayla agreed her job could be done anywhere. He'd heard the note of disappointment in her voice, as they both knew she wouldn't have the built-in opportunities in London that she'd have in Bitter Bark, but they did *not* want to separate. Not for a day or a night, so living on different continents seemed out of the question.

"What will she do there?" Gramma Finnie asked.

He shrugged. "We'll travel and experience a whole new world together." He looked from one grannie to the other. "I'd think you two would be pretty excited about this plan."

"I'm happy for you," Yiayia said, but for some reason, the words sounded hollow.

"Maybe the lass can find some way to practice over there what she does so well," Gramma Finnie said, sounding truly less than hopeful that could happen.

"You don't think she should go?" he asked the question slowly, as if he didn't even want to put it out into the universe. Of course she should go. They wanted to be together. This relationship was the start of something serious and wonderful. So why the look from his grandmother?

"She has a gift, Théodoros."

"I know that."

"It shouldn't be squandered." Yiayia's dark eyes narrowed as she reached down to pet Pyggie. "She helped me to understand how this dear dog feels about Aldo, and how to manage that. She can help people and animals."

He blinked at her, his heart feeling inexplicably heavy. "Then she'll help them in London."

"What about Clementine?" Yiayia asked.

"We might be able to take her and will try, but she does love the ranch."

Again, his grandmother's response was that brow flicked with silent disapproval.

"Yiayia." He leaned forward. "You think I should turn down an international nuclear engineering job that pays three times what I made in the Navy? Nuclear power helps people and animals, too."

"Hush, lad." Gramma Finnie patted his hand. "We're a couple of old dog lovers with a weakness for romance. What she did, helping those deputies take down the bad guys? It's a bit romantic, too, don't you think? And wonderful."

"Then she can do all her wonderful romantic things in Europe. They have animal communicators there. Or if they don't, they need one, and I'm bringing her."

The two ladies looked at him, silent. Before he could dive deeper into what they thought the problem was, the patio got crowded as the group from inside joined them.

His mother sat on the sofa next to him, smiling. "What are you all so serious about?"

"'Tis nothing, Katie." Gramma Finnie smiled at her daughter-in-law, never one to allow even a hint of conflict to go on for very long. "Did you settle the dog arrangements?"

"I think we did, but Ayla had to take a call, so we came out here."

"Another interview?" Yiayia asked.

"She didn't say," Marie chimed in. "Just that it was very important."

Daniel moved behind the sofa and put his hands on his wife's shoulders. "I bet it's the reward money," he said. "She seemed very excited and headed off to talk privately in my office."

"What a thrill for her," Marie said.

But the real thrill would be for Marie, Theo thought, who didn't yet know Ayla planned to give all the money to the ranch.

"You must be so proud of her," his mother said, patting his leg.

"I really am." Theo glanced at Yiayia, who was still looking a little displeased with him. "She's so good at what she does, and I'm sure she can *do it anywhere*."

The others started chatting over each other, so no one but Yiayia heard his subtle message.

But now they had him doubting everything. Ayla had said she was fine with moving to London. Did he misinterpret that? Would it be a disappointment to her? Because, he could find—

"You're not going to believe this!" Ayla came rushing out, holding her phone to her chest, her cheeks flushed, her dark eyes glinting with excitement.

Everyone on the patio turned to her, but her gaze went straight to Theo. Her smile faltered for a moment, but then she squared her shoulders and took a breath.

"Did you get the reward?" he asked.

"I got…a reward. A big one." She let out a little laugh. "I got a job offer."

"What?" several of them asked at the same time.

"Animal Network wants to launch a weekly show

called—are you ready for this? *Tailepathy*, featuring me as a pet psychic."

Theo stared at her, mind whirring with the implications, while everyone crowded around Ayla and peppered her with questions. But she didn't seem to be listening, her gaze on him, looking extremely…uncertain.

He stood, too, to give her a hug. "Ayla, that's amazing," he said.

"There's a caveat," she added, backing away to look at him.

"What is it?" he asked.

"They want me to do the show at the Last Chance Ranch."

"No!" Marie exclaimed. "You are kidding!"

"They think it would make a fantastic setting for the show, and they thought it would be fun to document the growth of the shelter and how many 'unadoptables' Marie takes care of. And they also want to include all of Bitter Bark, having me talk to residents and guests in town since this place is so…dog-forward. That's what they called it."

With each word, his heart dropped a little more as the plans they'd discussed evaporated like a cloud.

But this was her life, and her opportunity, and every bit as awesome for her as London was for him.

"I am so proud of you," he said, reaching out to pull her in for a hug.

She eased back again. "You understand what I'm saying, right? It's here," she said. "In Bitter Bark."

"I know. This is fantastic news for you, Marie, and the whole town." He hoped he sounded sincere. He *was* sincere, but at the same time, his heart was sinking. What would this mean for *them?*

"We'll talk about it," she said.

"Ayla. You can't even consider not taking this," he told her, his words drowned out by the celebration around him.

This family of animal lovers, along with Marie and so many others, had worked tirelessly to make Bitter Bark the most dog-friendly town in America. And now Ayla Hollis, animal communicator, was going to give the town even more national recognition.

They were overjoyed, every one of them.

As he held her against him, he looked over her shoulder and met Yiayia's challenging, warning, unwavering gaze.

He had no clue what she was trying to tell him, but he was already sifting through the ways to make this work for both of them. He didn't want to lose the love of his life, but if he even whispered to Ayla that he was disappointed, she might change her mind…for him.

He couldn't let her do that. He wouldn't let her do that. He would *not* be that man who disregarded what mattered to her, because he loved her too much.

The excitement finally died down after dinner and the football game, when some people headed home, others played games, and Daniel and several of his sons went to the kennels to take care of the dogs.

It was the first chance Theo had to be truly alone with Ayla since she'd announced her news, so he took her hand and suggested a walk with Clem.

"Let's see how she does at the picnic table after all this training," Theo said, but they both knew that wasn't the only reason they wanted to get away from the family.

They had to talk.

His emotions had been in a tangle all afternoon, but he hoped he'd hid that from her. This was her moment of glory, a recognition of her success and talent, and he didn't want to be the mopey guy who had to go to his massively high-paying job in London…without her.

They walked in silence for a few minutes, the sound of the dogs from the kennel and pen, as well as some laughter and chatter, fading as they made their way down the wide, winding path that left the homestead and headed for the small lake.

"I don't have to take it, you know," she said softly.

"Are you kidding? You were born for this job. This is an opportunity of a lifetime."

She leaned into him. "So are you," she whispered.

"I'm not in the equation," he said, sounding an awful lot like the engineer he was.

"Well, you're in *my* equation," she replied, looking up at him. "We agreed I'd go to London."

"Not when they want to shoot *Tailepathy* in Bitter Bark."

"You're so sweet," she said. "I know you're disappointed."

"Not in you," he assured her. "And we'll figure it out. I don't have the job yet. And you do."

She let out a sigh. "I should tell my family," she said as they walked.

"Do you have to?" he asked. "It's not like they're going to support you."

"True, but I have to pack some things, get my car, and talk to a real estate agent about getting my condo on the market. While I'm there, I'll at least see Trina and Mother." She groaned softly. "Who no doubt will insist I change my name to protect her reputation."

"Want me to go with you?" he offered. "I have a conference call scheduled, but I can change that."

"With London? It's the offer call, isn't it?"

He nodded. "I think so."

He felt her sigh. "Do the call. Marie's driving me over so she can visit the shelters, and I'll drive back so I can finally have my car here."

"How long will you stay?"

"A few days," she said. "I told the Animal Network people that I'll be here mid-week for a meeting. They're coming here with Colin Donahue. He was, apparently, a driving force behind the decision. Isn't that sweet?"

"Beyond sweet," he said dryly.

She elbowed him. "Don't be jealous."

"Of that guy?" he snorted. "Please. And are you sure you don't want moral support tomorrow? I can reschedule the Nova call."

"No, don't do that. I can handle it."

"I'll miss you." But he better get used to that.

She slid her arm around his waist and dropped her head on his shoulder. "I'll miss you, too."

"Oh man." He paused at the bottom of the path to rest his chin on her head, loving how she fit right into him. "Is this going to be our life? Missing each other?"

She looked at him, silent, but he knew the answer.

Life wouldn't be like this if he stayed in Bitter Bark. But how would that work? There was nothing for him here, no job, no real money, nothing but…Ayla. And family.

What was it about that equation that didn't add up?

At the sound of Clem's barking, they turned, only then realizing they'd forgotten about her, and she'd run ahead.

"She must see the picnic table," he said.

"I don't know. That's not very frantic barking."

They followed, hand in hand, stepping into the open area to see Clementine lying on top of the table, on her back, rolling around with unabashed joy.

"Look at her!" Ayla broke free and ran toward the dog. "What a good girl!"

Theo held back for a moment, watching Ayla run, her caramel hair swinging from side to side, her loving arms outstretched. Clementine got up, shook off, and jumped right into Ayla's arms, looking over her shoulder at Theo with that big goofy smile and her tongue hanging out with pure ecstasy.

Throw Clem into the equation, and…nothing added up right in his engineer's head.

Chapter Twenty-seven

Driving into Charlotte with Marie felt like a trip to New York City after a month in Bitter Bark. Traffic, buildings, people, and not a whole lot of dogs. After saying goodbye to Marie at the front entrance of her condo, she dragged her borrowed suitcase into the marble-floored lobby, getting a double take from Whitney at the front desk.

"Nice to see you again, Ms. Hollis," she said, her smile wavering. "I'm, uh, sorry about your wedding."

For a moment, she gave the woman a blank stare, not sure what she meant. That wedding seemed like a million years ago. "Thanks, Whitney. Do I have any packages?"

"Yes, and mail." The young woman slipped out from behind her desk and came back a minute later with a small bundle, her smile back in place. "I saw you on TV," she said. "I had no idea you could read animals' minds!"

"I sure can." She flashed a smile. "And I'm going to be doing a lot more of it."

Buoyed by a sense of freedom, she gathered her things and took the elevator to the fifth floor to let herself into her unit, which suddenly felt so big and empty.

In the entryway, she dropped the mail and looked around, feeling like an outsider in her own home after living at the Last Chance Ranch for so long. Everything was so white and shiny, missing dog hair, and a little black cat named Ziggy, and the sound of chickens, and goats, and…Theo.

He'd stayed at Waterford Farm the night before since his conference call was at nine today, and she and Marie had wanted to get an early start. Her mother and Trina would be here in about an hour, so Ayla headed right back to her bedroom, eager to start making calls and planning what she'd pack to bring to Bitter Bark.

She was going to stay with Marie until this place sold, then she'd—

A buzzer from the intercom interrupted her thoughts. Either she forgot something from the front desk, or Mother and Trina were super early, which was highly unlikely. And Trina didn't get buzzed in.

At the kitchen counter, she lifted the small house-phone that connected her with the front desk.

"Ms. Hollis, it's Whitney. Your father's here to see you."

Her *father*? He'd declined to see her when she'd texted him, confirming her suspicions that he wasn't going to speak with her for a long, long time. "Are you sure?"

The woman who ran the front desk with such efficiency probably wanted to roll her eyes at the question, but she was too professional. "Yes, ma'am. He's presented ID, too."

As if Whitney didn't know who Phillip Hollis was. "Okay, let him come up."

Bracing herself, she waited for him in the living room,

running through all the possibilities of what he could be here to say.

A bribe, most likely. All the money she could ever need if she would reconsider marrying EJ. No thank you.

An apology? Fat chance. As if he'd ever apologized to anyone for anything.

A plea for her to never, ever again do *that thing* with animals? *Sorry, Daddy.* That thing is going to be on national TV.

When he tapped at the door, she opened it slowly, not entirely sure what she expected other than a tanned, confident man who always had the world right in the palm of his hand. But she did a double take at the sight of him. Maybe his tan had faded since the wedding, but what had caused the circles under his eyes and the turned-down lips?

"Hey, Dad."

He didn't say anything for a moment, but slowly lifted his arms for a rare hug. She took it, of course, even more surprised by the squeeze he added. "Hello, Ayla."

Even his voice sounded a little…broken.

She drew back and took a hard look at him, stunned that he seemed like a shadow of the man she knew.

"Are you okay?" she asked him. "Can I get you something? Mother and Trina are going to be here soon, so…"

"So you think I should leave?" he asked.

"Of course not. I think you should…try not to fight."

He heaved a sigh and looked for a place to sit, falling into a club chair. "No, I don't want anything. Not that you can serve me, anyway."

"Dad." She sat across from him on the edge of the sofa, surprised by a wash of sympathy she rarely, if ever, felt for her father. "What's going on with you?"

He looked hard at her. “I built an empire on sand, Ayla. And the sand, if you must know, was owned and operated by Eugene Paxton Jr.”

EJ? That made no sense. “I know you and EJ’s father had plenty of deals together, but what are you saying?”

He stabbed his fingers into his hair and pulled it back. “It’s complicated, and there are a lot of smoke and mirrors involved. But, as you know, Eugene and I have been business partners for a long time.”

She nodded. “You built the pharmaceutical company together.”

“Not exactly ‘together,’” he corrected. “Eugene owned ninety-five percent.”

What? “I did not know that,” she said softly. But then, her father and EJ’s father never talked to her about money or the businesses they started and sold.

“Long story short, he’s going to yank the rug out from under me. He owned ninety-five percent of me, too. And when the wedding fell through…” He swallowed hard. “I’m going to lose everything, Ayla.”

She felt her jaw loosen. “Because I didn’t marry EJ?” Guilt punched first, then anger. “Eugene would do that to you?”

“Eugene didn’t,” he said. “But EJ has the control now, and he…well, he is being pushed around by lawyers, but I suspect he is gleefully getting his revenge.” On a sigh, he met her gaze. “He told me he saw you.”

“He came out to where I’ve been staying in Bitter Bark and…made threats.”

“Well, he made good on them.” He paused for dramatic effect. “Unless, of course, you change your mind.”

She choked softly. “Excuse me?”

“Ayla, please.” He propped his elbows on his knees

and leaned closer. "You've had your fun. You've had your little rebellion and your silly moment on TV and your… fling with some farmer. Trina told me all about it."

With each word, she felt her back straighten. "What are you asking me to do?"

"Reconsider your foolish decision." His frown deepened. "People's lives and livelihoods depend on it. Do the right thing for your family."

"And marry a guy who cheated on me, and threatens financial ruin if I don't?" Her voice rose. "What in God's name makes you think I'd do that?"

"Because I'm asking, as your father. As your *family*."

The words hit hard, and something inside her gut twisted. The woman she'd been for all but the last month of her twenty-nine years would have folded. She'd have taken the easy way out, given her family whatever it demanded, and pleased the people she needed to please.

It would have seemed like the right thing to do, for family.

But that woman didn't exist anymore.

"No," she said simply. "I'm not going to do that. And frankly, the fact that you'd ask is sickening."

"Ayla. We're talking *hundreds of millions* of dollars. Do you understand what that means?"

"It means you'll have to buy fewer homes, stop dating gold-diggers, and dip into savings and secret funds that I have no doubt you have. And you will not get me to change my mind."

He sighed, crossed his feet, and checked his watch.

"I have a ton of stuff to do, Dad."

He narrowed his eyes at her. "Ayla, you can't do this to our family. You can't. We're family. Do you know what family means?"

She almost choked. "I do," she said. "I learned all about it over the past month. And it's not this."

A knock at the door was the only answer, then Dad huffed out a breath like he'd been waiting for that.

"That's Mother and Trina," she said, knowing Trina didn't need to be buzzed up.

Dad nodded and looked at his watch again. "Late, as usual."

"They're actually early, but..." She put her hands on her chest. "You wanted to be here when they were, didn't you?"

"Ayla, we—"

"What is this? Some kind of intervention?"

"Ayla!" Trina called from the other side of the door. "Come on. Open up."

For a moment, she considered refusing, but how could she? Dad wasn't going anywhere. Damn it.

Huffing out a sigh, she opened the door to see her sister and mother looking almost as bad as Dad, except with styled hair and too much jewelry.

"She said no," her father said from the chair. "My own daughter plans to let us fall into financial ruin."

"Ayla." Her mother breezed in, her very aura taking ownership of Ayla's sanctuary. "This foolishness has to stop now."

Trina lingered in the doorway, her eyes tapered to slits. "You are not going to be a brat about this."

"That's rich, coming from the world's biggest brat."

"You want to know what's *not* rich? Us, if you screw this up."

Ayla turned, trying to process all this, plus the fact that Mother and Dad were apparently having a civil conversation. She wasn't sure if that was a sign of the apocalypse, or how dreadfully serious the situation was.

"Who would have imagined I'd be the one holding the family fortune in my hands," she mused, closing the door once Trina came in. "But y'all wasted your time."

"Y'all?" Her mother repeated the phrase with a shudder and an appalled expression. "You don't say *y'all*."

"I do now." She returned to the sofa and plopped down as Trina went to the open kitchen, looking for coffee, which Ayla was not about to offer. Her mother slowly walked the perimeter, no doubt searching for a mismatched pillow.

"How long is this going to take?" Ayla asked. "Because I have to call a realtor and start packing."

"Realtor?" Her mother whipped around. "You're selling this place?"

"Yep. Want to buy it?"

Trina snorted. "She might not be able to afford it if you don't do what you have to do."

"Trina, really? You want me to marry a man I loathe to make sure Dad's questionable business decisions don't come back to haunt us?" She looked from one to the other. "Are you serious about that?"

"Of course not." Trina came in without coffee and dropped into the other club chair. "You only have to fake it."

"Fake…what?"

"Trina and I have been talking, Ayla." Her mother abandoned her inspection and joined them in the living room. "You don't have to marry him. No one expects that."

"*He* expects it," Dad said.

"He needs to *think* you're going to marry him," Mother continued. "Just accept his apology, start dating him again, and give your father a month or two or three to restructure the businesses. Can you do that?"

"No." She almost laughed, except it wasn't funny.

"You can fake it," Trina said. "We all know you're a good faker. We saw you on TV. Was there ever a bigger fake-out?"

Dad's brows drew together as he glared at her. "You'll quit that psychic nonsense, too. Immediately."

The tone took her from mildly bemused to furious. "I'm not quitting anything. As a matter of fact, I'm going to be hosting a weekly show on the Animal Network that launches in the fall. It'll film in Bitter Bark, where I plan on living."

Three stunned expressions stared back at her.

"You cannot be serious," her mother whispered.

"As serious as three people who walked in here and suggested I fake a reconciliation with my cheating ex to save the family fortune."

"Well, of course you'd do that," Trina said. "All of our lives are on the line."

"Hardly." Ayla rolled her eyes at her sister's dramatics.

"Ayla Josephine." Her mother moved to the sofa to make her point. "You will not ruin this family's name by behaving like some kind of freak. Where is your pride? Where are your priorities?"

Priorities. How frequently she and Theo talked about them. "I'm not a freak, Mother," she said quietly. "I'm an animal communicator."

"You're a traitor to this family if you don't help us," her father said. "And if we walk out of here without your agreement, we're finished."

"Finished?" She barely got the word out. "What are you threatening, Dad? Spell it out for me."

"We won't speak to you again." He slid meaningful glances to Mother and Trina. "Ever. At all. Finished."

Her stomach tightened like she'd been punched. "Dad, we're family. We can't…not speak." She looked at her mother, whose gaze was downcast as she plucked at an imaginary thread on the white sofa.

Then Trina, who chewed her lip and looked…sad. "I love you, Ay, but you are being unbelievably selfish."

She was being selfish? They were telling her to lie, calling her a freak, and making demands about how she live her life. And at one time, she would have acquiesced. But that time was gone.

A cold chill passed over her whole body as she stood and crossed her arms, seeking some way to show them what family love is without giving in to their outrageous demands.

"I'll talk to EJ," she finally said.

They all exhaled, practically in unison.

"I'm not promising anything," she warned them. "But maybe I can get him to stop seeking revenge. After all, you three didn't leave him at the altar, I did."

Dad cleared his throat as if to say, yes, let's remember who's to blame, sending a shot of fury through her.

"After he had sex with one of the bridesmaids the night before," she added in a cutting tone.

Dad looked down. Mother was picking that thread again. And Trina stared straight ahead, still gnawing her her lip. Not one of them could respond, commiserate, express regret…*anything*.

Not one of this…*family*…who claimed to love her would even meet her gaze. Disappointment left a metallic, bitter taste in her mouth as she swallowed the lump in her throat.

Maybe she would have been better off not knowing how amazing a family could be. It wouldn't hurt so much to be a Hollis if she didn't know…there was better way.

"You can leave now," she said on a whisper, hating that her voice cracked.

They all stood and walked to the door. Dad left with a single nod. Mother managed to give a tight smile. Trina stood still for a minute, then lifted a brow.

"He must be amazing in the sack if you'd give all this up for a guy you met on a dog ranch."

Ayla closed her eyes. "I want Nana Jo's ring back."

"I want my trust fund back." She walked out, leaving Ayla to stand and stare at them as they disappeared around the corner to the elevator.

Then she closed the door, rolled up on the sofa, and cried.

Chapter Twenty-eight

The man behind the huge reception desk gave a cursory glance to his computer, another wary one to Clementine, then handed back Theo's driver's license.

He made a call, listened for a moment, then shook his head.

"I'm sorry, Mr. Santorini. Ms. Hollis is not answering, and pets are not allowed at the Chatham Arms. If you want to wait for her, I'm afraid it will have to be outside."

Didn't allow pets. How did Ayla ever pick a place like this? He couldn't even imagine her here.

"All right, thank you." He had no idea how long he'd have to wait, but it didn't matter. He had a plan, and nothing was going to get in the way of it. *Nothing*.

"You and I can practice our brain-train games, Clem," he told her as they walked outside of the five-story stone building tucked into an upscale residential section of Charlotte. The building wrapped around a large grassy area with walking paths and fake gaslights, so he found a bench that allowed him a view of the front door and the street, plus a clear shot of the parking garage entrance and exit.

With all his bases covered, he settled down with Clem and took the paper from his back pocket again, holding it in front of her.

"Get it in your brain, girl. I want her to see it, too."

She looked at Theo's pocket and barked. The treat pocket.

"Where do you think she is at eight o'clock at night?" he mused while Clem chewed the cookie.

Clementine looked up, her dark eyes communicating something. Probably thinking, *You should have called her.*

"I know, I know." Maybe he should have called, but some things had to be said in person. And after the day he'd had, starting with the Nova Nuclear conference call and the decision he'd made, he didn't want to tell her the news over the phone.

Marie had given him her address in Charlotte, and he'd expected to find her home.

Ten minutes later, he looked up at the sound of a car whipping into a handicapped spot right in front of the building. Not any car, either, but an over-the-top-expensive BMW he recognized.

What the hell was EJ Paxton doing here?

On instinct, Theo drew Clem closer, staring at the vehicle and squinting in the dim light to see…two people in the front seats. She was with him?

His heart dropped a little, not that he was worried Ayla had gone running back to that clown. But if she was getting closure or tying up the loose ends of a relationship, it couldn't have been easy for her. He watched, waiting, one hand on Clem's head.

When the passenger door opened, he spotted Ayla's dark golden hair pulled into a ponytail and watched her ex-fiancé get out of the car and come around to her.

They talked for a moment and then hugged.

Really? Was that just for closure? Of course it was. There was no way she'd go back to him. Theo knew that. But a shred of the green monster did threaten to rise up as they walked side-by-side toward the condo entrance. Not holding hands, not really talking, certainly not a couple.

Neither one of them noticed him in the shadows, and he fed Clem some more treats so she didn't get distracted, turn, and see Ayla. Let her finish whatever she was doing, and he'd go in after EJ left.

When they got to the door, EJ held it open, and in they went together.

Theo swore softly, staring at the entrance and considering all his options, which were dwindling and fast. Surely EJ was just walking her to the door…right?

"So much for timing and luck and the element of surprise," he whispered to Clem.

Now what? March in there and declare his love while they were up in her apartment having a "last" drink together? God, he hoped it was the last. But what if she'd decided that—

The door opened again, and this time, EJ was alone. He hustled down the path, a cell phone to his ear as he rushed toward where his car was parked in the handicapped zone.

"Okay, okay. Maybe it was the last hurrah," he told Clem, standing up. "He's leaving at least. That's good."

The BMW roared away, and Theo was about to head to the front door when his eye caught a navy sedan pulling out of the parking garage, almost as fast as EJ. Wait…was that Ayla?

He vaguely remembered her saying she drove a Tesla,

and even in the dim light, he could see that ponytail and recognized her profile.

Good God, could he not catch a break today?

On impulse, he tugged at the leash and jogged to his own car parked around the corner. He put Clem in the passenger seat and turned on the ignition just as the Tesla crossed the intersection in front of him, so of course he followed her.

Because that wasn't creepy or anything.

"People get restraining orders for this kind of thing," he said to Clem, who sat up in the front seat like they were on a grand adventure.

She cruised through a yellow light that was pretty damn red when he got under it.

"And they get tickets," he added.

Clem barked, panting a little because she sensed tension and excitement and probably smelled Theo's desperation.

And then Ayla rolled onto the interstate, making Theo let out a colorful curse. Was she going all the way back to Bitter Bark? Maybe he *should* call her. But he caught sight of her turn signal before he picked up the phone, so he followed her onto an off-ramp, staying far enough behind that she wouldn't spot him.

A few more turns, and she whipped into a parking lot under a sign that said Westside Animal Shelter.

"Now this makes sense," he said to Clem, his engineer's mind momentarily happy. He knew this was where Ayla went when things got tough. He knew she'd run here the night she tore out of her own wedding. And he knew that she'd only come here because she was upset.

Was she upset about EJ? Had they tried for

reconciliation? Nothing in him believed that, not for one minute. Maybe it had gone terribly with her family. Maybe she was sad about the long distance that was about to come between them.

Whatever it was, he had the power to make her happy, and that was all he wanted to do. He parked on the side of the building and watched as she went inside.

Wouldn't a shelter be closed at this hour?

"We might have to grease palms, beg night workers, and break some more rules, Clementine," he said, flipping off his seat belt. "Because we need to go get our girl and tell her the news."

Clem barked as they got out and headed to the locked front door, but Theo knocked loudly enough to get the attention of a night guard, who ambled over with a scowl.

"We're closed!" he yelled through the glass, his gaze dropping to Clem. "You want to leave the dog?"

Not in a million years. "We're here to see Ayla," he said. "Ayla Hollis is waiting for us." Not exactly, but it sparked recognition and got the man to open the door very slowly.

"She's in the back with the new arrivals," he said. "So you're not leaving this dog?"

Clem barked with an air of resentment that made Theo smile. "This is Ayla's dog," he said. "Ayla's and mine."

God willing.

The man smiled down at Clem. "Then you're a lucky dog, because Ms. Hollis loves the animals."

"She sure does," Theo says. "She knows what they're thinking, too." With a quick smile, he followed the direction of the guy's pointed finger and the sound of barking dogs. A lot of noisy, desperate, little orphans hoping for a home. He tried not to look at all of them, or things could get very crowded at the Last Chance Ranch.

The shelter was clean enough, but still a sad place with fluorescent lights washing everything in a dreary shade of grayish yellow. It made him want to build and paint more kennels and help Marie find the money to expand the ranch and open up the doors to all the dogs.

One rescue at a time, Theo.

At the end of the hallway, he looked left and right, listening between barks until he finally heard the sound of Ayla's voice.

Clem heard it, too, and immediately did a little dance on her back feet and barked, making Theo laugh.

"We haven't sealed the deal yet, Clemmie. Hang on."

He headed that way, certain that even if she heard Clementine bark, it wouldn't stand out in the cacophony of this shelter. He walked slowly, looking at each dog as they greeted Clem with a bark or growl.

Finally, he saw her ponytail through the bars of the last cage. She was sitting on the floor, her back to the aisle, leaning back against the bars like a prisoner. She spoke softly to a brown dog draped over her lap.

He gave Clem a good tug and a warning look, adding a treat and putting his finger over his mouth. It might work, or it might not. But either way, she was about to know he followed her here.

"So that must have been my good deed for the day," she said, stroking the fur of the needy creature in her lap. She was actually having a conversation with the dog, he realized.

And that was only one of the many things that made Ayla Hollis amazing.

"I know it's sad to be alone and not have a family. But

you know what, little dog that has no name? You'll get out of here. You'll find your family. They might not seem like yours at first, but then someone will let you sleep on their bed and eat their dinner scraps and…" She sighed. "Roll around on the picnic table."

He looked at Clem because that might be their cue.

"So, I fixed my broken family's problems." She dropped her head back. "But who's going to fix mine, doggo?"

"We are."

Clem barked, somehow sensing that since Theo talked, she could, too.

On a gasp, Ayla whipped around, her tear-stained face kicking him in the gut. She stared, her jaw loose, as Clem bolted toward her, barking wildly. Ayla blinked as the dog on her lap leaped up and barked right back at Clementine.

"At least, we hope we are," Theo added. "That's kind of why we drove all the way over here to find you."

"How did you know where I was?"

He winced. "We might have followed you when you left your condo."

"You…" She laughed softly, standing up to unlatch the door so Clem could launch in and cover her face with kisses, exactly like Theo wanted to do. The other dog pranced around, barking, more than a little jealous, so Theo came closer.

"Do you want me to take Clem?"

She looked down at the two dogs as they did a butt-sniff exchange. The light brown mix—mostly pittie, by the look of him—seemed no more threatening than Clem and about the same size. "I think they're fine. Why don't you come in?"

He took a step into the kennel. Still leaning against the bars, she slowly sank back to the ground as if her knees had given out.

"What are you doing here?"

He joined her, folding onto the ground next to her, while the two dogs barked at each other for a minute, then stopped.

"I came to deliver some important news."

"Really." She lifted her hand as if she wanted to touch him, but then thought better of that and lowered it. "What's the news?"

"First, tell me how you fixed your family's problems. Can you?"

"I can, but it's a pretty sorry tale of woe." She sighed and looked away, studying Clem as she flattened to the tile, looking up at the other dog, both of their tales flopping. "Oh, she likes Dog With No Name."

He laughed at the name and gave the dog a stroke on the head. "So? What is No Name thinking right now?"

She smiled and studied the dog. "He's trying to impress me, and suspects you have treats in your pocket."

"Safe bet." Theo fished out a few Milk-Bones and gave them to both dogs, chuckling as they pounced and chewed happily.

"So, your family?" he reminded her. Because he hoped like hell whatever it was would explain what she'd been doing with EJ Paxton.

"I had to mend a fence with my ex," she said. "Requiring me to be nice when I didn't want to be. But I pulled it off and convinced him not to be a jerk. A bigger jerk." She grinned. "And I saved the day."

"Then why"—he touched her cheek—"the tears?"

She sighed. "Because, as I have told you, I got so

cheated in the family department. They're awful, but they're all I have."

Not for long.

"So you got the offer?" she asked.

"I did." He gave a tight smile. "I thought I should come and tell you in person."

He could see more sadness in her dark eyes as she tipped her head. "Congratulations. I hope it was everything you wanted."

"Actually, I ended up with a little more than I ever thought they'd cough up, plus a nice office with a view."

"Looking out over the Thames?"

"Um, not exactly. But a great view of a really nice part of town."

She reached out and put her hand on his arm. "I know this was what you wanted, Theo."

"I didn't realize how much," he said.

"Oh. Well. Good. I'm…happy for you."

"Really? Because you sure don't sound happy. Faking it again, Ayla the Magnificent?"

"What do you expect me to say?" she asked with a wry smile. "Yay for London! See you twice a year, if we're lucky."

"Hey, I'm lucky. I always get what I want because I make it happen."

She dropped her head back against the wire cage, studying him. "You didn't get me to go to London."

"I know," he said. "But I think this is better."

Her eyes shuttered closed.

"You will, too."

"No, that's where you're wrong, Navy Guy. This is not better." She opened her eyes and looked right into his. "You want to know how I feel about this?"

"I want you to—"

"No." She stopped him. "No, I want to tell you. I have to tell you. I'm not holding back with people I care about. Here's the truth. I'm *devastated*."

"Ayla, I—"

She held her hand up. "Not even close to done."

"Oh, sorry."

"I'm devastated you're going to London, because…" She swallowed. "I fell in love with you."

His heart, already taking a beating today, folded in half.

"I don't know how it happened, but one day I woke up and realized that life without you wasn't, well, it wasn't so great. I wanted a life with you. I wanted to be with this smart, logical, funny, gorgeous guy with great abs. I did. All the time."

He smiled, but he wasn't about to interrupt her.

"You know what else? I love that you turned your life upside down for a dog someone shoved at you in a mini-mart, and took a gun into a meth house, ready, willing, and able to kill for that dog. I love that you are your grandma's favorite, and that you eat the way you make love—like you want to draw out every last morsel of pleasure."

Oh God, he had to tell her that—

"And I love your family. Every single person, from Gramma Finnie to the little ones and all of the people in between. I want to be in that family, kind of desperately. I want to be folded into Waterford and Bitter Bark and watch football games and dance at weddings, and oh my gosh, give me Bloody Marys on Sundays."

When she took a breath, he leaned closer. "Are you done?"

She wiped a tear. "Yeah, I'm done, except to say that I'd hoped you'd be the one, Theo. The one I'd live with forever in a house that was humble and cozy and had scarred maple dressers and lots of dogs and no… trappings. I hoped that because…" She blew out a slow breath. "I love you."

With that, he knew she was done, and so was he.

Instead of responding, he put his hand on Clem's head and drew her closer.

"Come on, girl, *think*."

Ayla gave a dry laugh. "What are you doing?"

"We practiced this." He turned the dog's head so she was looking at Ayla. "Think, Clem. Think about what I showed you."

She licked Ayla's hand.

"The paper, Clem. Remember that paper I showed you? The job offer? You were supposed to memorize it so Ayla would see it in her head."

"But it would be backwards," she reminded him. "Plus, I hate to break it to you, but she's thinking about the treat in your pocket."

He reached for two more and also grabbed the folded piece of paper he'd put there.

"Why do I need to see your London job offer?" she asked.

"Because…" He gave the dogs treats and held out the folded offer letter he'd signed late that afternoon, taking in a deep, slow breath. "It's not from London."

She looked up from the paper into his eyes. "It's not?"

"Read it."

Very slowly, she opened the paper, looking down. He followed her gaze as it landed on the stationery imprint with the elaborate Latin-looking letters.

"Vestal Valley College in Bitter Bark, North Carolina..." As she whispered the words, her voice cracked, and her fingers started trembling.

"Officially extends the offer to name Théodoros Santorini as head of a new Nuclear Engineering Department..." Biting her lip, she looked up at him, eyes damp with tears. "Theo."

He touched her cheek again, wiping a fresh tear. "They're creating the position for me, and I get to start the department from scratch and bring in professors and build an amazing organization."

Her jaw loosened. "This is what you want?"

"This..." He cupped her jaw and looked into her eyes. "This woman right here is what I want. I want to be where she is, all the time, three hundred and sixty-five days and nights a year."

"Oh, Theo..." She blinked and a tear fell. "But you wanted the money."

"I did," he acknowledged. "The money was always part of my formula. But then yesterday, I took money out of the equation, and all the answers were obvious."

"You're such an engineer," she said on a teary smile.

"And proud of it," he said. "But once I changed the formula, I knew. I could go all over the world and make big money and amass savings and be secure and free with all that money. And in an instant, it could be gone."

Her eyes flashed. "No kidding. Ask my dad."

"But nothing can take away a foundation of love and family. With you in my life, and my family around me, I'm way richer, way luckier, and my life is way more charmed than if I had a fat bank account."

She pressed her fingers to her mouth. "You're right. I couldn't agree more."

"Good, 'cause there might be a few scarred maple dressers in your future."

"As long as it's in a bedroom I share with you, I don't care." She threw her arms around him and squeezed, making the dogs bark. "Theo! I'm so happy!"

Inching her back, he looked into her eyes, knowing that showing her that paper wasn't enough. He had to lay it all out there, all the feelings, not only today but every day.

Taking another breath, he cupped her face in his hands.

"I love you, Ayla Hollis. I love everything about you. And I also would be devastated to get on a plane and move to another country, because you…are home to me."

She let out a soft whimper.

"Wherever you are, I want to be there. Whatever you do, I want to cheer you on and support you. I want you next to me at every Sunday dinner, and I want to stand on the set every time you mindread every animal, ever. I love how you make me *feel*, Ayla. Every crazy, unexpected, inexplicable feeling I didn't know I wanted but now can't live without."

He kissed her lightly, and Clem climbed right between them, curling in a circle on her lap. The other dog poked his head into the mix, too, making them laugh.

"He wants to come to the ranch," she said, petting his head. "Can we bring No Name?"

"Join the family, kid," he said to the dog.

"What do we call him?"

He put his hands on the dog's brown head and looked into his eyes, seeing gratitude and hope and a better life than the one he had. "London."

"London? As a reminder of what you gave up?"

"As a reminder of my priorities, because you are number one." He kissed her. "Also two, three, four, and five."

"Oh, Theo."

"I love you, Ayla. I hope you know how much."

"I do." She fluttered the offer letter. "I've got the empirical evidence right here."

Epilogue

Ayla always had a hard time deciding how to spend the lovely hour or two after Sunday dinner at Waterford Farm. Did she want to watch the touch football game from the blankets, with dogs, kids, and the rowdiest cheering section—with the added bonus of being close to the cute and sweaty quarterback for the Bloodhounds? Or should she stay on the wraparound porch for quiet conversation with the grannies, soaking up their tidbits of wisdom?

This late-September Sunday, the choice was easy, because the quarterback wasn't here. Theo had left her very early that morning with the announcement that he had a "secret errand" and would see her later at Sunday dinner. He'd taken off after a quick kiss that left her alone—and curious—in the spacious Bitter Bark apartment she'd rented a few months earlier.

He'd acted a little weird the night before, too. A tad preoccupied, but very happy, as affectionate as always, but also, after they'd made love, he wanted to…talk. About feelings, now that he'd really gotten the hang of that. But the conversation had left her glowing and certain and maybe even a little suspicious about what he might be up to today.

So, she chose the porch for the post-meal relaxation, but not because Gramma Finnie and Yiayia were there to entertain her. Today, the nonfootball gang included two of the tiniest, most precious creatures Ayla had ever seen.

When Declan and Evie welcomed their twins, Glory and Max, into the family in August, Ayla found it harder and harder to concentrate on football when the newborns were around to amuse and amaze her.

Right now, each baby was held by one of their great-grandmothers, covered in blankets, even though autumn hadn't really kicked in yet. The sun was warm and cast the whole porch in a golden glow that matched the true joy in Ayla's heart as she curled up in the corner of one of the sofas, soaking in peace and contentment.

Across from her, Ella looked to be sound asleep, stretched out on the other sofa with her feet in Darcy's lap and Gala tucked into her side, while Pyggie snored in the middle of it all.

Next to Ayla, Cassie had her feet up on the hassock, her hand on a five-month baby bump, her smile back in place after a rough first trimester.

Cassie and Braden's baby announcement had been a cause for great celebration with this crew, along with Alex and Grace's surprise elopement, which had been followed by one heck of a party at the winery.

"I can't believe it's almost October," Cassie mused. "It's been an amazing summer."

"A whirlwind," Ayla agreed, thinking of how she and Theo had slipped into their new life together, with him starting at the college while she worked with the Animal Network to plan her show, two episodes of which they'd already shot for the launch in October.

Days faded into lovely nights of cooking, laughter, and love. And every Sunday, they were here.

"Time sure does fly in this life," Gramma Finnie said, a sad note in her voice. "And then it's over."

"Hey." Darcy pointed at her grandmother. "Don't get maudlin on me, Finola Kilcannon. I know that tone in your voice. You have thirty more years, at least."

Finnie smiled, but her eyes did look cloudy behind her glasses. "'Tis the loss of Rusty that has me blue. I always thought that setter would live forever."

They all sort of sighed in unison. The one sad cloud on the otherwise perfect summer was the passing of the great Irish setter, Rusty, a few weeks earlier.

Daniel had been wrecked, but this weekend, he and Katie, and their retriever, Goldie, had taken off for a getaway, and everyone hoped their beloved patriarch would return in good spirits.

"No one lives forever," Yiayia reminded Finnie as she stroked Max Mahoney's tiny head. "But new lives start, and that's the beauty of it all."

"Listen to you, lass." Gramma Finnie gave her a sweet smile. "Soundin' like one of my embroidered pillows."

"How can I not?" she asked with a smile. "You've poured more Irish sayings into me than whiskey." She picked up her glass of "iced tea" and winked at Ayla. "And God knows she pours a lot of that, too."

"You know what you need, Gramma Finnie?" Cassie said. "Another match."

Gramma Finnie and Yiayia shared a look, staring at each other for an uncomfortable beat, then they each looked away, silent.

"Whoa," Darcy said. "Anyone have a knife so we can cut the tension?"

Yiayia slid a smug look at Gramma Finnie, who pretended to be very concerned with how Glory's tiny pink hat fit over her head.

"What's going on with you two?" Cassie asked.

"I bet I know," Ayla said softly as they all looked at her. "They want to close one chapter before they start the next."

"Ahh." Darcy nodded. "What is keeping Theo from popping the question?"

Ayla felt her cheeks warm as she laughed. "Something, but he won't say what. It's fine. I'm patient," she added.

"They're not." Cassie pointed at the older women.

"Well, we don't have forever, lass," Gramma Finnie said. "I'm staring down the barrel of ninety in a few years."

"Hush your mouth, Finola!" Yiayia said. "That number will never be spoken in my presence."

Gramma rocked, thinking for a moment, then she let out a noisy sigh. "Well, I, for one, have a wonderful idea for our next, uh, project."

"You, for one, have a *ridiculous* idea." Yiayia put her hand on the other rocker to stop it. "The issue is closed, Finola."

"Not as far as I'm concerned. We have to…" She bit her lip and adjusted her lime-green cardigan. "Talk to Ayla."

"Me?" She sat up. "How am I involved?"

"Do not go there, Finola," Yiayia warned. "This matter is settled."

"Will someone tell us what that matter is?" Cassie insisted.

"Shhh." Finnie put her finger to her lips and pointed

toward a sleeping Ella with the other. "'Tis a secret."

"From Ella?" Darcy asked in a hushed whisper. "Fair warning—you tell me, I tell her. Ella is my soul mate and cousin, as you all know."

"Then leave," Gramma Finnie said. "Because I have to ask Ayla a favor."

"I will not," Darcy sputtered, eyeing her grandmother. "Okay, fine. I'll…keep the secret."

Ayla smiled, very much doubting that, but terribly curious where she fit into the Dogmothers' next matchmaking scheme. "What is it, Gramma Finnie?"

"Finola," Yiayia ground out. "I told you, there is someone already picked out for the job." She gave her closest friend a hard look. "Someone Greek."

"Oh, Jace," Darcy said. "Well, he'd certainly love to be your next match. His crush on Ella grows stronger every time he's in town."

"Have I met Jace?" Ayla asked.

"You might have been too busy to notice," Cassie said. "He's my client from Family First Pet Foods. He's gaga over Ella and has been since the day he met her, and he's found every imaginable excuse to come to Bitter Bark."

"And…he's *Greek*," Yiayia announced. "What could be better?"

"Irish!" Gramma Finnie practically choked the word. "And I've found him. The perfect Irish match. I knew it the minute I laid eyes on Colin Donahue."

"Colin?" Ayla blinked at her. "The host of *Rescue Party*?"

"I met him on the set of your first show. Now that's an Irish boy." Gramma Finnie fanned herself. "Looks like he was born and raised on the Emerald Isle."

"I would imagine with a name like Colin Donahue," Ayla agreed. "And he is single." The host had become a good friend to her over the summer, having been instrumental in her getting *Tailepathy* and helping her to navigate the ropes at Animal Network. "And Colin's been here to shoot two more episodes of his show."

"Interesting," Cassie said under her breath.

"Why?" Ayla asked.

"Because he head of marketing for Family First Pet Foods, Jace the Greek god, is considering becoming Rescue Party's biggest sponsor." She waggled her brows. "The plot thickens with both those two men in town and working together."

Yiayia crossed her arms. "You can just stop at Greek god. That's what Ella needs."

"But Colin's blue eyes and black hair?" Finnie cooed. "The lad looks like my kin from County Wexford. He'd be perfect for Ella."

"Not as perfect as Jace."

Ayla laughed softly. "Doesn't Ella get a say?"

All of a sudden, Ella whipped the blanket off with a dramatic whoosh. "Apparently not," she proclaimed, standing up. "You…" She pointed at Gramma Finnie. "And you…" She moved her finger to Yiayia. "Are flat-out crazy. You know that?"

They stared after her, speechless, as she walked off the patio, dragging her blanket like a queen's train, off to watch football where, presumably, no one would be trying to control her love life or start a war between Ireland and Greece.

"Well, at least I don't have to keep a secret," Darcy said dryly.

Suddenly, someone squealed at an ear-shattering pitch

from the front lawn, followed by what sounded like a loud cheer.

"That game can't be over yet," Cassie said, putting her feet down and leaning forward. "What's going on out there?"

The noise continued, along with chatter and more high-pitched screeches that sounded like Destiny singing one of her high notes.

"Get Gramma Finnie!" one of the men yelled.

"Oh yes, she has to see this!"

Her eyes widened in surprise. "Gracious, that sounds serious."

As they all started to rise, Evie and Declan came rushing up to the porch, each of them taking a baby.

"They need you out front, Gramma Finnie," Declan said.

"Theo's looking for you, Ayla," Evie added.

Theo was here? She popped up, too, trying to imagine why or how his arrival had caused such a stir.

She joined the others as they headed down the stairs and around the drive to the huge lawn used for the football game, which had come to an end. Instead of a huddle, players and the smattering of family on blankets who'd been watching—every single one of the Kilcannons, Mahoneys, and Santorinis—were on their feet. They all gathered around Daniel and Katie, with everyone trying to get close to them.

The little kids, especially Destiny and Christian, were jumping up and down with uncontained excitement. Oh, and Marie was there, too.

As Ayla got closer, Theo came strolling toward her, that wide grin he usually wore after a Bloodhound victory firmly in place.

"Hey." Ayla reached out to him, and he hugged her so hard he brought her off the ground.

"Miss me?" he asked after a quick kiss.

"Terribly. What's going on?"

"I'm told this is a great Kilcannon tradition that only takes place about once every fourteen or fifteen years. And this time, I got to make it happen. Well, Marie did, but I held the little fellow all the way back."

"What are you talking about?"

Wrapping an arm around her, he brought her into the little crowd, close enough to see that Daniel held a tiny reddish-brown puppy who couldn't weigh much more than the newborn she had just been admiring.

Daniel's gaze was locked on his mother, Gramma Finnie, who looked visibly emotional as the family parted to let Liam and Shane Kilcannon slowly guide her to the center.

"Sweet Saint Patrick, I wasn't sure I'd live to see another Setter Day."

"Setter Day?" Ayla whispered to Theo.

"I think my stepfather is about to tell you."

To get some order in the chaos, Liam scooped up Christian, and John got hold of Destiny. All attention turned to Daniel and the puppy he held.

"This is a big day at Waterford Farm," he said, his booming patriarch's voice quieting the rest of the crowd. "For the immediate family, you all know what is happening. For the many of you who have joined us through marriage and love, welcome to your first Waterford Setter Day."

A cheer went up, most noisily from the Kilcannons, Ayla noticed.

"If you've spent any time with Gramma Finnie," he continued, "you know that when she and my father, Seamus, pulled up to the sign that said Bitter Bark, their Irish setter Corky barked so hard, they decided to this would be their new home."

"Maybe he could read," Shane said.

"Backwards," Theo cracked, making everyone laugh.

"Corky was the first of a long and great line of setters, starting a tradition that there would always be an Irish setter living at Waterford Farm," Daniel said. "And until recently…"

A soft moan rolled through the group.

"There was," he finished. "We have Goldie, of course, but she's used to another dog, and despite her color, she's technically a retriever. But there's always been a setter. Do you remember them all?" he asked his mother.

"Sure, I do, lad. Corky was the son of Fergus and Enya, who we left in Ireland," Gramma Finnie said, her eyes bright. "And there was Buddy, Laddie, and Murphy, too. Then our darling Rusty."

Daniel's eyes shuttered. "He was one of the great ones. But now…" Daniel stroked the puppy, who couldn't have been two months old. "Special thanks to Marie, who heard of a rescued pregnant pup in Charlotte and managed to snag us a little guy from the litter. Now we have…" He looked down at his mother. "Tradition says Finola Kilcannon always names the puppy on Setter Day. So, Mom?"

Gramma Finnie wasn't the only one fighting tears right then. She pressed her gnarled hands together as if in prayer and looked at the puppy, then out to the crowd, her blue eyes settling on Theo.

"You helped, didn't you?"

"I was with Marie today," he said, "but this is all courtesy of Westside Shelter."

Ayla sucked in a little breath, feeling a jolt of pride for her favorite place in Charlotte, followed by an unexpected kick of disappointment. Why wouldn't he take her along on this errand?

"Well, then, I think I have this wee one's name picked. We'll call him…Lucky. 'Tis a fine name for an Irish setter."

Daniel lifted the squirmy little guy *Lion King*-style over the crowd. "Family of Waterford Farm, I give you Lucky, the newest Irish setter to grace this home. May his life be as long and joyous as all the great setters who came before him."

They erupted with a cheer, clapping and high-fiving the new arrival.

From behind Ayla, Theo cheered, too, and wrapped his strong arms around her and pulled her into him, nestling his mouth by her ear. "Let's take a walk. Where's Clem and London?"

"They're in the pen and dying to see you," she said, sliding an arm around his waist and glancing at the crowd. "It'll be a while before I can have a turn with that puppy anyway."

They walked arm in arm to the pen, quiet until they were across the driveway.

"Why didn't you tell me where you were going?" she asked. "I would have loved to have gone to my shelter today."

"I had a few other things to do," he said. "Marie met Daniel and Katie at the shelter, and I… There's my girl!"

Clem tore from the other side of the pen at a full run, too fast to even bark, leaping into Theo's arms as he unlatched the gate. She slathered his face with kisses as they both fell to the ground, the two of them acting like they'd been apart for a year instead of half a day.

Ayla laughed, forgetting the conversation for a minute while she grabbed her phone to take a few pictures, then she greeted a much more mellow London, who barked and went back to his nap in the sunshine.

"All right, all right." He finally extricated himself and got to his feet. "To the table, Clem! Lead the way!"

No longer afraid of picnic tables, Clem bounded toward the path, stopped every few feet to make sure they were behind her, then led them down toward the field.

"This is a special place, don't you think?" Theo asked.

"Waterford Farm?" She laughed. "Yes."

"No, well, yes, but I mean that picnic table." He hustled her, moving almost as fast as Clem, down the hill. "That's where we had our first long conversation."

"When you suggested we fake liking each other to keep the grannies off our backs."

"Dumb idea," he acknowledged.

"What? Faking a relationship, or keeping the grannies off our backs?"

"Both. We can't fake anything, and those two are persistent." Laughing, they reached the table after Clem did, who climbed up and rolled over, ready for her picnic table belly rub.

Theo obliged while Ayla settled on one of the benches, the questions piling up. Why hadn't he gone to the shelter? Why hadn't he invited her? What was he up to?

But she waited until Clem was well loved and Theo sat next to her with a happy sigh.

"So..." He gave her a sly smile. "I know you are bursting to know everything."

"Of course I am. Where have you been, and why didn't I get to go?"

Once again, he let out a long, slow breath, bracing his elbows on the table behind him and looking up to the blue sky. "Oh, Ayla Jo."

She gasped at the name. "No one calls me that—"

"No one except your Nana Jo. I found out today that she called you Ayla Jo."

She blinked at him. "Today? Where…who told you that?"

"Your father."

"What?" she choked. "What were you doing with him?"

"He collected a box of things for me," he said. "It's in the car. Some pictures that belonged to your grandmother, more of her things, some clothes."

She stared at him. "Theo, what made you do that?"

"I knew you'd want that stuff, anything of hers, and I asked him to get it for you. He agreed."

Chill bumps blossomed over her skin. "I do want that, and that was incredibly thoughtful of you."

"I got something else, too." He gave her a sly sideways look and a smile, standing. "Something I know means a lot to you."

As he reached into his pocket, she inhaled sharply as she suddenly realized what that something might be. "You got it?"

He smiled and pulled out his hand, keeping the fist closed. "I got it."

"Oh! Theo! Thank you." She popped up, reaching for his hand. "I'm so happy—"

He held it to his chest, stepping back. "Not so fast, Ayla Jo."

She laughed at the name and the shiver of excitement. "Let me have the ring, Theo."

"You know, I've given this a lot of thought. A lot," he said. "And I know that glitzy, expensive things don't mean much to you."

"They don't," she agreed.

"So, after a great deal of consideration, and oh, by the way, getting a blessing from your father—"

"You…*what*?"

"I decided that we already have the right ring for this." Very slowly, he lowered himself to one knee and raised his hand to offer her the ring that Nana Jo had worn until the day she died. "You once told me this little piece of jewelry represents the love of a lifetime."

Looking down at him, she pressed her fingers to her lips.

"That's what we're going to have," he whispered. "If you will say yes and marry me."

For a long moment, she stood very still, looking into his eyes, lost and found at the same time.

"Ayla, I love you with my whole heart and body and mind…and soul. Please be my wife, and let me feel this way forever."

"Yes," she whispered. "Yes, I will marry you and love you as much as I do right now for the rest of my life."

He slid the ring on her finger, both of them trembling with the weight of the moment.

She held out her hand, seeing Nana Jo's fingers as clearly as she could see her own, through teary eyes.

"I'm so happy," she said as they hugged and kissed, and he twirled her. That made Clem bark and leap off the table to circle their legs. "And so is your other girlfriend," Ayla said on a laugh.

"Come on." Theo put his arm around her and led her back to the path. "Let's tell the grannies that the knee has hit the ground."

As they walked and Clem pranced ahead, Ayla looked up at the man she loved completely. "How do you feel, Théodoros?"

"Like I can't even put my feelings into words." He smiled at her. "But I will, Ayla, I promise. For the rest of my life."

"You know what? I believe you."

Want to know the release date and see the cover of the book for Finnie and Yiayia's next match?

Want to know the minute it's available?
Sign up for the newsletter.

www.roxannestclaire.com/newsletter-2/

Or get daily updates, sneak peeks, and insider information at the Dogfather Reader Facebook Group!

www.facebook.com/groups/roxannestclairereaders/

The Dogmothers is a spinoff series of

The Dogfather

Available Now

SIT…STAY…BEG (Book 1)

NEW LEASH ON LIFE (Book 2)

LEADER OF THE PACK (Book 3)

SANTA PAWS IS COMING TO TOWN (Book 4)
(A Holiday Novella)

BAD TO THE BONE (Book 5)

RUFF AROUND THE EDGES (Book 6)

DOUBLE DOG DARE (Book 7)

BARK! THE HERALD ANGELS SING (Book 8)
(A Holiday Novella)

OLD DOG NEW TRICKS (Book 9)

Join the private Dogfather Reader Facebook Group!

www.facebook.com/groups/roxannestclairereaders/

When you join, you'll find inside info on all the books and characters, sneak peeks, and a place to share the love of tails and tales!

The Dogmothers Series

Available Now

HOT UNDER THE COLLAR (Book 1)

THREE DOG NIGHT (Book 2)

DACHSHUND THROUGH THE SNOW (Book 3)
(A Holiday Novella)

CHASING TAIL (Book 4)

HUSH, PUPPY (Book 5)

MAN'S BEST FRIEND (Book 6)

FELIZ NAUGHTY DOG (Book 7)
(A Holiday Novella)

FAUX PAWS (Book 8)

And many more to come!

For a complete list, buy links, and reading order of all my books, visit www.roxannestclaire.com. Be sure to sign up for my newsletter to find out when the next book is released!

A Dogfather/Dogmothers Family Reference Guide

THE KILCANNON FAMILY

Daniel Kilcannon aka *The Dogfather*
Son of Finola (Gramma Finnie) and Seamus Kilcannon. Married to Annie Harper for 36 years until her death. Veterinarian, father, and grandfather. Widowed at opening of series. Married to Katie Santorini (*Old Dog New Tricks*) with dogs Rusty and Goldie.

The Kilcannons (from oldest to youngest):

• **Liam** Kilcannon and Andi Rivers (*Leader of the Pack*) with Christian and Fiona and dog, Jag

• **Shane** Kilcannon and Chloe Somerset (*New Leash on* Life) with daughter Annabelle and dogs, Daisy and Ruby

• **Garrett** Kilcannon and Jessie Curtis (*Sit…Stay…Beg*) with son Patrick and dog, Lola

• **Molly** Kilcannon and Trace Bancroft (*Bad to the Bone*) with daughter Pru and son Danny and dog, Meatball

• **Aidan** Kilcannon and Beck Spencer (*Ruff Around the Edges*) with dog, Ruff

• **Darcy** Kilcannon and Josh Ranier (*Double Dog Dare*) with dogs, Kookie and Stella

THE MAHONEY FAMILY

Colleen Mahoney

Daughter of Finola (Gramma Finnie) and Seamus Kilcannon and younger sister of Daniel. Married to Joe Mahoney for a little over 10 years until his death. Owner of Bone Appetit (canine treat bakery) and mother.

The Mahoneys (from oldest to youngest):

- **Declan** Mahoney and and Evie Hewitt (*Man's Best Friend*) with dog Judah
- **Connor** Mahoney and Sadie Hartman (*Chasing Tail*) with dog, Frank, and cat, Demi
- **Braden** Mahoney and **Cassie** Santorini (*Hot Under the Collar*) with dogs, Jelly Bean and Jasmine
- **Ella** Mahoney and…

THE SANTORINI FAMILY

Katie Rogers Santorini

Dated **Daniel** Kilcannon in college and introduced him to Annie. Married to Nico Santorini for forty years until his death two years after Annie's. Interior Designer and mother. Recently married to **Daniel** Kilcannon (*Old Dogs New Tricks*).

The Santorinis

- **Nick** Santorini and…
- **John** Santorini (identical twin to Alex) and Summer Jackson (*Hush, Puppy*) with daughter Destiny and dog, Maverick

• **Alex** Santorini (identical twin to John) and Grace Donovan with dogs, Bitsy, Gertie and Jack

• **Theo** Santorini and **Ayla** Hollis (*Faux Paws*) with dogs, Clementine and London

• **Cassie** Santorini and **Braden** Mahoney (*Hot Under the Collar*) with dogs, Jelly Bean and Jasmine

Katie's mother-in-law from her first marriage, **Agnes "Yiayia" Santorini,** now lives in Bitter Bark with **Gramma Finnie** and their dachshunds, Pygmalion (Pyggie) and Galatea (Gala). These two women are known as "The Dogmothers."

About The Author

Published since 2003, Roxanne St. Claire is a *New York Times* and *USA Today* bestselling author of more than fifty romance and suspense novels. She has written several popular series, including The Dogfather, The Dogmothers, Barefoot Bay, the Guardian Angelinos, and the Bullet Catchers.

In addition to being a ten-time nominee and one-time winner of the prestigious RITA™ Award for the best in romance writing, Roxanne's novels have won the National Readers' Choice Award for best romantic suspense four times. Her books have been published in dozens of languages and optioned for film.

A mother of two but recent empty-nester, Roxanne lives in Florida with her husband and her two dogs, Ginger and Rosie.

www.roxannestclaire.com
www.twitter.com/roxannestclaire
www.facebook.com/roxannestclaire
www.roxannestclaire.com/newsletter/